GARETH

LORD OF RAKES

GRACE BURROWES

GRACE BURROWES PUBL

CHAPTER ONE

"A Young Person to see you, milord."

The butler's very lack of expression was eloquent: Beyond doubt, a lady—unchaperoned and uninvited—awaited Gareth Alexander, Marquess of Heathgate, in the smaller formal drawing room.

Again.

Gareth walked into the drawing room still dressed in riding attire. That in itself was a bit of rudeness, but merciful saints, what could any decent woman be thinking to call upon *him* in broad daylight?

His visitor stood with her back to him, and his immediate impression, based on the resolute set of her shoulders, was that this was indeed, another desperate female looking for forgiveness of her husband's, brother's, or cousin's debts of honor.

The worst kind of helpless female too, he concluded as she turned—a *virtuous* helpless female. At first she did not meet his gaze, but aimed a martyred stare at his least favorite Axminster carpet. Her dress was an ugly, serviceable gray, her gloves faded black, and her person without adornment. Her russet-brown hair was pulled back into a large, simple knot at her nape. She was pathetically unremarkable.

Until she looked at him.

Amber eyes, slanting above high cheekbones and a wickedly full mouth arrested Gareth's dismissive perusal. He was *tempted*, though he'd refuse what she was offering as collateral for some man's debt.

Her features had a feline cast, an intelligence and alertness that made Gareth want to keep his eyes on her. He gained the impression she could move like a cat, think like a cat. The serious gaze she turned on him suggested that she probably, in keeping with solid English propriety, did *not* purr like a cat.

He approached her with a slight bow. "Heathgate." He'd purposely neglected to append the courteous *at your service*.

She curtsied. "Thank you for meeting with me, your lordship."

She did not offer her name, though she had a pretty voice. Gareth's brother Andrew would call it a candlelight voice.

He gestured to the settee. "Shall we be seated?" He ordered a tea tray—to appease his hunger rather than convention—and found his guest once more staring at the carpet.

"So, why have you come to see me, madam? You must know propriety is not served by a meeting under these circumstances." To his surprise, that blunt opening comment earned him a fleeting smile.

"Propriety is a luxury not all of us can afford." Her accent was aristocratic but musical, as if there might be some Welsh or Gaelic a few generations back.

Gareth paid attention to voices, to dress, to the tidy stitching on the index finger of her glove, to the details relevant when dealing with opponents in any game of chance. Hers were a challenge to add up.

"Propriety is a necessity if a young lady is not to lose her reputation, as others have in similar circumstances."

At that salvo, the lady removed her worn gloves—probably without realizing the symbolism of the gesture—to reveal, pale, elegant hands. The hands of a true lady. Gareth put aside further sermons for the moment.

The tea arrived, and as the footman withdrew, Gareth closed the door. That earned the lady's attention, for she leveled a questioning glance at him.

He mustered his minuscule store of patience. "You come to see me without invitation or chaperone; you will not tell me your name. I can only conclude you do not want the servants to overhear what you discuss with me. Will you pour?"

She gave a dignified little nod from her perch on the edge of the sofa. "How do you take your tea?"

"I like it quite strong and with both cream and sugar."

Her movements were confident and graceful; she knew her way around an elaborate tea service. She was a lady fallen on difficult times.

Oh, hell, not again. What was wrong with the young men of England?

"Shall we let it steep a bit, then?" she asked. "I wouldn't call it strong yet."

"As you like, but you will please disclose the nature of your errand. This appointment was not on my schedule." He wanted to get this over with, though his rudeness did not seem to perturb his visitor.

"I am without relatives, your lordship, except for a younger sister. My other nearest relation, a distant cousin, has recently passed away. Her will left me with a substantial source of income, provided I meet certain stipulations. The stipulations involve you. Should I fail to meet the conditions of her will in the immediate future, I am without a means of supporting myself, which is no great inconvenience. I could work as a governess or become a lady's companion. My retainers, however, are elderly, and my younger sister—"

She fell silent and poured a splash of tea into a cup. The lady must have decided it wasn't strong enough even yet, for she sat back and regarded him with steady topaz eyes. He saluted her mentally for meeting the challenge: They were quite down to business, thank you very much.

"How do the stipulations involve me?" Clearly, she wanted him to ask, to show some curiosity about her situation, while he wanted to leave the room at a dead run.

"My distant cousin was a madam, sir, and the source of income she left me was her brothel."

Gareth's visitor had his attention, drat her. He plucked a mahogany bay horse hair from the cuff of his riding jacket and flicked it away.

"And the conditions?"

"First, I may not sell the business for at least one year. During that time it is to be held in trust for me, and the profits available for my personal maintenance. That condition is problematic in itself." She paused, peering at the tea again. This time she poured as she continued speaking. "If it becomes public knowledge I am living off the proceeds of a brothel, my future is ruined—though that matters little. My younger sister, however, is blameless, and deserves some happiness from this life. She cannot be tainted by this association."

Gareth accepted the tea and took a sip. This difficult, inconvenient woman had made him a perfect cup of tea. Against all probability, he found his goodwill modestly restored.

"The second condition?"

The lady looked briefly away—toward the white roses on the piano—and he had the sense this mannerism was how she gathered her courage, though none of her trepidation was betrayed in her expression.

"I am to spend at least three months under the personal tutelage of the trustee, learning the skills necessary to manage a high class sporting house. I am to learn what the employees know, how the business works, how to gamble, and how the courtesan's trade is..."—she delicately lifted an eyebrow—"...undertaken."

Gareth stood, as genuine surprise—a rare and unwelcome emotion—coursed over him.

"Did your cousin dislike you so intensely, to put this choice before you?" Her cousin's generosity would be the ruination of her, whoever she was.

"She hardly knew me," came the reply. "She had chosen or been forced into her profession when I was but a girl. The family no longer received her, nor did she appear to want their acknowledgement. She probably felt entitled to her anger, if in fact this bequest is a display of anger."

Heathgate lowered himself beside his guest on the settee. He did not ask permission, and she did not shift away.

"How could this not be a posthumous tantrum? You appear to be a decent woman, and your cousin has made sure if you accept this bequest, then you won't be, nor, by association, will your sister be. I call that mean-spirited, particularly when your alternatives are what? To go into service, where your safety is none too assured anyway? This bequest is a diabolical gift."

The lady regarded him steadily, measuring him with cool, feline eyes. "My cousin was Callista Hemmings."

He leaned back against the settee, feeling a stab of loss. Callista had been the quintessential *grande horizontale*, and she'd treated him honorably. When all London had fawned over the newly invested Marquess of Heathgate to his face and laughed at him behind his back, Callista had been honest. She'd taken Gareth on as a project, educated him, refined him, shown him skills and weapons that had needed only the sharpening influence of time to see him into the peerage on his own terms.

She'd passed along tidbits about this peer, or that bit of business that had allowed him to make some brilliant investments. Then she'd dumped him flat, telling him she chose her clientele, and she was unchoosing him.

In hindsight, he'd seen the kindness in what Callista had done. Untried as he was, he'd been in danger of losing his heart to her. She was shrewd enough to know that wouldn't have been in her interests —or his. He was in her debt, and now she was gone. He'd felt the loss months ago when he'd been among few mourners at her funeral, and he grieved anew at the mention of her name.

"You knew her," his visitor observed dryly.

"My dear lady, much of London's titled male population knew her, and the remainder could only wish they had. Your cousin was quite a woman. Quite a lady."

"She was not a lady," his guest countered, the first hint of heat in her words.

He let that observation go unchallenged while he took another sip of wonderfully, hot, sweet, strong tea. "You resent this choice."

"I resent it, yes, even as I am grateful that it gives me options. Penury would likely cost me my virtue at some point in any case. I am resigned to traveling a safer road to ruin. Were my sister older, I could get her married posthaste, then slide into obscurity, but she is seventeen and that is...."

Her faltering resolve was interesting. "Seventeen is...?"

"Seventeen in her case is too young to marry."

Gareth's guest busied herself sipping her tea, apparently oblivious to his perusal. He sipped along with her, waiting to see where she was heading with her disclosures. At seventeen, without the first clue what she was getting herself into, *she* would have married to protect her sibling, had it been an option for her. He had no doubt of that.

"I am not the only one who might resent the way my cousin has arranged things," the lady said. She had pretty hands, but as she set her tea cup down, Gareth noticed a minute tremor in them.

"I expect the ladies in Callista's employ are not particularly pleased, and the trustee might find himself in a bit of a bind." The poor bastard would be in one hell of a bind, in fact.

His guest looked at him directly, and he realized all her previous glances and gazes had been oblique in comparison. Foreboding prickled up his neck.

"Do you?" she asked evenly.

"Madam?"

"Do you find yourself in a bit of bind?"

"Why would I do that?"

"Because Callista named you as the trustee of her estate, my lord, and thus the guardian of my virtue."

Bloody, rubbishing, perishing... Gareth stalled discreetly, calling for some cakes while his internal world righted itself. He was too taken aback at Callista's scheming to puzzle through the reasons for it —unpleasantly taken aback. Shocked, even, and it took a great deal to shock him—now.

He held his peace while his guest nibbled away at a chocolate éclair, and his consternation grew into monumental resentment. Miss Shabby Dignity eventually finished her tea and turned her unnerving regard on him once more.

"So, my lord, do you resent the task requested of you? Callista named an alternative trustee should you decline the position."

Reprieve. Maybe there was a way out—if Gareth wanted one. "Whom did she name?"

"Viscount Riverton."

"I see." Callista must have truly hated her cousins. Riverton was a confirmed deviant, sick at best, and evil, more likely.

No damned reprieve whatsoever.

"Riverton will not do." Did Gareth detect a slight relaxation in the lady's shoulders? "Any provisions for a substitute of my choosing?" And to whom could he delegate this project anyway?

She considered her empty tea cup, very likely some of the finest china she'd ever see, much less touch. "None. You take on the job or Riverton will, and I can tell you I do not relish the thought of his personal tutelage one bit."

His guest was a martyr of some discernment, then. How flattering. "What exactly does personal tutelage involve?" Because unless Gareth's distant recollection of Chancery law was in error, the will would have to be carefully worded to successfully skirt the illegalities of passing along a house of ill repute.

The lady remained perched on the edge of the settee, though she doubtless longed to get up and pace. "It isn't complicated, my lord. I

am to learn to be a madam. Your job is to teach me at least the rudiments of that profession, and the will stipulates that I have only so long
to complete this education. Make no mistake: My cousin's solicitors
were quite careful to explain that if I want the benefits of Callista's
generosity, I have approximately ninety days left to learn to whore."

The vulgar term in the midst of her polite diction landed like the
sound of breaking glass in a quiet library. Gareth sat forward, resting
his elbows on his knees and mentally sorting through curses in
French, though being a *lady*, she'd probably understand those too.
First things first. "Do you *want* me to teach you to whore?"

"I do not want to starve, and I do not want my sister to starve. I
hope to undertake this apprenticeship for the next several months.
One year from Callista's death you can sell the business for me, and
then this episode in my life will be over. The only one who will know
of it besides me and the solicitors is you, and I am hoping to rely on
your gentlemanly discretion."

He took a moment to digest her little speech. The course she
proposed was probably the most sensible, from her point of view.
And he could be discreet. A man on familiar terms with all manner of
vice had to be faultlessly discreet if he wanted to maintain his
privacy.

Which he did.

"Why do I not simply lie to the solicitors, tell them you have
fulfilled the terms, and let us go our separate ways in peace?"

She wrinkled her nose—and it was a pretty nose, in perfect
portion to the rest of her features. "The solicitors are to test me using
a list of questions and answers Callista devised, and if they suspect
I've not surrendered my innocence to their satisfaction, they implied
they could have me examined by a midwife. They would have me
believe myself fortunate that I was not asked to entertain a customer
before witnesses."

Gareth's eyebrow shot up because he knew Callista had been
capable of ruthlessness, and he'd damned near loved her for it, but

this was beyond ruthless. This was cruel, and not a bequest any court would have a part in enforcing.

"To summarize, then," Gareth said, "you want me to spend three months teaching you how to please a man, how to run a brothel, how to play various games of chance, and so on. I am to at least relieve you of your virginity, and I am to complete these tasks without anyone being the wiser? Moreover, I am to sell the brothel for you at the end of one year, all with utmost discretion. What do I get out of it?"

If this woman knew anything about him at all, she'd know to expect that question from him.

"My guess is Callista chose you for her own reasons, believing you would accept. I can't see that you get anything out of this other than the trustee's portion of the proceeds, which I doubt you need." She cocked an eyebrow, perhaps mocking him, perhaps inventorying his physical assets. "If Callista's faith in you is not misplaced, you will get the free services of a well trained whore, won't you? I doubt you need those either."

He suppressed a flinch at her continued use of the word, "whore." There were so many other ways to say it—soiled dove, courtesan, lady of the night, fashionable impure. His guest seemed to want to shock him, and maybe herself.

Two could play at that. He stood and locked the door.

"Why don't we gather a little more information before we decide what to do with this situation, hmm? Would you oblige me by standing?" She did, watching him warily as he stalked toward her. "Over here, away from the window if you please." He took her cool, bare hand in his and guided her across the room.

"What are you about, my lord?" She managed to put some indignation in her tone, but not enough to cover the unease.

Good, he wanted her unnerved. So unnerved and angry she'd stomp right out of the house and never want to lay eyes on him again. Let her swallow her pride and move in with dear old Aunt Besom or eke out a living on piece work from the modistes.

"Before you accept me as the guardian of your virtue, to use your words, you should have some idea whether you can even accept my touch on your person. Losing one's virginity involves a great deal of touching, done correctly. You have to know that much at least?"

She nodded once, suggesting that was the limit of her understanding.

"I will take on this trusteeship, if you conclude you can indeed find pleasure in my carnal touch. I will not force you." He would not force any woman, ever. To know he could still speak with conviction in this regard was a relief. "You decide if you can allow me to seduce you."

He purposely stood too close to her, letting her physically experience his six-foot-four inch height, the scent of horse and aftershave about his person, and the sheer masculine strength he had in abundance. Her pulse beat rapidly at her throat, and she was back to staring at the carpet.

He dropped his voice to a near whisper and leaned in even closer.

"You must be sure, my lady, because once your innocence is compromised, you will never regain it, whether your virtue is intact or not." He picked up her hand and rubbed his thumb slowly across her knuckles. Her gaze clamped on their joined hands, depriving him of any truths her eyes might have given away.

"Do you seek to take my virginity now?"

Brave lady. He awarded her points for that, and for amusing him —his reputation would suffer terribly if he allotted her deflowering only the few minutes available. "No time for that today, my dear, but I would ask of you a kiss to seal our bargain and begin your education. We have, after all, but a short time to complete it."

She glanced up long enough for him to see relief in her eyes, though such a proper lady could have no idea what manner of kiss he contemplated. His hands settled on her waist and he tugged her closer.

"Close your eyes and relax. You have nothing to fret about today."

She didn't immediately close her eyes, but watched him as he took both her hands in his, kissed each palm, then slipped them around his neck. He slid his hands around her waist, resting them at the small of her back. She was close enough to him that he heard the catch in her breath as his hold grew more firm.

She wasn't as cool as she wanted him to believe, and that realization gave Gareth a pause in his determination to rattle her. He started off by nuzzling her temple with his lips, and even that caused her to flinch. He repeated that caress, doing nothing more than inhaling the lavender scent of her hair until she relaxed minutely against him.

"I'll make you a promise." He moved on as he spoke, breathing against her hair, the curve of her ear, the silky skin of her neck, even as his hands went questing over her back in long, slow strokes.

"I will promise you if, at any point you want me to stop, no matter what we're doing, then I will stop. You have only to tell me." Gareth began kissing her, sipping at the spot where her shoulder and her neck joined, and he had to wonder if speech were already beyond her. Her scent was lovely, fresh and clean, without paint, powder, or the slightly singed odor of the curling iron.

Despite her prim and proper airs, despite the mad scheme she'd brought to his door, despite the niggling itch of what remained of his conscience, his body at least was enjoying itself.

"Kiss me," he whispered against her cheek. "Kiss me now."

She turned her face toward him, tensing up for what she no doubt expected would be a grinding, wet, teeth-bumping awkwardness. She was too pretty not to have suffered the attentions a callow swain or two.

So Gareth's lips were feather-gentle as they played at her mouth; he grazed her flesh with his, and slipped a hand to her nape. His mouth parted over hers and he was rewarded when she sighed, her body finally losing its starch against his. Her fingers drifted through the hair at his nape, and Gareth realized she didn't have to go up on her toes to fit him perfectly—more's the pity.

He traced his tongue over her lips, thinking not only to steal a taste of her, but also to distract her from the hand resting just north of her derriere. He molded her against the length of his body, and continued plying his tongue along her mouth. Tentatively, she touched her tongue to his, provoking him to growl in satisfaction at her overture.

She shyly tested the contours of his lips, and he let her explore while his hands stroked her back. Gareth sensed she was just becoming aware of the ridge of male flesh rising against her belly, when his instinct for self-preservation had him easing out of the kiss, and letting his hands fall still on her back.

Her breathing was slightly accelerated as she curled against his chest and rested her head on his shoulder. He tucked his chin on her crown and held her, there being no compelling reason to let her go.

"My dear woman, I should at least know your name."

She remained quiet against him, and he brought one hand up to massage the nape of her neck in slow circles. The kiss had grown a bit out of hand was all—he hadn't been expecting this particular variety of courage from her. This variety of honesty.

She stood unmoving for another moment then stepped away.

"You'll do it then—take on the trusteeship?" Her gaze was a little bewildered, which pleased Gareth inordinately.

"I'll take on the trusteeship for now, and I will be as discreet as possible. You must realize, though, if word of this gets out, I can do nothing to protect you from the terms of Callista's will. I doubt her solicitors want anyone knowing they've created such a bequest—one Chancery would scoff at, mind you—but given who I am, I won't be able to repair your reputation, nor will I try."

She nodded at him soberly. "If this becomes public, nothing will save my reputation, and I don't suppose you want people knowing you've taken on spinster protégé, either. Such a liaison hardly flatters you." She stepped back further and put her gloves on, donning another increment of reserve as she did.

She was wrong, of course. She would be ruined, while society, being stupid, venal and easily entertained, would regard this as another one of Lord Heathgate's titillating larks, nothing more.

"So how shall we go about this?" he asked, his voice holding a detachment his body did not feel.

"Don't scowl at me, your lordship. This situation is not of my doing or yours. I appreciate your willingness to comply with the terms of the bequest, but just as you asked me if I were willing to be seduced, you must be a willing seducer."

The women who would scold him were few in number. That this pretty, proper, spinster might be one of them suggested their dealings could grow interesting. "I can assure you, I am a willing seducer, enthusiastically and often. When do you next have your courses?"

"Wha...?! I beg your pardon!" She gaped at him, her self-possession gratifyingly absent. "What can that have to do with... Why would you ask such a thing?"

"How much do you know about the mechanics of copulation?" He'd chosen one of the more polite terms, and yet it raised a magnificent blush against the lady's fair coloring.

"It involves sleeping in the same bed, and probably some kissing, and touching. I know there is a maidenhead." Her blush deepened so he went to the door, unlocked it, and retrieved her wrap from the footman. He returned with her cloak and slipped it around her shoulders.

Without thinking, he turned her to face him and fastened the frogs of her cloak under her chin. Such caretaking was an intimacy, one he took completely for granted with any woman he'd kissed— until he noticed how stiffly *this* lady was standing.

"Intimate business between men and women involves a bit more than you perceive," Gareth said, smoothing down the lapel of her cloak, "and it will be my pleasure to educate you. I would remind you, though, I have promised if you at any time want to desist from this project, you have only to say so. I can probably find you and your dependents decent employment on one of my estates."

"That is generous of you, my lord, but having imposed on you to this extent, I would not seek employment from you. I have no doubt my mortification is just beginning, and you will be the last man I ever want to spend more time around once this situation is resolved."

He nodded, relieved, because having her in his employ didn't sit well at all. She'd then be under his protection in the *unavailable* sense, and that could only be awkward as hell.

"I will likely *start* Monday next." She looked around self-consciously, as if afraid of being overheard by the very furniture.

How long had it been since a woman had blushed in his company? "And how long are you indisposed?"

"Three or four days." Her answer was barely a whisper. She donned a bonnet that was the same color as old horse droppings, not at all flattering and years out of fashion.

When he taught her how to be a madam, surely he could dress her, too? He took her elbow and walked her toward the door.

"If you will send your direction to me, I will have my coach pick you up Monday afternoon at two of the clock, sharp. Expect to spend the balance of the afternoon with me, and at least several afternoons each week thereafter."

She paused at the door to the corridor and made an intense study of her gloves. "Will you give me some idea what to expect?" she asked, very much on her tattered dignity.

The only decent women he consorted with frequently were his dear mother and her aging friends, and even they—veterans of years of genteel warfare in the best ballrooms—knew not to reveal their emotions.

The lady in the ugly bonnet and mended gloves was afraid. Also affronted, humiliated, and many other things—likely including outraged—but under it all, she was afraid.

Of him, of what he would ask of her.

Gentlemanly sensibilities chose that inconvenient moment to rouse themselves from years of slumber. Of course she was frightened. Terrified—what if he'd refused her? What if he'd raped her? God in heaven, what had Callista been thinking?

Long ago, grieving and bereft, hating the lofty title that had made a laughingstock of him, Gareth had been afraid. As young men will, he'd used other terms for it: daunted, challenged, or when matters had been particularly bad, overwhelmed. In truth, he'd been terrified, and Callista had been his one ally against that fear.

He scowled at his visitor, resentment resurging, at her and at the bargain he'd been inveigled into honoring. "Remember my promise, madam. You hold the control, no matter what I or Callista's solicitors have planned. Considering your indisposition, why don't we start next week with the business aspects of the operation? The expenses, suppliers, ledgers, household budget, and so forth. Have you seen the property?"

"I walked past it."

Did everything make her blush? "Well, then we'll find things to keep us busy next week. Shall I notify Callista's solicitors I've taken the post?"

"If you'd contact them, I would appreciate it. They make me uncomfortable," she replied as he escorted her to the front door. She stopped before taking her leave. "My lord?"

Didn't *he* make her uncomfortable? "Yes?"

"Thank you. Riverton was not a prospect I could have endured."

Her gratitude was surprising and some part of Gareth also found it insupportable. Repugnant.

"I know." *Neither could I.* "Just one more thing, if you would be so kind?"

"My lord?"

"Your name."

She turned to go and beamed a smile at him over her shoulder. Her smile embodied benediction, relief, and pure female beauty all at once. Had he been a less experienced man, it would have bowled him over.

He was a very experienced man, and still, it stunned him momentarily witless.

"I am Felicity, your lordship. Miss Felicity Hemmings Worthington."

CHAPTER TWO

One of the marquess's liveried footmen hailed a hackney, and Felicity climbed in with a sense of unreality, as if watching herself perform on a stage.

She'd just kissed a man who hadn't even known her name, kissed him the way she supposed lovers kissed. It was, well, it was beyond words, though she admonished herself not to dwell on it.

Not dwelling on distasteful topics was a skill every English lady perfected long before she left the school room. Those same ladies would never admit, however, that a shocking kiss from a debauched marquess had felt not wicked at all, but rather, tender, intriguing, and *cherishing*.

And yet, Heathgate was precisely the sort of man to whom kisses given to strangers meant nothing, and such kisses from him should mean nothing to her. Moreover, before this situation had run its course—which it would do, one way or another, in the next few months—he would do a deal more than kiss her.

Already, Felicity was slipping into the pragmatic attitude of the professional impure: *He will have intimate knowledge of me, kiss me, touch me, and so on*—and she had some idea what "so on" was—*and I will have financial security.* In fact, she'd been terrified he'd decline the trusteeship, leaving her to face Riverton.

But the Marquess of Heathgate had a reputation for doing as he pleased and devil take the hindmost. To her relief, he hadn't refused her, as any decent man should have. But then, no decent woman would have asked for his help.

Felicity had spent months telling herself she and Astrid would manage somehow without this terrible gift from Callista, until the solicitors made it clear she'd have to refuse the bequest or meet its terms.

The hackney turned down the quiet lane running before the Worthington household, and Felicity deliberately smoothed her features as she exited the coach and turned to pay the cabbie.

"Hit's been tooken care of, mum," the cabbie informed her with a tip of his hat.

She closed her reticule and thanked him, flustered but honestly relieved. They had come to that—scrimping over cab fare—and would have soon come to worse.

The door opened as she approached the house.

"You're home! Oh, Felicity, what was he like? Will he help us?" Seventeen-year-old Astrid—petite, blond, and bubbling with energy —had Felicity's cloak untied and hung on a peg in an instant. "You must, you simply must, tell us everything—mustn't she, Crabby?"

Felicity was saved from responding by Mrs. Crabble bustling up from the kitchen with a tea tray.

"Now, Miss Astrid, give your sister a chance to get her bearings, for pity's sake. I'll set this in the parlor, and we can enjoy a nice, hot cup of tea while Miss Felicity tells us the news."

Felicity plunked the most horrid bonnet ever created onto a hook. She'd had tea and a sinfully rich éclair at Heathgate's, and found her digestion too unsteady to relish the thought of more, but Crabby tried hard to observe the domestic rituals, even as their financial ship floundered closer to destruction.

"Felicity, you must not make us wait any longer," Astrid declared as she thumped down on the most comfortable chair remaining in the family parlor. "Will Heathgate help us?"

Felicity lowered herself more carefully onto the sofa and watched as Mrs. Crabble poured. The marquess liked his strong and sweet she recalled—for no earthly reason.

"He will help us," she said, smiling purposefully at her sister, "but you must remember this matter requires utmost discretion, Astrid. No one is to know I am learning how to manage a gaming house."

That was only partly a lie—people did gamble at Callista's establishment—and since Felicity herself wasn't entirely sure what else *exactly* went on there, she couldn't have enlightened her little sister much further if she'd wanted to.

"Well, that's just fine, then," Mrs. Crabble said, handing a cup of tea to Astrid. "Things will soon come right now you've met with the marquess." Crabby sipped her own tea, the look on her round, worn face beatific.

A viscount's daughters did not take tea with their housekeeper. Perhaps if Felicity had paid Crabby's wages at some point since Christmas, she would have been better able to recall why.

"Tell me about his house, Lissy," Astrid prompted, "and tell me about him. What does he look like?"

He looked like every woman's vision of sweet ruin, blast him, and his kisses were the embodiment of same.

Which was some comfort. If a lady was to lose her every pretension to propriety, she should at least have lovely kisses to show for it.

"He carries the scent of sandalwood and something else— nutmeg, or clove, or something spicy, expensive, and oddly soothing. You'd pick it out easily, Astrid. He is tall, at least six inches taller than me, and I am taller than many men. He has blue eyes that... they do not invite question, is the best way I can put it. He is surprisingly dignified."

She sipped her tea—weak tea, an inevitable consequence of reusing the leaves. "No, not only dignified, but forbidding. I believe he enjoys an active life, based on his physique. His hair is dark, but not quite black—sable—and he wears it queued back." She had wanted to free his hair but hadn't dared. "He's in some regards old-fashioned. Different."

Though a man of Heathgate's consequence could be as different as he pleased, and his inferiors would ape him rather than judge him for it.

"Oh, good," Astrid said. "I cannot abide an effete man." A silence followed her pronouncement, and she set her tea cup down with a clatter. "Come now, you two. You are exchanging *that* look. I may be seventeen, but I do have opinions of my own."

Felicity and Mrs. Crabble had indeed been exchanging a look—one they often exchanged when Astrid's combination of adolescent directness and adult insight left them not knowing whether to scold or laugh.

"How would you know about effete men, dearest?" Felicity asked, unable to keep the humor from her voice.

"Father was effete," Astrid pointed out, "and look where he left us."

Mrs. Crabble heaved a gusty sigh in lieu of speaking ill of the dead—overtly.

"He did his best, Astrid," Felicity chided. "And he did not invent the process of escheat."

Astrid, never one for moderation of her opinions, leaned forward over her tea cup. "I was eleven when Father died. He had eleven years to find somebody who would bear him a male child, and he knew as well as the lowliest potboy that a peer who dies without male heirs will see his entailed property revert to the crown. Didn't he care any more for us than that? We were left with nothing! If Callista hadn't bequeathed us her business, where would we be?"

Another sigh from Mrs. Crabble, and another exchanged look.

"Astrid, Father didn't plan on having an apoplexy. Though it might not seem like it to you, two-and-fifty is not exactly decrepit. For all we know, he was trying to court an appropriate woman at the time, and he did manage to buy this house as personal property. We still have some nice things about us, and though we've had to economize a bit since Father died, there's no harm in that."

"More tea?" Mrs. Crabble asked.

Astrid shook her head, her expression mutinous. "You won't say it, Felicity, but I know it's true: Father didn't care for us. We have this house because he bought it for his mistresses, and even they didn't present him any children."

Felicity lifted an eyebrow and looked at her sister steadily. The silence stretched for several heartbeats.

"I am sorry." Astrid muttered this apology to her tea cup. "I have been so frightened—what if the marquess wouldn't help us? We've economized more than a bit—my dresses are becoming indecently short, you've let everyone but the Crabbles and the tweenie go, and we only have the pony cart left to get around in. Soon we will have to sell this house—"

Indecently short, suggesting even Astrid knew only streetwalkers flashed their ankles on purpose.

Felicity's heart nearly broke as she put her arms around her sister. This was why she would finally undertake the devil's bargain Callista had put before her. This was why she was resigned to losing her virtue, to accepting the guidance of the notorious Marquess of Heathgate. Astrid was innocent, and not even out of the school room. She did not deserve to go to bed at night wondering how long it would be before she slept in the streets.

"Astrid, don't upset yourself so." Felicity hugged her sister. "We are not as bad off as all that, nor will we be. Callista's will provides for us, now that I've agreed to learn her business. The marquess will do his part, and all will come right, just as Mrs. Crabble says. Finish your tea while I tell you about the marquess's house. His butler looked at least a hundred years old, and I thought he'd give me frostbite so chill was his disapproval of me for calling without a chaperone. But the house, Astrid, is beyond elegant."

She regaled her sister with the harmless details of her visit to the marquess, but noted from the corner of her eye that Mrs. Crabble's expression had become uncharacteristically thoughtful.

Felicity prattled on, knowing dear Crabbie was probably wondering how and why Felicity had got close enough to the marquess to note the delicate sandalwood scent of his soap and linen.

~

"HUGHES, have Brenner join me in the estate office at once, if you please." Gareth tossed the words over his shoulder as he left the soaring entryway of his town house. His encounter with Felici—*Miss* Worthington concluded, there was much to be done. He mentally put aside the developments ensuing from that interview, and turned his mind to the business he had planned for the day.

He let himself into the estate office, which overlooked the gardens at the back of the house, where a few brave purple crocuses suggested spring might eventually make an appearance. Gareth turned his back on the garden and began reading through the correspondence stacked on his desk. A discreet knock preceded the creak of the door opening.

Gareth did not look up from a long and whiny epistle from a land agent in Wales. "Brenner, take a seat. We have matters to discuss."

Michael Brenner, an auburn-haired young man who gave off an air of serious purpose, did as bid. Gareth paid him a tidy sum to do as he was bid, whenever he was bid, and without fussing or dramatics.

"I trust your journey was uneventful," Gareth said, putting aside his reading a moment later.

"It was, your lordship. The distillery is humming along in fine style, and you'll have my report by morning."

"You didn't have time to write it on the journey south?"

"I did draft it, but it requires recopying so as to be more legible."

Brenner spoke the truth—nobody in Gareth's employ for more than a day would lie, dissemble, euphemize, prevaricate, or otherwise attempt to bamboozle him. Those who tried were soon unemployed and in want of a character.

"Give it to the amanuensis. Your time is too valuable to spend copying reports. What do you know of a Felicity Worthington?"

Brenner shot his cuffs, which Gareth had long realized meant the man was arranging his thoughts.

"The Worthington family has weathered some difficulty, your lordship, as a result of Viscount Fairly's demise without male issue. I believe his wife predeceased him, leaving behind two daughters. The older is well beyond her come out, the younger still in the school room, though barely. Both were to have become wards of the crown, at least nominally, but at the time of the viscount's death, an older relation was prepared to take them in. I believe that relation, an aunt, has since died."

Brenner had nearly memorized Debrett's *New Peerage*, and could recite most documents he'd read verbatim—part of the reason Gareth had been paying him a princely sum for several years.

"How are the daughters supported, Brenner? Fairly has been dead at least five years." Gareth stared out into the garden, not seeing the brave crocuses, but rather, recalling a pair of serious topaz eyes.

"I am not sure how the Worthington ladies manage, my lord. The aunt left her nieces some money, but I believe their circumstances are significantly reduced."

"Is there a cadet branch of the family?"

"Not that I am aware of. One would think in a case of escheat, every line and branch would have been explored before such a radical step was initiated."

Escheat was the unthinkable tragedy threatening every titled family, the reason why the succession must be ensured at all costs. In Gareth's family, avoiding escheat meant his title had passed to him upon the simultaneous deaths of his grandfather, his uncle, his cousin, his father and his older brother. His was the kind of story that had the peerage fornicating like rabbits until the requisite heir and spare had been safely raised to manhood.

It was also the reason Gareth avoided visiting his family's distillery, and never overindulged in strong spirits.

He turned his attention back to the matters before him. Brenner, at least, did not seem aware Callista Hemmings was related to the Worthingtons, which was encouraging.

"You will investigate the situation of Viscount Fairly's surviving issue. I want to know the circumstances of the estate upon his death, and what the crown has done with the properties since. I also need to know whatever you can determine about the properties owned by the late Callista Hemmings, and don't limit yourself to the Pleasure House. Get some trustworthy eyes on the Worthington household while you're at it. Be discreet—but this account can be written."

"Of course, my lord." Brenner stood and bowed slightly, heading for the door, his expression suggesting he was already mentally organizing his assignments.

"Brenner?"

He stopped. "Something else, my lord?"

"My thanks for your efforts inspecting the distillery in Scotland. I would not have made the journey willingly."

"Glad to be of service, my lord, as always."

In the ensuing solitude, Gareth's mind wandered back to his interview with Felicity Worthington. Nobody, not the king, not the Prince of Wales, not the Archbishop of Canterbury, coerced Gareth Alexander into any task he didn't choose for himself. So why was he taking on the sordid business of ruining Miss Felicity Oh-So-Proper Worthington, and why for such plebian motivation as simple coin in the lady's pockets?

He'd find a way under, over, around or through the business, and for once in his life, he'd manage the situation without allowing himself the pleasure of bedding a pretty and willing lady.

Maybe.

AT PRECISELY TWO of the clock on Monday afternoon, Gareth's footman opened the door to his unmarked town coach to reveal

Felicity Worthington peering curiously at his equipage. Gareth kept his seat, and let the groom assist the lady up rather than risk the neighbors seeing him in her mews.

"Good day, miss. I am cheered to see that you value promptness." Gareth had taken the forward facing seat, while Miss Worthington arranged herself opposite him and smoothed her skirts so they did not touch his boots.

She was behaving like a chaperone rather than a potential conquest, leaving Gareth equal parts amused and annoyed.

"Good afternoon, my lord. Does one surmise from your tone you've had second thoughts? You sound anything but cheered." When she stopped fussing, she met his gaze directly, and he again felt that inconvenient frisson of arousal that had afflicted him when they'd first met.

"I have had many thoughts regarding this venture since last we met, but none of them what you would call second thoughts. I have agreed to serve as the estate trustee, and I do not break my word. Ever."

"How reassuring," she parried dryly. She held his stare unflinchingly, then started when he surprised her with a bark of laughter.

"Well done, Miss Worthington. You are capable of bravado, which will serve you well as you assume management of the Pleasure House." He thumped on the roof with his walking stick and the coach moved off.

"Is that what she called it? The Pleasure House?"

"Yes, though most men would simply refer to it as Callista's. We're headed there for an inspection of the premises if that meets with my lady's approval."

The shades were drawn, giving the coach an intimate feel though it was broad daylight. Miss Worthington wore the same hideous bonnet, also the same light, lavender scent.

"You refer to me as my lady, but I'm not a lady in the titled sense. When Father was alive, of course I was the Honorable Felicity Worthington and so forth, but the honorific means nothing without a viscount to inherit it. Now, it seems a reminder of ill fortune."

Gareth loathed small talk, and what she'd offered instead was something indicative of bravery—she'd offered him a place to start.

"I grew up as plain Mr. Alexander myself," he said. "I preferred to die in that happy state, but ill fortune, as you call it, had other plans."

That piqued her interest, as he'd known it would. One could fornicate enthusiastically with a complete stranger, but Gareth was fairly certain one could not seduce a proper lady without allowing her at least a passing acquaintance.

"What happened?"

He would tell her his tale of woe, mostly because she was bound to hear a version of it sooner or later.

"My family owns a prosperous distillery on an estate up in Scotland. The lot of us had assembled there at my grandfather's request. The estate is on the coast, and my grandfather fancied himself an expert yachtsman. I don't know if he was, but he invited us all out on his boat. My entire family went; I was the only one who declined the outing. My mother, father, older brother and younger brother joined Grandfather, my uncle, and my cousin as well as a guest or two. A bad squall blew up. The boat capsized, and most perished with it. My younger brother managed to rescue my mother, who at some point in her girlhood learned the rudiments of swimming."

He could manage this recitation in bland tones now, the signal accomplishment of nine years of effort.

"That's tragic!" Miss Worthington expostulated. "What a great blessing you did not drown as well, my lord. Surely you do not regard that as ill fortune?" Her great golden eyes shone at him with a world of concern, and she'd leaned forward to touch his sleeve.

He took her hand and absently raised it to his lips. The scent of lavender was stronger near her wrist, more bracing. He wished she'd been sitting beside him, so he might maintain possession of that scent.

"I don't regret surviving,"—he didn't regret surviving *now*—"but suspicion turned on me, because I'd had no stated reason for declining to join my relations on that boat. Some suspected I was guilty of foul play, and that rumor colored my first impressions of Polite Society, and—to be honest—theirs of me."

"But surely your mother and brother would have exonerated you?"

Miss Worthington's outrage was both comforting and disconcerting. She assumed he was blameless, and thought others should have as well, affirming his sense that Felicity Worthington was not simply proper, she was also, in the most sincere sense, decent.

"My mother eventually recovered, though she developed a serious inflammation of the lungs. By the time she healed from that, and from her grief, the worst of the gossip had died down. Andrew was fifteen, and I did not feel it fair to burden him with my problems in addition to his own difficulties."

The compassion in Miss Worthington's amber gaze could have melted any heart. This warmth in her was unexpected and not particularly welcome. Gareth's first impression of her had been one of starch and sensibility and for her to turn up *sweet* was not in his plans.

"Your brother blamed himself for not being able to rescue more of them," she said, drawing the conclusion on her own.

"He did, honorable little whelp that he was—at the time. Since the accident, he's grown into a bit of a rascal."

"And what of you, my lord? Are you a bit of a rascal?"

"The terms applied to me are not quite so charming, Miss Worthington, as you are no doubt aware."

She sat back, finely arched brows knit. "I'm *not* aware, your lordship. I was not out when details of your family tragedy would have been common knowledge. Because my mother died before my come-out, I never really moved much in society, even when I was old enough to do so. My father made a few attempts to introduce me around, but they never came to anything. I did not take, you see."

She smiled as she announced this. Smiled the same shy, proud

GARETH   27

smile another woman would have evidenced when referring to making a curtsey before the queen.

"I don't believe that bothered you much."

"It did not. I wondered if blond hair and petite stature might have served me better, but I did not wish for it. I had been running my father's household for some time before I came of age. I was happier to do something that made a difference to the family's wellbeing than to be out until dawn fluttering my eyelashes at callow swains."

He laughed again, a short explosion of sardonic mirth. "God help the swains if you'd determined they were useful for something more to your liking."

"Oh, I liked to dance, and I love music. But I am too tall for most young men to partner well, and they have not the patience for truly enjoying the music."

She was right, of course. The average exponent of well bred English young manhood was at best politely decorative in Gareth's opinion—also randy as hell, and completely inept at dealing with it. He certainly had been.

"I, for one, am glad not to be burdened any longer with excessive youth." Though at nearly thirty, he still had a little youth left, didn't he?

"I would say the same, my lord, except that as Callista's successor, youth would be an asset, would it not?" The coach drew to a halt as Gareth considered her comment.

"Now that is a paradox, Miss Worthington, and a complicated one." He preceded her from the coach and handed her down. "Most men frequenting establishments such as Callista's desire women who appear to be in the first blush of youth, but they do not want a partner who is inexperienced, inept, or immature. They want a woman, not a girl. I find the only men who persist in finding young girls attractive are old men, and they are likely intimidated by the idea that a mature woman could find their performance clumsy."

Gareth concluded from his companion's guarded expression that she did not entirely comprehend his comment. He started a mental list, a syllabus of corruptions he must perpetrate on her ignorance and innocence.

"Come. Your property awaits."

Miss Worthington looked around her—gawked, more like. Gareth had directed his coachman to let them off in the port cochere, which shielded them from public view.

"This is private," she murmured.

"You must assure discretion for the patrons who wish it, of course. Very likely, Callista chose this property with such considerations in mind." He ushered her through a side entrance to the large town house.

"Should I have worn a veil?" she asked, still peering around.

"Not today. I've given the staff and the ladies the afternoon off, with instructions to vacate the premises for the next two hours. We will tour the building, so you will have a more definite sense of what Callista left you."

And doubtless be shocked silly.

"I didn't expect it to be this decent," Miss Worthington said when they'd finished with the lowest floor and the public rooms.

"Many brothels are not so finely decorated, but Callista had, or developed, taste. She sought a clientele that wanted the same sort of surroundings they'd find at home. Comfortable, but refined. You should be grateful for that."

"Will you tell me why?"

The openness of Miss Worthington's expression took Gareth off guard, because clearly, she didn't know how perverted and even evil the oldest profession could become.

She would have to learn, and from him—drat her, Callista, the oldest profession, and human nature.

"Some people, Miss Worthington, make their living off the most indecent forms of the natural urges. They can do so because men—and women—who seek to indulge those perversions will pay handsomely for the opportunity. Callista chose not to offer such entertainments in her establishment."

"Such as?"

He turned a glacial stare on her—a stare that reduced Brenner to babbling—but she did not withdraw the question.

"Such as sexual arousal gratified by inflicting pain on someone helpless to protect themselves. Such as sexual congress with children. Such as those who enjoy being degraded as they pursue their pleasures; those who cannot find pleasure unless they are surreptitiously observing others having intimate relations. I do not begrudge two or four or ten adults what they choose to do in private, but many young girls and boys are inveigled into working in brothels because their alternative is starvation or repeated, uncompensated rape."

She looked shaken by the time he'd finished, which was all to the good, even if it left Gareth feeling as if he'd kicked a puppy. Thus Miss Purity Chastity Felicity Worthington could begin to see the reality of her cousin's gift.

He took her elbow and guided her to the higher reaches of the house, where she went quiet at the variety of rooms—a few bedrooms decorated in garish velvets, as well as the predictable sultan's tent, mock stable, and school room. She went quieter still at the ordinary, pretty bedrooms the women used for themselves on the next floor up, and abruptly, Gareth had shown her enough.

Though he'd become familiar with most of the house years ago, even he felt like a voyeur among the samplers, cutwork, dried flowers and embroidered cushions on the third floor.

When he handed his charge up into the coach he took a place beside her on the forward facing seat, as was his habit in his own coach. Miss Worthington bounced over to the chaperone's bench, making him feel like he'd kicked a kitten *and* a puppy while several small children looked on.

"Miss Worthington, if we have agreed to be physically intimate with one another, can't you bring yourself to sit beside me?"

She made a face, but answered him by resuming the seat beside him. "This is more than passing strange," she reflected, and it was not a sanguine observation. He took her hand, and in her preoccupation, she did not seem to notice his presumption.

"I ask myself," she continued, "is this what those women routinely do? They kiss men who don't even know their names? They stick their tongues into the mouths of strangers? It is decidedly odd."

He laced their fingers, wondering if he'd ever, ever, in his distant and prosaic, not-much-missed youth felt the same consternation.

"The ladies' trade operates within a ritual that makes it less bizarre. There is flirtation, sexual innuendo, mutual assent, and stages through which matters proceed. One becomes used to it."

She looked at their joined hands while Gareth braced himself for one of her difficult, fearless questions. "Does it ever become so commonplace it's boring?"

"Invariably." And again he felt a gnawing sense of irritation. It was one thing to swive a woman, and an entirely different and less appealing challenge to explain swiving to her. "Boredom is why men seek variety in their partners, and fantasies to enliven their interest. They use drugs, spirits, toys, and games for the same end. It's simply adult entertainment."

"When you kiss me, I'm not bored," she mused darkly. "I think you are accomplished at it."

"Your flattery, Miss Worthington, will surely turn my head."

She went quiet then, apparently content to roll along with her own thoughts, her hand casually joined with his. She had graceful hands, and soft, soft skin. Had she been so rattled she'd forgotten to don her gloves?

Had he?

Maybe seducing her wouldn't be all that much of a chore—not that Gareth should seduce her.

"What next?" she asked, looking at their hands as his thumb traced a pattern on her palm.

"Where would you like to go from here?" he countered, drawing her wrist to his lips.

She snatched her hand away.

"None of that. I do not know how to flirt, and I asked you a question. I cannot attend your efforts to educate me if I am in constant dread that this time, on this outing, or at this meeting, you have decided I must lose my virtue. I would like a schedule if you please."

What a magnificent scold she was. He recaptured her hand, admitting to himself she had a point: She was innocent and ignorant, and all manner of ghoulish fairytales were put into the heads of decent young women to ensure they preserved their virtue.

"We begin this week with the business aspects of your brothel."

"My brothel. I suppose it is. Dear me..."

"If I may continue?"

"Of course. My apologies."

So hopelessly polite. "We will start with the business aspects of the situation. You've seen the property, and you must have questions about it. We'll need to familiarize you with all of its finances, its staff positions, its assets and liabilities. You will need to learn the client list, the current staff, and so forth. That should occupy us for the next week or two."

He had her attention, at least—and he kept her hand as well. "We need to address your wardrobe, too, Miss Worthington. You are not attired as befits a successful woman of the world, and you must know how to clothe the women who work for you."

"Of course, but none of this is...." She blushed and might have glanced out the window except common sense dictated they were tooling through Town with every shade tied shut.

"None of this is getting us into bed?" he finished for her. "We'll have time for that. I propose when you have the business situation well in hand, say in several weeks, we begin on the more intimate details."

She looked him over, and not with the sort of interest he usually merited from the gentler sex. "You want me to become familiar with you first. That is kind of you."

The woman was daft. "Kind? I can assure you, deflowering a stranger who finds my touch unpleasant holds no allure for me. I intend to use the next weeks for us to become accustomed to one another's company."

She held up their joined hands. "That's why you do this? You touch me, when you don't have to?"

The carriage came to halt in the alley behind her house, and he regarded their hands. "Touching you serves that function, but in truth, I touch you because it brings me pleasure." And wasn't that curious? "I would ask one concession of you, however."

"What concession?"

He did not release her hand. She turned her head, so the brim of the awful bonnet obscured her eyes from him. The bonnet was going onto the rubbish pile at their very next outing.

"If we are to become intimate, then you must allow me the use of your given name, and I invite you to use mine as well."

"You have the eyes of a wolf."

He had just offered her the use of his Christian name and she came out with that?

"You have the eyes of a wolf, Gareth," he instructed.

"You have the eyes of a wolf... Gareth."

He gave her a terse nod, freed her hand, and let her leave the coach. He kept the vehicle waiting until she'd crossed the alley, made her way through a bleak, dormant back garden, and disappeared into her home.

The dratted woman was pretty, soft, fragrant and intelligent, and she appeared not the least bit interested in him on an animal level.

Despite all that, he could hope she'd at least been disappointed that he hadn't kissed her again—because *he* certainly was.

CHAPTER THREE

"I don't understand why we must spoil the customers so," Miss Worthington began. "They are provided with beautiful women willing to do their every bidding. Why do they need expensive drink, a French chef, and Flemish tapestries? It isn't as if these men pay attention to the furniture when they're ogling a décolletage."

Three weeks had seen a considerable thawing of the lady's reserve, and the emergence of an odd, protective attitude toward Callista's business. Miss Worthington had been introduced to the house staff and the ladies who worked there. She had accompanied Gareth to the milliner's, and learned about fancy French undergarments until her blushes could have lit a bonfire. She had won the argument over whether she should acquire some for herself, but lost when Gareth insisted on selecting evening gowns for her.

She had reviewed the wine list and the buffet menus, and could give a fair account of herself regarding several games of chance. She had learned the "guest" list, and made suggestions regarding the music provided each evening. Her aptitude for the managerial aspects of her role suggested that she had, indeed, been running her father's household since long before she'd left the school room.

Gareth met with his protégé in the library of his town house, because that space was more comfortable than his estate office, and better suited to the next phase of Felicity's education.

She wanted to know about spoiling the customers, while he was more interested in having her spoil him.

"You're not answering me, Gareth, and you have that calculating look in your eye that means something bad for somebody."

He had come to delight in her scolds—and in her use of his given name—but the woman was too perceptive by half. He rose from his armchair and stoked the fire burning in the huge fireplace before which they both sat.

"To answer your question, you don't need to spoil the customers to the extent Callista did. You may change whatever aspect of the business you wish because you're right: The important service is the one provided by the women. The rest is mere presentation. You should bear in mind, however, that prostitution is a competitive business. If all a man wants is a quick fuck, he can shove any streetwalker up against the nearest wall and be on his way in five minutes. The streetwalker keeps all the proceeds, and the same service is provided."

Felicity regarded him narrowly. "You use crude language to shock me. Get on with your point."

"My point,"—he jabbed again at the fire—"is that your establishment must remain competitive. Callista left you a thriving business, but it has little in the way of reserves. If a rumor were to get out that you're watering the drinks, your tables are crooked, or your women unclean, for example, then you would be forced to close your doors. The building itself is worth a fair penny, but the income over the long term is the greater asset. I would advise you to observe the business for some months before you attempt to improve it through drastic changes."

He finished speaking, but did not return to his chair. Instead he picked up a white quill pen from his desk, and began pacing the room idly, pulling out an occasional book and reshelving it as he wandered. Some distance—or something—was wanted, given the topic.

"I can understand that the supply exceeds the demand, Gareth, but can't we try a few things to improve profit?" she asked, staring into the fire as he paced behind her.

He brushed the quill over his lips. "Like what?"

"Couldn't we offer cognac in addition to champagne and other wines? It has class, you must admit, but is served in smaller quantities. Couldn't we use a piano soloist instead of a string trio some nights? The piano is beautiful, and sits idle most evenings. We could also—" She fell silent as he came to stand behind her chair, resting his elbows along its back.

"Go on," he urged, his mouth near her ear. He brushed the feather over her jaw, any number of games and diversions coming to mind that *we* might indulge in.

"What are you doing, lurking back there?" She remained facing forward because he'd arranged himself so that if she turned her head, her mouth would be in quite close quarters with his. She had good instincts, did Miss Felicity Worthington.

"Is my reprieve over?" she asked in a small, not-so-brave voice.

"Your reprieve?" When had the scent of lavender ever served as an aphrodisiac?

"You've given me weeks to accustom myself to our eventual intimacy. Have you decided the time has come for matters to progress?"

Gareth leaned along the chair behind her, breathing through his nose, and considering his reply. He'd taken things slowly with Felicity, finding himself reluctant to simply romp away her virginity. He disliked the position Callista had put him in—a position he'd agreed to—but no options were presenting themselves.

He brushed the feather over Felicity's lips and decided he would push the issue, scare Felicity witless, and she'd scurry off determined to find another way to keep body and soul together. She was decent to the bone; hence, his strategy was a foolproof way of extricating himself from a commitment he never should have made.

"I believe," he murmured in her ear, "you have the right idea. Some changes are in order at the brothel, but also in our dealings."

~

FELICITY CAUGHT GARETH'S CLEAN, spicy scent, felt his breath on her nape, and sensed the heat of his big, muscular body behind her. When Gareth nuzzled below her ear, her insides leaped about like March hares.

"What kind of changes?" *And please God, may they be made with my clothing on my person.*

"You have easily grasped the business aspects of your inheritance. We can move on to educating you in the skills plied by the women you employ."

Something warm and soft brushed against Felicity's neck—and not the infernal feather. The contact was faery-light, then came again, more definitely. *His lips.* For weeks she had dreamed of those lips, and watched them form one growling, precise, cranky word after another.

He wasn't growling now. "Do you mean right...today?"

"Today we begin." He straightened and came around to stand before her, his expression baleful. "You needn't sound so terrified, Felicity. Remember, no matter what we're doing, I will stop when you request it of me."

The daft man assumed she'd be able to speak.

"Would you like a drink?" he asked, tossing the quill pen onto his blotter. "Perhaps some cognac?"

This was Gareth's version of solicitude—to cross the room and give her time to gather her wits. He was, in his taciturn way, as kind as he could be, and Felicity wished not for the first time that they had met under other circumstances. His knowledge of commerce was encyclopedic, and for that alone, she could spend hours in conversation with him. He didn't condescend to her when she asked the simplest questions, and he never lost patience with her ignorance—about business, about *anything*.

"May I have some lemonade?"

"Certainly." He went to the dry sink and returned with two glasses—he was apparently in the mood for something cool and tart as well—then handed Felicity her drink and resumed his seat.

He regarded her over the rim of his glass. "We have not made much progress with your erotic education though we have covered other ground thoroughly."

Felicity sipped her lemonade, praying for fortitude. Gareth said naughty, forbidden words so easily. Shocking her was a sport for him, like skittles or bowls—and yet he was also drinking lemonade.

"I have allowed that part of our dealings to slip from my notice," she admitted. Shoved it under any handy rug, more like. "I've focused on learning what you set before me week by week, and ignored when you occasionally hold my hand, or touch my arm, or stroke my cheek. I suppose there will be more of that sort of thing?"

He treated her to a leonine stare. "You ignore my touch?" he asked, an odd note in his voice—humor maybe, or curiosity? Certainly not pique.

"I try. Sometimes I like how you touch me, but mostly it unnerves me. I am not from a demonstrative family." This was a falsehood—Astrid was nothing if not demonstrative.

He glanced upward at the Cupids cavorting among the molding, probably a rake's version of a prayer for strength. "What touches do you like?"

The answer was easy, the words were not. "I like your hands. They are beautiful hands, and you can touch with such assurance, such competence. Your hands make me think of the phrase that one is in 'good hands.' If I were a horse, I would trust your hands."

He looked absently at the appendages Felicity found so intriguing, his expression suggesting there was no explaining women's odd starts.

"What else?" If he'd been a cat, he would have been switching his tail so palpable was his impatience.

The sorry, lowering fact was that Felicity enjoyed *all* of his touches.

"You've on occasion tidied up my hair—I don't think you even know you're doing it. You tuck a loose strand back behind my ear, or smooth a lock off my shoulder. I like it, from you. I haven't had a mother about to fuss me for some years, and find it endearing."

He regarded her with the sort of consternation reserved for bad art purchased by a good friend for far too high a price, then seemed to come to an internal conclusion.

"We will start there, then, with your hands and your hair. Each time we meet, we will spend time on one particular part of the body —yours or mine, we'll get around to them all eventually, at least the ones that count. In this way, I expect you will lose most of what's left of those maidenly inhibitions, or send me packing."

He might have been planning the layout of his garden or compiling a guest list for a Venetian breakfast.

"You don't really care which, do you? It's all the same to you whether you get me into bed or scare me into a life of service."

The idea that her intimate education held no more interest for him than a choice of desserts was not cheering—and a life in service was not an option for Astrid.

Gareth took a sip of his drink, not a care in the world. "I am long past the point of taking sexual encounters any more seriously than I would a hot bath or a good meal, Felicity. We've touched on this before. If I take you to bed we will both enjoy it. For you, it will be a new experience, and one that makes certain options available."

"While it removes other options from my grasp." Options no decent woman parted with happily. He couldn't possibly think she'd lost sight of that reality.

He gave her a peevish look. "Yes, you will lose certain options when you lose your virginity. That is a matter for you to consider. My point is that when I make love with you, I will enjoy the physical pleasure, but I will also be discharging an obligation placed on me by Callista's bequest—no more, no less."

Philosophical lectures and sermons were delivered in this same dry, dispassionate tone, and his almighty lordship wasn't finished.

"If you want protestations of profound emotion from me, you are doomed to disappointment. I'll give you pleasure, and teach you how to please a lover. When I have discharged that obligation, I will wish you luck, and be on my way."

Felicity sipped her tart drink and did not ask the marquess the questions that had plagued her for weeks: How does it *feel* to take a stranger to your bed? How do you talk yourself into desiring me? How can you contemplate such intimacy with another and yet regard it as no more significant than sharing a bench outside Gunter's when the crowds are thick?

She offered him a placatory smile—she hadn't heard him call it making love before. He'd used a hundred vulgar terms in both English and French instead.

"I take your point: You are performing the service for me that Callista performed for you, and I will learn to perform for others. It's business. I understand that."

She did not understand why she felt as if she'd just insulted him gravely—he was trying to help her, and at her request.

He considered his lemonade, his expression unreadable. "Just so."

Felicity held her peace, lest the lump in her throat provoke her to more unhelpful speech.

"For the next part of our dealings," he said, setting his drink aside, "I request that you bathe thoroughly before we meet, forego your stays, and be prepared for me to seduce your hair."

He emphasized that pronouncement by running his fingers along Felicity's brow and smoothing her hair behind her ear—a gesture he'd performed a handful of times, but one Felicity had just admitted she enjoyed. Well, no matter. She'd been honest, and it meant nothing to him, regardless of the tenderness she perceived in his touch.

Was she supposed to hope that someday, that same pleasure would mean nothing to her as well?

"THIS FEELS SO AWKWARD!" Felicity protested for the third time.

She sat facing a vanity that took up an alcove in Gareth's dressing room, her reflected expression enough to daunt any man intent on seduction. Gareth put down the seven hair pins he'd managed to extract from her coiffure.

"I take it you don't have the regular services of a lady's maid?" Nor did she appear to have a seduce-able bone in her curvaceous body.

"Father thought it would spoil me, though I suspect the limitation was in truth financial," Felicity said. "Gareth, I'm sorry. I cannot be at ease with you touching my hair as if you were a servant or lady's maid. I know you have every right given the nature of our dealings, and I'm being ridiculous."

By pronouncing herself thus, she was attempting to be reasonable, but it was the sort of reasonableness that masked female upset. Gareth knelt beside her when he wanted to pour himself a bumper from the decanter.

"You can face down irate creditors, callow swains, and an ill-mannered marquess, but you're afraid of a hair brush?"

She looked away from him, the angle of her chin suggesting he'd lost control of matters entirely.

"Don't you be kind, Gareth Joyce Alexander. Don't you dare be kind."

He rose, the bitterness of her tone taking him aback every bit as much as the content of her accusation. "I was *trying* to be seductive."

A difference of opinion on that topic wasn't in his lesson plan for the day—for any day, for that matter, though he hadn't truly had to exert an effort with a woman since ascending to the title, and nine years of idleness dulled a man's reflexes.

"I was trying to be...." Felicity rose too, a fat, russet curl bouncing against her nape. "I don't know what. I've given you the right to deal with me however you please. Viewed from a certain angle, I've invited your attentions, but I simply..."

Insight struck with inconvenient certainty. Gareth passed her his handkerchief, and swept the curl over her shoulder—to which she did not object.

"This has little to do with permission, Felicity."

She dabbed at her eyes, confirming that she'd been on the verge of tears, and that he'd been the one to put her there. "What does it have to do with, then?"

So testy, a student who'd been certain she'd had the right answer.

"It has to do with *privilege*." Gareth scooped Felicity up and hauled her against his chest as he settled onto a divan along the wall. "I am not exercising contractual rights when I touch you, I'm enjoying a rare privilege you may revoke at any moment—though I rather wish you wouldn't."

That was the sort of honesty most women would have known to take advantage of. His admission should have sparked a spate of flirting on her part and wheedling on his.

Thank God the lady in his arms knew as little about flirting as he knew about wheedling. Felicity's upset was such that she didn't flounce off his lap and stride away while demanding a discourse from him on the difference between a right and a privilege. She instead snuggled closer on a sigh.

"You confuse me, Gareth. I had hoped you would find dealing with me pleasurable, but fear I'm just another duty for you: Meet with estate manager, attend opening of Parliament, deflower aging virgin." Felicity buried her face against his neck. "I hate that I'm crying in front of you."

"I don't like to see you upset either." This admission was more poor tactics, but also the ruddy damned truth.

"Maybe we should just go to bed and get it over with." Convicted felons spoke with the same enthusiasm about exercise at the cart's tail.

"Maybe not," he rejoined, letting one hand work its way into the thick braid coiled at her nape.

"Why not? I'm miserable at this seduction-by-parts you've embarked on, Gareth. I feel like a rabbit frozen at the sound of the approaching pack. I'm morbidly mesmerized by my impending doom. That feels good."

Gareth shifted her in his lap, the better to massage her scalp, and firmly resettled her against him. She stirred about as if trying to gather her wits, though Gareth had entirely different plans for her wits—perhaps for his own, as well.

"Behave," he growled.

She cuddled up again. "Why don't we just toddle along to that bed of yours, and be about it? Then you'll be finished with me and can be on your way, as you put it. Wish me luck, I think you said."

He considered her proposal and rejected it. Felicity was *not* ready. *He was not ready.* He was not ready to resign her to a complete loss of propriety, and what that said about his credentials as a rake did not bear examination.

"First, even if I did take you up on this daring proposal, there is much more to learn about copulation than the simple business of your quim being penetrated by an erect cock." He suspected she liked his blunt speech, and if nothing else it would distract her from her tears. "Second, a man must be in the mood to have relations, or he won't achieve a cockstand, much less satisfaction."

"You are speaking crudely again. I know the cock is the male breeding organ, and have overheard enough footmen to know that you also make indelicate reference to a female's privy parts. I am not precisely familiar with that other cock-business you mentioned." She sounded sleepy and bored.

Cockstand. You will soon be sitting on one.

"Have you ever seen horses mate, or flirt with each other in anticipation of mating?" he asked as he unraveled her braid.

"Once, when I was visiting my aunt and nobody was minding me. The whole undertaking seemed noisy and violent—until it was over. Then the stallion rested his neck along the mare's, and that looked sweet, though I can't imagine the mare liked having half a ton of exhausted male atop her. I will not countenance you biting my neck, Gareth."

Such an innocent. He sank his teeth against her neck, gently, and spoke from a lightly clenched jaw.

"A marquess bites whomever he pleases to bite." She tasted like the lavender ices he'd had at Gunter's, only better. He swiped his tongue against the pulse in her throat as her hair went tumbling down her back in thick, cinnamon waves. "Did you note anything about the stallion in particular?"

"He had what the stable boys called a fifth leg, though I'm sure they'd have been mortified to know I'd overheard that. I was certainly mortified. I will be quite cross if you tangle up my hair."

"Bother your hair. Your attention to the matter at hand would be appreciated, Felicity. I'm trying to explain procreation to you, for pity's sake. What you observed was the stallion's member preparing to pass his seed into the mare's womb, which is necessary for conception, I assume you know that much?"

He had the urge to laugh—at himself. Felicity's affirmative reply was muffled against his chest, suggesting he was amusing her as well, an improvement over provoking her tears. Gareth continued stroking her hair, finding those caresses relaxed the bundle of womanhood curled up in his lap.

Also the fellow holding her.

"A man's member also prepares for copulation by becoming rigid and erect."

"This does not sound very convenient when his breeches are tailored to reveal every detail of his manly physique, nor does it sound dignified." Her tone was amused, gleeful, maybe, at the thought of men relieved of their pride.

"Dignity has little to do with it, and when one is aroused that doesn't seem to matter so much." Felicity's attitude made it difficult to be matter of fact. The feel of her hand playing with the hair at his nape didn't exactly predispose him to sternness either.

"You are serious about this, aren't you?" Felicity said, humor still lacing her voice. "You aren't having me on about male parts enlarging with passion? One hears schoolgirl rumors, but they're hardly trustworthy."

"I would not lie to you, Felicity, ever. Though I must say, if I'd known the facts of copulation would amuse you, I would have mentioned them sooner." Why, in all the hours he'd spent in Felicity's company, had he never heard her truly laugh?

She scooted around on Gareth's lap. "This is not what I had expected today—it seems a strange undertaking. I'm not sure I can get my mind around it." The scooting was having a predictable effect on Gareth's mind, and his body.

"The whole situation would make more sense to you if you had experienced arousal. No." He put a forefinger to her lips to still her response. "Don't think about it. Allow me to demonstrate."

He replaced his finger with his mouth, kissing her without warning or preamble. He shifted her in his arms so she was cradled in his embrace, but reclining against the arm of the divan. This impulse on his part had taken her off guard—as it had him—and she stiffened in his arms predictably.

"Relax," he murmured. "I shan't leave off until you do." And very likely not then either.

Gareth exercised both his patience and his determination, the latter being one asset he possessed in abundance. Little by little, Felicity became pliant in his embrace. Her right hand wrapped around the back of his head, while her left rested over his heart, and her tongue made a timid foray along his lips as her eyes drifted closed.

Gareth, brought his hand down Felicity's arm in slow strokes. He moved back up to her shoulder, to her collarbone, to her throat, caressing elegant bones clad in worn, modest attire. When she seemed comfortable with that, he let his hand drift to her stomach, while he distracted her by sucking at her sweet, lemony lower lip.

His intention had been to soothe and arouse her with his touch, to start her a few steps up the long, lovely climb toward sexual satisfaction. To his consternation, he was the one soothed and aroused.

The problem was, he had to *pay attention* to her. He could not move through the same figures of the same dance and achieve the same results, as he could with any of his other partners. She was, drat the woman and her glorious unbound hair, *interesting* rather than convenient.

To touch her was a privilege, just as he'd said, and on an instinctive level, she knew not to allow him to assume anything less.

Slowly, so slowly, he inched his hand up to her ribs, at which juncture, her fingers came down on top of his. Undeterred, he eased a thumb along the underside of her breast, skimming the fabric of her dress. He teased and hinted and toyed, until she arched against him, sighing when he closed his fingers around her breast.

Gareth schooled himself to yet more patience, a difficult undertaking when Felicity was—at last—melting in his arms. She'd tiptoed across the divide between wary and wanton, though it had taken more stealth and forbearance than Gareth had shown any other woman in his shamefully vast experience.

She tried to sit up. "Gareth, I am uncomfortable... please..."

He responded by dipping his tongue into her mouth, and finding, to his pleasure, she met him open-mouthed. He lifted her against his body and slipped his hands around to unfasten the back of her dress. Felicity was apparently so enthralled with the sensations to be found by molding her breasts to Gareth's chest that the loosening of her bodice didn't register.

Until Gareth peeled her dress down from her shoulders and began kissing the flesh he exposed.

He'd wasted weeks trying to be gentlemanly, weeks arguing with the woman about menus, musical repertoire, and budgets. And all those weeks, he could have been devouring his very own lavender ice. Gareth moved his hand up to again cup her breast, but this time, his fingers closed on the flesh of her nipple through only the thin lawn of her chemise. Felicity gasped—or maybe it was more of a whimper—as he began a gentle, rhythmic pressure on her flesh.

"Oh-my-dear-gracious..." she murmured, though Gareth was drifting beyond measuring Felicity's reactions, beyond careful seduction. He briefly considered throwing up her skirts and plunging himself into her heat.

Alas, oh-my-dear-gracious was not an invitation to plunder.

He would have to stop soon.

But not quite yet.

Gareth considered himself due the satisfaction of taking her nipple in his mouth, and so he closed his lips around her flesh, and began suckling in strong, steady pulls. Felicity's hands cradled the back of his head, and she held him to her as if her life depended on it.

"Gareth, please..."

Please what?

Felicity grabbed at his hand, brought it up to her other breast, and closed his fingers over her nipple. He pleasured her for several more moments before forcing himself to ease up. His caresses became lighter, he slid his mouth off Felicity's nipple and rested his face along her bare, warm breast.

And found, to his fierce satisfaction, Felicity's heart was going like a rabbit's.

"My goodness gracious. My ever-loving goodness gracious," Felicity panted against his hair, wonder in her voice battling with disgruntlement. "You might bite me anywhere you please now. I'd have nothing to say to it."

Lovely thought, though she'd probably blather at him the entire time.

Gareth straightened, tucking up Felicity's bodice in the name of preserving the last shred of his sanity—because he'd been the fool to tell her all those weeks ago to forego her stays.

He regarded the spinster in his arms, the one with her russet hair cascading nearly to the floor, her lips rosy and pink, her bare shoulders a study in grace.

Privilege was a pale word for what she'd allowed. Courage came into it, and pleasure, and even an element of the sublime.

"You, my dear, hide surprising fireworks."

"Is that good?"

Probably not—for him or for her. Rather than answer that interesting question, Gareth scooted her to sit beside him, then turned Felicity by the shoulders so her back was accessible. "Let's get you organized." He fastened her hooks and planted a kiss on her nape. Such a soft, soft nape she had, and pale freckles dusting the tops of her shoulders.

"Please don't start again, Gareth. I don't think I could bear much more of that."

"You sound so stern, Felicity. I thought you liked it."

What he'd *thought* was that in some small degree, she had to like *him*, to permit him such intimacies. He kept that nonsense behind his teeth.

Felicity was quiet for a moment while Gareth finished with her hooks.

"I'm afraid I rather did like it," she said. "I was nervous before, Gareth; now I am terrified."

Woman, thy name is complexity. Though maybe she'd become so terrified she'd run screaming from the house, and all he'd hear from her was a polite note excusing him from further obligations.

This possibility did not bring as much relief as it ought.

"Passion is overwhelming until you get used to it," he conceded as he finger-combed her hair into a long plait. Part of him didn't want to receive that polite note, at least not quite yet.

"And when does one 'get used' to all that excitement and pleasure and intimacy and such?" she asked unhappily. He rose to fetch a green hair ribbon and the seven pins from the vanity. Felicity scowled at him as he padded across the room and said nothing as he sat behind her, tied off her braid and wound her plait up into a bun.

Though seven pins would not hold the mass of her hair in place for long.

"I don't think anyone wants to become completely blasé about sex, Felicity. It just happens. You go through such a variety of partners, you play with all the toys, explore all the games and drugs, and in the end, it comes back to a pleasurable bodily sensation. You asked if being full of fireworks is a good thing, and my answer is you will have to decide for yourself."

He pulled her against him, so her back rested against his chest, and his arms linked across her waist. While he blathered on about jaded palates and bodily humors, he ignored the creeping suspicion that the woman in his arms was near tears—again.

"The skillful prostitute knows how to appear aroused without actually becoming aroused, or only mildly so. She is hired to please her clients, not herself, and so her own satisfaction is not a priority. In your case, your sensuality makes my task easier. You may find, though, having had your passions awakened, it is inconvenient, as a madam, to seek relief from them with clients."

And why was he bringing this up now, when relatively tame play inspired the woman nearly to tears?

"You think I will need a male mistress?" she asked, clearly horrified by the very notion.

"A gallant of some sort. Society women often develop liaisons with discreet admirers for mutual pleasure. You need not concern yourself with this now."

Though being Felicity, she would. She would worry about it, and that made Gareth angry. With himself.

The idea of her hair unbound in some other man's presence also made him angry, which had to be a result of an empty belly and the certain knowledge Brenner had at least eighteen reports for Gareth to read.

Or something.

And yet, Gareth continued holding Felicity around the waist with one arm. With his free hand, he stroked her arm, her shoulders, her hands, because she wasn't ready to pop up and face the world.

"You have a mistress," Felicity stated, as if confirming a suspicion.

"I do." One he hadn't seen in several weeks, come to that. Worse yet, he hadn't *wanted* to see the woman, and hadn't given a thought to missing her company or her charms. "I enjoy regular sexual activity, and from all accounts, the ladies enjoy my attentions as well."

Though he wasn't in the habit of asking them if they were pleased, which realization he shoved to the back of his mind.

"I could hate you, you know." Felicity curled up against his chest. "You and all the sophisticated lovelies you'll meet tonight, while I'm playing backgammon with Astrid. Merciful saints." She fell silent and tucked herself more closely to him. He wasn't inclined to argue her out of her disgust of him, but neither would he deny her the comfort of his embrace while she nursed her hurt feelings.

"What was the sigh about?" Foolish question without any good answer.

"You are patient with me, Gareth. I appreciate that."

Not appreciation, not thanks, pray God. He kissed her temple and waited.

"But you, my lord, are no use at all in helping me to sort out my *emotions*. You have touched me in ways I would never touch myself, and I can only assume matters in this regard are only getting started. I have never been *aroused* before, you see. This changes me, and not in ways I was looking to be changed. I am not well pleased by what I am learning from you."

Women were hopelessly compelled to complicate what ought to be kept simple, and yet, Gareth offered the reply he suspected she'd sought.

"Felicity, any time you decide this course is not for you, you need only tell me to stop. You would make an excellent housekeeper, governess, or companion."

She stood abruptly and looked down on him as he sprawled on the divan. The perspective likely did not flatter him, because from her vantage point, he would look dark, decadent, and disheveled.

Spoiled, and yet to stand and loom over her just because he could would be spoiled *and* cowardly.

"You are wrong, Gareth. I would be adequate at those undertakings, just as I would be adequate at being some honest fellow's wife. I am excellent, however, at being a spinster. You are excellent at being a rake, and I'd wish you the joy of it, except I cannot escape the notion you are deserving of my pity."

Gareth watched her go, knowing it was rude not to see her out, but telling himself she needed the grand exit. Needed it, and deserved it.

CHAPTER FOUR

"Why are you in such a brown study?" Astrid asked as she bounced into the breakfast room.

"I'm slow to wake up today. You're looking quite presentable," Felicity replied. Astrid had been more consistent about putting her hair up in a coiffure lately, not a simple bun, and the result was fetching—and disconcertingly mature.

"I thought we might go for a stroll about the park today, sister mine. You've been so busy learning your wicked business that you have neglected me and Crabby shamelessly."

A mouthful of porridge lodged halfway to Felicity's belly. Her *wicked* business? Astrid gamboled on, clearly oblivious to her sister's distress.

"When will you teach me something besides how to bet on whist or vingt-et-un?"

Felicity passed Astrid the tea pot. "Running a gaming house involves more than playing cards, Astrid."

Lie upon fib upon fabrication upon deceit. The tea in Felicity's belly joined the general alimentary rebellion—strong tea, now that the marquess had arranged from some revenue to come their way.

"What do you do with Lord Heathgate when you're not playing cards?" Astrid asked with the blunt tenacity of the adolescent.

I complain about allowing him to touch my hair, then melt when he touches my breast.

"I learn the menus, the guest list, the preferences of each particular guest and how to meet them. I learn from whom I can buy good brandy at a reasonable price, and which musicians don't mind working later when the guests linger. I learn which footmen have quick tempers, and which are likely to bother the maids. I learn what it costs to cook those fancy menus, and what all the dishes and cutlery and glassware cost. In short, I learn to run the business, Astrid, and the fact that we will make money while others enjoy themselves doesn't mean I will enjoy myself."

Felicity delivered her little lecture with a very credible dose of longsuffering condescension, all the while hating that she was lying to her sister. If Astrid ever found out the truth, she'd be so disappointed... Young people could be idealistic. Idealistic and intolerant.

She poured herself more tea, wishing Crabbie wasn't brewing it quite so strong.

"You sigh too much, Felicity. I'm supposed to be the young girl afflicted with silly romantic notions." Astrid stuck her nose in the air with mock drama before cramming more sweet bun into her maw.

"You are seventeen, and that is too young to have romantic notions, silly or otherwise. I, on the other hand, am five-and-twenty years of age, and that is too old for any notions whatsoever."

Though eight short years didn't seem like enough time to explore, realize, and then discard *all* of one's interest in romance.

Astrid looked poised to score a riposte on that bit of sororal pomposity, when Mr. Crabble bustled into in the dining room.

"Letter for you Miss Felicity," he said, setting a missive down beside her. "Hit's got that marquess fellow's seal on it too, looks like."

"So it does!" Astrid cried, snatching up the letter and peering at the fine linen stationery and red wax seal. "Won't you open it, Felicity? We're dying to know that it says."

Felicity grabbed the envelope out of Astrid's hand—a marquess could afford the extra paper, just as Felicity could now afford fresh tea leaves—and broke the seal. "And you conceal your curiosity so nicely."

MADAM,

If you find it suits your schedule tonight, I would enjoy escorting you to Drury Lane. Appropriate attire will be delivered this afternoon.

Until tonight,

G.

"I'M TO GO OUT." Were they really going to the theatre, or was this Heathgate's subterfuge for some less savory outing? She did not trust him—look at how his attentions to her hair had gone awry.

"Out where?!" Astrid all but shrieked.

"Hush, Astrid," Felicity said. "Eat up, and I'll change into a walking gown. We have plenty of time for a turn about the park and some window shopping before the morning is spent. I am to go to the theatre with Heathgate, that's all. I'm sure we'll see something unremarkable, but I promise to bring you all the details."

Astrid was bouncing around the room at that.

"Oh, yes, Details! Those I must have. Can we buy you opera glasses this morning, so you might peer about the theatre and remark on the doings of Polite Society? I need ideas for my hair, Felicity, you can bring those back too." Astrid trumpeted on a while longer, but by the time they were at the gates of the park, she had quieted.

In fact, in the sudden mood changes for which her age was notorious, Astrid had grown downright serious.

"You know, Felicity, I appreciate the risk you are running to ensure our future," she said as they tossed some stale bread to the ducks.

Around Felicity's feet, ducks flapped and honked in an avian display of pique. "Whatever does that mean?"

"For a single young lady to run a gambling establishment is beyond the pale, and even I know that. You are hoping you can learn this business, as Callista required, then sell it with no one the wiser. You are having to trust Heathgate's discretion and hope not one word of scandal attaches to your name. That is quite a risk," Astrid concluded, throwing a small crust to a particularly tenacious gander.

"You are growing up too quickly, little sister." To this extent, at least, Felicity could be honest. "I am glad you see the need for extreme discretion regarding the time I spend with Heathgate. I believe we can trust his silence, but people will talk, and you are right: If word of this situation reached the wrong ears, I would be ruined in the eyes of good society, though at five and twenty, that hardly matters."

Astrid would be ruined by association, though, and that *did* matter.

"I would not like to see you ruined," Astrid said, firing a chunk of bread at a gander down the bank with the kind of steady aim no young lady ought to display in public. "You say you are five-and-twenty, Lissy, like it's some geological tragedy, but you aren't so old. You could still find true love. Besides, if you are ruined, I would insist on being ruined right along with you."

"Let's hope it never comes to that." Felicity dusted her gloved hands and hiked her skirts a few inches to allow her to scramble the few yards back up the embankment to the gravel pathway. Astrid was still tossing bread crumbs to the waterfowl, which she could do while chattering at a great rate.

"Felicity, have you noticed that the brown duck to my left bears a striking resemblance... Felicity!"

Felicity's mind was slow to add up what her senses screamed at her. That pounding sensation beneath her feet, the dull tattoo in her ear, came from a horse tearing across the green, its hoofbeats muffled in the damp grass. Though the rider sawed brutally at the reins, the animal bore directly down on Felicity.

Astrid was screaming in earnest when Felicity felt a pair of strong arms scoop her off the path and drag her behind the nearest tree, just as the horse thundered past, inches from where her rescuer shielded her.

"Felicity! Are you all right? Lissy!?" Astrid clambered up the bank and threw her arms around her sister. The gentleman obliged by wrapping an arm around Astrid too, while his words floated through the fog in Felicity's mind.

"Steady on, ladies. Catch your breath for a bit." He didn't seem to be in any hurry to release them, but stood with an arm around each sister. Unable to speak, Felicity closed the circle by wrapping her free arm around Astrid.

"Oh, Felicity, I've never been so frightened in all my life. That horse must have been mad." Astrid gulped back tears, and her voice became small and hesitant. "Are you all right?"

Felicity took one more slow, deep breath and pulled out of the stranger's arms.

"I am fine, Astrid, if a bit rattled. We must thank this fine gentleman for his timely appearance." She drew Astrid back with her as she stepped away from the man who had been holding them both. "Sir, I don't know why I exhibited such an inconvenient sense of indecision, but I do owe you my thanks."

Her voice shook, her knees felt unreliable, and she had the odd wish that Gareth were there to cling to.

"No thanks needed, ladies. Some fool trying to impress the world with his blood stock, no doubt."

The gentleman—his dress proclaimed him as such, as did his diction—was blond, tall and handsome in a severe, Nordic way. Felicity guessed his age as a bit older than her own. He was at that time in life when a man passes from being merely handsome into the realm of true attractiveness.

"Miss Felicity Worthington." She introduced herself with a

curtsy, though such forwardness was not strictly proper. Being nearly run down by a horse rather put proper somewhere in the middle of the pond. "And this is my sister Miss Astrid." Astrid offered a polite bob of her head.

"David Holbrook, my ladies. I would gladly escort you to either your carriage or your residence if you could suffer the company." Mr. Holbrook's smile did not make him more handsome, so much as it made him wonderfully human, suggesting bottomless depths of benevolence and charm all the more startling for the otherwise stern aspect of his countenance.

Felicity spoke at the same time as Astrid.

"I don't think that would be necessary..." from Felicity, but hardly audible over Astrid's, "That would be most appreciated!"

As Mr. Holbrook offered them each an arm, Felicity tried to puzzle out what in his expression was so remarkable. She would certainly know if she had seen him somewhere before, and yet, he looked familiar.

"You are noticing my mismatched eyes," Holbrook said. "I've been told that in more superstitious times, having one blue eye and one green eye might have cost me my life, being a mark of the devil and so forth."

"If they are a mark of the devil," Astrid replied, "they are quite beautiful nonetheless. I should die for one gorgeous blue eye and one delectably green eye."

"Astrid, you do *not* comment on the appearance of a gentleman of recent acquaintance!" Felicity remonstrated, though Astrid's predictable audaciousness routed the last of Felicity's physical unsteadiness.

"Oh, Miss Worthington, can't we allow her to comment just a bit, particularly when she's being so complimentary? It isn't my usual experience, I can assure you." Holbrook offered a tolerant smile, and Felicity had the sense he sympathized with both Astrid's youth, and the challenge it created for Felicity.

"The damage is done, I suppose," Felicity said, as they moved away from the honking, flapping waterfowl. "Astrid is nothing if not honest. You may be assured you are now in possession of her sincere opinion regarding your appearance."

"I am pleased beyond measure, Miss Astrid, to have your assessment. Will you ladies journey safely from this point? I can accompany you further, but you seem to have suffered no ill effects from your mishap."

"Oh, Felicity will bear up fine," Astrid said. "She always does, but I declare I shall feel faint if you leave us now."

Holbrook unlinked his arms from theirs.

"Miss Worthington, I cannot be sure, due to my inchoate decrepitude, but I believe this brazen child is attempting to flirt with me. I confess myself almost as flattered as I am... amused." He turned a sardonic eyebrow up at Astrid then, and she smiled right back, then spoiled the effect utterly by sticking her tongue out at him.

"You're not that old, sir."

"No, but you are that young, Miss Astrid, and you should have a care for your sister. Your liveliness could land you in a deal of trouble if you aren't careful, and that would aggrieve her, unless I miss my guess." The rebuke was delivered with a smile. Watching the exchange, Felicity was pleased some other adult had taken Astrid's high spirits to task.

The girl was only seventeen, God help her, but many a young lady became betrothed—or compromised—at that age.

"Sir, thank you for your escort, and your company," Felicity said, offering another curtsy. He bowed in response and studied the head of a walking stick carved into the shape of a crouching dragon.

"Perhaps we might encounter one another enjoying the park in future," he said, touching the dragon to the brim of his hat.

Felicity waited until they were out of the gentleman's hearing. "Astrid, what could you have been thinking, telling him you might feel faint?"

"I know I overstepped a little, but I felt as if with him, it was safe to carry on a bit. His eyes are beautiful."

"You won't develop a tendresse for him, will you?"

"No," Astrid answered, a frown puckering her brow. "I like him, Felicity, but he feels more like, I don't know, a potential brother-in-law? A man whose company I can trust."

Astrid had picked a fine time to have a grown-up moment. Felicity herself had had the same sense from Holbrook. He seemed absolutely steady to her. Completely beyond frivolousness or flirtatiousness. A serious, decent man. Not a fellow trolling for anything.

"He was very charming," Astrid went on earnestly, "and he did rescue you from that odious horse."

"Yes, he did," Felicity said as they reached their doorstep. "I've never felt so helpless in my life, Astrid. I knew I had to move, but my limbs wouldn't obey my mind. I could hear you calling my name, but it was as if I were dreaming. I still don't feel completely myself."

Astrid looked at her then, and said in all solemnity. "You must have...."

Felicity joined in, laughing with her sister as they chorused together, "a nice hot cup of tea!"

They went into the house, arms linked, exuding the good humor of sisters in charity with each other.

"PLEASE DON'T HANG over the balcony, Felicity." Gareth passed her a pair of opera glasses. "I doubt you want all of society to see you with your skirts over your head when I have to haul you back by your heels."

Felicity had merely peered about at the assemblage like any sophisticate would peruse the crowd, and yet, after the day's events, Gareth needed to scold her on general principles.

"My, but your lordship is grumpy tonight. I'm merely enjoying the spectacle created by the audience. Which reminds me: Why did you bring me here? I thought we had agreed discretion was absolutely necessary if my name is to be protected from scandal."

Fair question, which he'd thought to ask himself only *after* he'd sent his note on its way to her.

"It might surprise you to know that, like most gentlemen, I keep my personal vices separate from other aspects of my life, including my more proper socializing. On occasion, I am asked to escort the sister of an acquaintance, or my mother's friends' daughters to functions such as this. I do know how to behave, Felicity, and I know how to pay respectful addresses to proper young ladies."

To his own ear, his words held a faint but detectable note of defensiveness.

"I can well believe you are a proper escort when the need arises, and I meant you no insult, but what I was asking was this: Why on earth would you bother to escort *me*? I am seeking anything but respectful addresses, and in no manner can I be considered proper in your eyes."

He looked over at her, his irritation abating not one bit at her question. The real answer, that he'd brought her to the theatre largely to indulge a desire to bring her pleasure, was something he did not entirely understand himself.

"First, I respect you, Felicity. I find society's standards absurd in so far as a man is supposed to lose respect for a woman who permits him intimacies—unless she is his wife, in which case the same allowances are to result in his respecting her above all others, 'til death and so forth. This is hardly logical, and yet nobody seems to question it save myself.

"Second, you should become familiar with the other entertainments available to gentlemen who frequent your establishment. The theatre, in addition to being a subject of witty conversation, is also one of your competitors. The ladies performing on stage are as ostracized as the ladies at the Pleasure House, and frequently do give up the stage for the stability of a protector."

"Yes, professor," Felicity murmured, her observance of the crowd taking on a more thoughtful air.

"I am not yet finished," Gareth went on, quoting his first Latin tutor when that old worthy had been in a particularly loquacious mood. "A third reason we are being seen here tonight is to provide an alibi of sorts should anything untoward be bruited about regarding our other dealings."

"I do not understand." A breeze wafted through the box, and a portion of the candles in the nearest chandelier winked out, leaving the box in heavy shadows.

Gareth resented the need to spell out for her the type of subterfuge a more sophisticated woman would grasp easily—a more jaded woman.

"If rumors crop up that we are having illicit dealings, then it follows we should be seen skulking about the more notorious gaming hells, perhaps strolling the lovers walk at Vauxhall, or picnicking alone out at Richmond. Instead, we are seen in one of the few places I occasionally do the pretty with proper ladies. You are dressed most elegantly, and we will not—to appearances— behave like anything approaching a couple interested in one another."

As the orchestra struck up the overture, Felicity leaned closer— her lavender scent was laced with roses tonight. "What do you mean, to appearances we will not be interested in each other?"

"I mean that my fourth objective for this little outing, is that you add to your experience the sensual pleasures that make the theatre such a popular destination among the dissipated wastrels whom you will soon recognize as your best customers. Come."

As the orchestra played on amid the noisy bustle of the evening's socializing, Gareth took Felicity's hand and lead her to the back of the private box. The lighting was too meager to let him see her expression, even as he tugged her down beside him and removed her gloves.

"This is a sofa," Felicity whispered, much as she might have accused him of having lewd pictures on the walls of his best parlor. "Do you actually seduce women in your box?!"

Her question made him feel old, tired, and ridiculous. "No, Felicity, I merely have this very comfortable couch in the darkest corner of the least well lit box so I might bide here for the occasional nap."

She withdrew her hand. "You need not mock me." Her voice was quiet, but he heard the hurt.

"Come here," he coaxed, pulling her back against his side. What followed next would be as close to pillow talk as he was capable of. "I want to hold you for a few minutes. Tell me about your day—did you like the dress I picked out?"

"I love the dress. Astrid nearly fainted dead away at the sight of it. The color is rich, but subdued; the line elegant and simple. You are a genius with women's clothing, Gareth. It isn't fair."

"And you," he remarked as he resumed stroking her neck, "have the wisdom to bow to my refined judgment." *For once.* "Other than your outing to the park today, what labors have occupied you?" He pressed a soft kiss to the side of her neck, feeling the tension flow out of her as he did.

And perhaps a little out of him, too.

"It's the oddest thing, Gareth, but after the excitement in the park, I really wasn't very successful with the rest of the day's tasks. I played cards with Astrid—she wants to learn to wager, heaven help us."

Excitement. She referred to nearly losing her life as excitement, and that was assuming Brenner's report had described the situation conservatively.

"What excitement?" he murmured against her hair.

"Nothing much, really." She cuddled against him, slipping her hand inside his coat to run her palm languidly over his chest. "A horse bolted and a Mr. Holbrook assisted me in leaving its path."

Gareth let go of the earlobe he'd been nibbling, and turned Felicity's head so her lips were more easily accessible. "Promise me something, Felicity," he said as his thumb grazed the underside of her breast.

"I can't think when you touch me that way..."

About damned time. "Promise me if you have any more mishaps, or near accidents, you will tell me," he said, grazing her nipple through the fabric of her gown.

"Why?"

So I can keep you safe. Even in the relative darkness, he wasn't about to voice that sentiment, though frustration of it effectively banished any inchoate arousal.

Brenner had been unable to come up with much about the mysterious Mr. Holbrook, lately residing on an elegant little Mayfair side street. Gareth's man in the park had noted that the fool on the runaway horse hadn't taken the simple measure of turning the beast's head to bring it back under control.

"You will give me your word for two reasons," Gareth said, taking her hand and pressing his lips to her knuckles. "The first is that I take this safeguarding of Callista's bequest seriously. Her business is worth a small fortune, and to the extent someone could attempt to wrest it from you, you must conduct yourself with an eye toward your personal safety."

"That is absurd." And Felicity's tone was absurdly crisp, as if she hadn't been nearly trampled to death that very morning. "No one would want to take that business from me. I've barely inherited it yet, and Astrid would be my heir. Nobody even knows I'm taking Callista's place as owner, either."

In a conveniently shadowed theatre box, cuddled up against the worst rake in Polite Society, Felicity Worthington still managed to sound starchy and prim—and damnably ignorant of how quickly and irrevocably death could snatch a person from life.

Gareth tightened his grip on her hand and cradled his palm against her cheek.

"Felicity, you have lived a sheltered life, and you must trust me when I tell you people will commit evil acts for personal gain, and life can be risky." Highwaymen fired their pistols. Small pox decimated entire villages. Boats sank. "For that matter, I will ask you to ensure your housekeeper and even Astrid have my direction. I want to be notified if you ever don't come home when you should, or if they otherwise are concerned for your welfare."

Felicity turned her head, so her lips grazed the heel of his thumb. That she might have done so on purpose suggested he still had not impressed upon her the seriousness of the topic.

"I will comply with this request, Gareth, but you said you had two reasons for making it. What is the other?"

"I would be troubled if harm befell you." The rest of that thought wasn't for her to know: He was troubled to *be* harming her, ruining her reputation, destroying her innocence, taking away her chance for a loving husband and fat, chortling babies. The time for him to puzzle a way out of the dilemma was slipping by, and he very much feared he would end up completely debauching her—and enjoying the task. He purposefully turned his mind from that notion and linked hands with Felicity.

"I would be troubled if harm befell me, too."

"Good. Now, while the orchestra thunders on, let us at least appear to attend, shall we?" He kept his tone pure marquess, aloof and cool, but he continued to hold her hand and she continued to let him.

Gareth drew her to her feet at the interval. "We shall stroll for a bit."

In public, where his wayward thoughts were less likely to result in wayward behaviors. Felicity blinked owlishly at the relative brightness under the chandeliers in the passage. The performance was well attended, and the corridor rapidly filled with other patrons.

"Don't gawk," Gareth chided quietly as he smiled and nodded at an elderly couple proceeding in the opposite direction. "Head up, smile in place, and no hint that the man beside you wants to kiss you witless." And in a louder voice, "Good evening, Lady Quinn, Lady Dremel."

He bowed to the two matrons—his mother's best spies—and moved along rather than gratify their obvious desire to engage him in conversation. At his side, Felicity let herself be towed forward by the hand he'd wrapped over the fingers she'd placed on his forearm. She was being blessedly biddable—which state of affairs made him perversely nervous.

"Would you like some punch?" he asked, as they continued smiling and nodding along the passage.

"Good heavens, no thank you. I'm too excited to taste it," Felicity responded through her fixed smile.

He was about to whisper something naughty when he caught sight of a couple approaching.

"Trouble," he muttered giving Felicity's fingers a squeeze. "Play as sweet as you convincingly can."

"Why, Heathgate! How absolutely delightful to meet you here." Lady Edith Hamilton, decked out in fairy-pale blue and escorted by some doting young swain, extended her hand. Gareth took her fingers in his right hand and kissed her gloved knuckles. He realized his mistake when Felicity minutely stiffened beside him. A gentleman did not kiss a lady's hand, not in public, and certainly not when escorting another lady.

Truly, his instincts had grown rusty.

He embarked upon the introductions, bracing himself for Edith's brand of drama. Felicity produced an exaggerated curtsy accompanied by a convincingly sweet smile, while Lady Edith's smile would have cleaved leaded crystal at twenty paces.

"Why Miss Worthington, I don't believe I recall meeting you out in society. This is a pleasure. But where are my manners, you must meet Edward." She turned to the young man and wrapped herself around his arm. The poor fellow actually blushed. "Miss Worthington, Lord Heathgate, may I present, Edward, Lord Evanston. Edward, dear, the marquess and I have been friends for an age." She smiled a feral smile right at Gareth and touched the blue diamond nestled above her cleavage. "I haven't seen him for far too long."

Truly, Brenner was inspired when it came to parting gifts.

Edward stammered the appropriate pleasantries, but seemed

relieved when Gareth made polite excuses and resumed perambulations toward the balcony fronting the terrace.

"You're quiet," he remarked as they reached the double doors leading out to the chilly night air. "Shall we go out, or it is too cold for you without your wrap?"

"A little fresh air would be enjoyable."

"You will not make a scene," Gareth said as they came to a solitary bench on the terrace. "It is not my fault we ran across that woman. I don't even like her." In truth, he didn't *dislike* Edith. It was more the case he barely knew her.

Felicity allowed him to seat her near a convenient torch. When he came down beside her, he realized the bench was damned near freezing beneath his arse.

"How can you stand to join your body to that of a woman you don't even like?" she asked, and Gareth heard both confusion and misery in her quiet question. He wanted to take her hand, but didn't dare.

Blast all women to perdition, anyway.

"Women and men are different. We have discussed this on at least three separate occasions." He'd lectured her about it, at any rate. "I need no more like a sexual partner than I need to like the fellow who spars with me in the fencing arena, or races his horse against mine in the park. I can enjoy our exertions even though he and I have radically different politics, values, and stations in life. Lady Edith was a willing fuck, available on terms agreeable to her and me both."

He stood and blamed a need to move on having sat for too long entertained by little more than the opening farce. And yet, cursing was for men unable to express themselves through more sophisticated means, and referring to Lady Edith in such vulgar terms flattered nobody.

"Felicity, how can you contemplate making your livelihood off of the oldest profession and still have these silly romantic notions? Most men, most *gentlemen*, are simple-minded, randy bastards, and happy to be that way. Why do you insist on complicating matters?"

She looked up at him, and he was relieved to see her eyes were not glittering with either tears or malice. "Shall we go in, my lord?"

Brilliant. She had outgunned him with her composure, her evasive maneuvers, and her sheer, damned manners. He repositioned his hand over hers on his arm as she rose, but hesitated before rejoining the powdered, perfumed, bejeweled throng inside.

"If you must know, I broke off with Lady Edith several weeks ago, and I make it a practice never to resurrect old liaisons," he said, looking straight ahead.

Any other woman would have hugged that admission to her breast with visible glee—not that he would have made such an admission to any other woman.

"Why? If the lady met your criteria for an intimate partner, and if she is also clearly willing to continue the affair, why would you break it off?"

Felicity apparently did not understand that a marquess explained himself to no one. Gareth lost sight of that signal fact himself, though for only a moment. He did not stop as they approached the doors that would lead them back into the light, but admitted the puzzling truth as they walked along.

"To continue with Lady Edith would not have been kind. She was becoming possessive, and I was growing bored."

"WOULD you like to stay for the last act, or shall we take our leave?"

Felicity considered her options, and considered the ache in her bones that wasn't exclusively physically.

"Let's leave, if you don't mind. The day has managed to be long, though I did very much enjoy coming here." She stifled a yawn as Gareth helped her to her feet.

"Sleepyhead," he murmured, drawing her against him. "You must inure yourself to the long hours required by a life of wickedness."

She must inure herself to ignoring the teasing note in his voice, and the pleasure of simply leaning against his strength when she was tired, particularly when not long ago, she'd wanted to cosh him over the head.

"Take me home, please, Gareth, or I shall fall asleep even in your scintillating company."

"I would hold you as you slept, and treasure the moments."

Oh, to the very devil with him. He was trying hard to jolly her, when she felt like crying.

"You will please *not* start in with your flirting, your lordship. Were I to fall asleep, you would throw a carriage rug over me, and hie yourself off for a horizontal fencing match."

"Cranky when you're tired?" he asked as they once again moved toward the front doors of the theatre.

"Beastly," she replied, willing to elaborate on her sentiments at length. Further reply was cut off by an imperious voice from behind them.

"Heathgate, do you not greet your own mother?"

Gareth stopped and turned slowly, dropping Felicity's hand. So much for the pretense that their business with one another was proper.

"Mother, my apologies. I did not know you were in attendance. Andrew." With a bow, he greeted the younger man standing beside his mother. "A pleasure to see you, madam. Did you enjoy the performance?"

Gareth's mother was a trim, tidy woman who might never have been a raving beauty, though in her later years she could claim a dignified handsomeness and more sable in her hair than gray. Beside her two sons, she looked small, though Felicity and the marchioness were almost the same height.

"The performances, both on stage and off, were tedious," his mother replied. "Your manners, my boy?" For the second time, Gareth performed introductions, and Felicity found herself the subject of two thorough, if polite, blue-eyed perusals.

"You," pronounced Lady Heathgate, looking closely at Felicity, "are a good girl. See that you stay that way. My sons are not to be trusted."

Not knowing whether the woman was trying to be witty or simply rude, Felicity was at a loss for a reply. Lord Andrew spoke up, saving her the trouble.

"Mother, if we are not to be trusted, one must look to our upbringing." His voice was, like his physique, a younger version of his older brother's. He shared Gareth's muscular height, icy blue eyes, and thick sable hair. His tone, though, was patently teasing, and the light in his gaze humorous.

"Hah!" said his mother. "You are both the trial of my dotage; that you are accepted into Polite Society at all is a testament to my long-suffering and persevering nature. Now, go fetch the carriages, you scamps, while I interrogate Miss Worthington."

Gareth shot Felicity a look halfway between a warning and an apology. She waved him away, all too happy to see his best laid plans knocked asunder twice in one evening by sheer happenstance.

"Lady Heathgate and I will enjoy a short visit."

"So, Miss Worthington," the dowager began as she took Felicity's arm, and lead her in the wake of the retreating brothers. "What is my son's business with you? You are not his usual type."

The mystery—had there been one—of where Gareth came by his blunt speech and imperious airs was thus solved. "His usual type?"

"Don't be tedious, dear. You needn't mince words with me. We both know he usually disports with the likes of the Hamilton creature. Bored, vacuous, tedious females who trespass on his generous and randy nature."

Felicity chose her words carefully, not wanting to deceive Gareth's mother. Lady Heathgate was a woman who had survived unimaginable grief, and she was entitled to protect the family she had left.

"Your son is assisting me with a business matter a woman in my circumstances could not resolve on her own," Felicity said. "His interest in me is mostly charitable, and I appreciate his generosity."

Deceitful but not quite a pack of lies. Perhaps one grew more accomplished at dissembling the more one practiced. Gareth was generous, he was also too shy to admit such a thing.

The dowager displayed the same cocked eyebrow Felicity often saw on her son. "That's a pretty speech," she conceded. "All the ladies appreciate his confounded generosity. He is seldom charitable, in the true sense. The man is nigh thirty years old and needs to set up his nursery. Given his bachelor proclivities, I wonder if any decent woman would have him. There is the title, of course. I don't suppose you're interested in that?"

Felicity caught sight of "the Hamilton creature" across the lobby, laughing on the arm of yet another man who looked ten years her junior. "My lady, I doubt Lord Heathgate intends to set up a nursery. I believe he is relying on his brother to ensure the succession."

"Told you that much, did he? Did he also tell you he never wanted the title and still doesn't?"

Felicity stopped walking, hearing something more than grief or a mother's meddling in the words. Lady Heathgate was *worried* for her son. He was a great strapping, brash, handsome, growling, beast of a man—and yet, his mother worried for him.

Which was both dear and sad, also a relief, because Felicity worried for him too. "I know of the accident, your ladyship, but not of the specifics to which you refer. Surely family confidences should not be exchanged with a mere acquaintance such as myself?"

Lady Heathgate continued her scrutiny, but seemed to accept Felicity's remonstrance.

"Ask him," was all she said as they emerged from the building. "Ask him for those confidences, then." She straightened, and looked about for the approach of the carriages. "Your breeding does you credit, Miss Worthington. You may call upon me. I do not attend many of the social functions of the approaching Season, but I am at home on Wednesdays. Ah, the knights approach with their chariots."

Felicity saw Gareth alight from his carriage, while Andrew emerged from the one behind it. Andrew approached the ladies and offered each one an arm, while Gareth exchanged a few words with his coachman.

"Miss Worthington, it was a pleasure meeting you," Lord Andrew said. "No matter what my brother tells you about me, you must not forget his lamentable tendency to habitual mendacity—and he, alas, is my example in all things."

Felicity let Gareth hand her into the carriage, bemused by the encounter with his family. She was struck too, by the sense of familiarity she felt as Gareth settled himself beside her. His physical presence was becoming a comforting fixture in her life, and she would miss it when they parted.

She would not miss his aloofness, his arrogance, and his sexual pedagogy. Well, maybe she would miss those a little, but she most definitely would miss the solid reality of *him*.

CHAPTER FIVE

"How bad was she?" Gareth took Felicity's hand and stroked his thumb across her knuckles. Felicity had a habit of taking her gloves off when she settled into a carriage with him, something he liked about her.

He also liked that Felicity had met his family, which made no damned sense at all.

"She restrained herself, though I would not want to be in her path when she's in full sail. She rather put me in mind of you, and Lord Andrew is very handsome."

He was. And no longer a boy. When had that happened? "There's a family resemblance."

"Not that you aren't also very attractive, my lord, in your own way." Said so very earnestly.

He bit her knuckle. "Women who tease me can also be turned over my knee, Felicity. We'll consider it part of your intimate education." The education he'd failed to advance much in an entire month of regular meetings.

"To blazes with my education. I had a lovely evening, Gareth, and you have my thanks for that. The dress is beautiful, the orchestra was in good form, and I had you all to myself, even though we were out among the Beau Monde. Thank you." She kissed his cheek—the first kiss he could recall her giving him, and what good cheer he could lay claim to dissipated.

"I introduced you to a woman who's barely received, Felicity. I do not want your thanks for that."

He wanted the next two months with her to be over. He'd introduced her to his last mistress, for God's sake, and the dress was merely something he'd seen in a shop window earlier in the week.

"Well, you have my thanks. I saw at least four new hairstyles for Astrid to try. You can't know how that will contribute to our domestic tranquility."

She spoke of hairstyles, when their real agenda was her ruin.

Inspiration struck, low, mean, and appallingly appealing. They'd dithered and dallied long enough, and Felicity would either have to send him packing or take him to bed soon.

"I thought this evening would be an opportune time to explain to you the pleasures of cunnilingus," he said, kissing her palm, when what he wanted was to put his fist through a window.

Her breath drew in sharply when his tongue flicked out to touch the webbing of her thumb. "That sounds—Latin."

To lick the cunny. "It is. It refers to the use of my mouth on your sex for your pleasure. We left the theatre early—there is time—and I think you might enjoy it." Though perhaps he shouldn't have admitted that, lest she refuse him on that basis alone.

"Must we?"

She could not have sounded less enthusiastic, which suggested confronting their bargain in this manner—a vulgar, purely physical encounter in a moving coach—might free Gareth from further dealings with her.

"We don't have to, but I want to." As much as he wanted free of his obligations to her, the male animal in him also wanted to put his mouth on her sex and experience her reactions. He wanted to give her the kind of shocking pleasure no decent, plodding husband ever would, even if it was only this once.

"May we douse the lamps?"

"All but one," he allowed, because he wanted to see her face when she found her pleasure. He should be allowed that much for his sacrifice. He took off his hat and extinguished the carriage's interior lighting, save one lantern he turned down to a small flame. Next, he draped a lap robe on the floor—sore knees being no kind of addition to arousal—then lowered himself to kneel before Felicity's tightly clenched knees.

He hadn't dallied in a coach for years, which suggested sheer novelty had something to do with the arousal coursing through him.

"Your job, Felicity, is to relax. I will not touch your breasts, though you should certainly touch yourself if you feel so inclined." He dropped his voice to a sensual near-whisper, lest the damned coachman be entertained. "I will explain to you what I'm about as we go along, and you should ask questions if they occur to you. You must, of course, tell me if you are at all uncomfortable."

He gave her a moment by unfastening his cloak and folding it up beside her on the seat.

"Why do you spring these maneuvers on me when I'm not expecting them?" She sounded peevish, much as he'd felt peevish when she'd sprung her situation on him those weeks ago.

"I spring them on you so you will not fret in anticipation, sweetheart. Anxiety is a close cousin to pain, and I would not for the world bring you discomfort." He slid her slippers off both feet and began massaging her feet, which were, literally, cold.

"I am uncomfortable," Felicity muttered as she braced herself back against the squabs, one hand covering her stomach. Beneath her skirts, Gareth slid his hands along her calves, then around her knees.

She would, of course, make him work for it. He should have expected nothing less, and yet, even the woman's *knees* were silky.

"Let me rephrase myself: It is no end of diverting to make you uncomfortable, Felicity, but I would never bring you physical pain, though I'm sure we'll have more to say on that topic as it relates to your clientele. Now, hush, close your eyes and relax. You have much to learn and it is my privilege to disabuse you of your ignorance."

Though hopefully, not of her innocence, not entirely.

She concurred with a terse nod.

"Permission granted," he murmured, letting his hands trail up under her skirts as far as her thighs. "There are relevant terms with which you are unfamiliar, so attend me." In the coach's deep shadows, Felicity's face was set in lines of dread and steely resignation, her eyes closed tightly, and her hands fisted on the seat.

She was braced for him to toss up her skirts and fall upon her like a starving wolf, which in some ways, might be kinder to her, though he simply wasn't capable of it.

Not with her, not tonight.

"The surface of a woman's inner thigh," he began, stroking both thighs and pressing them wider as he spoke, "is a sensual delight to both man and woman. I enjoy touching you here, because this terrain is so smooth, warm, and forbidden. You enjoy my attentions because my touch *here* evokes anticipation of my touch *here*."

He slid his hand higher, so he was almost brushing her curls. Again he brought a slight pressure to bear, pushing her legs gently apart. He contented himself with stroking and kissing around the top of her thighs for a bit, while he slid her skirts up to rest just over her knees.

He wanted to pleasure her, and he wanted to leap out of the coach.

He could devour her, and he could kick himself for getting entangled in the whole infernal mess.

She shifted on the bench, slid an inch closer to him, bringing the scent of clean, intimate female wafting past his plans and intentions. His cock liked that fragrance exceeding well, his resolve to shock her witless was rather distracted by it too.

He moved his thumbs in small circles, massaging, exploring, and all the while gently pressing Felicity's legs open with his forearms.

Still he did not bare her to his gaze, but let her skirts trail over her thighs.

His forbearance was not a sop to her modesty, but rather, a nod to his flagging self-restraint.

As his hands trailed across Felicity's flesh, the dread in Felicity's expression was replaced by something else—curiosity? Inchoate arousal? Her lips were slightly parted, and her breathing a bit accelerated.

She deserved better than this. Better than him.

"What do you feel, Felicity?" Gareth asked, bringing his thumbs together and limning her outer folds, while in his head trying to recall the geometric proof for bisecting an angle.

"Restless," she muttered. "Itchy under my skin."

His touch on her told him she was aroused, but not to the degree of torment his attentions to her breasts seemed to cause. Interesting, because he, poor, randy sod, could have closed his eyes and come with no further provocation than she'd already provided.

"Restless is a start. You can learn to touch yourself the same way. We'll practice as often as you like." His set of antique jade phalluses came to mind, none of which were any harder than the appendage behind his falls.

The need to feast on her had become tearingly urgent, and her folds were wonderfully slick, but she wasn't writhing or moaning. Not yet.

For a few minutes, he limited his touch to Felicity's outer flesh, but when her hands began to open and close on the leather seats, he carefully slid a thumb higher.

"This, small, hidden little jewel here,"—he punctuated his words with a sudden increase in pressure—"is a source of much pleasure." Felicity gasped, and relaxed her hips forward.

He took shameless advantage of her discomposure, inching her skirts up until he could see what he was touching. The sight of her was almost enough to make him spend, so wet and pink and lovely was she by the light of the single lantern.

"Gareth." She was asking him for something—relief, understanding, he knew not what.

"Relax, Felicity. There's no rush, and I'll do whatever you want me to." He kept up the pressure on her, moving his thumb in slow circles and letting her feel the small surcease of a gratifying rhythm. "I think you might feel a little better, love, if I also touched you inside, though."

He slid a single finger in and out of her body, shallowly, slowly. Her breathing accelerated further, and she tossed her head against the leather seat. What he would give to replace that finger with his cock.

And yet, he was relieved too, that it was only his finger, that he was suffering torments of arousal rather than truly deflower her under these circumstances.

"Gareth... it's too... I need..."

God, so do I.

Felicity was wet, tight, hot, and denying him nothing. Cautiously, he slid a second finger into her and penetrated just a bit deeper. The deuced woman *liked* that, rocking her hips into his fingers, and showing not the smallest sign of being appalled, disgusted, or brought to her proper senses.

"Still not enough, is it?" Gareth asked, coming up on his knees, and moving Felicity's skirts up to her waist. "Maybe this will help."

He found her with his mouth and drew firmly in a slow, relentless rhythm. Shock rippled through her, then her hips shifted and her legs parted wider. He slid his hand under her derriere, lifting her against his mouth more firmly as he plied her with steady, skilled precision. She was squirming and rocking against him helplessly when Gareth realized she was trying to speak. He lifted his mouth from her, frustrated at the interruption of what he was convinced was the closest she'd been to waking satisfaction.

"You are torturing me," Felicity managed. "I don't want you to stop, but I can't... this is unbearable."

"*Shall* I stop?" He was frankly looking at her spread flesh, toying with her damp curls, and running a finger over her wet folds. He did not want to stop, and not out of any generous impulses toward her and her limited experience of pleasure. "It's your decision, love."

He'd promised her this, that he'd stop, because he was sly, manipulative and nowhere near as clever as he thought himself to be. He'd thought himself experienced with women, and he was—with the Ediths of the world—but Felicity was not like them.

Yet.

"I need to..." Felicity licked her lips while Gareth clenched his teeth. "I need to rest."

Well, of course. This was Felicity, and he'd been so sure he could shock her into abandoning their agreement. He laid his cheek against her mons, wanting to howl, get drunk, and curse—or swive her until neither of them could walk.

Felicity stroked her hand over his hair, slowly, as if the contact soothed her.

"It helps that you don't just pop up here beside me, all tidy and dapper and full of more vocabulary."

Helps whom with what? "I am," he said without moving, "also a bit undone. These are the precise circumstances underwhich a man might be well advised to see to himself."

Her hand on his hair went still. "See to yourself?"

"Masturbate, self-gratify, bring himself off." He raised himself to sit beside her, and noticed Felicity didn't immediately twitch her skirts back into place.

He was making a wanton of her, and that did not please him at all.

"I don't mind if you want to do that here."

So bloody damned gracious of her, but Gareth didn't want to go prowling through the night for a partner and he was hard *now*. They had talked about self-gratification, about how his father's generation regarded it as a harmless pleasure, and a growing sentiment in the present day regarded it as sinful.

"I will trespass on your generosity." On her courage, on her determination.

Her damned stubbornness.

Felicity did smooth her skirts down, with a single, casual brush of her hand. "You will embarrass me but not humiliate, Gareth, and the rest is just overwrought dignity on my part. Couples all over Town are fornicating as we speak, every alewife and baroness, and all London seems to have known it but me. What would you like me to do?"

He would like her to find some other way to meet the terms of the damned will, a will he should have had Brenner read by now.

He undid his falls instead, extracted himself from his clothing, then sat back and wondered if there was a particular corner of hell for men who corrupted aging virgins.

"Watch," he said, letting his gaze drop to her mouth, then to the tented flap of his shirt-tail. He wanted her mouth on him, wanted her hands on him, and yet all he could manage was to ask her to watch.

Nothing more, simply watch.

She was a damned spinster virgin bluestocking excuse for a madam in training, and she was driving him absolutely barmy.

GARETH WAS in dishabille on the cushioned seat and gazing at Felicity with all the inscrutability of a large, hungry cat. *This* was personal tutelage. This was exactly what she was supposed to gain from him, though the transaction felt as unbusinesslike as anything Felicity had ever undertaken.

Her body felt damp, soft, and alive with sensations she had no words for, while her heart... she'd let him down, somehow, and he was disappointing her as well.

He was a rake, disappointing women was what rakes did.

"I suppose you want to flaunt your wares?" she asked. She'd seen drawings of the male parts in Gareth's library, and suffered through his lordship's bored lecture about erections, testes, and other peculiar terms. Male anatomy had struck her as a collection of oddments, flesh affixed to the general scheme after the fact to accommodate procreation at the expense of aesthetics.

"Felicity...."

He might have been having second thoughts, while Felicity had no doubt she wanted this encounter behind them.

"We have plenty of time, Gareth," she quoted him as she leaned over to inspect him intimately, "and I'll do whatever you want me to." She brought a hand up to stroke his *balls*—his term for them, though he spoke the word rather like an endearment—and began teasing through the hair at the base of his shaft with her other.

The texture of his hair here was different from elsewhere on his body, both springy and soft. And his testes were soft too, while his shaft was hard as a lance.

Not that she'd ever stroked a lance before.

Gareth's expression was both resigned and annoyed. "I have created a monster."

The very point of the undertaking, to Felicity's way of thinking, though not very diplomatically phrased. While curiosity warred with an odd irritability, she brought her hand over his—over *him*, and gently began to explore the length of him.

The texture of his skin was smooth along his shaft, and smoother still on the crown—velvet smooth, petal smooth. Why did none of the clichés refer to being as smooth as man's parts?

She ran her fingertips over all of his curious contours, tracing the indentation of the crown, then down to the sturdy base of his shaft. All the while, she listened for his breathing to change—Gareth professed a great enthusiasm for monitoring a lover's breathing—and kept a hand on his thigh, attuned to the tension in the muscle there. Gareth's hips began to rock, a small, slow motion, but one that thrust him through the sleeve of her palm and fingers.

That little movement, spontaneous and uninvited, sent a bolt of confidence through her, and something not far removed from vengeance. She circled her fingers around his shaft and kept the pressure firm with her hand—he'd prosed on at length about that too.

Gradually, the relaxed, rocking motion became more focused, more thrusting. Gareth moved a hand over his nipple and tipped his head back, making the tendons in his neck stand out.

Felicity felt an urge to do something—kiss him, on the mouth, *there*, somewhere— but didn't want to deprive herself of the sight of him in these unguarded moments. The eruption of a wet warmth over the back of her hand was a surprise, for Gareth had uttered not a sound. She eased the pressure on him, but didn't turn loose of him entirely.

For reasons she surely did not fathom, she was reluctant to let him go. They remained thus for several moments, the only sounds the rasp of Gareth's breathing and the clop of shod hooves on cobblestones.

"You can let me go, you know," Gareth said, still not opening his eyes.

Her tutor sounded unhappy. Felicity sat up and fished a handkerchief out of her sleeve. She tidied him up then glanced over at him. In the dim light of the single lantern, *he looked* unhappy too. He arranged his clothing, then sat back, staring out the window, his expression bleak. Some of the sense of wellbeing and confidence Felicity felt ebbed away as she realized he wasn't even going to take her hand.

The disappointment surged back, in herself, in him, in the entire outing. "Is something wrong?" she asked after several more minutes of silence and staring.

"Why do you ask?"

So blasted cool. At least his tone helped banish the temptation to cry. "Normally, when we are private, you hold my hand, Gareth. You put an arm around my shoulders, you offer me—at least—a token of physical affection. Normally, when we have been in company with each other, you tidy my hair, you look over my clothing, you offer encouraging comments on my progress, you chatter. You don't simply stare out the window, ignoring the fact that a woman has been intimate with you in your very coach, and that woman is wondering what the *bloody hell* she could have done to provoke you thus."

Men were sleepy and agreeable after finding sexual pleasure. He'd assured her of this, and Gareth's promises were utterly reliable.

He looked at her then, as if he'd forgotten she was there—but at least he looked at her.

"I do not chatter." He tugged on his gloves, beautiful white leather gloves that fit him like a second skin. "You have not provoked me."

Felicity sat beside him in silence as he continued to regard the night beyond the coach window. Gareth would give nothing away. He kept his own counsel about every blessed thing, and only told her what he wanted her to know, when he wanted her to know it. Nonetheless, Felicity sensed in her bones that from Gareth's perspective, something also wasn't right, and that something related to what she'd just done with him.

Well, damn, to use his word. She had touched him, had learned intimate things about him, had learned to hear the way his breathing changed. His privy parts were fascinating in their contradictions: soft and hard; mighty and vulnerable... Gareth interrupted her musings by knocking three times on the carriage roof with his cane, with the result that the horses swung into a trot.

Still he did not touch her.

She fluffed her skirts and pulled on her own damned gloves.

"Do not be concerned, Felicity. I was not anticipating the direction of our dealings tonight, and I am merely reconsidering my plans."

The coach turned left, the first left turn it had made since leaving the theatre. "You didn't think I'd be willing, did you?"

"I wasn't sure, no." Still, he did not touch her, and she was determined not to touch him uninvited, even if he'd all but admitted she'd foiled whatever *direction* he'd had in mind.

"You found your pleasure." The confines of coach bore the scent of his pleasure, and yet she'd asked a question nonetheless.

"I most assuredly did."

They did not speak again. He helped her down from the coach, bowed over her hand, and climbed back in, tapping on the roof before the footman had the coach door closed.

～

"YOUR MENSES SHOULD ARRIVE the end of next week?" Gareth asked as he consulted a calendar. He sat at his late grandfather's massive desk, the fireplace crackling merrily, while Felicity wandered the room. She nodded her answer, no doubt thoroughly bored after spending almost two hours with him. He'd drilled her on everything from erotic Latin terms, to the price of a good bottle of claret.

She had answered every query accurately, though she had not, to use an apt term, cried off—damn her and bless her.

Still, she was subdued, and to his expert eye, pale, and that made him uncomfortable. But then, the whole bloody business was making him increasingly uncomfortable, so uncomfortable he'd left her in the cold and dark of night nearly a week ago, thought of nothing but her for intervening days—and nights—and hardly knew what to say to her now.

Please forgive me came to mind. *I am taking coin I do not need in exchange for ruining a decent, good woman who is too stubborn to accept charity instead.*

He rose from the desk, as if he could gain physical distance from that admission.

"We must eventually see that you are no longer a virgin, and you are almost ready to take that step. I will teach you the use of various contraceptives, but to minimize the risk of conception, we should be about our task either early next week, or immediately at the end of your bleeding. That will leave us about ten days to meet with the solicitors, and complete our dealings."

With a few weeks to spare, and his wits possibly intact.

Felicity looked up at him from some little red book of erotic poetry, her expression nonplussed, but as he watched, she roused herself to concentrate. "When is there the least risk of conceiving?" Her tone was admirably businesslike, just as brisk as his—damn it all.

"Immediately before you bleed, according to the midwives and ladies whose judgment I trust. The physicians debate the matter." He crossed the room to where she was standing. It was the closest he'd come to her in a week, but some things shouldn't be declaimed from twenty paces.

"Felicity, you must know that if there is a child, I will provide for you both, for so long as you live. I do not seek an heir, you know this, but I take my responsibilities seriously. You would want for nothing." Much to his surprise, he'd never meant anything more.

Felicity smiled up at him, her expression wistful. "Oh, I know first hand you do not avoid your duty, Heathgate."

Heathgate.

She reached up to touch his face, but he flinched before her fingers met his cheek, uncomfortable with a caress when she ought to slap some sense into him.

Felicity dropped her hand and stepped back. "What is *wrong* with you, my lord? Last week, you were stuck to me like a barnacle, and now you recoil as if I'm diseased. What did I do to displease you?"

He said nothing, but stood looking down at her, feeling something heavy and miserable in his guts.

"You must tell me, Heathgate. I cannot countenance the thought that in a week's time I will be as intimate with you as a woman can be, and yet you cannot bear my touch. If the burden is so onerous to you, I would not ask it."

She was near tears, he could sense it, feel it, hear it in her voice, felt something in his chest go tight with the knowledge of it.

Would she cry when he was inside her body? He could not ask her that, could not tolerate the thought of it, and could not bear another moment without her in his arms. He reached for her silently, and she folded herself into his embrace as the tears broke free.

"I have felt so awful," she whispered, clinging to him. "I cannot stand to have you angry with me, Gareth. I don't know what I did, I don't know what's wrong."

He walked her over to the reading chair before the fire and pulled her onto his lap. As Felicity's crying gradually subsided, Gareth came to an uncomfortable realization: The part of him that wanted their dealings concluded wanted her willing, but only willing to swive in the general case, not willing to bed only *him*, specifically. Some other godforsaken part of him, though, had decided her exclusive attention was surpassingly to be treasured.

Damn, damn, damn the woman to hell and back.

He nuzzled her hair and tightened his arms around her. "Take my handkerchief."

She complied, but refused to look at him.

"Felicity, listen to me, please."

That earned him a nod.

"I have hurt your feelings, and for that I am sorry." Women were always grateful for an apology. "You must realize however, that thirty days from now, sooner if I can arrange it, we will once again be as strangers to each other. Should we meet in public, you would be well advised to give me the cut direct—you know that don't you?"

Another nod, and thank goodness she wasn't arguing with him on that point.

"So you must not take on so when I approach you in a less personal fashion." His logic was unassailable, and the wording both deft and direct.

No nod, though.

"You take my point, don't you?"

Felicity raised her head, and the anger he saw in her magnificent topaz eyes had him shifting back against the chair.

"You *hurt* me, Gareth Alexander. You hurt me, and frightened me with your coldness and distance when yours was the only reassurance I could possibly seek. You were avoidably cruel, and though I have apologized for offending you, I still don't know what the problem is. It wasn't well done of you, and you will not use me so ill again."

She glared at him, until, not knowing what else to do, he dipped his head to rest his cheek against her hair.

He fell back on the recitations of naughty schoolboys and inattentive husbands, neither of which he'd ever been. "I'm sorry. It will not happen again." Unlike many schoolboys and husbands, he meant every word.

As he held her in his arms and watched the fire slowly die, Gareth told himself he couldn't wait to see the last of Felicity Worthington.

Honestly could not wait.

DAVID HOLBROOK WAS neither impatient nor indecisive, but as he sat before the hearth in his office, stroking the tabby cat in his lap, he was most assuredly frustrated. Yesterday, he'd waited in his coach, as he waited almost every morning—rain or shine—for the Worthington sisters to appear in the park.

To no avail.

He set the cat down, but the wretched beast sprang onto the desk and took itself on a tour of the surrounds.

Perhaps Miss Worthington's appearance last week at the theatre with the Marquess of Heathgate was not the potential disaster Holbrook feared, but his men were bringing him reports of Heathgate's coach in the Worthington mews, and that, Holbrook could not like.

A gold handled letter open clattered to the floor, while the cat ran its cheek over an arm of the wax jack.

"Wretched beast." David tucked the letter opener into a drawer and his abacus as well.

By all accounts, Heathgate had succeeded to the title under suspicious circumstances. No less than *five* other family members had been killed in the same accident that had resulted in Heathgate becoming the marquess. Interestingly, Heathgate's intended had also lost her life in the same mishap.

That had to be some kind of tragic record, and Holbrook did not envy the man who held it, assuming that man was not the author of those deaths.

Which he might have been.

The cat sat upon a pile of bank drafts and commenced its ablutions.

"I'm concerned that a decent lady is consorting with a rake and murderer while you wash your ears."

The cat offered no comment, but instead shifted to lick its own belly.

Heathgate's reputation was one of ruthless business acumen—no doubt a function of his plebian antecedents—and unflinching self-indulgence in the personal sphere. While not known as a drunkard or wild gambler, the man did cut a wide swath with ladies of a certain description.

A *very* wide swath. Rather like the damned cat now in a purring sprawl over David's open household ledger.

David allowed the cat to remain right where it was, while Heathgate's proximity to the Worthington sisters was something to be watched very, very carefully.

CHAPTER SIX

"He has some blunt," Brenner said.

"His name is Holbrook, and he has some blunt," Heathgate repeated. "It doesn't seem our investigation has progressed very far, Mr. Brenner."

The interview was taking place in the estate office, and as with many of his interviews with the marquess, the occasion visited upon Michael Brenner a compelling urge to dive out the window.

"As you say, your lordship, this fellow is turning out to be deucedly difficult to investigate. He has no markers out; he doesn't even gamble, for that matter. He keeps prime horseflesh, and drives conveyances that are all the crack, but nobody knows where he or his money came from. His household servants have all come into Town with him, and they keep to themselves. If the help won't gossip, your lordship, it is nigh on to impossible to get the particulars on the employer."

Oh, blessed Saint Bridget, there goes the Eyebrow.

Brenner soldiered on. "He doesn't receive many invitations that we can see, and he's had no company to the house since we've been watching him—not one caller of either gender. He takes his coach to the park in the morning, and he sits there and watches the foot traffic. A prodigious amount of correspondence seems to come and go from his town house, and messengers come and go at all hours, but they arrive and depart on horseback, Lord Heathgate. Hard to see what's in their satchels, if you get my drift."

Heathgate scowled, which qualified as a sort of Double Inverted Eyebrow.

"Rifling satchels, Brenner, would be premature, and ill advised. For all I know, Holbrook is merely a country squire hiding in Town from his wife's relations, keeping a close eye on his interests at home. His interactions with the Misses Worthington might have been purely incidental."

Would to God his lordship could content himself with such an innocuous explanation.

"Don't think that's the case, your lordship. Holbrook has taken his rig to the park every morning since that horse almost ran down Miss Felicity. Mostly, he sits there. We suspect he's reading correspondence. Yesterday, he got out of his coach as soon as the young misses came into the park. When some other folk paused to offer pleasantries to the sisters, he stopped, and got right back into his coach, and took up his watching again. When the ladies left, he left—not before."

His lordship stared into the fire, something Brenner had seen him doing a lot lately. "Brenner, good decisions are made..."

Brenner couldn't help himself—he interrupted his employer to finish the oft-repeated saw. "Based on good information, yes, your lordship. I will bring you better information. Until then, we keep the ladies under watch, and their house as well?"

"You do, and the Pleasure House. Keep Holbrook under close watch as well. He may be simply an inconvenient coincidence, but something tells me his interest in Felic—In Miss Worthington is not the obvious."

"Very good, sir."

BY THE TIME Gareth finished interrogating Brenner, reading his correspondence, and sorting through his situation with Felicity, the clock was striking an hour after midnight. He heard the front door slam, and recalled with a start that Andrew was temporarily sharing quarters with him. The office door opened and through it strode Gareth's surviving brother, fresh from a night on the Town.

"You, brother," Andrew drawled in disgust, "are positively stodgy. Not thirty years of age, and all the fun has gone right out of you. Here it is, a fine if frigid spring evening, and you have no doubt spent the past hours sitting right where you are, balancing columns, and reading reports from the home farm. I thank God above every night of my life you stand between me and the title." He plopped his thankful self into one of the armchairs and began tugging off his boots.

"Edith the Insatiable was asking for you," he went on "I gather you've thrown the little schemer over."

"A gentleman doesn't spank and tell, Andrew, but I did have Brenner find her a bauble to console her in her impending loneliness." Along with the bauble Gareth had also sent the requisite apologetic note, explaining that the press of business would render him unable to share her company for the foreseeable future, and she should not limit her enjoyments out of any misplaced sympathy et cetera, et cetera.

She'd appeared to like the diamond, at least.

"Don't know what you saw in her, Gareth." Andrew padded sock-footed over to the dry sink. "There's only so much of her carrying on a fellow can find amusing. Brandy?" He gestured with the decanter.

"Please. It's been too long since I joined you in a nightcap." Gareth folded the spectacles he used to read late at night and slid them into a drawer, then accepted the glass from Andrew and settled himself in the other armchair.

"I think,"—Andrew paused to swirl his brandy glass slowly in his palms—"you saw nothing at all in the fair Edith, and that's why you took up with her. Your taste in women these past few years has given me considerable worry. What kind of example are you setting for me?"

"Worry about yourself, Andrew," Gareth growled, wondering when his little brother had become such an astute observer of the human condition. "I look to you to secure the succession."

"I will if you ask it of me. Just don't ask it of me quite yet. I am a young man, you know." He sipped again. "Where do you find this stuff? I've never come across its like elsewhere, anywhere."

"It's six-and-forty years old, Andrew. You will never come across its like, so enjoy. I certainly am." He savored the drink, and savored the quiet conversation with his brother.

"Oh, and speaking of your taste in women..."

"Which I was not."

"What on earth is this I hear about you setting up that Worthington woman at Callista's old place?"

"*What?*" Gareth hadn't yelled, but the single word reverberated in the quiet office like a pistol shot.

"I was, shall we say, enjoying the healthy good spirits common to young men when one of the ladies present said she'd heard it from another cust— gentleman that the Worthington woman had retained you to buy a brothel for her. It's just the kind of thing you'd do, Gareth, but having met Miss Worthington, I can't picture it."

How had this happened? "Andrew, you are my brother..."

"Oh, no," Andrew groaned. "You're doing it aren't you? She seemed like such a decent sort. What were you thinking, introducing her to Mother? I can't say I find that amusing. This goes beyond what I expect even from you."

Andrew set his glass down with a thump and gathered his boots to leave.

"Andrew, hear me out."

Andrew turned, and Gareth was treated to what one of his

mistresses had termed the dreaded Alexander Eyebrow. Coupled with Andrew's height and dark good looks, the effect was surprisingly daunting.

"I am relying on your discretion, Andrew."

Andrew set his boots down. "Spare me your insults."

"I am not buying Miss Worthington a brothel. If she can meet certain conditions of Callista Hemming's will, she inherits the brothel." Which was, to quote the solicitors, a distinction without a difference. "She cannot meet those conditions unaided, and Callista specified the assistance should come from me."

Andrew's face was a mask of disgust. "That is scandalous. I never knew Callista well, but she struck me as hard, not evil. Why would she leave her business to a proper young lady like Miss Worthington?" He did not resume his seat, but remained standing over Gareth like Headmaster with the first form. "Well, is she a proper young lady? You did introduce her to Mother."

How did one put a presentable face on unpresentable facts?

"Miss Worthington is the daughter of a viscount and well bred. Her father, however, died without male issue, and barring the last minute appearance of a long lost heir, his estate is in the process of reverting to the crown. For reasons I do not understand, the young ladies were not made wards of the crown, nor were they granted a competence from the incomes during their minorities. I don't understand it—Brenner is checking—but I think this is simply one of the many details that have fallen beneath royal notice in recent times."

Andrew appeared to consider Gareth's words: King George had been mentally slipping for many years, and it was common knowledge, hence sentiment grew ever stronger in favor of a regency for the Prince of Wales. Two penniless female orphans were hardly of concern to a monarchy that had all it could do to wage war against Napoleon's ravenous ambitions.

"But why her?" Andrew persisted. "Callista could have left the business to some other whore, and directed an income to be paid to the Worthingtons. That could have been handled discreetly enough."

Never once, by word or action, had Andrew ever betrayed his brother's confidences. Fortified by that fact, Gareth answered his brother's query honestly.

"Callista is a cousin of some remote degree to the Worthingtons. I assume she did not direct a stipend be paid to her cousins because over time—over decades, possibly—that would have involved others who had no loyalty to Felicity and Astrid. Callista was not in the business of trusting to others' noble natures."

He fell silent, while the fire crackled, Andrew retrieved his drink. Again, Gareth had to wonder what could have motivated Callista's cruelty toward her only female relations.

"I *liked* Miss Worthington, Heathgate. She seemed like such a nice change of pace for you," Andrew said, sounding cross. "If she inherits that brothel, she's ruined. If she doesn't, I suppose she's destitute—not a complicated choice when one's belly is empty and there's no coal in the hearth. What will you do?"

Andrew had ever been a bright lad—damn him.

"What I thought I'd do is provide the assistance requested of me so she does inherit, then manage the business for her until it can be sold one year from Callista's death. I had hoped the whole matter could be handled quietly, as had Felic—Miss Worthington. But you tell me there are rumors?"

Andrew nodded, finishing his brandy.

"Only rumors and only among the ladies of the night. I, of course, laughed uproariously at the very absurd thought, and explained you had quite properly escorted the woman in question to the theatre, introduced her to Mother, upon whom she would be calling Wednesday next... 'ha-ha, how these things do get garbled in the minds of the less intelligent...' says your loyal brother. I'll try to find out where it came from, but Lucifer's balls, this is a mess."

Andrew assumed the mess was one they now shared, and that warmed Gareth more effectively than the fire or the brandy.

"A mess, indeed. I took Felicity out the other night precisely to create a proper impression. I suppose now she will have to call on Mother, though for the love of God I cannot like the idea."

Not for himself, not for his mother, and most of all, not for Felicity.

"You underestimate our dam, Gareth. She would like nothing, *nothing*, more than to be of use to you in unraveling a scheme like this. She has good instincts when it comes to people, and she liked Miss Worthington on the spot. Her good offices could go a long way toward scotching rumors and avoiding scandal. For all we know, Mama knew the late viscountess, or some such rot."

Not even the marchioness of Heathgate could scotch this scandal if the particulars became public, and yet, that wasn't what bothered Gareth most.

"There's more, Andrew."

"Only you, Heathgate."

"Shut up, brat. I have reason to believe somebody wishes Felicity harm." He outlined the incident with the runaway horse, and the strange lack of information on Felicity's "rescuer," when a knock interrupted him.

"Enter."

Brenner appeared, uncharacteristically disheveled and out of breath.

"Begging your pardon, your lordship, Lord Andrew, but I thought you'd want to know now: There's been a fire at the Worthington residence."

FELICITY SAT at the worn work table in the kitchen, icy fingers clutching at a mug of tea. Her mind was unaccountably concerned with the question of why in the aftermath of a fire, she should be so cold. Though she had a dressing gown wrapped around her night-gown, she couldn't stop shaking. Astrid sat beside her—right beside her—pale as a ghost and for once beyond chattering.

"Close that damned door, Brenner," came a familiar growl from the hallway.

Gareth. Relief flooded her, unreasoning, physical, emotional relief.

"What are you doing here, my lord?" She stood as Gareth and his brother tromped into the kitchen, followed by a red-haired man who looked a bit the worse for wear but closed the door at his lordship's barked command.

Relief gave way to a need to hit something, or somebody.

"I wanted to air out the smoke in here, my lord, and you haven't answered my question." Felicity gripped the table to steady her unreliable knees. The Crabbles rapped on the now closed door, then joined them in the kitchen.

Gareth walked right up to her and opened his arms, spreading his cloak wide. He enfolded her in its depths by virtue of wrapping his arms around her, then tucked her face into his shoulder without acknowledging her in any other way.

She took a big, shaky breath, and loved him for bringing warmth and the scent of spices, flowers and safety to her cold, smoky kitchen.

He began speaking while Felicity listened to the beat of his heart beneath her cheek.

"You'd be Crabble, I take it? Was anybody hurt? No? Thank God for His mercies. Andrew, please take Miss Astrid upstairs and have her gather what the ladies will need for a short stay elsewhere. Send the tiger with a message to Mother telling her she will have company for the balance of the night, possibly longer. Crabble, you and your missus will present yourselves at my town house tomorrow morning that we may discuss this unfortunate situation in detail. For tonight, I want you to secure this residence after we leave. My man Brenner will assist you once you've shown him the damage."

The whole time he'd been issuing orders, he'd stood with his arms around Felicity, wrapping her close. His scent, expensive, masculine, and complicated, pushed the acrid smoke from her nose.

Lord Andrew followed Astrid toward the stairs, while the Crabbles, looking relieved to have somebody taking charge, bid Felicity goodnight, and bustled out the back door with Brenner in tow.

Only when they were alone did Gareth kiss Felicity on the cheek and sit her down at the table.

"I'll freshen this up," he offered, taking her mug of tea. While Felicity drank in the sight of him in her kitchen, he rummaged, finding the fixings and preparing two cups of hot tea, then he sat at Felicity's elbow and pressed the mug into her hands.

"Can you tell me what happened?" He folded his hands around hers as she cradled the hot mug. His hands were warm and cherishing, his blue eyes full of concern.

Which he would not want her to see, much less acknowledge.

"I couldn't sleep," Felicity murmured, looking at their hands rather than at his eyes. "I came down to make myself some warm milk, and I saw a kind of a glow from the back of the house. When I opened the kitchen door to investigate, I realized the back of the building was on fire. Fortunately, the cistern was full because we've had so much rain. The others heard me screaming, and we managed to beat it out by wetting the sheets Mrs. Crabble had left out to dry on the clothesline."

She took a sip of her tea and saw her hands were shaking. She could not feel them shaking, but she could observe it.

Gareth pushed her hair back from her brow, a gentle caress that made her long for his arms. "Go on."

"This fire was a near thing, Gareth, and Astrid was unbelievable. She can be far more fierce than I had realized. Her hands..." Felicity looked down, and Gareth squeezed her fingers. "We put some salve on them, but those burns are going to hurt like the very devil. She'll have scars."

Astrid's hands were so pretty. Felicity knew she'd cry for her sister's scars, but she couldn't seem to cry just yet.

Gareth shifted closer, his arm coming around Felicity's shoulders.

"I am angry," he said, in perfectly civil tones. "I am enraged that somebody would attempt to hurt *this* household—a couple of doddering servants and two defenseless young women. There is no explaining or defending such an act."

He added a second arm, so Felicity was cocooned in his embrace. "You cannot stay here tonight, my dear. It's freezing and the house reeks of smoke. Besides, you are in need of some cosseting, and my mother's physician will see to Astrid's hands."

Felicity could barely make sense of his words, so comforting was the mere sound of them. Gareth had a beautiful voice to go with his beautiful body and beautiful sandalwood scent. Why hadn't she appreciated that about him before?

Andrew and Astrid returned to the kitchen and Gareth did not withdraw his arms, sit back, or otherwise accommodate the proprieties.

Astrid at least seemed to be regaining a little color, perhaps as a function of Andrew Alexander's company.

"We've retrieved a small mountain of necessities, each of which Miss Astrid assures me is indispensable to a lady on a visit, Heathgate. I'm prepared to escort the ladies to Mother's, if you like."

Gareth did shift away then. He stood before Astrid and took her hands in his.

"Ouch," he said, surveying the burns across the backs of her fingers and knuckles. She nodded jerkily, but didn't withdraw her hands.

Felicity knew Astrid was making a heroic effort not to cry, but she suspected Gareth was equally challenged not to roar with outrage at Astrid's red fingers and skinned knuckles.

"Because you are injured—and barefoot,"—Gareth shot a look at his brother—"I will ask you to allow my brother to carry you to the coach. Felicity and I will join you shortly. You'll find some spirits in the boot, Andrew. I think a medicinal tot for Miss Astrid is in order."

Andrew wrapped his fingers around Astrid's wrist, leading her from the kitchen. She put up about as much resistance as an exhausted puppy and that, more than the reeking house, the ruined sheets, or the Crabbles' dismay, broke Felicity's heart.

"He'll put her at ease," Gareth said. "Are you barefoot too?"

Felicity looked down.

"Oh dear," she muttered, as the pain in her feet made itself known to the rest of her. "I forgot to put shoes on before I went outside, and then my feet were so cold, and I thought we were going to lose the house...."

And even with the income Gareth had insisted they be allowed from Callista's solicitors, Felicity shuddered to think of replacing the ruined sheets, much less paying for repairs to the house itself.

"I cannot leave you unsupervised for a minute," Gareth grumbled, pouring hot water from the kettle into a basin, then grabbing a towel and soap. "Give me that foot."

Gareth washed her feet, and the several small cuts she'd suffered trying to put out the fire. He'd certainly handled her feet before and she'd seen him barefoot—feet were on his list of pedagogic topics—but having him *care* for her feet exceeded the intimacy of any of their previous dealings—even their odd, uncomfortable interlude in his coach.

And the whole time, he kept up a soothing patter of male disgruntlement, muttering about unsupervised females, damned mischief, the blighted watch, and the realm going to the dogs.

"I don't want to leave you down here alone, or I'd rifle your belongings for some slippers," he said, taking off his boots and peeling off his thick wool stockings. "These are clean," he muttered as he put his stockings over Felicity's feet.

He sat back, surveyed her feet, put his boots on over his bare feet, then scowled at her.

"I don't like this Felicity; I don't like this *at all,*" was all he said before scooping her into his arms, and walking with her out to the coach. There, they found Astrid cuddled up under Andrew's arm, his handkerchief clutched in her hand.

"We've had a nice, ladylike little bout of the sniffles," Andrew reported, patting Astrid's shoulder. "We'll be feeling much more the thing once we get some hot chocolate and raspberry crumpets under our belt."

"I'm glad you're feeling better, Andrew," Gareth snapped. He rapped on the roof, and soon the horses were trotting on. Felicity sat beside Gareth, realizing she was at long last warm. She'd been so cold and afraid sitting in the kitchen with Astrid, and then Gareth had arrived.

Later, later when they were alone, she'd ask him how a woman was supposed to cope when a man diligently planned his exit from her life, then showed up in her kitchen in the dark of night, poured tea down her throat, tended to her feet, then bundled her off to the safety and luxury of his very own mother's household.

And later still, she'd ask him how she would have coped, how she would have ever managed, had he *not* come in the dead of night, growling, snapping orders, and fixing her tea.

TWO DAYS AFTER THE FIRE—BY which time, Gareth's staff had already seen the damage repaired, painted, and aired—Gareth summoned Felicity from his mother's house, and introduced her to erotic literature. The images in his naughty books provoked her curiosity, and she challenged Gareth to prove that indeed, a man and woman could pleasure one another orally at the same time.

He'd offered to take her to a room in the Pleasure House where one could watch, unobserved, while the parties in the next room engaged in perversions with each other.

She had declined.

He treated Felicity to a particular expression, a single lifted eyebrow that conveyed a sardonic challenge—and made her want to kiss his arrogant mouth. "If you will not indulge in the pleasures enjoyed by a *voyeur*, then perhaps you'll oblige me with a game of chess."

Chess? "Do I get to keep my clothes on?"

He appeared to consider this. "Not entirely."

"You are planning wickedness." She hoped he was planning wickedness, and feared it as well. They were running out of days, and yet, the timing was such that she might well conceive. Gareth had not broached the topic of her virginity since the fire, which had been a relief. He'd been full of orders for Mr. Brenner, about how footmen were to be awake on the Worthington premises round the clock, and arsonists deserved the hangman's noose.

Felicity rather enjoyed those pronouncements, and had to wonder again how she'd manage when he wasn't on hand to make them.

He stalked up to her, bringing the scent of horse with him, and memories of their first encounter.

"I am planning on getting out of my riding attire. Brenner ambushed me in the very mews this morning, we worked through luncheon, and now..." He sat and stuck out a booted foot. "I will teach you how to be a proper valet."

In the privacy of his suite, he taught her how to be an *improper* valet. She could not tug his boot off unless she faced away from him while doing so. To untie his cravat, she was to stand close enough that he might catch her scent, but not close enough that her breasts touched his chest. Removing his sleeve buttons was an excuse to place the back of his wrist on her thighs, and while all this seduction appeared to have no impact on *him*, his gloriously naked body certainly affected Felicity.

"I don't suppose you'd like to learn how to bathe a man today?" he asked, scratching his bare chest and cracking his jaw.

Did nothing unnerve this man? Though, if nothing else, his display meant Felicity wasn't fretting over arsonists or extra house staff.

"I've bathed babies. How different can it be?" Except babies were delightful little armfuls of humanity, not six feet plus of male beauty and frank sexuality.

He caught sight of himself in the mirror and dragged his fingers through his hair. "I need a haircut. Perhaps I should bathe you."

Felicity's knees threatened to buckle. "Perhaps you should put on a dressing gown, lest you take a chill."

A dressing gown, a loincloth, *anything*. His chest, shoulders and belly might have been rendered by some master out of Carrara marble, so articulated were the muscles thereon, and his arms were the same. Corded, moving in layers of powerful muscle under smooth skin.

His legs put Felicity in mind of paintings and myths, of charioteers and gods. No human male should be this well put together.

He prowled closer. "My dear, I am proud of you. You are staring at my cock."

He was beautiful, true, but Felicity suspected every woman ever to see him thus told him as much. "You and your vocabulary, my lord, are tedious."

She grabbed him by that appendage she could not name without blushing, and went up on her toes to kiss him. His surprise was palpable, but then—wicked, wretched, oddly dear man—Felicity felt him smile against her mouth.

"Naughty woman. Lovely, naughty woman. Are you sure you don't want me to show you how that business in the little book works?"

He wasn't only proud of her, his smile said he approved of her, and for that, Felicity was almost willing to surrender her clothes.

Almost. "And what of our chess match?"

His smile faded from a grin—and a disconcertingly charming grin at that—to something horrendously tender. "I shall win, that's what of our chess match. You will be too unnerved by your state of undress to concentrate on the game."

Felicity's command of the King's English deserted her. Naked, Gareth resembled a lithe, relentless predator, one intent on making a meal of her wits. When he stalked right past her to snatch a blue velvet dressing gown from his wardrobe, she could not help but admire the view of him from the back.

"You're allowed to look you know," he said as he shrugged into the dressing gown and straightened the collar and sleeves. "I enjoy you looking at me, particularly when your expression suggests you'd like to revisit that notion of getting your mouth on me."

He stood by his vanity fussing with the cuffs, turning them back, apparently inspecting his image, and then frowning at nothing Felicity could fathom.

And abruptly, the moment turned sweet.

"You, my lord, are stalling." He *was*—he was dithering, shilly-shallying, and generally not being about his stated business of undressing her, mostly or otherwise. Gracious heavens. The notion that Gareth Alexander might be reluctant to embarrass her warmed Felicity to her very toes.

She set about exposing those toes, appropriating his reading chair to unlace her half boots. "You need not be so delicate, Gareth. The naked female form is hardly novel to you, after all, and one antici-pated that in the course of our dealings at some point one might be subjected to your—gracious!"

Between getting one boot off, and bending to start on the second, Felicity found herself lifted from the chair and deposited on Gareth's bed.

"Hush." He growled this while climbing onto the bed and getting to work on her remaining boot. "You chatter when you're nervous."

She chattered, he growled. They should share a cage at the menagerie.

Gareth tossed her boot in the general direction of the reading chair, her stockings followed.

Felicity hiked herself up on her elbows. "In case you're inter-ested, this is not how I'd imagined a gentleman bent on seduction would undress his lady."

Gareth sat back on his heels. "A *gentleman* wouldn't *be* bent on seduction."

The exasperation in his tone was at such variance with the care in his touch that Felicity remained silent. He eased her garters off without comment—plain, dingy garters no madam would admit she owned—then tugged her to sitting so he might sit behind her and undo the hooks of her dress.

"What you said before..." He leaned in, and Felicity thought he would kiss her nape. Instead he looped his arms around her waist and rested his chin on her shoulder.

"I have it on good authority I was chattering, my lord."

"You were."

Felicity's dress and stays were undone, which meant she could breathe freely. Amid the soft press of his velvet robe and her disheveled clothing, she could also feel his bare chest against her naked back. The intimacy of it was stunning, and yet she had the sense Gareth remained draped around her so she might be denied the sight of his eyes as he spoke.

He kissed her shoulder, a lovely press of soft lips followed by his hand skimming her hair aside. "You said the female form holds no novelty for me."

"The naked female form." For he must have seen dozens—hundreds, in fact, Scads and troupes and hordes of naked females. This thought ought to make her jealous when mostly it made her sad, for him. Felicity covered Gareth's hands where they linked at her waist and did not chatter though she was nervous.

"You were wrong, Felicity."

Another kiss, while Felicity tried to review what, exactly she'd said.

"You were wrong that the naked female form holds no novelty for me. For a long time, it hasn't... I stopped seeing... What I'm trying to say..."

He dropped his forehead to her shoulder, and Felicity grasped what he could not admit. *Her* naked form held novelty for him.

He'd seen legions of naked women, but he'd never seen her naked, and this unnerved him.

"You are the only man I've seen as God made him," Felicity said, rising from the bed. "I consider myself fortunate that if I'm only to see one man thus, that man is you, Gareth Alexander."

She stood beside the bed letting her dress and stays sag down to her hips. Gareth said nothing, though even in her inexperience, she knew she had his attention. She had his complete, unblinking focus as she pushed her clothes to the floor and went to work on the bows of her chemise.

"Let me." Gareth's voice was hoarse, and though he hadn't phrased it as such, Felicity knew he'd asked her a question.

Asked her permission.

She let her hands fall to her side. "Please. My fingers have become clumsy."

And her heart had filled, because Gareth's touch went from careful to reverent as he undid one small bow after another. He pushed the fabric off Felicity's shoulders and closed his eyes, his hands settling on either side of her neck.

Warmth coursed through her, from his touch, from the angle of his head as he learned the contour of her jaw with his fingertips. This was personal tutelage too, but Felicity was not the pupil.

Not the only pupil.

"So soft." He tugged her closer, so she stood between his thighs. "A marvel of softness." For long moments, Felicity reveled in the sensations he evoked with his hands. He traced her features, making her feel beautiful to herself—her eyes, her nose, her chin, her eyebrows, nothing escaped his tactile inventory.

He palmed her breasts, cherishingly, slowly, as if he'd never touched a woman's breast before. He measured the span of her waist and the flare of her hips. His thumbs brushing over her nipples seemed to fascinate him—and nearly brought her to a swoon.

He knelt at her feet.

Oh, no. Not this again. "Gareth, I thought we were planning to play—"

He rose up, like an incoming wave climbs the cliffs that try to stand against it, and enveloped her in an embrace. "I concede. I goddamn concede."

His concession included a hot, open-mouthed kiss that didn't stop until Felicity was naked on her back beneath him, his weight a glorious and strange comfort over her.

"Gareth, I want you now."

He kissed that place where her neck and shoulder joined, the spot on her body where Felicity most wanted his mouth, though she'd gone a lifetime not realizing it. In retaliation, Felicity ran the soles of her feet up his hairy, muscular calves.

"Now, Gareth. I concede too."

"Hush, love." He got an arm under her neck to cradle her closer, and that was lovely. "You'll tempt me past reason."

Felicity curled up against him. "To blazes with reason."

He raised up on his elbows, Felicity caged in his embrace, and laughed. The damned man laughed, though at least it was an unhappy laugh.

"We cannot copulate now, Miss Worthington. I do not typically conduct my liaisons here, so certain accoutrements are not at hand. You will laugh to find it so for I certainly find the humor ironic." He dropped his head and nuzzled her ear. "I will not risk getting you with child any more than needs must."

And he managed this, this prodigious feat of responsible thought, with his cock a hot, hard reality between their bodies.

He kissed her brow, and Felicity realized that though they could indeed copulate now—her body regarded this as a capital notion in fact—because Gareth was a gentleman whose private quarters did not boast sheaths, vinegar and sponges, they *would* not.

Or so he'd have her believe.

"Gareth, I want to cry." The feeling was one not only of emotional upset, but also of real, physical torment. "I honestly do want to cry."

"I cannot abide the thought that I've moved you to tears."

When he moved against her, the sensation was at first one of comfort. Welling up beneath the comfort, though, was that urge Felicity had voiced—a wanting that sought to murder reason, commonsense, and all sane notions, until the only thought remaining was to join her body to his.

She rocked her hips against him, and tucked herself more tightly beneath him. "Please, Gareth..."

He pressed harder, his cock slicking itself to Felicity's wet sex so snugly she thought it must pain him.

"Must. Not."

Must, must, must... Felicity directed that terrible, straining frustration to the place where their bodies were nearly joined. She poured it into a fusing of their mouths, she let him feel it where she sank her fingernails into his muscular backside.

A wet heat spread over her belly as Gareth held himself hard against her, and then, a mighty male sigh breezed past her ear.

They breathed in counterpoint, Gareth above her, Felicity pinned beneath him and running her nose over the soft skin of his inner arm. He eventually shifted, collapsing on the blankets beside her, to pant some more.

Just as Felicity would have dozed off, myriad questions fluttering in her brain like so many trapped moths, she felt the rim of a glass pressed to her lips.

"Drink." She obeyed, and heard him moving away, her eyes already drifting closed. Gareth had protected her, and he hadn't exactly pleasured her, which pairing of decisions, she could accept. The next thing she felt was a cool, wet cloth being pressed low on her belly, and that had her eyes flying open.

"Too cold?"

"No," she managed. "It feels comfortable, it's simply..."

"Simply?"

"Odd," she subsided against the blankets. "Most odd." Her gaze glanced off of Gareth's, and she knew they were feeling the same thing: Surprise, physical upheaval, and emotional disorientation. He hadn't shown her the greatest pleasure, but she'd been more aroused than at any point previously, and Gareth would certainly have divined that. Then too, she was fairly confident his own pleasure had been noteworthy.

"Cuddle up, sweetheart."

Now the idea that he'd been with legions of other women bothered her in a more predictable sense. Did he call them all sweetheart so he didn't have to recall their names?

And yet, when he tugged her into his arms, she hiked a knee over his thighs and lay passively against him, eyes closed while his fingers roamed over her face.

"You don't seem upset," he commented softly.

She was beyond upset, in several directions at once, and also oddly at peace. "I am not upset, precisely, but maybe in awe of the magnitude of my own ignorance. Why should I be upset?"

Gareth kissed her temple, and smoothed her hair back, then shifted them, so they were on their sides with him spooned around her back.

"I am upset," he said at last.

CHAPTER SEVEN

Felicity forced herself to remain relaxed, to breathe evenly, to *not* whip around and stare at Gareth for what he'd just said. His voice held no irony, only a kind of unhappy bewilderment.

"Why?" Felicity asked with as much indifference as she could feign.

"Felicity, you just allowed me good old-fashioned humping," he began, anger creeping into his voice. "Not well done of me. The lady's pleasure always comes first."

The courtesan's pleasure was supposed to come when she was paid. Felicity did not share this observation, because, God bless the man, Gareth did not see her in that role.

"Did you enjoy it?"

"You were supposed to be the one enjoying herself. I was determined to win the chess match."

Whatever that had to do with anything. "You sound resentful."

And why shouldn't he? Brenner was probably waiting below with another five hours or paperwork.

Gareth was silent for so long Felicity was certain he'd fallen asleep, in which case she might have a chance to study him in slumber.

"I don't resent you. I *desire* you."

Her patience with him and his moods gave up. "You don't have to be polite, Gareth."

He cuddled closer, a big, hot, naked weight of male moods and passion Felicity could not read at all. "Are you fishing for compliments, Felicity?"

"I am trying to delicately state the obvious," she replied with studied calm. "I am a virgin of little skill. You can amuse yourself with my body because you do know what you're doing—Callista likely chose you for that, after all. I don't flatter myself I have much at all to do with your pleasure, when it's all said and done."

She was learning to read his body. He did not allow himself to tense, but in the careful stillness of his limbs and muscles against her, Felicity felt him considering her words.

"You're wrong, you know," he said. "Wrong again." He hitched his leg over her hip, as if she'd scamper away from him. "You haven't the experience to understand, Felicity, but the trust you show me, and the openness with which you respond to my caresses, they have as much to do with the pleasure I feel as any naughty toys or novel positions. I am not enjoying only myself, you see, I am also enjoying *you*."

Which probably bothered him, because in his world, such emotions were messy. Felicity did not like messes, but she very much liked him. The notion surprised her, though it seemed all her revelations regarding him were tinged with sadness.

He kissed her nape. She loved it when he kissed her nape, all scratchy beard and soft lips.

"Your family died almost a decade ago, Gareth. Why are you still so alone? You are charming, handsome, and intelligent. You are loftily titled, well to do, and in possession of all of your considerable faculties. I don't think, though, that you are particularly happy, and I can't see why you keep yourself so apart."

His cock against her bum suggested he was recovering from their latest bout of passion, and she expected him to start back in with the lectures on arousal and positions, and all his silly whatnot. In the alternative, he might climb out of bed and tell her the hour grew late when he had plans for the evening.

He kissed her nape again, so tenderly she shivered.

"While your good opinion of me is cheering, Felicity, it is not shared by all and sundry. No man with a title can afford to trust others very easily. I am alone, as you put, unencumbered by friendships, basically because, I have grown prudent."

He arranged her, wrestling her so she straddled him, then pulled her down onto his chest. His handling of her was so matter of fact, she might have been swathed in her grandmother's winter nightgown, and yet to cuddle with him skin to skin was lovely.

"You want to see me with a wife, a chubby baby on my knee, and a lordling or three in the nursery studying to be my heirs. You think I should dance attendance upon my aging mother and donate conspicuously to charities—is that it?"

He did dance attendance on his mother, and he did donate to charities, though not conspicuously. Felicity had seen both his calendar and enough of the correspondence piled on his estate desk to know this.

"I want to see you happy, Gareth." She wanted this badly. "I have known you more than two months, and I've never yet seen you laugh for pure joy. Do you resent the title that much?"

Another silence, while Felicity wondered how a man could go for years with no one to simply talk to. Rain started up against the windows, and off to the south thunder rumbled. Gareth's hands on her back started drawing patterns that felt like vines and flowers.

"I did resent the title that much. I never wanted it, and then to have people accuse me of murdering five of my own family members to get my hands on it... I thought the world was a generally fair, pleasant place, Felicity, where family loved you, and friends were honest to your face. When I became the Marquess of Heathgate, I realized that world, if it had ever existed, was no longer mine."

His heartbeat was soft and steady, like the rain on the windows. "And now?"

"And now I am older and wiser and worlds more cynical. It is too much effort to cope with the aftereffects of misplaced devotion or betrayed trust. I simply do not traffic in those commodities any longer."

Oh, but he did. "I wish your heart had not been broken, Gareth. I wish you had not had to suffer so." She wrapped her arms around him and buried her face at his throat, wishing there was more comfort she could offer, any comfort at all.

~

MICHAEL BRENNER EXPERIENCED a rare moment of optimism because he'd been closeted with the marquess for almost an hour, and had seen no sign of the Eyebrow. In fact, his lordship seemed distracted to the point of appearing uninterested in their dealings.

Brenner was not deceived. His lordship was merely contemplating one problem while discussing another.

"So, Brenner,"—the mild tone nonetheless riveted Brenner's attention—"what else have you managed to uncover about our friend, Mr. Holbrook?"

Brenner had known the calm was too good to last.

"Precious little, your lordship. I can tell you he owns property in Kent—good farmland, a commodious manor house, grazing, a mill, a dairy, that sort of thing. Typical prosperous country holding. His correspondence goes there, but also to Bristol, Manchester, Leeds, Scotland, the Continent, the Americas. He is a man of varied interests, one would conjecture."

Conjecture was not the best word for the moment. The

marquess's riding boots hit the floor. "Who are his people? If he's that much of a businessman, I should have heard of him."

"Well you should ask, your lordship. He appears to have no family. He lives quietly in the country, keeps no mistress that we've been able to locate, does not socialize with the titles in his area. He's well liked by the tradesmen, pays his bills scrupulously on time, takes excellent care of his staff, and supports the local living generously."

"Why would he do that? Kent is thick with earls and viscounts and old families with plenty of funds."

His lordship had the knack of seizing on small details that could unravel complicated patterns. Brenner both marveled at and dreaded his employer for this instinct.

"Not in his little corner, it appears. He bought the estate almost a decade ago from some earl or other who was short of funds—the property wasn't entailed—and he's managed it well since coming into possession of it. Can't find anybody to say much about him, your lordship, but nobody who does know of him says anything unflattering."

"What is such a virtuous yeoman doing in London, Brenner? It makes no sense."

Brenner sent up a prayer to St. Jude, patron saint of lost causes, because his lordship was about to conclude this interview where he had the last one: Bring me better information.

"Holbrook has gone out a very few times while we've had an eye on him, your lordship. Twice to meet with solicitors, and we're working on the clerks to see if we can't loosen a tongue or two in that office. Occasionally, he'll still lurk at the park, and he hacks out in the early morning when the weather is fine. He did visit a brothel once when first we began to keep track of him, but he didn't stay long, and he hasn't gone back since."

"Which brothel?"

"I'll have to inquire of our man, your lordship. I did not think to ask."

The Eyebrow went to about half mast. Any single gentleman of means, just up from the country, might make a brief stop at a brothel upon arriving in Town.

A discreet scratching on the door interrupted the discussion.

"Come in," Heathgate commanded.

"A note from the Worthington household, your lordship." The footman bowed and withdrew leaving a silver salver on the desk.

Brenner watched while his lordship regarded the simple white envelope warily. If it had been an emergency, a threat to life or limb, one of Heathgate's men would have come directly. His lordship opened the envelope without asking Brenner to leave him, which was in itself more an indication of worry than of indifference to Brenner's presence.

A single, Anglo-Saxon curse erupted through clenched teeth in such a vicious undertone Brenner wished himself Anywhere Else.

"Brenner, excuse me, and have my horse brought round immediately on your way out, please."

"Of course, your lordship." Brenner bowed, only too happy to leave the room, and the house. His lordship had received disconcerting news from the Worthington household. It wasn't Brenner's place to wonder what could have prompted that oath from the lips of a man whom he had never, ever known to use it in the past.

THE DOOR to Felicity's bedroom swung open quietly, and she stifled a sigh of relief. Gareth was here now, and they could discuss matters, and be done with it.

"His lordship, Miss Felicity, to see how you're getting on," Mrs. Crabble explained unnecessarily. "Right kind of him to come," she added with a worried frown.

For him to be in Felicity's bedroom was right indecent of him, and all three of them knew it—though only Crabbie ought to have been dismayed by it.

"Crabbie, if you would fetch us some tea?" Felicity noted that Crabbie left the door open a few inches—a scant few inches.

Gareth stared down at her, looking about eight feet tall in his boots and riding attire, his expression unreadable.

For her part, Felicity was glad he hadn't caught her in bed—that would not have done at all. In fact, Mrs. Crabble would probably have insisted on staying—until Gareth, oozing charm and sweet reason, threw her out.

He came over to the day couch where Felicity had been using the natural window light to read. She swung her legs to the side, thinking to stand, but he called her bluff and took a seat beside her.

"I rode here, temper blazing, ready to thrash you for this clumsy maneuver, Felicity," he began quietly. To her surprise, though, he took her hand. "And I am still prepared to do that, should it be necessary, except on the way here, it occurred to me that, in the first place, you would only stoop to an *elegant* subterfuge to gain your ends, and second, you probably would prefer to have today's scheduled dealings concluded as much as I would."

Scheduled dealings. Thus a man of the world referred to demolishing a spinster's virginity.

That he wouldn't verbally thrash her was a relief—he never raise a hand to a woman in anger—but that he admitted to wanting to conclude his *dealings* with her, well, that hurt a bit.

More than a bit.

"You look pale," he commented, smoothing her hair back from her face. "And tired. Do you really have a headache?" he said, clearly ready to believe her if she replied in the affirmative. "You might be suffering overwrought nerves, you know."

She hated seeing him unsure. "Your arrogance is deserting you, Gareth. Why would I be nervous when I can anticipate only the greatest of care and expertise at your hands?"

Which sally only provoked him to frowning more fiercely. "Because once we do this, you will never, ever, under any but the most unusual circumstances and calling upon the greatest possible good luck, be able to contemplate the life of a respectable wife and mother. I had hoped I could find you a way around this, Felicity, but I don't believe I tried hard enough." He treated her to a ferocious scowl. "I must want too badly to sin with you."

"At last," Felicity said, "a compliment, I think." Though one that left her sad and him in a temper.

At the sound of Mrs. Crabble's ponderous tread on the stairs, Gareth stood and moved off a couple paces. He kept a polite distance while Crabbie set down a tea tray laden with the service, sandwiches, and crumb cake.

"Mrs. Crabble, you shouldn't have gone to such trouble," he admonished her as he pulled a chair over from the hearth to the low table beside the day couch.

"It tweren't no trouble, your lordship. Since you sent over those lads to help out, I've finally had some proper appetites to cook for. The larder is stocked and my kitchen is busy again,"

She beamed at him, apparently ready to nominate him for sainthood—which he would loathe.

He winked at her. "No doubt they'll all come back into my employ two stone heavier and complaining about my cook."

When Crabbie had gone blushing and beaming on her way Felicity let the tea steep rather than have Gareth know she had, by virtue of forced economies, acquired a preference for drinking it weak.

He all but closed the door after Mrs. Crabble, then resumed his place beside Felicity. "What is this indisposition you referred to in your note?"

Her body betrayed her. A blush crept up her neck, and Gareth's brows drew down than up.

"Got your menses early, did you?" he asked, sounding if anything amused.

Felicity gave a small nod. "You aren't angry with me?"

"How could I be angry with you? These things are mysterious, even to the medical experts. I had in my employ at one time a woman who never bled, not once in her adult life, if her husband was to be believed. She was the mother of five healthy children. You do not control this, and nor, it appears, does the Marquess of Heathgate."

"But Gareth, what does this do to the bequest? There are time constraints..."

"You've shown enough good faith progress with its terms I should be able to bully and intimidate our way to some lenience. It's not like anybody wants to see the damned thing examined in Chancery."

Felicity was reassured by his casual unconcern, but she'd be more reassured when his bullying had borne fruit. To come so close to meeting the terms of the will, only to be thwarted by nature.

"I don't think we should consummate our dealings until you've had the proper assurances from Callista's solicitors." Commonsense was back in her grasp, at least to that extent.

Gareth had been busying himself with preparation of the tea, and Felicity had been so preoccupied she'd allowed it. He handed her a cup with two sugars and a tot of cream, just as she preferred.

"Thank you."

"You're welcome. Shall you have a sandwich or some of this crumb cake as well? I did not eat before coming here, so I will be able to do respectable damage to Mrs. Crabble's offerings if you're not up to eating."

"How good of you."

"One makes sacrifices." He served himself a sandwich and a piece of cake, but set the plate down rather than tucking into the food. "How do you feel, Felicity?"

"Awkward." Awkward, sad, pleased that he'd come himself to investigate and not sent Brenner around, or demanded a report from her in writing.

"Still? You are the most determinedly proper woman I have ever met, and I have met some formidable dames. You have no need to feel awkward with me."

"Oh, no none at all," she replied. "My own sister doesn't know my bodily cycles. Mrs. Crabble isn't sure just how much milk I take in my tea—though there's cream on the tray when the marquess comes 'round. No man, not even my own father, has sat in this room with me in my dressing gown, and casually taken tea with me...."

Gareth sat back, his expression puzzled.

"I can't tell whether you are angry at them, because they didn't see the genuine article of you, or angry at me, because I won't let you be invisible."

A vexingly good question. "Both?"

"Or maybe,"—a faint twist of humor came into his mouth—"you are angry with yourself, because you let them *not* see you, and you enjoy when I look at you?"

Look at her, with her clothes on, with them off, and any state in between. "Oh, that too," she conceded. Her strong, rich, sweet cup of tea abruptly felt like no comfort at all. Whatever reprieve the solicitors granted, it was only that—a reprieve, not a general pardon.

"Will you miss me, Felicity?"

She stood, wincing because she'd risen too quickly. "Of course, I will miss you." She turned her back on him and stared out the window at the chilly, gray expanse of the garden and mews. "I will miss intelligent adult conversation, I will miss your affection, your humor, your moods. I will miss..."

He stood as well, and came up behind her, wrapping his arms around her and pulling her back up against his chest. She wasn't supposed to answer him this truthfully, not give him a litany so honest, it hurt her—and possibly him as well.

"What else will you miss?" he asked, his lips at her nape.

"I will miss having you for a friend."

Surprise rippled through the man holding her so carefully, and Felicity knew in her spinster-virgin-budding-madam bones, he'd been certain—bet-his-best-morning-hunter certain—that she'd been about to say: I will miss having you for a lover, seeing you naked, kissing your naughty, handsome mouth. Some saucy, stupid, flirtatious reply she could not produce.

"I will always be your friend, Felicity." He spoke with conviction, but the dratted man did not hush up and let her treasure the fiction that they could be friends.

"I have wished I could offer to be your protector, and that you could accept," he said, still holding her gently.

"And I have wished I could accept too," she said, leaning back against him. If it weren't for Astrid, and hopes that Astrid might make a decent match... But he wouldn't offer, and she wouldn't accept, making their words a mere exchange of wishes, after all.

"Where do you hurt, my dear?"

"My..." she took one of his hands and placed it over her womb. "Here."

He began slow circles low on her abdomen, while Felicity stood leaning back against him and accepting the consolation he offered.

"You must have been up last night feeling uncomfortable."

"I was up late reading, and then the cramps started, and I knew I was in for a night of it."

"Does laudanum help?"

"Not really. It can dull the pain, but then I'll wake up with a pounding headache, a parched throat, and a lingering, muzzy feeling. I'll feel better by tomorrow." In two or three days, at any rate. Or two or three years.

"We can copulate when you're bleeding, it's a slightly less tidy proposition."

He was offering her a conclusion to their dealings, because he was considerate and not because he wished to hurry her from his life. She drew away and cocked a glance over her shoulder, wondering if she wished to hurry away from him.

She ought to wish such a thing.

"You are very unlikely to get pregnant if we do." Wretchedly helpful of him to add that.

"Will it be more uncomfortable?"

"It could be, somewhat, but for your first time, I will restrain my more exuberant impulses in any case."

His exuberant impulses would be magnificent.

"And what would you advise?" Because he'd advise what was best for her, regardless of any inconvenience to him.

"I am undecided," he said, regarding the dreary garden. Felicity raised a hand to cradle his cheek, and he turned his head to kiss her palm.

"We can reschedule this assignation for tomorrow or the next day, Felicity, and be done with it. It will be, as you can imagine, a bit messy, but not much more than it would be otherwise. You would probably be more self-conscious, though, than if we wait another few weeks, and that self-consciousness will, I believe, reduce your ability to...."

He sighed, an indication of the effort even a sophisticated man must make to sustain such a discussion.

"I will be less able to appreciate your efforts to make the experience pleasant," she suggested.

"Just so."

"Gareth?"

"Hmm?" He used both hands to stroke her now, and let one stray up to her breasts, where he fondled and kneaded with extraordinary gentleness.

"I would rather wait, if the solicitors will give us the grace period, and I would like to explain my reasons."

Mrs. Crabble's voice sounded somewhere belowstairs, but Gareth's hand neither paused nor faltered. "Explain, then."

"I expect this encounter with you may be the only one I have with anyone, ever, and if it is to last me a lifetime, then I would like it to be as pleasantly memorable—as opposed to self-consciously memorable—as possible."

"And I would want that for you as well, though I sincerely hope you do not limit your amorous encounters to this odd time you've spent in my company, Felicity. Considering the price you are paying, you deserve more return on your efforts than a single encounter."

He sounded testy—every bit the marquess whom she tolerated,

not the friend whom she cherished—though his hands were bringing her marvelous comfort.

"I can contemplate illicit intimacies with you because I understand it is necessary to secure my future and that of my household. No less compelling motive could induce me to such behavior." A fine speech, and mostly honest. It had been more honest even twenty minutes ago.

"Determined to be proper." Gareth slipped away from her and resumed his seat beside the table. "Your scruples would be admirable, Felicity, if they weren't such a waste of you," he said, biting into the sandwich.

Felicity took her seat on the day couch and finished a tepid cup of tea. After watching him eat for a moment, she sat back, her hand on her stomach.

"I feel better."

He shrugged as he demolished his crumb cake. "It's your breasts. They are quite sensitive, and any attention to them seems to arouse sensation in your womb as well." Felicity was prepared to ask him if there was a name for this sort of thing when they were interrupted by a knock on the door.

"Lissy?" Astrid barged right in, clad in a walking dress with a pelisse and reticule over her arm. "Oh, it's you."

She collected herself and curtsied, grinning. "If I'd known it would bring you a-visiting, your lordship, I would have become indisposed today too."

Gareth did her the grown up courtesy of standing and bowing, returning her smile as well.

"Hello, Miss Astrid, and what brings you to your sister's bedside? Sororal devotion to the sick, perhaps?"

"Not a chance." Astrid flounced into the room without further invitation, and appropriated a piece of crumb cake.

"Astrid, please do not consume that while sitting on my bed or standing about in my boudoir," Felicity warned. "Here." She handed her sister a plate.

"Why thank you, Felicity. You are looking a bit more comfortable," she said around a nibble of cake.

"I appreciate your concern."

"I did not have a nice walk, if you must know," Astrid said, assuming a chair. "It is too cold, damp, and windy, but I swear I would have lost my very mind were I to have stayed here playing cards with you."

She bit off a sizeable hunk of crumb cake and chewed with the focus and energy of a squirrel, while Gareth shifted to a seat beside Felicity.

The habit of taking his hand nearly overcame Felicity's commonsense. She reached for her tea cup instead, finding it empty.

"I had a mishap," Astrid pronounced dramatically, though the twinkle in her eyes belied the grave tones. "My everyday bonnet, the one I have hated since I was twelve years old, well, the wind grabbed it right off my head, and off it went, sailing toward the pond. I was certain I was seeing the last of the wretched thing—burial at sea and all that—when that charming Mr. Holbrook appeared and snatched it from the jaws of the gale. Bad timing on his part of course, but we had a lovely chat nonetheless. He even tied my bonnet back on my head, though I received rather a scolding in the process."

Felicity was torn between wanting to tear a strip off her unruly sister, and wishing Gareth would.

"Oh, come, Felicity," Astrid chided. "That bonnet truly is horrid, and Mr. Holbrook is an ever-so-comfortable fellow to pass the time of day with."

"Miss Astrid," Gareth's voice was soft, relaxed, even casual, but with an undertone of disapproval that put a sting in every syllable. "If all goes well, in a very few months, you will be presented to society, if not at court, and then, and only then—under strict chaperonage—will you begin having lovely chats with ever-so-comfortable fellows."

Astrid gaped at him, her last bite of crumb cake poised before her mouth, while Gareth went on.

"You know nothing about this Mr. Holbrook, if that is even his real name. He could be planning to kidnap you, extort money from your family, or do you personal injury. I know you took a footman with you to the park, but all the footman will do is tattle on you to your sister, unless somebody actually does attempt to do you bodily harm. No footman can protect you from the harm you do your own reputation—and your future—by behaving like a careless child. Do you comprehend me?"

Gareth had neither raised his voice, nor risen from the day couch. Instead, he sat across from Astrid, maintaining a calm, almost bored demeanor. His words, however, had apparently landed like a series of well placed blows to Astrid's adolescent self-regard, and she gaped at him in consternation.

"You allow him to speak to me thus?" she asked Felicity, indignation and hurt in her voice.

"Any adult who cares about you is welcome to speak to you thus," Felicity told her, and apparently even Holbrook had offered some remonstrations. "You take chances, Astrid, and sooner or later, there will be consequences. His lordship does not want to see you hurt any more than I do."

Astrid put down the last of her crumb cake carefully, keeping her gaze on it as she rose.

"Excuse me please, Felicity." She bobbed a curtsy. "Your lordship. I'll be about my lessons now." She stalked out of the room, spine straight and shoulders set.

"Was I too hard on her?" Gareth asked when Astrid's steps had faded up to the third floor.

The question, the immediacy and uncertainty of it, elevated him yet further in Felicity's affections.

"It's so hard to know, Gareth. Maybe Mr. Holbrook merely handed her the bonnet, and wished her a fine morning. Astrid is lonely, and Mr. Holbrook did seem to be a perfectly pleasant man. He, in fact, has chided Astrid almost as strongly as you have, but that's not the point, is it?"

"The point is that she's rash, and probably shouldn't be trusted on her own in public, or all your efforts to secure her future will be wasted."

"You're angry." And while Gareth was frequently irritable, he was rarely angry.

Gareth stood and paced to the hearth. "Andrew was two years younger than Astrid is now when our father died. His entire youth was over that day. I couldn't protect him from the rumors, the gossips, the petty cruelties that followed that incident for years. You uncomplainingly jeopardize your entire future, and Astrid is *oblivious*—"

He jabbed at the fire with the wrought iron poker, sending a shower of sparks up the chimney.

"She isn't as oblivious as you think," Felicity countered. "I believe she pulls these stunts to make sure I am paying attention to her. Our circumstances have been greatly reduced in recent years, and she needs to know I still, to use your words, *see* her. Then too, she's at an age in life when emotions can seem ungovernable. A year from now, she could be engaged. That doesn't seem possible to me, and I have no idea how the notion would sit with her."

Felicity rose to stand beside Gareth at the hearth, and put a hand on his arm.

"This is part of the reason I do not sire children," Gareth said, pulling Felicity into his arms. "Bad enough that I became responsible for Andrew. The concept of parenting a female..." He shook his head, a man who apparently could be daunted by the common human undertaking of raising a child.

Felicity leaned into his embrace, and he settled his chin on her crown. They remained thus for long moments, the only sound the ticking of an ormolu clock on the mantel and the hiss and pop of the fire.

Felicity pulled away first, feeling as if this day—with its biological inconveniences, and petty domestic drama, somehow drew her closer to Gareth than all of their erotic nonsense, and that was not necessarily a good thing.

He peered down at her. "I hope you feel better."

"I shall." Bodily, in any case. "Assuming the solicitors will give us more time, what will you want of me in the intervening weeks? I have learned much of what Callista wanted me to know, and I have certainly become acquainted with her books, her customers, her—"

His finger pressed against her lips.

"I have considered this while we've talked. I want you to hear me out before you pass judgment on my idea." He stepped away before continuing. "I should use the next few weeks to give credence to the fiction I am interested in you socially."

"Why, when a month from now, sooner, in fact—" They would be done with each other.

"Consider, Felicity, that I bear the title, am considered remiss in my duty for not having sired a few heirs, you are well born enough to aspire to a good match, and if rumors do crop up that we might be having illicit dealings, then the best way to combat them is to appear as a legitimate couple."

"Look at me, Gareth," Felicity said matching his cool tones, because he was reasoning with her, using the same voice in which he'd cajoled her into tasting far too much wine and parting with far too many confidences.

He complied with about as much visible enthusiasm as if she were a one woman firing squad.

"What aren't you telling me, Gareth?"

"That this is the best I can come up with, to prevent your modesty from resurging where I'm concerned, address potential rumor, and assure the solicitors you are not blowing full retreat."

He was improvising, telling her half truths, which strongly suggested the rumors had already started, and he could not bear to tell her so.

"Very well. I trust you, and we'll handle this as you choose." Though how she'd endure another four weeks in his constant presence was a mystery not easily solved.

Gareth accepted her capitulation with a smile that, to Felicity, looked suspiciously more relieved than pleased.

CHAPTER EIGHT

To be seventeen was to suffer, and to be treated like a child when one was old enough to marry, bear children, or run a household was insupportable.

Astrid did not intend to suffer in silence.

"I hate him, Felicity, and don't try to reason with me and sweet talk me," Astrid warned. "Heathgate is officious, overbearing, pompous and just plain mean."

Astrid had waited until the officious, overbearing, pompous man had quit the premises because what needed to be said was *private*. She confronted her sister in the third floor school room to ensure even the Crabbles wouldn't overhear.

"I agree, Astrid, his lordship can be all those things, as can you or I." Felicity took a seat on a window bench, though in her dressing gown and robe, she looked cold.

"Except you're not, Felicity. You're decent and kind, and when you scold me, I know it's because you truly do care. He scolded me simply because he could, the wretch. And you let him."

That last part was what truly hurt, that Felicity had abdicated her authority to a man who ought not to be under their roof at all.

Felicity looked troubled, but she did not appear contrite. "We have been living here since Father's death without the guidance or protection of any man, Astrid, and I think you are simply unused to the fact that most men, most good men, believe delivering a scolding is their duty when those they care about err. And," she added, standing and facing Astrid, "you were imprudent."

Felicity was not merely an older sibling, she was a good six inches taller than Astrid, and that she'd try to use her height in this argument was dirty tactics.

"I was *not* imprudent, Felicity! How can you say that? I have been introduced to Mr. Holbrook, he was most proper and well behaved in my presence. We were in public at all times and we quickly parted. I went nowhere private with him, I did not allow him to inappropriately touch my person, and I *will not* tolerate remonstrance from the Marquess of Heathgate of all people on the propriety of my manners!"

It felt good to state her position, and it felt even better to do so without raising her voice.

Felicity glanced at the closed door, but Crabbie's bad knees meant no adult reinforcements would be arriving, and Astrid had stopped lighting a fire up here months ago in any case.

"What is the matter with you, Astrid? Heathgate was only imparting the same message I'm sure Mr. Holbrook tried to convey more gently."

This was the outside of too much. "What is the matter with *me*? Felicity, you were sitting alone with the man in your bedroom, with the door all but closed, in your dressing gown. *What is the matter with you?* That man is compromising you, I know it. I know it in my bones."

Astrid let the rest hang between them unsaid: Felicity disappeared to the marquess's townhouse unchaperoned for hours at a time. She came home distracted, her hair occasionally arranged in a different style than when she'd left. She hadn't given Mr. Holbrook a second glance when he was both handsome and dashing, and worst of all, she wasn't railing against Astrid's accusations.

Fear, acrid and bitter seeped up from Astrid's middle to clutch at her lungs.

"Astrid, I don't know what to say."

"You don't deny it." And for the first time in Astrid's life, Felicity sounded uncertain.

"Why, Felicity? It isn't worth your virtue, whatever he's paying you. We can sell this house, and find a cottage, take in laundry and mending, put in a larger garden. We could manage."

Brave words, though Astrid knew well Felicity had been managing for years, and she also knew why. Felicity could make a competent governess or companion but Astrid wouldn't last until sundown in service.

"I have underestimated you, Astrid," Felicity said at length. "Will you sit with me?"

She held out a hand and led Astrid to the window bench, her fingers cold in Astrid's grip. Astrid had learned to love books reading on that bench, learned a lot of useless Latin, and had learned lately that the only subject she was interested in sketching was Lord Andrew Alexander. Now, she saw a spider's web occupied a high corner, though the spider was mercifully not in residence.

"This is complicated," Felicity said.

A ferocious wave of protectiveness toward her only sibling threatened Astrid's composure. "You are my sister. No complication on this earth will affect that one whit, not even if it's a compromising sort of complication."

"Thank you. I am not yet compromised, but it is imminent, and if you are willing to listen, then I think you are ready to hear the explanation."

The explanation was that Felicity had to support her younger sister. Misery joined fear and despair in Astrid's vitals as a gust of wind came moaning down the chimney. "I am listening, Felicity."

Felicity had pretty, graceful hands, and they were clenched in her lap like a martyr's in anticipation of an Inquisition. Astrid wanted to haul Lord Heathgate into the school room, and make him listen to what was to follow.

"Callista Hemmings owned a very high class brothel—do you know what a brothel is?"

"I know exactly what a brothel is, and that they're thick on the ground in some of the best neighborhoods."

Felicity gave her a look, but that look had lost its power to daunt six months ago.

"Well, I do and you asked, so please go on."

"Callista left her brothel to us—the assets of the brothel, the legalities being somewhat complicated—on the condition that I learn to manage it, and that I learn to perform the services procured there. She further provided that my instruction should be in Heathgate's hands, and I may not sell the business for one year following her death. There are other stipulations, mostly intended to see that I don't try to avoid the conditions I just described."

Astrid did not doubt those other stipulations were onerous, and yet she could not bear to make Felicity recite them. She took out her handkerchief, the one sporting silver edging on a border of purple crocuses, and passed the linen to her sister.

"I'm listening."

"Heathgate could have turned his back on me, in which case I would have been relegated to the tutelage of Viscount Riverton, a wastrel whom you may recall as a former associate of Papa's. Heathgate offered me a position on one of his estates as a housekeeper, but I declined."

This was bad. This was very, very bad, because Lord Pomposity was not the author of Felicity's impending downfall, some wretched relation Astrid had never met deserved that honor—after Papa, of course.

"You are trying to convince me Heathgate's role in all this is virtuous."

"I am trying to explain to you that all of my options are bleak,

Astrid, and I don't want you to hate me for the one I have chosen. The path I have selected is not honorable, but it offers the only hope I could find of safeguarding respectability, eventually."

Felicity started blinking, and Astrid wondered if there was a special circle of hell for ungrateful little sisters.

"Oh, Lissy..." Astrid slipped an arm around her sister's waist. "I could just kill Papa. Kill him and kill him again. This is so unfair to you. He could have done more, but he simply didn't care. I hate him more than I hate Heathgate."

This earned her a wan smile.

"Gareth has been as decent as I've allowed him to be, Astrid, and he really is a kind man."

"His variety of kindness leaves me unimpressed." Though the night of the fire, even Astrid had been glad to see him—and to meet Lord Andrew. She'd been very glad about that.

"And as such," Felicity went on, "he's convinced the fellow in the park on the runaway horse, and the fire we nearly had could be somebody's efforts to do us mischief. If we inherit Callista's business, we will be well set up. Someone might not be happy about that."

Astrid would not be happy about it if it cost Felicity her self-respect.

She squeezed her sister's hand. "If it becomes known we have inherited that business, we are both quite ruined, though if Heathgate's suspicions have any merit, then somebody already knows. I gather he suspects Mr. Holbrook?"

"Dear God...." Felicity got up and paced to the empty hearth, then turned to pace back across the room. "Astrid, you could be right, and yes, I suppose Gareth is suspicious of Holbrook. His lordship is not a very trusting man."

More and more, Astrid wanted a word with His Lordship—or *Gareth*. "I don't think Mr. Holbrook will do us much mischief by handing me my bonnet, or plucking you from the path of a galloping horse, Felicity. Why is Heathgate such an untrusting person?"

The question 'why' had ever been one Astrid's favorites, and something about the man was inspiring—the soul of gentility—to break every rule of decorum.

Felicity resumed her place beside Astrid on the chilly window seat.

"I don't know all the details, but it has something to do with how he assumed the title. He was fifth in line for the marquessate, behind his older brother, father, uncle and cousin, when they all perished in a yachting accident. Gareth became the subject of unkind speculation. At the time, I don't think his mother and brother were in any condition to help him either assume his duties or deal with his grief and guilt. It's a wonder he has got on as well as he has."

Beyond doubt, that dark, taciturn, interfering man had Felicity's sympathies, which was puzzling.

"He has everything a man could want, Lissy. He's dashing—if a bit long in the tooth—rich, titled, landed and not bad looking. What is so difficult about that?"

Felicity drew her knees up, looking to Astrid more like a younger sister still in the school room than an older sister on the verge of ruin.

"He was a plain mister, Astrid, one of his grandfather's lowly men of affairs, and then overnight, he became wealthy and powerful. From that point forward, his friends were not his friends, and, for reasons that aren't reasons, he had enemies and his private business became grist for the gossip mill. I don't think Gareth enjoyed having his life thrown into turmoil."

Gareth. Felicity called him Gareth, and he'd marched into their smoky kitchen at midnight and wrapped himself around Astrid's sister with every evidence of terrified relief.

"I certainly haven't enjoyed having my life thrown into turmoil," Astrid conceded. "And I am a nobody. Why don't you marry him?"

The question had to be asked, mostly because if Heathgate had offered, and Felicity had refused, some shrieking on the part of a certain younger sister was directly in order.

"I don't want to be married, Astrid," Felicity said. "More to the point, he hasn't asked. And if he did, I would not accept."

"Whyever not?" Though Astrid would have turned him down flat, Felicity clearly favored the man, and she was a far better bargain than *he* deserved.

"Because I am not suited to being a marchioness, for one thing, and because Gareth does not love me. I don't think he is capable of loving a wife the way I would need to be loved."

And yet, at midnight, he'd come at a dead gallop, and been prepared to do murder most foul to protect this woman he wasn't capable of loving.

"Then make him capable. He's overbearing, but he isn't stupid. He could be taught to love just as he is teaching you other things."

"Oh, Astrid." Felicity sounded torn between amusement and heartache. "I hope this situation works out, so we can sell the business and get you properly—and I do mean properly—launched. You will be an Original, and I will be so proud of you."

The chances of such a scenario were between nil and nothing, and yet Astrid gave her sister a smile. "I shall be, you may depend upon it. But you should bring Heathgate up to scratch, Felicity. My prospects would improve, you know."

"I could not be happy married on his terms."

As if one could be happy when ruined?

"How much longer must you suffer Heathgate's company, Felicity, and why must he come around this house? The footmen and gardeners and grooms he's sent over are all very nice, but your good name will not be long preserved if it's known he visits you in your own bedroom."

"That was a mistake, Astrid. I canceled an appointment with him at the last minute, and he was concerned. Mrs. Crabble knew he was in the house, and the door was not closed."

Heathgate's most recent version of concern needed some significant refinement, which thought Astrid kept to herself.

"Heathgate has proposed that our best strategy to combat any rumors of illicit doings is to appear to be a legitimate social couple," Felicity explained.

"He's preparing to *court* you?"

"He's preparing to appear to court me, or appear to think about courting me. He should be courting someone," she added, frowning. "It will only be for a few more weeks."

The daft man should be courting Felicity.

"Astrid?"

"Yes, Lissy?"

"I don't believe we are in any danger, but Heathgate is not similarly convinced. Would you be offended if I asked you not to go to the park without me, or to market and so on?"

She was asking, sincerely, asking, and while that was flattering, it was also upsetting. Outside, the wind picked up, and a cold draft swirled into the school room.

"For the next few weeks I can agree to limit my outings, but Lissy, why doesn't Heathgate simply ask Mr. Holbrook what his interest in us—if any—is?"

"I will put that question to him, Astrid, and suggest that in the future, if he wants to remonstrate you for your manners, he do it somewhere besides my bedroom, hmm?"

"See that you do, and you may also tell him that if Lord Andrew accompanied him on the occasional call, I would contrive to be on my best manners."

~

"I WILL WALTZ you out the door on the next series of turns. You *will* follow my lead, Felicity."

Gareth had bent his head to whisper his orders into Felicity's ear; she beamed him a gay smile he knew to be false, and soon he had her, as promised, out in the brisk night air. The terrace was dimly lit with well spaced torches, and other couples were moving in the shadows.

"Will you be chilled out here?" Gareth asked, giving her his arm as he walked them toward a descending set of steps.

"Probably, if we stay out long enough. But for now, the cool air feels wonderful."

The cool air smelled wonderful too, of lavender and Felicity, rather than underwashed, over perfumed bodies in a poorly ventilated ballroom.

Gareth led her, literally, down a garden path, stopping in deep shadows before a stone bench facing a small fountain graced with naked stone cherubs. When Felicity seated herself on the bench, he dropped his evening jacket around her shoulders.

"Thank you."

And the daft woman was truly grateful. "Felicity, you are such an innocent."

"I am no longer *such* an innocent in anything but the technical sense. I fail to see what my thanks for such a thoughtful gesture has to do with anything."

Oh, delightful. She was in the mood to scrap—too. Gareth lowered himself to the bench beside her.

"A gentleman lending you his jacket is not a thoughtful gesture, Felicity, it's a move in a game. No proper gentleman appears before a lady in his shirt sleeves. Under the guise of a solicitous gesture, he can get away with that, and envelope you in his scent. He can begin the process of disrobing before you, and begin disrobing you when he retrieves his jacket from your body."

Increasingly, Gareth's attempts to enlighten her regarding illicit amatory matters came out sounding like scolds. She hadn't walloped him for it yet, and he hadn't apologized. "Gracious, all of that? And here I thought it had something to do with my health, or your fine manners."

"You are driving me to distraction," he muttered, skimming his lips over her jaw. That was a mistake, because she angled her neck to allow him her throat, her lips, her shoulders...

"I have missed your touch," she whispered, bringing her hand up to the back of his neck. "I have missed touching you," she added, just before their lips met, a soft re-acquainting of mouths, scents, and tastes.

His response was to slide a stealthy hand under the jacket that sat loosely around her shoulders, and stroke her abdomen in feathery caresses. Felicity abetted this nonsense by sifting her fingers through his hair and making soft, female noises of longing that called directly to Gareth's breeding organs.

Which had developed damnably good hearing where she was concerned.

Before those same breeding organs drowned out the last clamoring of good sense, Gareth stood and held out his hand to help Felicity up. When she placed her hand in his and he drew her to her feet, he brought her hand to his lips, kissed her gloved knuckles, then tucked her fingers over his arm, and lead her back up the steps.

Twenty-one more days, he reminded himself. Then he could take her to bed and indulge every whim and fantasy either of them had ever dreamed. The past week had been difficult, to say the least. With the collusion of his mother and brother, Gareth had observed the fiction of a proper interest in Felicity.

All of the mincing and bowing was enough to gag him, and Felicity obviously wasn't enjoying it either.

"I wonder," Gareth said quietly, "how I ever found this ...." He gestured vaguely toward the ballroom, "of any interest. It's beyond intolerable, now."

"You enjoy the acquaintances you make in these surroundings," Felicity reminded him. Her comment was aimed at his sexual recreation, but Gareth shared her distaste.

"I have," he rejoined mildly.

"Well, well, well," came an amused voice from their left as they regained the terrace. "If it isn't Heathgate, out trolling for a fresh catch. Lady Edith is quite relieved she needn't suffer tedious attentions from you any further, old man."

Beneath his hand, Gareth felt unease creeping through Felicity, and applauded her instincts.

"Riverton." Gareth gave him the barest nod. "You will pardon me if I don't pause to introduce the *lady*. Too much night air can be unhealthful, and I must return her to company."

"I beg you pardon, my lady." Riverton offer Felicity a slow bow, his thinning hair flopping over his brow as he bent.

Gareth walked them back across the terrace silently, pausing only long enough to whisk his evening coat from her shoulders and urge her back into the ballroom.

"Give me a minute to button this damned thing up and get my gloves back on," he muttered. "I will find you in the refreshment room, where, I have no doubt, you will also find my brother."

Felicity looked as if she might engage him in further discussion, which was not precisely convenient. Gareth offered her a wink, which had her moving back into the ballroom, her expression more puzzled than pleased. Abandoning any pretense at humor, Gareth crossed the balcony to find Riverton lounging against the balustrade.

"That one looked tasty enough," Riverton commented, "if a bit prim. But the prim ones can be the most fun, eh?"

Gareth considered his options while making a production out of removing a cigar from a nacre case he carried in a pocket of his evening coat. They were a prop his valet insisted on—Gareth never had, and he never would, smoke the damned things.

Fifteen years Gareth's senior at least, Riverton was among the barely tolerated effluvia one encountered when moving in certain social circles. He had the sallow complexion, thinning hair and thickening gut of the aging roué, and no Lady Riverton to curb the worst of his excesses. Gareth generally offered the man terse civility when they crossed paths, but no more.

And yet, Riverton was named in Callista's will. What did Riverton know, and how was Gareth to find it out?

"Riverton, an apology is in order from you, but I would not have you address my companion directly to deliver it. Your observations were rendered in inappropriate company." Gareth adopted a mild, almost humorous tone.

"As if any female in your company would be expecting the pretty, Heathgate. Your reputation alone damns the woman."

Gareth let a silence stretch until even Riverton had to feel the awkwardness.

"Even such as I, Riverton, must eventually do my duty to the title, and when I am thus occupied, you can be assured the fortunate object of my attentions is all that is deserving of *prim and proper decorum.*"

While that little speech wafted about on the night air, Gareth mentally located his dueling pistols, then set them aside: A duel fought over Felicity's honor would ruin her every bit as much as what Gareth had planned for her.

"You don't say! Well, apologies all around then," Riverton wheezed. "You don't say, indeed!" He spun on his heel and went chuckling off into the night. Gareth pitched his unlit cigar into the bushes and wondered if Felicity would consent to leave before supper.

"Well, that ought to get the tongues wagging," came a voice from below the balustrade.

"Andrew, quit lurking like a sneak thief. Nothing I had to say to Riverton was worth eavesdropping on anyway."

Though Andrew might also have seen Felicity with Gareth's jacket around her shoulders, which had been pure stupidity on Gareth's part. More pure stupidity.

"What prompted an exchange with that weasel in the first place?" Andrew asked as he ambled up the steps.

"I took Felicity out for some air and Riverton made an untoward comment." Though the weasel's comments about Gareth's usual company were not inaccurate.

"An untoward comment *regarding* Felicity?" Andrew asked sharply.

"Not quite. He described me as trolling for a fresh catch and

informed me Lady Edith was relieved to be spared my tedious attentions. I should have called him out on Edith's behalf but he isn't
worth an extended visit to the Continent. Moreover, he might well
know who Felicity is and why she is in my company."

"Why wouldn't he know?" Andrew asked, propping his elbows
on the stone railing beside Gareth.

"Because he's tiresomely stupid and concerned only with the
pursuit of his own tawdry pleasures?" Gareth suggested, feeling a
pang of regret on Edith's behalf that this should be so. "I wasn't aware
Callista had involved me in her schemes until Felicity appeared on
my doorstep. If Callista didn't see fit to gain my prior consent, I doubt
she would have troubled to inform Riverton he was the proposed
alternate."

"Riverton is tiresome, Gareth, but he is not completely witless.
Yes, he's stupid enough to fornicate, drink, and gamble his way into
an early grave—the same affliction affects half the peerage—but he's
cunning."

Andrew was no longer a pup just down from university, and
Gareth could not tolerate the notion he might be causing his brother
worry.

"What if he is cunning? I am fulfilling the request Callista made
of me, and Felicity will meet the terms of the bequest. In a very few
months, the brothel will be sold, and it all will have been none of
Riverton's concern."

"One hopes."

Two words, each towing a bargeful of fraternal censure. "One
will do more than hope, Andrew. I have given Felicity my word, and
thus it shall be." Gareth kept his voice down, because a couple was
strolling beneath the balustrade, the woman plastered to her escort,

"You were giving her more than just your word, brother mine,
when I spied you down by the fountain a few minutes ago," Andrew
retorted, albeit quietly. "I thought the idea was to show the lady
proper attention, not make her out to be yet another one of your illicit
conquests."

Every word of which, was also damnably, rottenly true. The couple below paused in the shadow of some rhododendrons and stood far too close to each other.

"Is there something you want to tell me, Andrew?"

"Oh, don't pull that with me, Gareth. You took a risk with Felicity in the garden tonight and you know it. She is in an extremely vulnerable and difficult position; take advantage of her and you shame yourself while she pays the price."

"Andrew...."

"Oh, yes, I know. She needs you to ruin her, but Gareth, you don't have to make sure the whole of society is in on the joke. I'll marry her myself before I'd let you do that."

That his brother would hold him accountable for honorable behavior was an occasion for pride, and for far less comfortable emotions.

From the direction of the rhododendrons, somebody giggled.

"Do not judge where you have only some of the facts, Andrew," Gareth said. "Felicity is a problem thrust upon me by circumstances and I am trying to deal with her as expeditiously as possible."

"For God's sake, Gareth, cut line. You are not the victim in this farce, she is. But if you continue to take chances like you took tonight, I won't be marrying Felicity to protect her from the cruel scorn of her peers. I'll be marrying her to protect her from what you've let yourself become."

Andrew made his exit on that uncomfortable note, leaving Gareth staring after him in disbelief. The conversation had been startlingly awkward, particularly because Gareth grasped Andrew's point all too clearly.

If Andrew were the one ruining a decent woman so she could become a silent owner of an indecent business, Gareth might very well be treating his brother to a memorable round of fisticuffs.

The realization was sour, stark, and inescapable.

Gareth considered going after Andrew, when the sound of a palm slapping stoutly against a cheek came from the shadows below. The notion that somebody else was being soundly scolded for a lapse in judgment brought a smidgen of comfort.

"I won't marry him, you know."

Oh, lovely. The evening needed only Felicity's selfless propriety. "Everyone has taken to spying and lurking in shadows," Gareth observed. "I find myself sadly out of fashion, standing here where all and sundry may note my presence."

Felicity came away from the door to stand beside him, peering up at him in the dim light.

"Andrew was not in the refreshment room, and somebody told me I could find him out here. I knew you were also here, so I returned. I'm sorry I overheard, but you mustn't be perturbed with your brother, Gareth."

They fell silent as a young lady stalked past, a gentleman sporting one red cheek beside her, but not touching her.

"Well, he's more than perturbed at me," Gareth replied. And that was intolerable, also completely understandable.

"He'll get over it, and it's good for you to occasionally hear something besides, 'yes, your lordship,' and 'certainly, your divine perfection-ship.' He's a dear man, and you are fortunate to have him for your brother."

Andrew was dear. Dear to Gareth like no other; a loyal brother and a patient, tolerant friend. They had been at outs before, but this last discussion had a disturbing depth to it.

"Would you mind very much if we departed before the supper?" he asked Felicity as they regained the ballroom.

"I would not mind one bit. I am not used to society's schedule, and I am uneasy leaving Astrid home with only staff at such late hours."

She would worry about her sister, while Gareth, if asked to bet on little Miss Astrid or a she-wolf, would not have bet on the wolf. Gareth escorted Felicity through the crowd, nodding and almost-smiling with just enough distance that those who would have approached were dissuaded.

Until a cultured male voice cut through the hum and buzz of the ballroom. "Why, Miss Worthington, what a pleasure."

Gareth looked to their right to find David Holbrook smiling at Felicity. In return, she was gifting the man with one of those rare, genuine, smiles that dazzled with the sincerity of her warmth and pleasure.

"Mr. Holbrook, what a delight to see a friendly face. May I perform the introductions?" She blithely proceeded with proper introductions in the proper order, during which two grown men made proper replies at the proper times.

Though what Gareth wanted was to properly black the eyes of friendly Mr. Holbrook merely for the way he smiled at Felicity.

"I haven't seen you in the park of late Miss Worthington," Holbrook said. "Your dear sister has been allowed to prowl without supervision a time or two, but so far she seems content to harass the ducks and attempt felony assault on her bonnet."

"Astrid hates that bonnet, but she mentioned that you'd foiled her efforts to be rid of it," Felicity replied.

"I did wonder," Holbrook said. He turned to Gareth, his smile undergoing a subtle transformation. "And you, my lord, do you enjoy the pleasures of the park?"

Gareth smiled as well, infusing his expression with barely enough charm to fool a halfwit. "I do, Holbrook, though I'm more likely to enjoy them mounted."

"I enjoy a brisk ride myself," Holbrook countered. "Miss Worthington, are you fond of mounted recreation, or do you prefer more pedestrian leisure activities?"

Holbrook was staring at Gareth as he asked the question. There was something off about the man's eyes, and patently intolerable about his innuendo.

While Felicity was still beaming at the damned blighter. "I haven't had time to ride much in recent years, though as a girl I enjoyed the stables tremendously when we lived on the estates. I cried for a week when my old pony died. Astrid is the one who must have her outings to the park, and fresh air is good for her."

"You must let me take you ladies driving, then, so she can have her fresh air with your company," Holbrook offered.

"Perhaps sometime after spring has more reliably graced us with her presence," Felicity said. "And I will not mention this offer to Astrid, who would pester you into immediate compliance with her wishes."

"At your pleasure then."

"Holbrook," Gareth cut in, having exceeded the limit of his meager supply of patience. "You must excuse us. We were on our way to fetch the lady's wrap. The evening has grown tedious."

Holbrook displayed a lot of handsome white teeth. "Oh, I agree, Heathgate, tedious beyond belief. I am inspired to follow your example and make my apologies to our host and hostess. Your servant, Miss Worthington." He bowed over Felicity's hand and departed.

Gareth resumed their progress toward the main doors, his hand clamping Felicity's glove firmly to his arm. She maintained her silence until they were, at last, at the curb and waiting for his carriage. Gareth handed her in wordlessly then seated himself beside her. She'd no sooner arranged her skirts than Gareth settled an arm around her shoulders.

Then he was kissing her—truly kissing her, with pent-up passion and longing and—had he completely lost his reason?—anger. When she made no move to pull away, but stroked her hand softly over his jaw, he gentled his attentions and eventually settled back to encircle her with his arms while she rested against him.

"Is this as difficult for you as it is for me?" The question hadn't formed in his brain, it had come tripping directly out his idiot mouth.

Felicity took her time. There was no bullying this woman, no cowing her or intimidating her. "Yes, but in a different way."

He did not pounce on those words, but instead focused on the feel of her beside him, the scent of her lavender fragrance, the calm she brought him by her simple presence.

"I cannot for the life of me figure Holbrook out, Felicity. Don't trust him, please." He stripped the glove from her right hand and stroked his thumb over her bare palm.

"You don't trust him. Why not?"

"I have a sense he isn't what he appears to be, and his intentions toward you and Astrid are not altogether honest." Gareth offered a half truth, because he had more to go on than his instincts, though not as much more as he'd like.

"Has it occurred to you he might simply be seeking to pay me his attentions?"

"He had damned well better disabuse himself of that notion, at least for the next several weeks." But yes, it had occurred to Gareth. Late at night when his eyes were too tired to read any more damned reports, the idea that Holbrook might be smitten occurred to Gareth rather a lot.

"You are being ridiculous" Felicity chided, humor in her voice. "If you hop from one wench to another at your merest whim, then you can't expect I won't be dancing with other swains, should they ask."

Wench-hopping had lost its appeal the day he'd found Felicity in his formal parlor, staring at his ugliest Axminster carpet.

"Dancing is one thing, Felicity, but you and I have an assignation in three weeks' time. I would request that you restrain your urges until then." The comment was unfair. She'd never once indicated an interest in indulging her urges without his personal provocation.

He heard Felicity sigh in the dark confines of the coach.

"Gareth, I've already told you I have no intentions of taking up with other men, not now, not ever. It would not be... It would not be right for me."

He had the dread suspicion she was trying to comfort him.

"You will come to see it differently, Felicity," he said, closing his eyes, the better to breathe in her scent. "You might start out intending to remain celibate, but you will grow lonely, and frustrated, and some fellow will come along who demands little of you and offers you respite from your discontent. You will take him up on his friendly offer, and realize to your surprise, it wasn't so difficult after all."

Self-torture being a fine diversion from lust, Gareth went on. "You will realize the encounter was more enjoyable than you'd thought, though less than you'd hoped, and the man, if you chose well, did bring you some pleasure, and some companionship. The next one will be easier, the next easier still, until you are adept at finding just the man, and just the circumstances to suit your *whim*."

She rubbed her cheek against his shoulder, reminding Gareth that he'd thought her a feline sort of woman from the moment he'd laid eyes on her.

"And is that how you came to be in your present state of gentlemanly debauchery? You gradually allowed these people, these peers of the realm, to relieve you of your dreams, your integrity, your scruples, until you amount to little more than a series of gratified whims?"

Her arrow buried itself all the deeper for the casual tone of her question.

"Christ, Felicity... You and Andrew both in one night?" And yet, Felicity saw clearly. For all her innocence, or maybe because of it, she saw clearly. "You perceive me as jaded. I see me as the inevitable result of growing older and wiser in the ways of the world into which I was thrust."

"Gareth, you mustn't trouble yourself," Felicity said, lacing her fingers through his. "This situation with me is not of your doing, and it will soon be behind us. I cannot abide to see you upset when all you're doing is trying to help me."

He was silent. He hated it when she made excuses for him, apologized to him, or tried to placate him. He deserved none of her kindness and all of her scorn. Andrew, at least, saw that much.

Felicity kissed his knuckles, a startling reversal of the chevalier's role. "I could love you, you know."

For the first time, Gareth heard bitterness in her tone, and it stung like acid.

He said nothing, and he held her hand for the entire journey to her home.

CHAPTER

CHAPTER NINE

Gareth waved his butler and valet off to bed and settled into the library with a small glass of brandy. To his surprise, Andrew was waiting for him, boots off, cravat undone.

"If you must further remonstrate with me, little brother, the lecture would have better effect were you fully dressed. Brandy?"

"I am not here to lecture. I came to apologize," Andrew said, accepting a glass with two fat fingers of Gareth's finest sloshing gently in the bowl. Gareth leaned a hip on his desk and considered the handsome younger brother who'd offered—or threatened—to marry Felicity.

"You have nothing to apologize for," he said, regarding his own drink. "Besides, Felicity wouldn't marry you even were you to ask." *Thank God.*

"Well, there's a blow to a fellow's ego. Why not?"

"You aren't me." Of all the damned, unfathomable reasons.

Andrew tossed a pillow onto the raised hearth and took a seat with his back to the fire. "And haven't I thanked the gods for that bit of fortune often enough. Will Felicity marry you?"

"She said she could love me, but she won't marry me." Her illogic and her courage provoked him to smiling, and because Andrew looked comfortable perched before the fire, Gareth took a second pillow from the couch and sat beside his brother.

Andrew touched the glass to his lips, but didn't drink. "She said she loves you—Felicity Worthington said this. And what did you say?"

"Nothing."

"I see," Andrew replied, looking thoroughly confused. "You are, meaning no disrespect, the biggest tomcat on the stinking wharf that is polite society, and a decent woman declares her love for you. You offer her no agile response, no gently humorous comeback, no polite expression of regretful flattery. You say nothing?"

All Gareth could do was shake his head, for the situation was worse than Andrew grasped: No agile response, humor, or flattery had even *occurred* to Gareth.

Andrew moved his boots away from the heat of the fire, though he was clearly warming to his topic.

"Get your hands off the reins of all the damned business you transact and take her away on some travels. I'll mind the tiller here, you romance her, and she'll come around. God knows the marquessate can't be that hard to manage, not when I've watched you bugger it up for nearly a decade." Andrew concluded his homily with a magnificently casual swallow of his brandy.

"Bugger it up have I?" Andrew was teasing, wasn't he? Or goading, which qualified as teasing between them. "And how do you equate trebling the family's worth in ten years to buggering it up? Could you do better?"

"I wouldn't have to, Gareth. You've set us up so well we'll be wealthy until hell freezes over." Which did not seem to impress Andrew in the least.

The fire was warm at Gareth's back, the brandy beyond excellent, and this conversation, as difficult as it was, was a comfort in some way, too.

"Do you want me out of sight that badly?" Gareth asked,

wondering if he'd misjudged his brother all these years. Not *seen* his only surviving brother.

"I despise the title, Gareth, and all it's demanded of you, and well you know it. I've seen it eat you alive, steal your sense of joie de vivre, and make you into someone who is content to be miserable and call that his life. You do your duty to it, and then you take your revenge on yourself. It breaks my heart, and I don't know how much longer you can keep it up before you turn into something as pathetic as Riverton."

Andrew sounded not disgusted, not taunting, but sad.

"This is a night for revelations. I did not realize you felt so strongly, Andrew."

Andrew pinned him with a gaze that had Gareth looking away as a silence rang loudly in the library.

"The discussion of travel is moot, Andrew. It isn't the scenery Felicity takes exception to, it's me. And I agree with her. I would make her a sorry husband, though I believe I've become quite proficient at being the marquess."

"Do you want to marry her?" Andrew asked, because somewhere, in the handbook given exclusively to little brothers, they were tasked with charging in where angels—and marquesses—feared to tread.

For Gareth did want to marry Felicity. A small, sentimental, inconvenient part of him did indeed want to marry her. The lateness of the hour was taking a sorry toll.

"I would make her miserable and she would turn me down did I offer. She deserves a real husband, not a casually intimate business associate, which is what I'd seek in a wife. I would break her heart, and then you'd have to call me out in truth."

Andrew passed the drink under his nose—a handsome nose, and not the least bit arrogant. He did not correct Gareth's summation of the situation.

"Do you really think I could ever be as pathetic as Riverton?" Gareth asked taking another small sip of the brandy.

"Worse, Gareth, because he never had potential, and you do."

Holy God. Gareth rose to refresh his drink, and because the fire's heat was becoming uncomfortable. "I don't know, Andrew. Riverton was once young and probably attractive, his manners can be fine, and he keeps a handsome house."

"Yes, and maybe some interesting company," Andrew suggested. "Did you happen to notice he and Holbrook exchanged a few words before you and Felicity 'ran into' Holbrook?"

Gareth paused, his hand on the cool, cut glass of the decanter. "I did not." Though thank God, Andrew had been paying attention. "How long did they speak, and was anyone else privy to the conversation?"

"I could not overhear them, and the exchange was little more than a nod and a greeting, but how do they know each other? Holbrook would seem to be new to Town, and if he's moving in Riverton's circles, that cannot be good."

Gareth lifted his glass to take a drink, then realized it was empty. "It cannot be good, particularly when Holbrook is exerting himself to charm Felicity. I want to dislike the man, Andrew, but I find him worthy. Suspicious, but worthy. He has dealt decently with Felicity and Astrid thus far."

"Whatever that means." Andrew tossed Gareth's pillow back to the sofa rather forcefully. "Astrid's judgment is hardly to be trusted when it comes to gentlemen. Witness, she likes *me*."

Perhaps self-loathing was a family trait. "Why shouldn't she? You have been all that is avuncular and pleasant to her, and you will have a chance to charm her further the day after tomorrow."

Andrew sat a little straighter, his instincts apparently in good working order. "I shall?"

"Mother has decided we will picnic, weather permitting. You, Mother and Astrid will accompany Felicity and me, though I am tempted to take Felicity up in the curricle and leave you to manage in the vis-à-vis."

"I take it back, I'll dice you for the title, and you can sit backward with the dowagers and schoolgirls," Andrew said. "Where is this bacchanal to take place?"

An older brother with potential was entitled to indulge in a bit of needling. "I don't suppose there's anyone you would like to bring along?"

"Don't be droll. I have no need of a fiancée, wife, heir, or spare, if you'll recall. I am in the process of enjoying my youth, not that you'd recognize such a pursuit if it bit you on your skinny arse."

"We're rusticating at Willowdale for luncheon. You won't be trapped in the carriage long." A mere two hours each way, in good weather.

Andrew rose, fired the second pillow at the sofa, and rubbed his derriere with his free hand. "I haven't been to Willowdale for years, Gareth, not since Father banished you after your first year at University."

"It's a pleasant little place." And Felicity would love it. The old-fashioned Tudor manor house boasted eight bedrooms, lovely gardens, and several thousand acres of attached farm, pasture and wood. Gareth had always enjoyed it, and allowed himself several weeks of peace and quiet there every summer and fall.

Andrew tucked his boots under his arm and put his glass on the sideboard. "My time has been bespoken, so I'll see you the day after tomorrow, but Gareth? Think about what I've said. You've suffered enough for the title and obligations to family. The past nine years have taken a toll on you I don't think you clearly see. Mother and I both would rather see you happy than titled, and I mean that."

"Thank you, Andrew," Gareth said, considering his empty glass as Andrew left for his bedroom.

Felicity's hair in a certain light was the same color as very good brandy.

Felicity, who loved him.

Oh, she'd phrased it carefully, in deference to his delicate sensibilities, but the truth had been aired, despite all common sense and convention to the contrary. She loved him, and Gareth knew better than to disparage her sentiment as a silly infatuation. Felicity Worthington was a grown woman, one who had faced adversity for much of her life. If she said she loved him, then she did.

If she said she wouldn't be taking up with other men, then she wouldn't be, at least not while Gareth was associating with her.

So how in the hell, how in the ever-loving *hell* was he to take her to bed knowing she felt as she did? To permit himself those intimacies with her would be cruel beyond measure, and yet he knew he would do it. Worse he would do it and make the occasion as memorably pleasurable for himself—*and for her*—as he could.

He owed her that, at least.

"THIS IS ABSOLUTELY LOVELY!" Felicity exclaimed as Gareth handed her down in the drive of a cozy Tudor manor. "How can you stand to dwell in Town when you have this alternative so close at hand?"

"Come." Gareth slipped her hand over his arm, "I'll show you around inside. We keep a skeleton staff here unless I'm in residence, though Mother warned the housekeeper we'd be coming today."

He'd dodged her question, but Felicity allowed him to lead her into the house anyway. Willowdale was as charming on the inside as it was outside, with mullioned windows shedding light on gleaming wood floors and hothouse bouquets. The estate, both manor and grounds, glowed with a serene contentment from age and ceaseless good care.

"What are you thinking?" Gareth asked. He'd brought Felicity to an upstairs bedroom to freshen up, a room much like the one Felicity had enjoyed as a girl. The high four poster sported a patchwork quilt in Dresden blue and white, morning sun poured through the windows, and the room was suffused with a peaceful stillness. Gareth leaned against the jamb of the door as Felicity wandered the room.

"I would like to live in a place like this," she said. "The house has a benevolence, and a sense of dignity. It's pretty but unpretentious, much like our former family seat." She would enjoy the thought of Gareth dwelling here, in this quiet, serene place, though it would pain her to know he was two hours from London.

"I've always loved this property," Gareth said, crossing the room and tugging her wrist until she sat beside him on the bed. "I feel more at home on this small estate than I do anywhere else. One of the last summers my father was alive, he bade me spend here with only Andrew and the staff for company. We had the time of our lives, fishing, riding, staying up playing cribbage until all hours, and making the acquaintance of all the local lads. I tried to get Andrew drunk but he has a very thick skull, and more commonsense than I gave him credit for."

"He would have been little more than a child."

"He matured early. It's a characteristic of the males in my family."

And then, with no warning at all, he gently shoved her back onto the mattress, and Felicity found herself pinned beneath him as he nuzzled at her neck and breasts. Her heart kicked into a canter, and her bodice abruptly became unbearably tight.

"If I don't get my hands, and my *mouth* on your breasts in the next minute, I will tear your dress off, and devil take the hindmost," Gareth growled, rolling her over and unfastening her dress without further preamble.

She felt him start on her stays, and made a feeble bid in the direction of commonsense. "Gareth, your mother will be here any minute, and Astrid and Andrew as well."

Feeble protest, indeed. She didn't roll away, or otherwise impede his busy, competent fingers when he lowered her bodice. He untied her chemise next, and within the prescribed minute he had exposed her breasts to the lovely light of day.

"Ah, God, Felicity, what you do to me," he said, molding her breasts with his hands and bringing his nose to her cleavage. "I promised myself I'd leave you alone for these few weeks, but for the love of God, I cannot."

He wedged her up so she lay fully on the bed, the pillows beneath her head, then attacked his own clothes with one hand, even as he continued to fondle and shape her breasts with the other. Perhaps his reference to their few remaining weeks together preyed on her self-restraint, because Felicity wanted nothing, *nothing* as much as she wanted to strip Gareth naked and get her hands on him.

She reached up to help him free himself from his breeches, and he groaned at the touch of her fingers on his arousal. He fell silent as Felicity wrapped her hand around him and began to stroke in firm, rhythmic caresses intended to bring him pleasure in short order.

"Love, slow down," he rasped, head thrown back, eyes closed. "I'll spend."

"I know," Felicity said, not slowing down one bit.

Gareth scrabbled backward away from her, shot her an exasperated look, and sat breathing heavily on the edge of the bed.

"Come, Gareth," Felicity said, reaching around his waist to fondle him again. "You said we have some time before the others arrive. You're wasting it when I am offering you some ... 'Respite from your discontent'." She slid one hand up under his shirt to brush her fingers over his nipples.

She was supposed to learn the erotic arts from him, but all she was really learning was to desire him, and to cast her dignity aside at the least provocation. Sometime soon, she would regret this state of affairs. Right now, she wanted only to touch him.

"Merciful everlasting saints," he muttered, yanking off his boots. His breeches, cravat, waistcoat and shirt followed, while Felicity hoped he'd locked the door.

"I ought to exercise some damned restraint," he groused, climbing back onto the bed. "I ought to at least nod in the direction of a little discipline. I'm not a school boy." He came to a stop, naked and directly over her on all fours. "If I must spend the entire day ignoring the uproar created in my breeding organs by the very sight of you, I won't answer for the consequences."

He was not happy about that uproar, and Felicity shouldn't be pleased about it either. But what honest spinster wouldn't be a little impressed to have such an effect on a mature man of the world?

"You've said a couple intent on their objective can fornicate in less than five minutes." And they'd used at least two minutes getting his clothes off, and hers into complete disarray.

He crouched lower, his blue-eyed gaze boring into her. "When we consummate our dealings, madam, it will require considerably more than five minutes."

"Then why are you nak—?"

He kissed her soundly, and while it was a kiss to curl a lady's toes and make her breasts feel heavy and tender, Felicity tasted temper in his kiss too.

And she did not want him angry, because under that anger—under most anger—would be some hurt, some grief, some pain he would not allow her or anybody else to see. She caressed the plane of his chest, past the flat musculature of his belly, to grasp his erection. When she wrapped her fingers around him, he broke off the kiss and hung over her, his forehead resting over hers.

"Finish me, Felicity. It won't take much."

His tone was harsh, though she made her touch gentle. She *toyed* with him, easing up, then bearing down, then easing up again. The pleasure of handling him—and the power of it—was fascinating. And while she wished she could spend hours on that bed, they had only a little time before the others would arrive.

"I said to goddamn finish me."

"Hush." She kissed him, realizing that he wasn't in a hurry, so much as he sought to limit his pleasure to a quick servicing. "I wish we had all day."

Her wishes went well beyond that prosaic notion, so she put

them into her kisses and her caresses, into the way her hand gripped his cock, and her body yearned to share more with him than this quick gratification.

He reared back with a groan to kneel between her legs and bring himself off in a few hard, jerking strokes. His pleasure was not pretty, but rather, looked more like torment—magnificent, robust, intimate torment.

He opened his eyes. "You will pay for that."

Unease skittered through Felicity's vitals. "You would *punish* me?" He'd told her all about people who enjoyed an element of pain with their sexual diversions. She didn't comprehend it, and intended to die in that blessed state of ignorance.

"I would punish *myself*." He swabbed at himself with a handkerchief, balled it up and tossed it in the direction of his boots.

"Gareth, that makes no sense whatso—" She fell silent when he put a hand on her knee. Something in the quality of his touch was different, less polite, though no less cherishing.

"Lie back, Felicity, and let me pleasure you." Then, more softly. "We have time. We have time for your pleasure, too. Damn me if I'll let you turn me into a selfish lover."

Comprehension dawned. He was annoyed with himself, annoyed to have indulged himself when they had little privacy and Felicity's bodily calendar was unobliging.

"You don't need to do this, Gareth."

The naked, growling man between her legs was surely bent on some mischief that did not comport with a pleasant day among family in the country.

"I will be the judge of what I need, and what you need too. That is exactly what you came to me for. Close your eyes."

Felicity lay back and gave up listening for the sound of a carriage on the drive. The Eighty-Second Foot could come trooping up the steps and Gareth would not let her off the bed until he'd achieved his ends with her.

"You are wearing a red silk chemise. Have I made a strumpet of you?"

The words were meant to be teasing, but something about the way he caressed her breasts through that chemise and the pain in his eyes suggested he felt regret—possibly even shame.

So much for her daring experiment.

Felicity sat up, wiggled and scooted until she had the chemise off. "I made it myself. I would not ask a modiste to fashion such clothing for me."

He kissed her, gently, not like his earlier kisses. "Let me touch you."

His hand rested on her bare calf, and Felicity realized that once again, he was asking permission. She lay back and let him arrange her skirts so she was bared to him from mid-thigh down.

"This time, I want to see you," he said, easing her skirts higher. "I want to feast my eyes on you."

Felicity endured his inspection by virtue of keeping her own eyes closed. He stroked and petted and caressed and generally acquainted himself with her most intimate anatomy, while she....

Thought.

About the frustration she'd sensed in him earlier, about the pain in his eyes, about the red chemise.

He kissed her sex. A shocking, soft, application of his mouth to the bud of flesh that had some Italian name Felicity could not recall. She stroked a hand over his hair, felt the way the sunlight warmed it, and knew an urge to weep.

"We have time," Gareth said again, nuzzling her palm before renewing his attentions to her sex.

Within moments, her body was quickening with arousal, the yearning becoming a writhing beast beneath the pit of her belly.

They did not have time. They had nothing but an agreement of some sort, and that would soon be concluded. "Gareth, stop."

Perhaps he didn't hear her. Perhaps he didn't want to hear her.

"Gareth, stop *now*. I am not asking."

He went still, then eased up, so his cheek lay against her breast. "Why in God's name are you unwilling to let me give you this pleasure?"

His question was bewildered, his hand on her breast exquisitely gentle.

"This is not the time. Gareth. When I have my pleasure of you, it will require considerably more than five minutes." And it would take her considerably more than five minutes to recover from the experience.

He didn't immediately leave her, but remained resting over her, a comfort against the throb of unappeased desire and impending heartbreak.

"I do not understand you, Felicity."

What he did not understand was that a woman might want to give him pleasure, that she might enjoy providing him a few moments of indulgence for no reason except that it gratified her to so do.

She caressed his hair, letting her fingers trace the shape of his ear. "Then ascribe the hesitation to my nerves. I am a fully articled spinster, I'll have you know."

He closed his eyes, so she felt the brush of his lashes against her breast. "And I am a confirmed rake. I'll thank you not to forget it."

They remained like that for a few minutes longer, until Gareth rose and dressed, Felicity watching as he buttoned himself up into the marquess once again. He laced her stays and hooked her dress, the consummate lady's maid—or rake—and even tidied her hair without her having to ask.

"I hear a carriage," Felicity said, wondering why the thought of their families arriving brought no joy.

He glanced around the room, and frowned at Felicity's red silk chemise on the floor near the bed. When she thought he'd hand it to her, he instead kicked it under the bed and offered her his arm.

~

FOR GARETH TO have his paramour-in-training underfoot at his private estate along with their families ought to have been awkward as hell. When the scheduled picnic was cut short by an abrupt shift in the weather, Gareth comforted himself that his mother had not asked for the worst details regarding the folly he'd embarked on with Felicity.

Which did not explain why seeing Felicity and Lady Heathgate, heads bent over the same embroidery hoop, both pleased and pained him.

Dinner had been an interesting exercise in playing lord of the manor, and in watching Andrew gently flirt with young Astrid—and wouldn't that be a lovely complication if those two took a fancy to each other?

"Do you require solitude while you brood the night away," Andrew asked, "or might I have the pleasure of watching you?"

"You may build up the fire if you've come here to nag and gloat."

Andrew's smile was sardonic, very different from the teasing smiles he'd offered Astrid, but he did add a pair of logs to the fire. "Mother likes her, you know."

"Astrid?"

Andrew came down beside him on the couch. "Her too. If this scheme does work, and you can sell the damned brothel before anybody's the wiser as to its ownership, then Mother will likely present Astrid at court."

God in heaven. If that came to pass, Gareth could well find himself sharing a coach with Felicity on the appointed day.

Gareth put his book aside, a particularly pompous translation of Marcus Aurelius. "I might develop a pressing need to inspect the properties in Scotland, should Mother remain determined on that objective."

"You haven't been back there since the accident."

The word *accident* rattled off the window panes, like a gust of cold, wet wind. "Neither have you. I send Brenner when needs must."

Andrew stretched his feet out toward the fire, though upon those feet were a pair of Gareth's riding boots. "I get drunk each year on the anniversary."

Which would come up in a few weeks. Rather than put an arm around his brother's shoulders, Gareth rose. "I leave the brooding to you, little brother, and my thanks for keeping the ladies smiling at dinner."

"You're managing all right, then?" Andrew's question was casual, and quite personal.

Personal enough that Gareth could have left the library without answering it. Instead he returned to the sofa, retrieved old Marcus, and shoved the bastard between two volumes on French cuisine.

"I am losing my goddamned mind, Andrew. What is wrong with me, that I want Felicity to see that I'm a cordial host, a dutiful son, a decent brother, a conscientious landlord? She knows exactly what I really am."

Andrew tugged off his boots—Gareth's boots—and tossed them toward the door, then stretched out full length on the couch and folded his hands over his belly like some carving on a royal tomb.

"What's wrong with you, that you'd try to hide all those parts of yourself from a woman you're going to great lengths to help?"

By swiving her? Because he would. When the time was right, very soon, he'd take what she offered and then turn his back on her, just as she'd asked.

"Good night, Andrew. Pleasant dreams."

Andrew snorted, blew Gareth a kiss, and closed his eyes.

TO BE around Gareth's family was perilously nerve wracking, though his lordship's savoir faire appeared easily sufficient for the challenge. Felicity punched her pillow against the headboard, and debated whether she respected Gareth's sophistication in this regard, resented it, or lamented it.

Probably all three. He was so handsome in his country gentle-man's attire, so patient with his mother and Astrid.

And probably sleeping so soundly a few doors down the hallway, while Felicity—

Her door eased open, a familiar shape looming in the meager light. "I suspect you're awake, Miss Worthington. Are you receiving callers?"

Gareth used that ironic tone when he wanted her to think he was teasing. "Assuredly not. I am fast asleep and dreaming peacefully." Though she truly wanted him to stay. Now that he was here, she could acknowledge that she'd been waiting for him, hoping he'd wander into her bed, where they'd...

Not be able to indulge in her wildest fantasies.

"And I am sleepwalking," Gareth said, his weight dipping the bed. Felicity heard fabric rustling, and caught a scent of sandalwood and spices on the cool night air, suggesting he'd used his scented soap before he came calling.

"I have not invited you to sleep with me."

The rustling paused. "I thought we'd talk, Felicity. Just talk."

Perhaps they would indulge her wildest fantasies after all. "What shall we talk about?"

"You were upset at what passed before us in this bed earlier today." The mattress rocked and Felicity felt the covers lift, her only warning before Gareth tucked himself in beside her. "Tell me why you were upset."

He used the same tone he might use to ask for a report from Brenner, suggesting he was honestly in want of an explanation.

So she'd give him one—just as soon as he was done draping himself around her from behind.

"I cannot comprehend, Gareth, that this whole business is so casual to you, while to me it is overwhelming, lovely, and so very inti-mate. That you don't find it so only makes me sad for you. I wish I could restore..." She fell silent, as Gareth stopped fussing the covers and rearranging pillows.

He pulled her into his arms and fitted his chest to her back. She might have been a pillow for all the delicacy he used, though the man gave off heat like a toasted brick.

"What do you wish you could restore?"

"Whatever it is that has been taken from you, Gareth. I don't know exactly what, I lack the sophistication to put a name to it, but that you have lost something precious, or let it be taken from you... it isn't fair, or right."

He made no reply, but after a few minutes, his hand began to wander, kneading her breasts, flowing down her back, over her hip, her shoulders. She suspected he was trying to distract her, was desperate to distract her, so she wouldn't have the mental fortitude to wonder what he was thinking.

What he was *feeling*.

"Don't waste your concern on me, love," he said at length. "I cannot afford the luxury of the sentiments you allude to, but I appreciate you would want them restored to me. I, for one, do not miss them."

He rose over her and rolled her onto her back, then wedged himself between her legs, and took the weight of his upper body onto his forearms.

"Kiss me, Lissy. I want to come against your tummy."

"This is not talking, Gareth."

He bunched her nightgown up above her waist. "Hmm. Shall I regale you with a list of names for what I'd rather be doing? Swive, roger, blow the grounsils, at clicket..."

She kissed him to stop his naughty words, and because talking was indeed, difficult.

His hips rocked slowly, and Felicity grew damp as he moved against her. He kissed her more carnally, sealing her mouth with his own, breathing into her and through her. She startled when he dipped his arousal against her slick folds, wondering if he would attempt penetration.

But he was content to rub himself along her flesh until he too was slick with her desire. Then he changed the angle so he was once again sliding snugly against her belly.

He held her tightly, and Felicity reveled in his closeness. She wrapped her arms around him and anchored herself under him as he began to thrust against her more rapidly.

"That's it," Gareth whispered, sliding his hands down to cup her backside. "Hold me tight, love. Don't let me go."

He increased his pace, and Felicity did as he bid, wrapping her arms and legs around him, folding herself tightly to him. When a quiet groan escaped him, she fastened her mouth around his nipple and suckled gently, until he spent in a rush of warmth between their bodies.

His thrusts subsided, and yet Felicity held him to her, the urge to weep and the urge to destroy something rioting through her. Gareth kissed her, probably to prevent either of those impulses from finding their way into words. When Felicity let her limbs go slack, he rose from the bed and retrieved a damp towel from the bowl and pitcher by the fireplace.

He tended to himself first, while Felicity watched him from the bed. When he'd finished his ablutions, he rinsed and wrung out the towel, dampened it again, then hung it on the fireplace screen to warm.

Several moments later, he sat on the edge of the bed to use the towel on her belly.

And still he said nothing.

At least he made no offers to pleasure her, no threats of retribution. He swabbed his seed from her belly, and then sat back and regarded her without covering her up.

"Felicity, I know I said we'd talk, and if it's any comfort to you, I wish..."

By the light of the fire, Gareth looked weary and haggard, not sated. If she demanded it of him, he'd stay, and he'd listen.

He would not talk.

Without speaking a word, Felicity held out her arms to him and Gareth brought his body down to rest against hers. She flipped the covers up over them both and offered him in her embrace a silent comfort even he was unable to refuse.

CHAPTER TEN

Gareth stole down the dark hallway to his own room about an hour before dawn. He sat on the four-poster for a long time, listening to rain patter against the windows. If the rain kept up, there would be no attempting a return to Town today. One washed out bridge, one strained tendon on a coach horse, and they would be stranded on the road, prey to whatever harm pursued them.

Because the traveling coach had been followed out here. The spies Gareth had set had reported after dinner, and even now, even in this downpour, somebody might be watching his house.

His world had become complicated. Concern for Felicity's safety consumed him every bit as much as lust for her body. For a man who valued his own comfort highly, he'd arrive to a miserable state of affairs.

He would never forget the way she'd clung to him in bed only hours earlier, pushing him into mindless ecstasy with an instinctive use of her mouth—a trick he'd not shown her, because it worked especially well with him.

Felicity was lovely, and worse than that, she was becoming dear.

The longer he dealt with her, the angrier he became over his role in her life, over the dirty trick Callista had played on her.

And for what? Was Callista striking a posthumous blow at the family that had turned her out? It wasn't Felicity's fault Callista had been indiscreet with a heartless cad. And it didn't strike Gareth as true to Callista's nature to exact a vengeance so cruel on an innocent party.

Andrew had made the same observation weeks ago: This scheme did not comport with Callista's nature. Callista would have been the last person to victimize another woman, much less a woman left without male relatives to intervene on her behalf.

The whole business made little sense, and not for the first time, Gareth drifted off to sleep with the conviction he was missing a piece of the puzzle, a set of facts that would put the whole situation in a more understandable perspective.

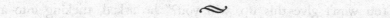

WHEN GARETH ROSE a few hours later, the sense of niggling frustration still haunted him, but for all that, he also looked forward to the day. He made his way downstairs to break his fast, hoping to catch Felicity at the table.

To his pleasure, she was there, and there alone. She looked up and smiled when he joined her. The room being otherwise empty, he responded by kissing her cheek lingeringly—lavender was a lovely scent on a damp morning—and taking a seat beside her.

"Good morning, my lord," she said, pouring him a cup of tea.

"So it's to be like that?" Gareth replied, serving himself eggs, bacon, toast, and an orange.

"Like what?" Felicity asked, and Gareth realized he liked her this way. Tentative, off-balance, blushing—and fetching as hell.

"You're milording me again, Felicity. Am I such a stranger to you?" he asked, accepting the tea from her.

"You are less of a stranger than ever." Her delicate little pink and white Sevres tea cup apparently fascinated her, perhaps because the pink nearly matched her blush.

"But you are still shy." Which pleased him.

"You have been patient with me," she said, topping up her tea, "and I do appreciate your forbearance, and yet I am disconcerted by what we do. You blithely sit down to tea, prepared to discuss the weather, or Astrid's bonnet. I am quite in awe of your sang froid, Gareth. Disconcerted, but in awe. Are you really so indifferent as you seem?"

Felicity was not angry—he wondered what could anger her—but Gareth detected genuine bewilderment in her tone, and this topic, this business of her consternation, apparently needed addressing—again. She'd brought it up last night, and he'd dodged. Ducked like a boy who knows he's earned a proper caning, and takes the long way home to delay it.

"You won't give this up, will you?" he asked, tucking into a steaming serving of omelet.

"I have *no one* else whom I may ask, Gareth. And I am quite troubled by what has transpired between us. Our activities no longer seem to be strictly in aid of my education, and yet I allow them."

She pushed a bite of eggs around on her plate, and Gareth realized she'd waited here in the breakfast parlor for him. Waited for him to come and make sense of the notion that he'd not merely had his pleasure of her twice without seeing to her satisfaction, but he'd stayed in her bed, wrapped around her like a presuming housecat.

While she'd cuddled up the livelong night, like an exhausted kitten.

He put his fork down, as the fluffy, delicately spiced eggs turned to so much ashes in his mouth. "You look so damnably pretty at my breakfast table."

The smile that had taken him so aback weeks ago reappeared, a ray of feminine benevolence on a gloomy morning.

"Your compliments might be easier to spot, Gareth, if you didn't scowl so thunderously when you doled them out."

She looked worse than pretty, she looked *appropriate* across his breakfast table. As he watched her enjoy her tea, it hit him that he'd become the sort of man to take advantage of a guest under his own roof, while his family slept in the very next wing.

He'd *never* spent the night sleeping in a lover's bed.

Never introduced his casual amours to his mother, and they were *all* casual amours.

He'd never brought a woman he was intimate with to his townhouse, much less to his favorite country estate.

"More tea, Gareth?"

"Please."

The picture of Felicity pouring the tea for him, all prim and tidy with just a hint of color on her neck where his beard had abraded her skin, would remain with him for the rest of his life.

He had lost his heart to a virgin spinster. "I do like you, you know."

She added cream and sugar to his cup and passed him his drink. He more than liked her, and she more than liked him, and it was up to him to avert the disaster looming as a result.

"I like you too, sir. Will the roads dry out enough for us to get back to Town today?"

Did she have to sound so hopeful? "Very likely, so you needn't worry that I'll trouble your slumbers again. That wasn't well done of me, and you have my apologies."

She didn't want his apologies. He could see that in the way her brows drew down. She wanted an *explanation*, which would not be forthcoming because he bloody didn't have one.

"I didn't mind, Gareth. I just... it confuses me. What we do confuses me. There are the terms of the bequest to meet, which I understand, but then there's this other... "

What she *felt* confused her, and that was his fault, and his responsibility to rectify, though it would make kicking puppies seem endearing by comparison.

"I know you are troubled, and no, I am not completely unaf-

fected, but you must trust me you will find your balance with this.
These little pleasures we indulge in are normal, adult behavior where
the bodily passions are concerned."

"Passions?" she murmured, clearly not liking that at all. "You are
saying I am wanton?"

Kicking puppies *and* kittens, then.

"You are passionate," Gareth said, and that much was the truth,
"but I don't refer to merely physical passion. You are a woman of
substantial heart. You are not designed in your nature to be frivolous
with your affections. May I fix you a plate?"

"No, thank you. Are you frivolous with your affections then?"

The question challenged his logic, because the idea that Lord
Heathgate, scourge of lackadaisical clerks and napping backbenchers,
could be frivolous about anything was ludicrous.

"I am designed to bring a certain detachment to all that I do."
Though last night, that detachment had been sadly absent.

As it had been earlier in the day, as it had been since Gareth had
laid eyes on Felicity Worthington.

She studied him from behind her tea cup, topaz eyes taking in his
expression, then flicking down to the substantial portion of food
grown cold on his plate.

"You will excuse me, please. If we're to return to Town, I'd best
let Astrid know."

He bowed as she left the room, and then made himself sit back
down and stare at something—racing results, the society pages, he
could not have said what—for another five minutes before removing
himself to the library.

The problem was not that he'd become a man who would accost a
guest under his own roof, when his family slept in the very next wing,
but that he'd made Felicity into a woman complicit in such behaviors.

And yet, Gareth had treated her to that display of obnoxious
pontification over tea not only because her reputation was jeopar-
dized by proximity to him, but also because proximity to her could
well be his undoing too.

IN A COUNTRY where it could rain for days, the heavens obliged for only an afternoon and a night, and thus Felicity found herself beside Gareth in his traveling coach, bouncing and swaying back toward Town, and the inevitable end of her dealings with him.

The more intimate she became with him, the more tightly dread twined around her heart. She would miss him, and as for this detachment he brayed about so insistently, she would learn it at the cost of a broken heart.

Gareth shifted beside her, pushing his spectacles up his patrician nose.

"You have been staring at Mr. Brenner's report for the past half hour. What on earth are you thinking about?"

"I was thinking about Riverton," he said, taking his glasses off and folding them up.

"I do not know Viscount Riverton well, Gareth, but I cannot like him. He and Father were companions of some sort for a time, though if I knew he was coming around, I made it a point to stay in my room."

"I didn't know he was acquainted with your family," Gareth replied, tucking his glasses away. "How well did your father know him and do you think he recognized you when our paths crossed a few weeks ago?"

Felicity glanced out at the damp, drab countryside. Now, the perishing man was happy to talk.

"I do not think he recognized me. Ten years ago, I was a good deal shorter, barely putting my hair up, and generally kept my nose in a book. I avoided Riverton if possible, so he might have caught a glimpse of me, but we never spoke."

"And yet, your father knew him?"

So it was to be an interrogation, and regarding an uncomfortable topic.

"For a short while they were great friends, out of an evening in

each others' company most nights. Then less, and then, for some time
before Father died, they no longer associated. At least, Riverton no
longer came to our house."

Gareth did not take her hand, and Felicity wished he would. She
took her gloves off whenever they were private in a coach in hopes he
might.

"Why didn't you like him?"

Why don't you take my hand? "He never touched me, never said
anything directly to me. But when he looked at me a certain way, I
felt unclean. He never gave me that look when Father could see it."
She was quiet for a moment, though she found Gareth's hand with
her own. "I could not have borne having to comport myself with
Riverton as I have with you. Would not."

This provoked a frown, but in the vast lexicon of Gareth's frowns,
his expression was thoughtful rather than disapproving.

"I have wondered what Callista was about, leaving you with him
for an alternative."

"She was probably forcing me into your company," Felicity
replied. "By comparison, anybody would seem more acceptable than
Riverton. My father once alluded to the idea it was Riverton's lasciv-
ious tendencies that had undermined their association. He said the
man would keep company with any species if there was sufficient
money and drink involved, though I don't think I was supposed to
overhear that."

Gareth brought her knuckles to his lips. "You weren't. Riverton
once screwed a pony on a bet, and there were many witnesses."

Unease congealed into nauseated dread. "You are not serious."

"I most certainly am. I departed before the deed was done, but
that little mare did not leave the mews without knowing Riverton in
the biblical sense."

"That is. diabolically offensive." Though that Gareth would share
such a thing with her was a measure of how far they'd come with
each other. "I am glad you left, but that poor little horse.... Why
would a man do such a thing? And how could others watch?"

"You are so innocent, so good." His tone carried both affection and despair. "I don't know what motivates some men. If it's any comfort, Riverton was barely received after that. Sometimes, boredom can become an enemy that demands excesses of vice and a banishment of decency. Bad company becomes no real company at all, and soon what began as an effort to find pleasure or drown sorrow becomes a cultivation of evil."

He sounded so bleak, so weary of his own life. Felicity kept hold of his hand and wished she could climb into his lap.

"Why would Riverton have been received at all, Gareth? He abused an animal, he abused the dignity of his acquaintances, he debased what it means to be human—and this was for *sport*?"

She wanted to cry and wanted to destroy the thing in Gareth that understood Riverton, even if he didn't approve of him.

"It was neither for sport nor purely for money, though money changed hands. I can't explain it, Felicity. Men, particularly inebriated men, do stupid things to prove themselves daring, reckless, *manly*. I found it disgusting, but some part of me was also shocked at Riverton's audacity. What he did made me notice and remember him."

"For God's sake, Gareth, you notice offal in the street. I suppose I should be grateful I am not the unwilling successor to an unwilling pony."

His gaze shifted, sweeping over her with imperial thoroughness. "I would not have let that happen. I will never let that happen."

She would become a madam, a brothel-owner, and her reputation would be at risk long after the day Gareth sold the wretched establishment to someone else. He could make all the decrees and speeches he wanted to about safeguarding her wellbeing, but in less than a month—after he'd destroyed the last of her innocence—they'd once again be strangers.

Felicity snuggled against him and remained quiet.

GARETH STARED at Brenner's very thorough report on some damned situation or other, glad for the care the coachy had to take on this journey back into Town.

Since their unlooked for time at Willowdale, Felicity regarded him with emotions that eviscerated his ability to concentrate: protectiveness—not his protectiveness toward her, but *hers* toward *him*. She held him as if he were precious and admitted feelings for him no woman ought to own up to.

She was also angry, though he could not tell if she was angry for him, or with him, or both.

And worst of all, her eyes communicated a bottomless sadness he could hardly stand to acknowledge.

"You have gone quiet, Felicity. At this rate we won't make Town for another hour at least. You must share your concerns with me."

He couldn't force her to, of course. He was the man who'd offered to talk with her of a night, only to take advantage of her, and deliver a lot of hypocritical speeches in the morning.

She rested her head on his shoulder. "What is our plan, Gareth, for the next two weeks and beyond? I will be less anxious, if I know what to expect."

"Do you want me to be imperious now, Felicity, or shall I make suggestions?" He honestly could not read her mood.

"Be imperious, please," Felicity said, nuzzling his shoulder. "If your ideas are not to my liking, I will speak up."

She would, which was some reassurance. Gareth carried her wrist to his lips, in need of a fortifying whiff of lavender.

"You will always speak up—I rely on you for this." He returned her hand to her with a pat on the knuckles when he wanted to haul her into his lap.

"We will return to Town," he began in the most prosaic tones he could muster. "I will arrange an appointment with the solicitors for say, two weeks hence. I suggest you leave your schedule free for the preceding afternoon, so we can dispense with your virginity, whether your feminine cycle cooperates or not. In the intervening two weeks,

I intend to go driving with you in the park, perhaps escort you to the theatre once more, and finally, I will join you at one of Mother's at-homes. If you deliver me a rousing set-down at my mother's house, then we will justify untangling ourselves from each other in the eyes of society."

Felicity rode beside him in silence for a damp, jarring half mile. "I suppose that will do."

"I am not finished." Which came as something of a surprise to Gareth, because he'd honestly put off thinking through these maneuvers.

"I will oversee the running of the brothel, until such time as it can be sold. I believe it best if we have no direct interaction once we're done with the solicitors. I would not risk your reputation any further." Nor his own sanity. "If you would permit me to maintain the staff I have in place at your house until the brothel is sold, I would appreciate it. Should we need to correspond, it can be done through Brenner."

He wanted her to argue with him, to find excuses for them to remain cordial. He wanted her to hint that she might discreetly continue as his mistress. He wanted her to slap such thoughts from his idiot mind.

She leaned into him as if weary. "I am glad, Gareth, that you can think through these considerations, really I am. I absolutely cannot see past the day we meet with the solicitors. I try, but I can't."

The heartache in her tone nigh undid him, but all he could think to do was squeeze her hand. "We will endure this, Felicity. One day at a time, one hour at a time, one breath at a time, if that's all you can manage." He rested his cheek against her hair and thumped his fist once on the roof of the coach.

The horses came down to the walk from their unambitious trot.

Gareth did this not to reduce the jolting and bouncing of a well sprung coach on a muddy road, he did it so he had a few more moments with Felicity before they once again said good-bye.

"MR. HOLBROOK HAS GONE to ground, your lordship,"
Brenner said. "He no longer takes his coach to the park, and hasn't
left his house for three days."

Three long damned days since they'd returned from Willowdale.
That had been Thursday, and now Sunday afternoon had arrived
brisk and blustery. Since Gareth had dropped Felicity off at her residence, he'd thrown himself into work.

Or tried to.

A knock heralded the arrival of a footman, bearing a note on a
tray. The epistle wasn't from Felicity, which was a relief and a disappointment both.

Cecelia, Countess Evansley, begged the pleasure of Gareth's
company for supper that evening at eight of the clock. She was one of
his duty escorts, or she'd started out that way when her husband had
died, leaving Gareth with an obligation toward a deceased former
schoolmate's wife. Of course, that had been years ago, when a few
lingering associations from university still qualified as friends.

Cecelia was a lady, though, and Gareth speculated she'd heard he
was no longer keeping company with Edith Hamilton. He genuinely
liked Cecelia, and her company was restful. The thought of a liaison
with her left him peculiarly unmoved, though he ought to be lining
something up to occupy his spare time once his business with Felicity
was concluded.

Something besides work, work, and more work.

He set the note aside.

"Brenner, attend me. Holbrook is a mystery I want solved. Go
back over everything you know, look at his deeds and records again,
interview his neighbor's coachy over a pint, bribe the boot boy, flirt
with the tweenie, but get me some answers. I want to know what his
connection is to Felicity Worthington, and I want to know yesterday.
Do I make myself clear?"

"Very clear, your lordship."

"How do the Worthingtons fare?" he asked as he straightened a sheaf of papers, each one an eloquent plea from some charity or other.

"They appear to be well, sir. Crabble has the men cleaning out the gutters, re-thatching the stable, mending harness, that sort of thing. The house is coming along, and Mrs. Crabble says it hasn't looked so well since the last viscount was alive."

Gareth decided Brenner wasn't being deliberately obtuse. "And the ladies?"

"They have remained at home, as you requested. Mrs. Crabble does the marketing, and if the young misses need to go out, they take at least two footmen."

"Why would they need to go out?"

"They went to services this morning, sir."

Because that's what decent young ladies did of a Sunday.

Gareth fell silent, unable to think of any other way to press Brenner for details without sacrificing his own dignity. Instead, he directed his staff to have the coach available at half seven that evening, his evening clothes laid out, and his brother notified he would not be joining him for dinner.

"SHE TOLD YOU *WHAT*?" Andrew spluttered as Gareth paced the library early Monday afternoon.

"Cecelia, Lady Evansley, invited me to dinner for the sole purpose of politely warning me she'd heard a rumor to the effect that Miss Felicity Worthington had inherited Callista's brothel, and I was managing it for her. The other element to this on-dit was that Felicity is my current paramour, and Lady Evansley is enough of a friend she thought I should know what's said sooner rather than later."

And thank God, that had honestly been her agenda.

"That must gall," Andrew said, perusing the shelves as Gareth paced. "Being hung for sheep, and all that. No pun intended. What will you do?"

Break every valuable in the house as loudly as possible.

Get drunk for the first time in nearly a decade.

Marry Felicity so none of this gossip or mayhem could touch her.

Gareth stopped pacing directly before a miniature replica of Canova's *Psyche Revived*, noticing that one of Eros's manly wings was sporting a chip.

"I'll have Brenner chase down the rumor to its source, I'll see that Felicity meets the terms of the bequest, and I'll ensure she and her sister enjoy disgustingly good health so long as it is in my power to do all of the above." This recitation had the quality of a vow, but didn't settle Gareth's mind the way a vow ought.

Andrew helped himself to a drink. "I don't envy you. Do you suppose Mother might be some help?"

"She will be invaluable in muddying the waters of gossip, as will Lady Evansley, but they can merely buy us time to ferret out the origin of the ill will. I can't help but think Holbrook is wrapped up in this. Lady Evansley knows him," he added. "She reports he is quite the honorable fellow, though it's rumored he's regrettably, if discreetly, illegitimate."

"Interesting," Andrew commented, sipping his drink. And then, when Gareth's guard was down and his focus on a lone, wispy cobweb dangling from the central chandelier, "Brother, do I detect a note of fatigue about your countenance?"

Gareth was exhausted, and damn Andrew for noticing, because he would report the situation directly to their dame. "I don't sleep well of late."

"You know you have only to ask and I'd lend any assistance requested."

Gareth should thank his brother for those words, and for the genuine sentiment behind them. "I know that, Andrew, but some matters I cannot delegate or entrust to anyone—even you."

Andrew looked like he might say more, then passed Gareth the remainder of his drink and departed.

Leaving Gareth to stew in thoughts of Felicity.

He wanted to keep her close, and wanted to swive her until neither one of them could stand. But he would hate himself if he did that to her—and she *should* hate him, too, though she wouldn't. Not at first, anyway.

Realizing his fretting was getting him nowhere, he saw to his attire, bellowed for his phaeton, and arrived at Felicity's door minutes later. His tiger held the team while Gareth went to fetch the lady, though to his surprise, Astrid was the one opening the door.

"You don't look quite in the pink, Heathgate," she observed. "Are you in good health?"

"I haven't been sleeping so well of late," Gareth admitted, because by all accounts, dissembling before Miss Astrid was arrant folly.

"I'm sorry," Astrid said. "Warm milk with a finger of brandy is Felicity's recipe for the same ailment."

Gareth peered down at her curiously—he did not mistake the girl for an ally—but she merely winked at him as Felicity came down the stairs.

"This bodes ill, the two of you with your heads together," she said, smiling at Gareth and surprising him by offering her cheek for a kiss. He bent to comply, and the scent of her fragrance wafted up to him, along with a wave of something sweet—relief, comfort, longing. As he kissed her cheek, some of his fatigue fell away.

"Shall we make haste before the weather decides to change on us again?" he asked, offering his arm.

"By all means. Astrid, behave yourself, please," Felicity directed over her shoulder.

The day wasn't warm, but that gave Gareth a pretext for sitting close to his lady on the narrow seat of the open carriage. Because the air was brisk—and because he was in no mood to conclude their outing—Gareth kept the horses to a walk.

"So how fare you, my lady?"

"I miss you dreadfully," Felicity said, sounding peevish. "I sleep poorly, I am jumpy and crabby. I wish I'd never gone to Willowdale and I wish we were still there. And yourself?"

"The same," he said, his heart lighter for hearing her recitation.

"Lovely. When will I get over you?"

Gareth was silent a moment, considering a question she couldn't ask anybody else and ought not to be asking him.

"It's like this," he said, while in the back of his mind, puppies whined, kittens mewed and small children covered their eyes. "You suffer with these sorts of things, until you are sick of being unhappy with it, then common sense, or pride, or something asserts itself, and you stop clinging to your suffering. Then one day, you realize you've gone maybe two whole hours without pining, or moping, and you come to the conclusion if you can manage it for two hours, then you can try for two days. The blasted business simply takes time."

Felicity bumped him with her shoulder. "It breaks my heart that you know such hard lessons from experience, Gareth."

More of her protectiveness, which he did not deserve. "They're only hard lessons the first time you learn them. After that, they're valuable lessons."

"Hmmph. At least we do have a peek of sunshine."

She smiled over at Gareth, and he simply could not rise to the challenge. He could not offer her a false smile, a glib rejoinder, a flirtatious aside while discussing the bloody, blighted weather.

He would miss her, *terribly*, for a long, long time. This realization manifest itself in a leaden ache in his chest, much like what he'd experienced for months after the damned accident.

A pigeon fluttered close to the offside gelding's ears, and before Gareth could wave the idiot bird away with his whip, the horse propped, the carriage lurched, and Felicity pitched against him.

"Apollo, Mars, settle."

Like the fine animals they were, the horses obediently resumed a placid walk—and Felicity straightened away from him.

"What is it, Gareth? Something is bothering you—something to do with me."

Many things were bothering him, most of them to do with her. "Recall, please, that we are in public, soon to be joining the throng at the fashionable hour. I have unpleasant news, and I don't wish your expression to betray its nature. We are still, to appearances, a potentially courting couple." He related the gossip shared with him at the previous evening's dinner, all the while keeping an eye out for persistent pigeons that might benefit from a taste of his whip.

"Steady on," he remarked, as if to the horses, before continuing. "I am investigating the source of the rumors, Felicity, but words can do more harm than bullets."

"What harm can rumor do? Astrid and I were bound for obscurity in any case. It isn't as if the dictates of Polite Society were much of an influence on our lives when the coal cellar was empty."

"That's my lady," he replied, though from her—from the tenaciously proper Miss Worthington—this recitation bore an air of nervous self-deceit. "Obscurity is one thing, and total exile another. Even if you plan to eschew the state of holy matrimony, you harbor hopes for your sister."

"I do—I did, anyway." Felicity sank against him. "The right man will not marry her for her title, her fortune, or her spotless family history—each of the foregoing being nonexistent."

"You're suggesting," Gareth said, tipping his hat to a passing carriage full of dowagers, "what more harm can come from a few nasty rumors? That reasoning holds some merit, but I am troubled, nonetheless. This gossip is an attempt to hurt you, *another* attempt to hurt you. And if the rumors are to be believed, then any man will consider you and Astrid fair game for dishonorable advances. This has to be intentional."

At an angle to the path they rolled along, Edith Hamilton held court in a phaeton parked beneath a shady maple. Gareth turned his conveyance before either lady could notice the other.

"Maybe you see a pattern where there is none," Felicity said.

"The rumors could be just what they appear to be: juicy, idle gossip. You do, however, look troubled. Tired, at least."

It was on the tip of Gareth's tongue to ask Felicity if he might drive her back to his townhouse for a substantial, leisurely tea, and yet, he knew better. He'd have her upstairs within minutes, and naked in his bed within more minutes—and she'd allow it.

He had done that to her, made her available to him on request in the broad light of day, and it had only taken him a handful of weeks to bring her to this state. Before he could open his fool mouth, he turned the horses off the Ring, and dropped Felicity directly at her door. Perhaps he'd use the balance of the afternoon to learn the neglected art of the solitary nap.

~

FELICITY SAW GARETH not the day following their outing in the park, but the day after, at his mother's regular Wednesday gathering. He still looked tired to her, and still had a restless, discontented quality lingering beneath his company manners. She caught Lady Heathgate eyeing him with puzzled concern, but her ladyship said nothing.

With Andrew, Felicity was inclined to be blunt.

"Your brother looks peaked to me," she whispered as Andrew took a turn with her about the upstairs gallery.

"You mean, he looks like hell?" Andrew rejoined as they stopped to admire a be-ruffed, goateed Alexander ancestor's portrait. The man's legs were muscular, putting Felicity in mind of—

"Gareth looks weary, and ruffled, beneath his elegant clothing and sophisticated manners," Felicity said, not rising to Andrew's teasing. "Who's this?" she asked, nodding at another figure who wore an impressive wig and gorgeously embroidered coat.

"The first earl of Heath. I believe the family was one of the few to financially support Charles II during the Protectorate, which elevated the title to its present exalted status."

"It's an old title."

"Very old," Andrew said. "Not quite back to The Conqueror, but almost. Longshanks bestowed the barony, and the succession had been unbroken through the primary line—until Gareth."

"My heavens, who is this?" They had stopped beside a portrait of a young man and a young woman. The gentleman stood with his hand on the young lady's shoulder, while she sat slightly angled before him, a picture of blond, blue-eyed beauty. While the young lady was smiling broadly, the young man's expression was solemn. His features bore the handsome stamp of the Alexander family— height, thick, dark hair and snapping, vivid blue eyes. The artist had captured a sense of energy about the fellow, a sense that the sitting couldn't be over soon enough, because this man had business to be about. From the dress, Felicity gathered that the portrait had been done during her lifetime.

"They make a lovely couple, though the gentleman looks very serious," she remarked. Beside her, Andrew was silent, and when she glanced over at him, he looked uncomfortable—and a great deal like his older brother.

"I didn't know Mother had hung this. Otherwise, I'd have spared you."

"Spared me?" Felicity examined the portrait again, a leaden feeling congealing in her insides. "That is Gareth, and his *wife*?"

CHAPTER ELEVEN

"Miss Ponsonby was Gareth's intended, not quite his fiancée," Andrew said, tugging at Felicity's arm. "And I refuse to reveal his confidences, Felicity, other than to tell you the young lady perished in the same boating accident that nearly took my life and Mother's."

Felicity allowed Andrew to lead her on around the gallery when she wanted to plant herself before that one portrait.

"Was this engagement a secret?" She kept her voice just above a whisper.

"Not even quite a fact, the negotiations were barely begun. We don't speak of it and I doubt Miss Ponsonby's family does either. The circumstances were unusual."

Judging from Andrew's expression, the circumstances could not have been worse.

"To have lost his beloved so tragically..." Felicity murmured, her heart hurting for that young man, and the brutal grief fate had handed him.

Andrew ran a hand through his hair in a gesture reminiscent of his brother, while across the gallery, two dowagers pretended to study a painting of some lady in a powdered wig with a pair of spaniels panting at her tiny feet.

"It wasn't like that." Andrew kept his voice down too. "Theirs was not an easy match, not even a formal engagement when they spent a couple weeks sitting for that painting at a family gathering in Scotland. That's all I intend to say on the matter."

"Heathgate loved her." And he'd lost her, and Polite Society had likely blamed him for her death too.

"He cared for her," Andrew said uneasily.

"And I am not to ask him about this lost love?"

"I wouldn't advise it. He has much on his plate now."

Andrew's tone held reproach, and rightly so. Gareth was coping with enough problems from Felicity already; she didn't need to resurrect his painful past into the bargain.

"You are particularly quiet," Gareth remarked as he escorted Felicity to his town coach nearly an hour later. Astrid was making her farewells to Lady Heathgate, giving them a moment of privacy.

"Still not sleeping well." And wasn't it a relief that with Gareth at least, Felicity could be honest. "And you?"

"I did have an amazingly good night Monday, but last night I counted nearly every sheep on our Scottish holdings to no avail." He still held her hand, but Felicity was too preoccupied to object to the impropriety. He began to rub his thumb over her gloved knuckles.

"Are you looking forward to joining me at the theatre on Friday?" he asked, dropping his voice as he leaned closer to her.

Alerted by the seductive note in his voice, Felicity snatched her hand away. "Shame on you, my lord."

"I'm supposed to be considering making you an offer," he said, all offended innocence. "A man should be able to hold his betrothed's hand." He grabbed her hand and kissed her bare wrist, and all she could do was glower at him.

"Don't take me so seriously, Felicity," he said, a touch impatiently.

"Not take you so seriously? Is that like you shouldn't react so peevishly when I mention your other women?"

"Touché."

"I will give it my best effort, sir, if you will do likewise," she replied with some asperity. How she wished there weren't a touch of real distress in her voice.

"Sweetheart, let's not argue, please? This next week will be difficult, but we will manage. You are not intimidated by what lies ahead?"

Sweetheart—and he'd made it sound so genuine, just as genuine as his concern for her. Worse yet, as he was wont to do, he'd focused on at least one source of Felicity's anxiety.

"Must we speak of that here?" she asked, looking over his shoulder for Astrid—for anybody.

"I don't want you to worry," he said quietly. "You know I will take greatest care with you, and you mustn't fret about this. I have it on good authority that alewives all over London copulate regularly with no ill effect. Surely we can manage it once."

Felicity glared at him.

"What?" More innocent bewilderment, though this time, genuine.

"*Once*? You expect me to believe you'll leave it at that? You expect me to content *myself* with that?"

He did laugh then, loud enough that his mother and brother, standing on the terrace, exchanged a wondering glance, and Astrid came sauntering down the stairs to investigate.

"Whatever is that sound, Lissy? I hear something strange, a rare, wonderful sound... Can it be?" She goggled, earning her a swat on the arm with her sister's glove.

"You are a bad girl, Astrid Worthington, and you have no manners," Felicity said. "Heathgate is overcome with mirth at the thought anybody might find your company acceptable."

"Verily, and Andrew doesn't count because he's a worse case than you, Miss Astrid," Gareth said. In his serious expression, and the mirth dancing in his eyes, Felicity found confirmation for her worst fears:

She loved Gareth Alexander. The Marquess of Heathgate she could often take or leave, but this other fellow... She would adore making love with Gareth Alexander, and it would shatter her heart for all time.

"Bother you both," Astrid said airily as Gareth assisted her into the coach. "I heard Heathgate laughing. You will have to warn John Coachman to be on the lookout for flying pigs. They could spook the horses."

~

"FELICITY, HOW LOVELY YOU LOOK," Gareth rumbled from the bottom of the stairs. The appreciation in his eyes reassured her he wasn't offering idle flattery. "I would not have thought to dress you in brown," he continued, taking her hand for the last few steps, "but the shade becomes you well." He kissed her hand, and eyed the chocolaty velvet swathing her from head to toe. "This is new," he concluded, approvingly.

"It is." And the dress was more than decent, and she positively loved the entire outfit, though prior to meeting Heathgate, she never would have indulged in such a feminine design. "I had a few things made up when we went shopping for Astrid."

"I will be the envy of every sighted man tonight, and," his smile shifted, becoming naughty, "and because you smell so good, every man with a working nose. Shall we be off?"

Gareth was more than usually attentive, bundling her into her cloak and fastening the frogs with myriad casual touches to her neck and chin. He wrapped his hand over hers on his arm as they descended the steps, and took her hand in his immediately upon seating himself beside her in the coach. He was attractive enough when he was casually affectionate, but this display coupled with his evening attire and concerted good manners had Felicity's heart speeding up.

I will remember him like this. Handsome, gallant, affectionate, and subtly possessive—no, protective.

Gareth helped her alight, and again drew her hand onto his arm and secured it with his other hand. As they approached the doors to the elegant establishment, he leaned down, as if to hear something Felicity was saying.

"Stay close to me, Felicity," he whispered, "We're in public, but a crowd can hide a wealth of mischief."

She nodded and tucked herself more snugly to his side, more than welcome for an excuse to feel his body heat, and revel in his scent. In one week's time...

Gareth seated her in the front of his box. He took her hand again, as she used his opera glasses to scan the crowd.

"I spy some acquaintances of yours." she said, handing him the glasses.

"Sweetheart, I am acquainted with most of the gathering tonight, including the drunken swells in the pit. To whom do you refer?" Out of sight of the crowd around them, his thumb circled on her palm in small, lazy strokes.

And there was that endearment, landing right in the middle of Felicity's heart, where it sank beneath her composure like a stone disappearing in a still pond.

"I see Riverton, and seated, if I'm not mistaken, next to Edith Hamilton." Some of her pleasure evaporated at the simple sight of the woman, for Gareth had no doubt called Lady Edith sweetheart too.

"You appear to be correct." His thumb did not cease its caresses, though his grip became more snug. "I am forced to admit I am sorry for Edith that she is keeping his company. She doesn't deserve that— no woman does."

"And I am forced to agree with you." Felicity could not imagine having been close to Gareth, and then succeeding his attentions with those of a dissolute scoundrel. Maybe Lady Edith had learned to keep her heart out of the bedroom, and one lover was much the same as the next to her.

How sad—but practical, wise even.

The farce began and Felicity wondered at what point—if any—Gareth would suggest they find refreshment, stroll the corridor, or otherwise support the pretext that they were a potential couple. To her surprise, he sat beside her, giving every appearance of enjoying the play. At the interval, they strolled the passage, and again, they left before the final curtain. In the coach on the way home, Gareth wrapped an arm around her shoulders and held her hand.

"You won't invite me to come back to your house with you?" Felicity asked.

"I will not."

"Whyever not?" Because she wanted to be with him. Even if all they did was share a bed for the entire night, she wanted to spend the time with him.

"Felicity, I am trying to behave." His tone suggested this was an onerous undertaking, for which he blamed her. With his free hand, he extracted a small, silver flask engraved with a sprig of heather and offered it to her.

She shook her head at the proffered libation. "Why are you trying to behave now, when you made no effort in that direction when last we visited the theatre?"

To uncap his flask, he had to retrieve his arm from around her shoulders and use both hands. "I am trying to behave to make amends for being so inconsiderate previously. I have comported myself like a damned ass with you on more than one occasion." He sounded impatient, but amused too. The way he tossed back a swallow of aromatic brandy suggested displeasure, despite his amusement.

"Did it ever occur to you, Gareth Alexander, maybe what you think is inconsideration does not strike me as the same?" Felicity asked in a low voice. "Does it occur to you to ask how I want to be treated, to even *listen* when I tell you how I want to be treated?"

They passed the occasional street lamp, so his face flickered in and out of shadow, making his expression impossible to read. He did not put the flask away, but rather, cradled it in his ungloved hands.

"You are saying you'd like me to take you home with me, so I can thrust my cock up your ass, or perhaps down your throat, or maybe have you bring me off, and that will restore your good spirits?"

His words, delivered with lazy condescension, were intended to hurt, and hurt they did. Felicity wanted to rail at him for his trivializing of what did not feel trivial to her at all, but then she recalled him looking worried and tired for most of the past week.

"So," she said, forcing some amusement into her voice. "You are in one of those moods." She took his hand in hers, and sat back, willing herself to become the picture of calm.

"What moods?" The words were dragged from him, laced with a prudent quantity of male foreboding.

"Sometimes, you dodge our physical intimacy; other times, you dodge the emotional intimacy, and sometimes, you use the one to dodge the other. I have only to figure out what we're dodging on a given occasion, and I then I can comport myself accordingly."

"That," he said, slowly, looking at their joined hands, "was a perfectly catty thing to say."

Felicity smiled at him, willing to have an intimate argument if she couldn't talk him into any other variety of closeness.

"I do not dodge intimacies." His tone suggested he was trying to convince himself rather than her.

"I simply wish you could inform me of your preferences, my lord. You could have told me at Willowdale that we would bounce around in bed of a night so you didn't need to cope with the burdens of conversation. Tonight, you might have said I wasn't to be granted any privileges, because you are in fact, weary of this whole exercise. When we go driving on Monday, you might consider simply being honest, you know."

"Honesty is highly overrated. I was trying to be considerate of your ladylike sensibilities."

And abruptly, Felicity was tired—exhausted—by his savoir faire, his moods, his incessant flow of sophistication.

And heartbroken by his dissembling, because the man who'd held her through the night was not present with her in the coach, and he'd been a more honest, likeable fellow than the handsome lord beside her.

"Cling to the fiction that you're being considerate of me if you must, Heathgate. I would really rather we were clinging to each other."

Felicity's voice did not break on that admission, a small sop to her dignity.

The horses clip-clopped along through the darkness, while she silently admitted that having the last word was a cold comfort, compared to having Gareth's body wrapped around hers in a warm bed.

"Fine, I'll be honest with you, Felicity," he muttered, just before tossing his flask onto the opposite seat, and fusing his mouth to hers in a ravenous, open-mouthed kiss. Her arms went around him as her tongue met his, and her body arched up against him. She pulled back a moment later, the scant half inch necessary to permit speech.

"Better, Gareth, much better," she said, before resuming the kiss.

And while the horses plodded patiently around London's better neighborhoods, from Felicity's perspective, the situation grew better still—much, much better.

FROM HIS SEAT at the back of a borrowed theatre box, David Holbrook had watched the Marquess of Heathgate pay court to Felicity Worthington. They were a handsome couple, both tall, attractive, and elegantly turned out.

And yet, something was off. A man acted one way with his mistress, and another with his proper companions. Felicity and Heathgate had acted somewhere in between, or rather, Heathgate

acted, and Felicity allowed it. Holbrook pondered the possibilities for
the duration of the drive home, mostly fretting that Heathgate was
privy to Miss Worthington's secrets, and taking advantage
accordingly.

On the one hand, Heathgate had no need to coerce a decent
woman into his bed, on the other, rumor was, his lordship lacked
sufficient conscience not to.

Holbrook let himself into his study, lost in thought. At first he
didn't see the man sitting on a cushioned window bench, but when
the fellow cleared this throat, Holbrook glanced up.

"Jennings," he said, nodding with the briefest of smiles. "I see
you've helped yourself to the brandy. Am I advised to do likewise?"

"A tot wouldn't go amiss," Jennings said, rising to stand before the
fire. He was a handsome man—as tall as Holbrook, but dark where
David was fair. Jennings, however, had perfected the art of looking
forbidding. When he chose to, Thomas Jennings could be surprisingly charming, an aspect of him all the more interesting for the
contrast it made with his usual demeanor.

Holbrook had known Jennings for years, however, and knew that
in whatever guise—gracious, civil, or ruthless—Thomas Jennings was
at the very least, loyal.

"You have news for me?" Holbrook asked. He wanted a brandy
and for that reason denied himself the pleasure. Discipline was not so
much a habit as a hobby, and encounters with Thomas late at night
merited a clear head.

"I haven't news, so much as information, though I wish it weren't
my task to pass it along."

"You are too careful of my sensibilities, Thomas." Holbrook
leaned against a table near the window, leaving Thomas to bask in
the fire's heat. "What information?"

Rather than admit to any anxiety over Jennings's late night
report, David comported himself like a man who had all the time in
the world.

Which he did not have, as they both knew.

"I came across a rumor you should know about concerning Miss Worthington."

The table scraped back a few inches under David's weight. "This rumor also concerns the Marquess of Heathgate?"

"It does, tangentially." Thomas was choosing his words, and this did not bode well.

"Out with it."

"There's word in low places that Miss Worthington has inherited a brothel from a distant relation, and to perfect her title to it, she has to take on the responsibilities of the brothel's madam. Heathgate is said to be assisting her in this regard." Jennings made his report while appearing completely absorbed in the study of the fire. Thomas had once confessed to enjoying the sight of dancing flames the way some men enjoyed watching women promenade.

"That is an ugly rumor, Thomas. What facts have you to back it up?"

Jennings swirled his drink, took a delicate whiff, held it up to the firelight, while David's hip began to ache from the cold coming off the window.

"The facts are few, but what we do know is this: Until a few months ago, Heathgate knew nothing of Miss Worthington's existence. The young ladies, as you know, do not go about in society. Callista Hemmings did own a brothel here in London, a very exclusive place that continues in operation some months after her death—as you also are aware.

"Heathgate and Miss Worthington have been seen on the premises on at least one occasion. And I need not remind you both the Misses Worthington were Heathgate's houseguests at his estate in Surrey, that visit having been chaperoned by his mother."

Which had been some comfort when David had had Heathgate's party trailed to the wilds of Surrey, though no comfort at all when David realized some third party had also been interested in keeping the marquess's coach in sight.

"Why would the marchioness lend her presence to something as sordid as you are implying?" he asked, his mind buzzing with the ramifications should this rumor gain wider circulation. "And what aren't you telling me?"

"As you know, Miss Hemmings was a relation of the Worthingtons, though her immediate family had long since cut her off prior to her demise. It is also of note that if Miss Worthington were to inherit a profitable business, that might provide us a motive for whoever is bent on harming her."

Jennings's reasoning was sound, as usual. As always.

"We don't know somebody is trying to harm her."

Jennings's tone shifted from deferential to ironic. "Right. But you, yourself saw that the idiot in the park was spurring his 'runaway' horse right toward Miss Worthington, and I was the one to tell you Heathgate's coach was followed from London to Surrey by a man on horseback carrying rifle and shot. You are aware as well that the cause of the fire at her house—in the middle of a damp night—was never discovered. Heathgate's man Brenner sniffed around the entire block and every tavern for a mile in any direction and came up empty handed."

All damnably true. David gave up on his hobby and poured himself a drink, but rather than joining Thomas before the fire, he evicted the cat from the seat behind his desk and appropriate the warmed cushion.

"Could Heathgate be orchestrating these incidents to somehow get his hands on the business?"

The cat stropped itself against Thomas's boots then hopped onto the desk, skidding a few inches on a stack of reports from David's land agent in Kent.

Thomas finished his drink, then tilted the fire screen back a few inches to shake drops of brandy on the flames.

"Heathgate might be the author of Miss Worthington's ill fortune, but his personal worth matches your own, and that doesn't include the holdings of the marquessate. Why would a wealthy man scheme to get his hands on a brothel? In the first place, he commands plenty of willing attention from the ladies without paying for it. In the second, he could buy any damned brothel he wanted with his pocket change."

All woefully true. "What about the younger brother? Lord Andrew's in a close orbit around Heathgate these days. Maybe he resents the marquess's consequence or has a gambling problem?"

Jennings prowled across the room to set his empty glass on the sideboard, then leaned a hip on David's desk and scratched the cat's chin. Callista had liked Thomas, and Thomas had liked Callista. More than that, David had not wanted to know.

"The younger brother, Lord Andrew, is the current heir, so you'd think, if anything, he might be trying to end his brother's life. Nonetheless, this family did not expect to inherit the title, and I don't think either of the brothers really wants it. If Lord Andrew is in a close orbit anywhere, it's around Miss Astrid."

Well, blast and perdition. David had missed that.

"She's not even out of the school room, for God's sake." But who was David, to decide what the Worthingtons should and shouldn't be doing with their social lives? He was no one to them, no one at all— and might always have to remain in that posture.

"I noticed this evening that Heathgate's men are still parked on my doorstep," David said as the cat made a half-hearted swat at Jennings's hand. "Any luck getting a peek at Callista's will?"

Jennings took a white quill pen and began to tease the cat. "We're working on that. She used a small, family-owned business of solicitors, and while they are marginally decent, they won't be as careful as a more prominent firm might be. I can't imagine their reputation will be flattered if news of this situation begins to make the rounds, assuming the rumors are true."

The cat caught the quill in its claws, looking comically surprised to have wrested the prize from Jennings's grasp. Jennings slipped the feather free of the cat's paws and set it down on the other side of the blotter.

The cat yawned, reminding David that he, too, was tired. "Callista once threatened to leave her damned business to me. I treated it as a jest, which probably hurt her feelings." Because Callista, despite all appearances to the contrary, had been a sweet and generous woman. Too sweet, and too generous.

"The Pleasure House is profitable," Jennings said. "There are worse investments."

"Some man of business you are. Every penny earned in that trade takes a toll off a man's reputation, regardless of his station. Funds, we can replace, but one's good name—"

Thomas glanced at the clock, and from him, that single flick of his gaze was the equivalent over others taking out their gold watch, flipping it open, and studying it at length.

"Thomas, I have a sneaking suspicion your rumors are true, and Miss Worthington was driven to accept this bequest because her household coffers were empty. That is my fault, though I have yet to ascertain how to rectify the situation without causing difficulties. I will puzzle on this, though I hope it wraps itself up damned soon."

Jennings regarded him with a hint of a smile as the cat rose and padded across the desk, then paused, likely to contemplate exactly where on David's evening finery cat hairs would make the most telling statement.

David scooped the cat onto his lap and finished his tirade. "I am sick of slipping out of my own house dressed as a footman, and skulking around London after the marquess and his lady love. And one more thing," he added, as cat's claws sank into his thigh.

Jennings shoved off the desk. "Yes?"

"I saw Riverton at the theatre tonight in the company of a lovely, petite, if slightly brittle blonde whom I believe to be Lady Edith Hamilton, widow without fortune. The woman regarded Heathgate with open bitterness—or perhaps regarded Heathgate and Miss Worthington with bitterness. I'd like to know what grudge she carries. Hell hath no fury, and all that. What's afoot could be nothing more complicated than an amatory triangle, and the whole issue of the brothel is beside the point. I cannot think

Lady Edith is in happy circumstances if she's consorting with Riverton."

"I'd missed that possibility," Jennings said. "Will that be all?"

"It will, Thomas. Thank you, as always. Seek your bed and keep me informed, please. Trouble is brewing for the Worthingtons, and that is the last thing I wanted to add to their lives when I came to Town. And Thomas? Mind you be careful. The whole situation leaves me uneasy, and you have a knack for being in the thick of trouble."

While the cat, rumbling happily in David's lap, shifted around in a slow circle, making sure to stomp David's cods with at least three paws.

Jennings's rare smile flickered into view as he thumped the cat once gently on the head. "I cannot recall a single time when, across the years and continents and oceans it has been my pleasure to travel with you, your intuition has ever been wrong."

"YOU FINGER that little diamond as if it's a noose," Riverton observed. "Do your sentiments regarding the marquess become murderous, or is it the young lady with him who has put such malice in your eyes?"

Edith Hamilton stopped toying with the gem nestled at her cleavage, stopped thinking of how the color matched Heathgate's eyes when he was displeased.

"The hour grows late, and I've changed my mind," Edith said. "You may stay up all night losing coin you cannot afford. I'd prefer to go home." Prefer to be anywhere but at Riverton's side.

They were in a hackney, for God's sake, the scent of horse hair and urine thick in the air, and Riverton wanted to make the rounds of every den of vice in Mayfair.

"One needs one's beauty sleep as one ages," he remarked mildly —meanly.

She let the comment pass, though Riverton was certainly showing signs of wear—signs of disease, if the rumors were to be believed. Then too, mercury treatments were expensive.

"Who is Heathgate's latest diversion?" Because to his lordship, they were all diversions. Edith nearly pitied the red-haired woman, for she'd had a decent look about her, and Heathgate would toss her over the same way he did every other female to end up in his bed.

"I'm not supposed to know," Riverton said, patting Edith's knee. The gesture made the punch she'd swilled at the theatre lurch in her belly. "But I do know. I know a great deal people don't give me credit for."

Riverton was arrogant—most titled men were arrogant, and their womenfolk no better—but his tone bore a nasty gleefulness that boded ill for both the lady and her escort.

"People might give your credit for your cleverness if you paid your bills, Riverton. Will you signal the jarvey to take me home, or must I pay the fare for you?"

Because that was clearly Riverton's plan. He was that much pockets to let, he would have her drop him on St. James Street first, and thus stick her with the fare.

Heathgate had never expected her to take a malodorous cab, had never quibbled over funds, had never treated her with less than perfect courtesy in public, and perfect consideration in private.

"You can afford the blunt," Riverton said. "I know you've earrings to match that necklace, and a bracelet as well. Enjoy Heathgate's largesse while you can."

The earrings were already gone, surrendered into the dubious keeping of Edith's solicitors, whom she suspected of fleecing her outrageously as they turned her assets into coin—the firm had been Riverton's suggestion, come to think of it.

"You know very well I'm finished enjoying anything from the marquess except his polite greetings." Riverton and all of society expected scorn from her toward the marquess, and yet, something in Edith still enjoyed merely watching Heathgate. Society could go to blazes as far as he was concerned, and that monumental self-assurance had been as appealing to Edith as the size of his various assets.

As fortifying. As comforting.

"Soon, the marquess himself will be finished," Riverton said. "Did you ever know a girl named Julia Ponsonby?"

Julia had never been a girl. She'd been one of those females born knowing, naughty, and unhappy with it, determined to snabble as high a title as possible—no mere viscount for her if the heir to a marquess came waltzing by.

"We made our come outs together," Edith said. "A restless woman, though I'm sure her family has missed her all these years."

"A woman with better taste in men than you've demonstrated my dear."

Riverton was Edith's present male company, for the evening anyway, though his jibe was intended in Heathgate's direction. The coach rattled along its stinking way for another two streets, while Edith made a decision.

She would sack the gang of thieves now handling her business, buy a cottage, and retire from a life that put her in hackneys late at night with the likes of Riverton. Even in these confines, his breath bore a stench she could not stomach.

"Riverton, what are you planning?"

"Justice," he said, all smugness gone from his tone. "Justice for me, and for those who can no longer seek it for themselves."

The notion that Riverton could be an instrument of justice might have been laughable, but for the cold—mad?—certainty in his tone.

"Leave me out of your crusades, please. I'm taking a repairing lease, before my own debts become ruinous."

Heathgate had forever been telling her to take her finances in hand. She even missed that about him, though Edith had never deluded herself that he was courting her. He had been blunt to a fault on that point.

"You must be carrying," Riverton observed. "A woman like you does not leave Town at this time of year unless she's made a significant mistake and must hide the consequences. You will miss what I have planned for your handsome marquess, but one understands your need for discretion."

Another pat to her knee, and she really was going to be sick. Alas, Edith was not carrying. She would never be carrying, something Heathgate had probably known when he'd deigned to consort with her.

Perhaps she should warn Heathgate he'd made an enemy, though Riverton was hardly a match for the marquess.

"Play whatever little games you must," she said, opening the slot that communicated with the driver. She gave the man her direction, then sat back, letting a chilly, marginally fresh breeze into the confines of the coach. "I'm going home to Dorset, there to stitch samplers and gossip in the churchyard."

Riverton laughed, a nasty, rusty sound Edith would not miss. This plan meant she'd have to sell the bracelet too, but she refused to part with the necklace. The gem was beautiful, she'd earned it, and when she was an old woman kept warm only by a handful of memories, she'd be glad she'd not sold Heathgate's beautiful necklace.

CHAPTER TWELVE

"What time did you say Heathgate would be here?" Astrid asked.

"Around two." Felicity turned so Astrid could do up the hooks on the back of her gown, only to find Astrid had flown to the window to peer into the street.

"Well somebody's carriage is pulling up, but it isn't Heathgate's," she said scampering toward the door.

"Astrid!" Felicity called her back. "Do me up before you go haring off, please."

"Oh, of course." Astrid made short work of Felicity's dress before dashing from the room.

Felicity went to the window in time to see David Holbrook alighting from a quietly elegant uncrested town coach. He spoke to his driver before opening the front gate, and the driver set the horses to ambling around the block.

A gentleman caller was not convenient, particularly not at this moment—and yet, Holbrook's arrival was interesting. Felicity put the last touches on her hair, and checked her appearance in a mirror before following Astrid down the stairs. Today, she'd dressed with particular attention in anticipation of going driving with Gareth, but the thought that two gentlemen might have occasion to admire her finery was pleasant nonetheless.

Astrid was admitting Holbrook into the foyer when Felicity came down the stairs.

"Mr. Holbrook, this is a pleasant surprise," Felicity said, offering him a respectful curtsey. He bowed with equal courtesy and came up smiling.

"The pleasure is mine, Miss Worthington, Miss Astrid. I hope I am not too forward, to be calling on you without warning this way? I was perfectly willing to leave my card if the timing wasn't convenient." His smile was that beaming, charming benevolence Felicity had seen once before, the one that suggested his soul glowed with a warmth his expression could only hint at.

"Let me take your hat and cape," Astrid offered, holding out her hands.

"We are delighted to have your company," Felicity said. Holbrook had a quiet, solid quality that appealed to the quiet, solid part of her. Unfortunately, she couldn't imagine ever doing more than liking him.

Holbrook was glancing around the entryway, trying to be discreet.

"This is a lovely house," he remarked as Felicity led him to the parlor and Astrid—with a timely display of maturity—ducked back to the kitchen to fetch the tea.

"This used to be a lovely house." If the man was fortune hunting, he'd best be aware the Worthingtons had nothing to offer. "Now it's a little worn, though Mrs. Crabble battles relentlessly to restore it to its former grandeur. We're comfortable here, though." Particularly now that the marquess's personal army had put the place to rights.

"The neighborhood is pleasant," Holbrook said, though he had to know there were more pleasant neighborhoods for families with more pleasant finances. "The park would be even more pleasant."

"You are about to invite us to go driving with you."

Holbrook's smile became muted, retreating mostly to his mismatched eyes. Despite those eyes, he was a handsome man, handsomely attired.

"I am found out. The park beckons, as does your company."

"You should smile more often, Mr. Holbrook," Felicity said as Astrid reappeared with the tea tray.

"Perhaps," Astrid said as she set the tray down, "Mr. Holbrook needs a reason to smile. Shall you pour, Felicity?" Felicity watched as Astrid took her seat on the settee, close to Mr. Holbrook, but not quite touching. The china on the tray all matched, another indication of improved circumstances, though it was merely Jasperware.

"Astrid, why don't you do the honors?" Pouring out would give Astrid something to do besides aggravate their guest.

"I would smile," Mr. Holbrook said as he watched Astrid arrange the tea cups, "were you ladies to accept my invitation to go driving."

"Oh, that would be lovely," Astrid crowed, replacing the lid to the teapot with a loud *plink*! "I'll get my bonnet—"

Astrid was halfway off the sofa before Felicity could catch her eye.

"Though first, perhaps we should finish our tea," Astrid said.

"Unfortunately, Mr. Holbrook, my afternoon is already promised to another, though I appreciate the invitation." Felicity expected Astrid to expire from frustration, but her sister seemed to understand that for Astrid to go driving with the gentleman alone would not do.

"Perhaps another day?" Holbrook asked as he accepted his tea from Astrid.

"Perhaps," Felicity demurred as the sound of carriage wheels halted before their gate.

"Uh-oh," Astrid said, popping up half-way through preparing Felicity's tea. "Heathgate is here." She went to the window and reported over her shoulder. "He's driving a pair of handsome bays today. I don't think I've seen this team before." Astrid was out of the parlor without a parting curtsey, leaving Felicity equal parts embarrassed and amused.

Holbrook set down his tea untasted, a reflection of manners, doubtless because Felicity had not been served. "Lord Heathgate is your regular driving partner?"

"He is my escort for today." Had the question been about her availability in general, and not merely for outings to the park? She sensed Holbrook wanted to interrogate her further, but the sound of Gareth's voice in the foyer spared her.

"Felicity!" Astrid called with an excess of cheer. "Look who's here!"

Heathgate loomed in the doorway, looking coldly beautiful, and entirely unhappy to see their guest. Holbrook rose and offered him a perfectly correct bow.

"Lord Heathgate."

Gareth nodded, barely civil. "Holbrook, I thought you were rusticating."

"My lord!" Felicity remonstrated, surprised at his rudeness.

Holbrook smiled—a smile unnervingly devoid of charm. "I have plenty to occupy me in Town, at least for the present."

Why don't you be about it, Gareth's expression suggested, which was brilliant, when Felicity hadn't had a caller in ages, and Astrid was taking in every word.

"Town does have its appeal," Gareth responded, "such as the opportunity to take a lovely woman out for a drive."

"My very own thought," Holbrook said, "though I see you've beaten me to the invitation, and my presence has become *de trop*. I will take my leave, Miss Worthington, Miss Astrid, and thank you for a pleasant visit. Perhaps on a future call, my timing will be more *opportune*."

Amid more proper bowing and curtseying, he took his leave, though the occasion left Felicity with the realization that both men wore a similar fragrance: rich, exotic, and spicy. Heathgate's choice tended toward sandalwood, while Mr. Worthington's leaned in the same direction but included a hint of floral subtleties.

"Astrid," Felicity said, shooting Gareth a warning look, "would you be so kind as to take the tea tray back to the kitchen?"

Astrid, after one glance at Gareth's scowl, picked up the tray and took her leave.

"You have frowned my sister into submission. That is no small feat."

Gareth had the door closed and his arms around Felicity before the words were out of her mouth.

"What was Holbrook doing here?" he asked as he buried his lips against Felicity's neck.

"I've missed you too," Felicity said, for it was the truth. "Mr. Holbrook paid a perfectly correct social call, and followed up on the invitation he issued when we met him at the ball. If he was up to more than that, you will have to query him directly. Shall I get my bonnet and wrap?"

Or should she do as she'd prefer and linger in his embrace?

His arms slipped away and he took a step back. "Soon. We need to talk about tomorrow."

For once, Felicity did not want to *talk*. Gareth still looked tired and harried to her, perhaps even a trifle gaunt, and she wanted to cling to him.

"We can have this discussion in the sunshine and fresh air. Will I be coming back here after our drive?"

"I don't know."

Felicity regarded his reflection in the mirror as she settled a pretty green toque on her head. "Gareth, what do you *want* to do with me?"

He flashed her a grin of such pure, wolfish lust, she couldn't help but feel a thrill of alarm—and pleasure.

"Besides that, which we will get to in a couple days." Less than two days, really. Forty-five hours and—she glanced at the clock—twenty minutes, give or take.

"Perhaps we could make our plans en route?"

"Fair enough." Felicity would have swung her cloak over her shoulders, but Gareth took it from her grasp, draped it around her, and stepped in close to tie the frogs.

Felicity bore up under his manners, even when he lingered a moment to kiss her cheek.

"This is new, too," he said, stroking a hand glancingly over her chest. He withdrew his hand before his fingers glided over her breast.

"The cloak is new." That her finery was a result of funds received from her cousin's brothel only diminished her enjoyment of it more than a little.

"Shall we be off then?"

"We are fortunate in our weather today," Felicity remarked as Gareth settled beside her—close beside her—on the bench of a phaeton. What did it say, that she was reduced to platitudes with him, when they had only hours left to be together?

"In our weather, yes, but not so your recent company," Gareth groused. "My men told me Holbrook has not been in Town for the past several days, and then he pops up on your doorstep. Do not get into a carriage with him, Felicity, and tell Astrid she is forbidden to do so as well."

Felicity treated him and his commands to a trenchant silence.

He sighed a put-upon male sigh. "I am *asking* you ladies to deny him an opportunity to whisk you away to parts unknown. Your cooperation with this request would be appreciated."

Gareth was making an effort, at least. For her. "I wouldn't let Astrid go anywhere with any man alone, except perhaps you or Andrew. As for me, I will respect your request until such time as you're satisfied that I am safe."

"Thank you," Gareth replied, sounding more pained than grateful. "Now, about Mother's at home tomorrow." He paused to feather the vehicle around a flower seller's wares, a moment of rare, colorful fragrance among the street's other offerings. "You are to give me a clear set-down, if you please. This will be difficult, because you don't want to insult your hostess, but you do want to insult her son. Can you manage, or should we plan something specific?"

He'd discussed the Latin names for intimate body parts in the same brisk, businesslike tones. How she wished...

"I can manage." To offer Gareth insult before his peers would break her heart. "I don't relish the prospect, though."

This earned her another smile, not quite as buccaneering as the previous version.

"Felicity, I will know you don't mean it, and you will know you don't mean it. You mustn't let this subterfuge trouble you. By next week, Society will have found plenty of fresh game to dine on. It means nothing."

"I know." To him her set down would mean nothing, Edith Hamilton meant nothing, his title meant nothing. "Gareth, is there no other way I can secure the income from that brothel?"

He drew the coach to a halt right in the middle of the street to allow an elderly crossing sweeper time to complete his task.

"It would not matter, Felicity, if your objective was to secure the income from your business or not. You must be seen to spurn my advances in a convincing, public manner. Gentlemen, walk on." The horses obliged, though Felicity noted the sweeper had not gathered up all evidence of the previous team's passing.

"I will decline your advances," she said as they rolled through the crossing, "because you say I must."

"Certainly, you must. Beyond a certain point, no matter how correctly we behave in public, if we continue to spend time together without there being a betrothal announcement, you will be assumed to have surrendered your virtue to me. I don't think you want that," he finished with surprising gentleness.

"I do not want to hurt you. Not even fictionally."

"Love," Gareth said quietly, "you will hurt me if you *don't* do this. I could not bear to see your reputation in tatters, your company limited to your sister and your servants, your hope for a decent future turned to bitterness. You deserve more, Felicity."

The marquess, with his calculation and lectures had departed, leaving Felicity on the bench with the man she loved, and would not hurt for the world.

She wanted to rail at him that the company of her sister and her servants had been more than adequate for the past five years, but she knew what Gareth was trying to do: He was trying to preserve for her the hope—ephemeral, but real—that she would someday have good companions, as Lady Heathgate did. That she would someday have gentlemen callers who took her driving, as David Holbrook seemed inclined to do. That she would someday see her sister happily wed.

Did a gallant knight ever bring his lady anything more precious than hope?

Gareth flicked his whip at a hovering pigeon, sending the bird flapping away into the trees. "Stop brooding, Miss Worthington. Will you have dinner with me?"

He was apologizing for their quarrel, and his charm tried her composure far more effectively than his difficult moods.

"I would enjoy that, Gareth."

The more memories with which to break her heart, the better. Truly, being in love was a sort of sickness of mind and heart.

Gareth allowed the horses to complete their circuit of the park, but when they regained the street, he put them into a brisk trot, and was soon escorting Felicity through his back gardens.

"May we linger here?" she asked. Behind his house, the walled garden was sheltered and private. Bulbs of every description were putting on a show of color that begged to be appreciated. Daffodils, narcissus, tulips, hyacinths... Whoever had planted this garden had intended for it to be enjoyed.

"Let me alert Cook to the addition of a guest for dinner. You don't mind waiting out here?"

"I will enjoy it."

And she did. The sun was warm, the air redolent with the scent of daffodils, and the scenery lovely. In a few more weeks, lilacs and early roses would bloom in profusion, rhododendrons would blaze. Somebody had loved this garden, and were it hers, she would love it too.

As Felicity found a gazebo in a shaded back corner, she had the thought that she might be Gareth's mistress for a while and put off

the parting that loomed so close at hand. In the moral labyrinth that
was his sense of honor, he'd likely be appalled if she suggested such a
thing.

As appalled as she'd be, when Mr. Brenner or some equally
discreet, well paid intermediary presented her with a tasteful, expensive parting gift.

She bent to sniff the gentle, sweet fragrance of a daffodil—the
floral symbol of chivalry. Better by far to love a garden, than to love
the passionate, difficult, dear man who owned it.

~

WHEN GARETH RETURNED, he found Felicity sitting on a
bench, knees drawn up, her expression thoughtful.

"You designed this garden, didn't you?"

How could she know such a thing? And could she look any more
lovely and sad, perched on a simple bench? He took a seat on the
bench, not touching, so he might fix the picture of her in his mind
more firmly.

"The design is mine. As a younger man, I fancied myself the next
incarnation of Capability Brown, only better than he, of course. I
loved to be outdoors, though even in my family, if I'd announced my
intention to become a gardener, it would have raised eyebrows. So I
designed gardens, and when nobody was looking I planted a few."

"You should resume your hobby, Gareth," Felicity said, twirling a
lemony daffodil between her fingers. "You have talent, and correct
me if I'm wrong, but I think you were happy, digging here in the dirt.
How old were you?"

What odd advice, and yet he'd situated all of his offices, estate
rooms and personal chambers where they would afford him a view of
the gardens. Why hadn't he noticed this earlier?

"I would have been fifteen when this garden was put in. Somebody has done a good job with it, though. Since then, everything has
clearly been dug up, divided, fertilized. A garden is a lot of work."

She closed her eyes, and tipped her face up to the afternoon sun, probably courting a crop of freckles and heedless of her peril.

Gareth tried to imprint that image on his heart, too. "We have some time before dinner is served. How would you like to spend it?"

"You are trying to make amends for our quarrels, but this charm of yours... I have defense against it. None."

Is that what he'd been up to? "I never mean to quarrel with you. Your silences shred my defenses, Felicity."

He'd meant to please her with a confession—a man could make confessions to a woman from whom he'd soon part—but she looked more sad than pleased.

"I would like to sit out here with you, maybe on a blanket, and talk, I know this is no small boon I request of you. Your staff will likely remark it, that we're spending time in a manner wholly unproductive of anything except, possibly, a greater understanding of one another."

"I would like that too." He'd *love* it, though her suggestion was as ill-advised as it was brave. "I'll be back."

When he returned a few minutes later, he had a thick quilt folded over his shoulder, and a small wicker hamper in his hand. "Miss Worthington, choose your spot."

When she had proper suitors—regular, proper suitors—they would address her as such.

She took the request seriously, picking out a place in dappled sun, the trees around it having not finished leafing out. A hedge starting to flower ran around three sides, making her choice—at ground level—quite private. She led him over to her preferred location, and he spread the blanket, handed her down, then joined her.

He started to tug at his boots, then paused. "Do you mind if I take off my boots?"

"I won't mind if you don't mind me doing likewise," she said, unlacing her half-boots. When they were in their stocking feet, Gareth realized that callow-swaining was something with which he had no recent experience.

"Now what?" he asked, leaning his weight back on his arms.

Felicity smiled at him, that soft, benevolent, glowing smile. Then she curled herself up to rest her head on his thigh.

"Now," she said, sighing and closing her eyes, "we have a nice visit."

He smoothed a hand over her cheek, feeling a welling tenderness for his favorite spinster, and inconvenient envy for the swains who would court her properly.

"What do we visit about?"

"Suppose you tell me about your father? You never talk about him, but I gather he was a fine gentleman."

"I have shied away from thoughts of my father," he said, tracing the feathery contours of her hairline. "He was, as you say, a fine gentleman. But I am curious why you characterize him thus?"

"Because Lady Heathgate loved him so, and hasn't found his like in almost ten years. I doubt she's even thought to look. I also know he was a fine gentleman because of how you and Andrew are with each other, and how you have both turned out. And you miss him."

"That, I do," Gareth agreed, plucking a stem of grass and tickling her nose.

She batted his grass flower aside. "What about your older brother? Stop that, Gareth, or I shall be forced to take stern measures."

"Merciful saints, not those again," he teased back, then fell silent for a moment before answering her question. "I missed Adam the most, of all of them. He was a lot like Andrew, a more blithe spirit than I, even to the point of lightheartedness. He looked like Andrew too, not quite as hulking as me."

"You are not hulking, Gareth. You are more muscular than Andrew."

"Adam was a peacemaker, full of charm and kindness," Gareth went on, accepting her chiding. "When he died, I was at an age when an older brother was a boon. There are certain things having to do with how to go on in life that an older brother is ideally suited to convey. Adam had a grace, an ease. He could explain to me how to deal with losing at cards, how to parlay with a lady of easy virtue, how to treat an overindulgence of spirits, and he did it with such a generous nonchalance I never felt like the gauche stripling I was."

"And you provided that same guidance to Andrew," Felicity guessed, shielding her eyes to peer up at him.

She had the most beautiful, sincere eyes. "I tried, but to be honest, I avoided Andrew after the accident. He would come down from university on holidays, and I knew he wanted to spend time with me, but I was too busy, or off trolling at a house party, until he gave up on me."

To put that history into words caused an ache in the vicinity of Gareth's heart, but gave him a goal, too.

"I don't think Andrew gave up on you so much as he grew up on you," Felicity murmured. "Do you and he ever talk about the accident?"

"We've mentioned it in passing to one another occasionally. He blames himself for not being able to save more than just Mother. I don't bring it up because I don't want to cause him hurt."

"And he doesn't want to cause you hurt, so the whole topic sits there like a lame horse," Felicity said, rubbing her cheek against his thigh. "You make a very firm pillow."

"Well, then here," Gareth laid himself out flat on his back at right angles to her, so she might make a pillow of his stomach. "Better?"

"Marginally." She said in tones suggesting she was being diplomatic. "So what happened that the boat capsized?"

The sky above was a beautiful canvas of blue and white, the breeze scented with flowers, and Felicity's voice a melody against Gareth's body. In nearly a decade of being haunted by the accident, he had discussed the details of the accident with no one, and yet he wanted to answer Felicity's question now.

Needed to.

"I have never questioned Andrew about this, but there was, of course, an inquest. The court concluded it had simply been a matter

of sudden rough seas and high winds overcoming a pleasure vessel
that should never have been out in such weather, and certainly not so
far from shore. What the court discreetly omitted from its report was
that an enormous quantity of alcohol had been consumed, at least by
those gentlemen older than Andrew, and the family had been quarreling bitterly for much of the day before this outing."

"Was that why you remained ashore?" Gareth felt Felicity rolling
to her side so she faced his feet. Her change in position allowed him
to stroke her hair, teasing the occasional pin from its assigned
location.

"I don't know why I stayed on shore," Gareth said softly. "I've
puzzled over it at great length. I am not a good sailor, for one thing,
and being very proud at that age, I did not want to be the butt of the
ribbing I would get. I was also quite disgusted, as only young people
can be, with the inebriation and posturing of my elders. And finally, I
wanted badly to be alone. Even then, I had little tolerance for being
told what to do, what to wear, and with whom to dance. My parents
cut me a wide berth, but my uncle and my grandfather tried to
improve upon me constantly."

Felicity pushed up onto her elbows and regarded Gareth with a
frown.

"You describe the family gathering from hell. What was everybody quarreling about?"

"Family matters." He laid his forearm over his eyes, blocking out
the lovely sky. Beneath the perfume of the flowers, he caught a hint of
lavender. "They quarreled about me, about Andrew, about investments, about my cousin's education, about whether the little creature
who spooked the horse was a hare or a rabbit, about where to gather
for the holidays and which horse won what race eight years ago,
about anything and everything. My own family was not much of one
for undignified discourse, but grandfather was a shouter, and I
believe my uncle and my cousin became shouters in sheer self-
defense."

"I am forming a picture in mind," Felicity said, "of the young man you were: Shy, determined, smart, hardworking and serious—a fellow who loved peace and quiet, flowers, and order. A fellow who would sit for a family portrait obediently enough, though he'd rather be off inspecting the home farm or reading an improving tome when he wasn't—cautiously, and under the protective watch of his older brother—dipping his toe in the tamest of vices young men indulge in."

She stopped, though Gareth realized that was kindness on her part. She'd described a young man completely unprepared for the cruelty and artifice of titled society. Something turned over in his mind and in the center of his chest.

Viewed through Felicity's eyes, that young fellow deserved not scorn, but compassion. He deserved to be respected for surviving the tempest of Society's cruelty, for making his way to shore in any condition at all.

"You," Felicity said, sitting up and lifting a leg over Gareth's belly, "have endured much." She snuggled down onto his chest, right, exactly where he wanted her. He settled his arms around her and kept his eyes closed, the better to feel the glory and comfort of her in his embrace.

"This recitation of yours makes me feel protective of you, sir, and quite angry with all those relatives who left you alone to face the lions."

"I suppose I was angry at them too," Gareth said, his hand cradling the back of her head.

"You *suppose?*" she shot back. "They left you to face an inquest, shoulder the title, parent Andrew, comfort your mother, and learn how to deal with the predators of Polite Society, when all you should have been doing was designing gardens. If they weren't dead, I'd be tempted to see to it myself."

He smiled and did not open his eyes. Felicity would make somebody a wonderfully protective mother, and a very loyal wife, but not him. Never him.

"You are so fierce," he murmured, leaning up to kiss her briefly, because for all the misery of their discussion, he also felt curiously happy. "What about you? Are you angry with your parents for dying?"

Felicity nuzzled his throat, then sighed. Her hair was gathering the afternoon sun, warming Gareth's fingers as he loosened her braided bun.

"I was furious, particularly with my mother, because I was quite young at the time. She was an unfashionably involved mother, spending far more time with me than was thought wise. My father left my upbringing to her, of course, but I don't think he disapproved."

Felicity young, motherless, and angry. How he wished their paths had crossed sooner—much sooner. "Was your parents' marriage a love match?"

"Good heavens, no." She fell silent, thinking thoughts Gareth was not brave enough to probe. "They came to have affection for one another, but my mother's general approach toward my father was gratitude that he would have her, for she brought only a dowry to the match, whereas he had the title. She made no demands on him whatsoever, and went out of her way to make sure I knew what a worthy man he was."

"Was he? Worthy, I mean?"

The answer mattered more than it should. The fellow was long dead, but his inability to manage was indirectly responsible for the dubious manner in which Felicity had come to Gareth's doorstep.

"Like another young man we recently discussed, he resented being told whom to marry, where to live, when to produce a son, and so forth. He had a rebellious streak he did not outlive," she concluded. "I do know he came to regret how little effort he'd put into his marriage. He told me once, shortly before he died, he'd wasted the love that could have grown between him and my mother, trading it in for reckless pride. He made poetic statements like that frequently, but he didn't live a particularly poetic life."

"Were you upset to see him go?" Gareth asked, sliding his hands down along Felicity's rib cage.

"Of course, I was. He was the only parent I had left, and he wasn't a bad man or a bad father. Fortunately, it took some time for the financial ramifications of impending escheat to manifest—we had an aunt of last resort, at the time—or I probably would not have been able to cope at all."

An aunt of last resort, and Felicity had been comforted by that.

"Which means you have, what, another year before missing heirs are disinherited in favor of the crown? I really don't understand why you and Astrid weren't granted something at least during your minorities." And why hadn't he put Brenner on the question already? "Do you want me to look into this, Felicity? It would be no trouble."

No trouble at all, and give him an excuse to remain at least marginally involved in her life.

"Gareth, when has anyone, *ever* succeeded in collecting a debt from the crown in a timely fashion?"

Particularly with the king's sanity in doubt, and Wales spending like a sailor on shore leave. "Point taken."

"What's the sigh about?"

Lying on his chest, even with her eyes closed she could no doubt feel as well as hear his sighs—as he could feel hers.

"Self-recrimination," Gareth admitted. "If I'd had the foresight to chase down the crown's agent managing your father's estate, you might have seen some revenue by now, but it simply didn't occur to me." Though it wasn't likely—but why hadn't he tried?

Felicity raised up to glower down at him. "And I should have married any man who offered while my father was still alive, and petitioned the crown to pass the title on to my firstborn male child? Lived and traded on the expectations generated by such a farce?"

She looked both fierce and delectable, silhouetted against the sky, her hair tumbling down her back.

"I am content with what is, Gareth, and I am not sure father's estates were even realizing a profit at the time of his death, suggesting those efforts might have so much wasted effort. My legs are going to sleep."

She shifted, so she was sitting on him, then treated him to a frown worthy of a seven-year-old hellion's governess. "Oh, you bad man."

"What?" He was a bad man. It had never troubled him much before he'd met her.

"I saw that look in your eye, you rapscallion. You had an impure thought," she accused, hoisting herself and her voluminous skirts off of him.

He levered up on one elbow. "Only just the one, and more an appreciative thought than an impure thought."

"Wicked, wicked, bad man," Felicity told him rubbing her feet. "Scandalous, shameful, scoundrelous bad man."

Gareth smoothed her hair back, thinking this was one of her finer, dearer, scolds. "Is scoundrelous even a word?"

"When you're in the vicinity, it should be. I need to get up, but my legs are not awake yet."

Gareth surged across the blanket to tackle her onto her back, and crouched above her. "No running off yet."

"I can see the time has come for those stern measures."

"That it has," he replied, before he sternly kissed her senseless, and had her panting and laughing on the blanket in broad daylight.

CHAPTER THIRTEEN

Felicity stretched and yawned, nagged by a sense that the day she faced held something onerous. Yesterday had been so lovely, with memory upon memory to treasure. Gareth had given her hours of his time, and a touching amount of himself as well. They'd lazed around in the back garden on a blanket, shared a quiet private dinner, played cribbage after dinner, and taken a moonlit stroll through the same garden.

The day had been different from any other time they'd spent together, rich in both affection and conversation, but also in self-reflection. Felicity came to see how her father's lifestyle and untimely death had robbed her of a girl's most fanciful years, forcing on her a practicality that might not have been completely true to her nature.

And Gareth had been so quiet, unusually so for a man who never seemed to stop moving, and *doing*. The sexual tension had been present, as it always was with them, but subdued by something sweeter.

Romance. Gareth had given her a few hours of romance. Or they had given it to each other, a precious parting gift to warm her heart for years to come.

And then, like a rumble of thunder on the horizon, her agenda for the day emerged into her awareness: Today was the day she would publicly end her association with the Marquess of Heathgate. She would insult him, humiliate him if possible, leaving no doubt further association with him was unwelcome.

Drat him and his stratagems. Drat him for his unwillingness to risk her reputation one iota more than circumstances required. Drat him for his very chivalry.

Felicity had resolved to roll over and go back to sleep when Astrid came along, chirping determinedly about an outing to the park after breakfast. Felicity capitulated, because spending the morning cooped up in the house would only exacerbate her sense of anxiety—and Astrid had been trying so hard to be good lately.

They walked to the park arm in arm, footmen trailing closely, and the day promising to be every bit as lovely as the previous one. As they gained the duck pond, Felicity looked up to see David Holbrook sauntering down the path.

"Hello, Miss Worthington, Miss Astrid. Glorious morning, isn't it?"

Astrid waved enthusiastically from where she was tossing bread crumbs on the water several yards down the bank. Ducks and geese honked at her feet, and made quite a racket, splashing out into the water in pursuit of the bread.

"She is the picture of feminine innocence, is she not?" Holbrook asked, watching Astrid with a quiet smile.

"Mr. Holbrook, are you entertaining ideas about my sister?" Felicity tried to keep amusement in her voice—enough to convey that such a notion couldn't possibly be serious, not so much as to insult the man.

His expression when he answered her was all gravity. "While I am sure Miss Astrid is lovely in every regard, she is, in the first place, not yet receiving gentleman callers, and in the second, not appealing to me in the manner such attentions require. And," he added, looking abruptly quite severe, "if you are wondering if I am harboring *ideas* regarding your own person, be assured I am not."

Felicity's smile faded in surprise. "That is an interesting declaration." And more of a relief than it should be.

He further startled her by bestowing on her a warm, thoroughly transforming smile. "I rather surprised myself by making it. I do not want you to worry that you or your sister might have to fend off my unwelcome designs. You ladies appear to me to be without the protection of a properly motivated male relation. Having been raised myself with some deficits of familial support, I am concerned to see you thus."

Felicity puzzled through that, and searched his face for nefarious innuendo. "You are offering friendship?"

"If ever a friend you need," he replied handing Felicity a card engraved with his address—one street off Grosvenor Square, no less. He turned from her, distracted by a commotion along the bank the pond. Astrid was flapping the empty bag of crumbs over the hissing and weaving head of a particularly cantankerous gander.

"Try flapping that bonnet, Miss Astrid. If you're lucky, he'll snatch it out of your hand," Holbrook called.

"Astrid Worthington, you will do no such thing. That is a fine, serviceable bonnet, and until such time as it no longer fits, you will not use it on helpless waterfowl."

Astrid grinned at them, and fingered the bow under her chin, but left her bonnet on her head. Shooing the gander off, she rejoined her sister on the walkway.

"Mr. Holbrook, how pleasant to see you again. I have missed your company, among that of my other companions in the park."

"Your other companions?"

"She means that lot," Felicity said, gesturing to the honking, flapping crowd on the bank. "They know she brings them treats, so she is a great favorite with them."

"I am to be compared to a goose?" Holbrook mused. "It won't be the first time, I'm afraid. Shall we stroll, ladies, or would you like to linger by the water?"

The pond, while picturesque, bore a certain scent that did not agree with Felicity's breakfast. Then too, the daffodils here were all past their prime.

"We should stroll," Felicity said, before Astrid could take charge of matters. "Astrid and I have a call to pay this afternoon, and cannot tarry here with her many admirers much longer." Though she wanted to tarry amid the sunshine and greenery, despite all the misgivings Gareth had about Mr. Holbrook.

"You look wistful, Miss Worthington," Holbrook said, offering them each an arm. "Are your duties so burdensome?"

"Her duties are burdensome," Astrid said. "She must disentangle herself from old Heathgate today, and in the home of the man's own mother. We'll be relieved when we've sent him on his way."

If Holbrook was surprised at that revelation, or at Felicity's gasp of indignation, he didn't show it. "And will *old Heathgate* accept his set-down with good grace, or will the situation become awkward?"

"Good grace," Astrid informed him cheerily. "He and Felicity have this planned to stifle the gossips. They actually rub along together quite well, though he simply won't suit, will he, Felicity? There's really nothing else for it."

"Astrid," Felicity said through clenched teeth, "*that is really quite enough.*"

"Miss Worthington," Holbrook addressed Felicity with a twinkle in his mismatched eyes. "When I spoke earlier, I referred to the burden a lack of family can bring. I see in your circumstances, family can also be a burden."

Bless him for his gallantry, though Astrid didn't deserve it. "Mr. Holbrook, you are entirely right. At this moment, having less family appeals quite strongly."

"Miss Astrid?" Holbrook prompted.

"I suppose I should not have said something so forward to Mr. Holbrook, Felicity, but with the way Heathgate acted yesterday, I didn't want Mr. Holbrook to think you were spoken for when you are not."

And never would be at this rate. Felicity closed her eyes, and leaned on Holbrook's supporting arm. And to think some people endured siblings by the dozen.

"Astrid, you were doing less harm before you attempted that apology. What am I to do with you?"

"Miss Astrid," Holbrook said, bringing them to the gate of the park and looking back over the lovely, green space, "I do not envy you the dressing down you're due for once your sister gets your home. I'd sooner face Barbary pirates unarmed in a high wind."

"I am sorry, Lissy," Astrid mumbled.

Holbrook surprised them both by reaching out and tweaking one of Astrid's blond curls from where it had escaped from the dreaded Ugly Bonnet.

"She knows you are, miss, but she has earned the right to sulk and glare and make you pay a bit, don't you think?" he suggested, smiling at Felicity as he spoke.

"I think," Felicity agreed, offering Astrid the barest smile.

Having apparently satisfied himself that they had exchanged an olive branch—an olive *twig*—Holbrook tipped his hat, bowed, and strode away.

GARETH DECIDED to walk the eight streets to Felicity's house. He'd watched from the corner of his eye as she'd navigated the social waters at Lady Heathgate's at home, and when she'd embarked on a tête-à-tête with two of his mother's most gossipy cronies, he'd known his term as a marital prospect had summarily ended.

Which should have been a relief.

He let himself into her back door, and found her in the kitchen preparing dinner. Wordlessly, he held out his arms to her, and without hesitation, she went to him.

"I hated doing that."

He kissed her temple, thinking of a cold spring night when this same kitchen had smelled of smoke and fear rather than freshly baked bread and lavender. "The deed is done, and I never felt a thing, thank you."

Felicity pressed her nose to his cravat while Gareth inhaled lavender and peace. "It wasn't as hard as I feared in some ways, and in others, it was harder, too."

He should have stepped back, instead he kissed her cheek. "What exactly did you say?"

"That I lacked the worldliness to take on a marital project of your, er, *proportions*, as you are too sophisticated, and your estates too well *endowed* for one of my retiring and reserved nature."

Gareth smiled at the ceiling, where pots hung gleaming from nails in the rafters. "Merciful saints. We don't suit because I'm too mighty a swordsman?"

"I gave them a version of the truth." Felicity slipped away, her smile forced. She went to the hob and poured a fresh pot, and Gareth considered her as she shared a cup of tea with him in her humble kitchen. She looked lovely in her old dress, flour dusting her hands, and she looked so *dear*.

It hurt; it hurt nigh unbearably, to think he would never again have the privilege of stopping by, letting himself in through her back door, and being offered a perfect cup of tea like any other adoring swain calling on his lady.

He had more wealth than most men could dream of, but there was something in this kitchen, something in this household, something in this *woman*, he would be forever impoverished without.

Felicity had hated maligning him in any fashion. He had hated forcing her to do it, and that was their version of common ground.

The silence stretched between them, comfortable, warm, and sad. Felicity eventually rose, took Gareth's empty mug from his hand, and leaned down to kiss the top of his head. He wrapped an arm around her waist and pulled her to him, pressing his face to her midriff.

"Are you worried about my swordsmanship tomorrow afternoon?"

"Not worried," Felicity replied, "More... I don't know. This time tomorrow night, I will be different. I will not be the person I am now, and the change is irrevocable. I think I see it as something like riding into my first battle. I will know things tomorrow I don't know now, and the knowledge will not necessarily make me happier."

Gareth rose at her words and steadied her—or himself—with a hand on each of her shoulders.

"Felicity, love..." He searched for the right words, words that would be honest, but comforting. "You will be different, that much is true, but you will not be *less*. You will be *more*."

She looked unconvinced. "And what about you, Gareth? If you do this with me, feeling as you do, will you be more as well, or will you be less?"

He framed her face while he offered her a kiss of more tenderness than he'd known he had in him. When she might have moved into his embrace, he stepped back.

"That is to remind you that this business we undertake tomorrow will be for your pleasure," he said, tapping her nose with an index finger. "Sleep well tonight, for you'll need your rest."

"See that you do likewise, Marquess of Too Much," Felicity said, beaming him one of those sudden, brilliant smiles. "For I plan on taking many stern measures with you."

"On that comforting assurance, I will take my leave," Gareth replied, grabbing his coat, and strolling out into the pleasant spring evening.

As he made his way home, he tried but failed to come up with a satisfactory answer to Felicity's question: If he made love to her, completing the destruction of her innocence but securing her future, if he allowed them both to create a memory as painful as it would be precious, if he engaged in intimate pleasure with a woman for financial reasons, would that make him something more or something less than the man she'd kissed, held, and greeted so warmly tonight?

A SOFT, incessant clicking woke Gareth before dawn, less than three hours after he'd finally dropped off to sleep the night before. *Sleet*. About the ugliest of the many varieties of ugly weather London offered, but typical of the season. Glorious spring weather one day, and a dirty reprise of the winter the next.

Today he would be Felicity's lover in fact, no longer merely her tutor in all the peripheral bed sports. The concept left him as unsettled now as it had four months ago. He craved intimate congress with her body with a cross-eyed, mindless lust he hadn't experienced since he'd been a university boy in a state of perpetual rut.

But he also treasured Felicity's womanly decency, that something about her that was fine and good and proper. The same something that in her eyes would be diminished—if not destroyed—by what they did today.

The room was freezing, so Gareth stirred up the fire, grabbed his blue velvet dressing gown from the foot of the bed, and went to the French doors leading to the balcony.

He stood for long minutes before rousing himself to put the morning, at least, to some use. Brenner had managed to find a copy of Callista's will, and Gareth had yet to actually read the damned thing, which lately had niggled at him, as details sometimes did.

So he rang for hot water and his morning chocolate, washed, dressed and shaved quickly and without assistance.

As he sat at his desk intending to hunt up Callista's will, he was assailed by the memory of Felicity, curled on top of him in the warm sunshine of his back garden. He'd never spent time like that with anyone, much less a lover. Their afternoon had been enchanted, imbued with a sense of peace and privacy that in some secret, wistful corner of his jaded heart, he knew would haunt him for the rest of his life.

He rose, considered pouring himself a drink regardless of the hour, and decided against it. His stomach was probably tentative because, for him, he had been drinking substantially more lately than was usual. He had no sooner started rifling the papers on his desk in search of Callista's will than somebody rattled his office door.

"Gareth, if you're in there, open up," came Andrew's none-too-cheerful voice.

Gareth obliged because Andrew was emphatically not an early riser. "You've made a night of it," Gareth observed with wry amusement. Andrew was unshaven, his cravat hung askew, and fatigue lined his handsome features.

"I have, and I've a craving for some of your finest," he said, throwing himself onto the couch with an air of dejection.

Gareth poured his brother a drink, and took it to him, then leaned back against the desk, crossed his arms, and waited for Andrew to start on his drink—and whatever else he needed to start on.

"I know you have a lot on your plate," Andrew said, tossing back the drink, "but I've a favor to ask."

"Ask." Andrew had never asked him for anything, at least not since he'd graduated and come into his own fortune. Andrew would always watch his brother's back, but Gareth was not to be afforded the same opportunity.

That privilege being, somehow, another casualty of the boating accident.

"I think it's time I did some traveling on the Continent," Andrew said, running a hand through damp hair. "What with the Corsican wreaking havoc, I've never had the chance, but if I avoid France and the Peninsula, I could take in some sights, see the capitals, that sort of thing."

As queer starts went, and rotten beginnings to difficult days, that would do nicely. "And the favor you have to ask of me?"

"Could you send someone down from time to time to check on Linden Hall?"

"This sounds serious, Andrew." Gareth shoved away from the desk to take his brother's empty glass. He put it on the sideboard and went to stand by a window, seeing the sleet had changed to a pattering rain.

"It isn't serious. It's simply time," Andrew said. "My education, you know, and all those charming foreign ladies, the great art, the food and drink, the sights. Might even hie on down to Egypt, take a boat up the Nile."

This had to do with a woman, very likely a married woman, or some female otherwise unavailable.

"I can't enjoy the thought of you leaving, Andrew." That Gareth's brother would announce plans to leave him, today, was too much. "What drives this decision?"

Andrew rose to retrieve his glass, stumbling a bit on the fringe of the carpet. "Take your pick, Gareth. I play around at lord of the manor between furious bouts of drinking and wenching here in Town. I am of no use to you in managing the estates. I am doomed to dance attendance on Mother and her cronies when she can't inveigle you into serving. I am, in short, leading a boring, pointless life. Maybe travel will help."

Andrew hated anything that put him in sight of open water, much less at sea.

"I often felt the urge to travel abroad when I first assumed the title. But travel for me then would have been an escape." *What are you running from?* "I will, of course, take the best of care of your properties, and if you want me to attorn for you in your absence, I can do that as well. I have a favor to ask too, however."

Andrew poured a shot, tossed it back, and sent Gareth a haunted look.

"Please delay your departure until the Worthingtons are safe," Gareth said, noting the wince crossing Andrew's features. "Felicity and I will meet with the solicitors tomorrow, and if all goes well, title to Callista's assets will be transferred shortly thereafter. If somebody is trying to stop the transfer, then their opportunity will thus be at an end. And if that's not the motivation for various incidents of mischief, I hope we soon know what it is."

Andrew poured yet another tot—though this one he did not so much as sip—and took his turn at the window surveying the weather. The day had turned nastier yet by virtue of a billowing wind that sent chilly gusts moaning down the chimney.

"I'll stay for a bit. Don't ask me to attend the ladies personally if it can be avoided. As you've said, the need for direct dealings between you and Felicity will soon be at an end."

"It's Astrid, isn't it? You are running from Astrid."

Andrew did not turn, but something that was probably intended to be a laugh escaped him.

"Astrid is formidable," he replied. "Don't think she's the sole reason I am inclined to travel. I like the girl exceedingly, and wish her many handsome, driveling beaus, with big incomes and small brains. She will twirl them all around her dainty finger and they'll never suspect a thing."

As Astrid likely suspected nothing of the effect she was having on Andrew. The notion brought concern for Gareth's brother, and—oddly—for the girl.

"She'll be hurt."

"She might be puzzled," Andrew conceded, turning from the window. "That will slow her down for about five minutes before she's on to the next conquest. Did you know she saw Holbrook again in the park before they came to Mother's?"

And thus the subject *changed*. Gareth took pity on his brother, and followed this gambit.

"No, I did not. Neither of the ladies said anything, but I expect Brenner will brief me on it when he shows up. He won't be here for another hour, so tell me what you know."

"Not much," Andrew said, crossing to the decanter, setting his full glass down and moving to the hearth. "Astrid said they went to feed the ducks, and there he was, out for a stroll. He walked with them briefly, long enough for Astrid to tell him you and Felicity were not honestly *interested* in one another, and Felicity would be giving you a public set-down to stifle growing speculation to the contrary."

"Merciful drunken saints," Gareth muttered, eyeing the dwindling contents of the decanter. "I spent a good half hour in Felicity's kitchen last night, and she never mentioned this. Astrid may have just given Felicity's enemy all he needs to destroy both sisters' futures."

Andrew smiled the first real smile Gareth had seen on that morning, a small, mostly private smile, but real.

"If that's Holbrook's plan, he is slow off the mark," Andrew said. "I've been out all night, and visited no less than two bordellos and three gaming hells, as well as my club. A certain topic has caught everyone's interest, and it isn't the true purpose behind your acquaintance with Miss Worthington."

"Bloody, rubbishing hell." Gareth returned Andrew's smile with a sheepish grin. "The idea was Felicity's."

"You wish it had been. Felicity's plan has worked. Your personal assets, your tireless *energy*, and your *prodigious imagination* regarding contractual matters were the talk of every venue last night. You wouldn't believe the number of women claiming they sympathize with poor Miss Worthington's concerns because you are quite a nice change of pace, but really, as a husband you'd be just *too much*. The men, of course, are wickedly envious that you're considered *too much* man by at least one pretty lady. If Felicity thought to spare you the humiliation of being jilted, she's done a bang-up job."

"A delightful job," Gareth replied, which did not explain the urge to hurl the decanter at the fire. "I am not a pathetic reject, but I am an object of ridicule."

"Not ridicule, Brother, but envy," Andrew assured him, his smile gaining a hint of commiseration. "Shall you come to darkest Africa with me?"

"Give me a moment to pack and say good-bye to my horse." *And a lifetime to say good-bye to Felicity.*

Andrew peered at him more closely, looking damnably sober, which suggested bad things about his habitual consumptions of spirits.

"You've been an object of gossip ever since you acquired the title.

What about those Dutch triplets, hmm? Even Prinny got in his digs about that one."

"The triplets were Danish; the twins were Dutch." The triplets—three young ladies with large breasts, big smiles, and small English vocabularies—had been more than five years ago, but God in heaven, what had he been thinking? No wonder Felicity's unwillingness to marry him had been so credible.

"I weary of this subject, Andrew. If you are to travel, you will need letters of introduction, proper documents, embassy contacts, and suitable bribes to ensure your safe passage. Tell me what I can do to help, and it shall be done. I'll look in on your estates myself," he added, realizing he'd never seen Linden Hall, and Andrew had owned the place for years.

"That won't be necessary," Andrew said, heading for the door. "If you go to Linden, Mother will want to come, and there's no telling how long she'll ensconce herself. Just send Brenner, and I'll be grateful."

"Andrew?"

Andrew stopped, his hand on the doorlatch, his back to Gareth. "Yes?"

"I really will miss you," Gareth said, squeezing his brother's shoulder. Everything in Andrew's posture gave warning he did not want to be dissuaded from this course, but it seemed to Gareth at least a gesture of affection was in order. He'd wasted so much on empty physical pleasures with women whose faces he could not recall, and here was his brother, suffering. "And if there's anything I can do...?"

He let the question hang, while Andrew flinched, shook his head, and walked away, closing the door with a solid click behind him.

The silence left behind was larger and lonelier than it had been before Andrew's arrival. Gareth would not have been surprised had his mother waltzed in and announced she'd become betrothed to some nabob, soon to decamp for the Orient. And then here he'd be, the possessor of one string of titles, much wealth, and a very tarnished reputation.

And now, recalling Felicity's parting words, he would be lucky not to be assigned the sobriquet Marquess of Misbehavior. He'd barely resumed his search for Callista's will when another knock disturbed him, and Brenner, uncharacteristically early, joined him in the library.

"Morning, Brenner. Have a seat, and I'll ring for tea, unless you'd like to help yourself to breakfast when you take your leave?"

"I'll grab some tucker before I depart, your lordship," Brenner said, "There are developments relating to the Worthingtons, and you should be apprised of them."

Gareth leaned back in his chair, thoughts of nabobs, an errant brother, and sobriquets gone. "Out with it, Brenner. I did not sleep well last night, and my customary good cheer has deserted me."

Brenner muttered about Blessed Saint Jude while sorting his notes, then cleared his throat. "Holbrook accosted the sisters in the park yesterday as they walked out to feed the waterfowl, but I expect, if you've seen the ladies, you know that."

"I have seen the ladies, as you are well aware, Mr. Brenner, but it was Lord Andrew who apprised me of Holbrook's latest appearance among the dramatis personae. What else can you tell me?"

"He waited in his town coach, back in his usual spot, until he saw the ladies, then took a path to intersect theirs on the way to the duck pond. They chatted, and he walked them back to the gates before taking a proper leave of them. The footmen were on hand at all times, of course."

Gareth toyed with a white quill pen—the same feather he'd once considered using to intimately annoy Felicity.

"You, Brenner, should be aware Miss Astrid took it upon herself to inform Holbrook her sister would be publicly dropping me later in the day, and to further inform him such an arrangement was our mutual scheme for deflecting gossip. What do you suppose Holbrook will do with that information?"

Brenner's expression turned thoughtful. "He might well do nothing with it, your lordship. Everything we uncovered about him suggests he is simply a successful country gentleman—albeit with unfortunate antecedents—up to enjoy Town life. He might keep his own counsel."

"And how was such an innocent fellow out strolling in the park when your men told us he wasn't even in Town any longer?"

Brenner rearranged his notes, though Gareth would have bet his favorite pair of matched bays the notes were in perfect order.

"Mr. Holbrook was taking his leave of the house in disguise."

"And our fellows couldn't see through a disguise? Was he posing as a chambermaid?"

"A footman, your lordship. Our men are stationed where they can see the house, and its various points of ingress and egress. They are not close enough to see the features on a man's face beneath his hat brim when his collar is pulled up against the evening chill. Given that limitation, they have done as we've asked."

Gareth denied himself the useless recriminations boiling up inside him. "You said everything we uncovered about Holbrook suggested he was merely a wealthy rustic with excellent taste in clothing. Why did you use the past tense?"

"A detail has come up, your lordship. You directed me to recheck all the land records, among other tasks, and so I did. You will recall Holbrook acquired properties in Kent at various times since attaining his majority. One of the larger estates, close to ten thousand acres, he acquired from Viscount Riverton some years ago. The detail that has emerged is that Riverton won the property from one Viscount Fairly, whom you would know as Felicity and Astrid Worthington's father."

Gareth twirled the feather. "Was it a crooked game?"

"No way to know, your lordship. Riverton does not have a reputation as a cheat, but the best ones don't. He and Fairly were some kind of friends at the time, and it was a game that had included several other players, all of whom dropped out as the stakes went up and the hour grew quite late. Come morning, Worthington—Viscount Fairly, rather—had written his vowels to Riverton to the tune of what must have been the bulk of his personal fortune. Riverton then transferred the property to this Holbrook fellow."

"So dear Papa Worthington gambled away the ladies' security several *years* before his death and still made no provision for their welfare?"

"And it's a prosperous piece of land, too," Brenner added mournfully.

Gareth twiddled the feather while struggling with the realization that Felicity's father hadn't done anything—not one thing—to preserve his daughters from a life of penury and worse.

"Brenner, how long did Fairly live after he lost this property?"

"Several years, your lordship."

"So *how* did he live? If he'd sold his most valuable private real property, and Felicity claims the entailed estates weren't profitable, where was his money coming from? The London merchants will extend credit to a title, but only so far. If you can't throw a man into the hulks, you tend to watch how much you lend him."

"I'll look into that," Brenner said. "The viscount was only the third title holder, so I doubt the title encompassed much of a fortune, substantial jewels, an art collection, or extensive stables. I don't know what Fairly was living on, but I will find out. One thing is apparent, he was not a professional gambler. After that game with Riverton, he wasn't seen much at the tables at all."

"Interesting." Frustrating, more like. Bloody damned frustrating. A silence lengthened as Gareth stared out at the rain and brushed his finger over the quill's feather.

"Brenner, for the next several days, I want your men living in Holbrook's pockets. I don't care if he knows he's being watched, or if he sets men to watching our men. He is not to make a move—in disguise or as God made him—that we don't know about. Is that clear?"

"Very clear, your lordship."

"And the same goes for the Worthingtons. Astrid is not to go looking for Jehoshaphat's kittens unless two footmen haven't found them first."

"Jehoshaphat's kittens?"

"The feline strumpet living in the stables. The ladies are not to sneeze without being offered two handkerchiefs, they are not to set foot out of any door without two pairs of strong arms to protect them. If the fellows are competent with pistols or knives, arm them."

"I'll see to it, your lordship."

"Good, now to breakfast with you. One other question."

Brenner paused in a near-dash for the door. "My lord?"

"That saint you mentioned is a new one. St. Jude? In the celestial clerking office you Papists have organized for the receipt of prayers, what is St. Jude's specialty?"

"My granny was the last Papist in the family, my lord. St. Jude is the patron saint of lost causes. I assigned you to his care early in my association with you."

Michael Brenner was smiling, and Gareth could not recall having seen the expression on the fellow's face before.

CHAPTER FOURTEEN

With no little astonishment, Gareth revised his characterization of Brenner's expression: The man wasn't smiling, but rather *smirking*.

"If you turn that expression on the young ladies, I will soon lose a competent man of business to the distractions of holy matrimony. Be off with you, I have a will to read."

Gareth's hunt for the damned document was interrupted a few minutes later when his butler brought him the morning post, the newspaper, and a breakfast tray upon which Cook had "insisted."

The morning was advancing, though the day grew no lighter.

"Hughes, I will be meeting with Miss Worthington this afternoon. I know most of the staff takes their half-day on Thursdays, but make sure they know not to go above stairs for any reason once the lady has arrived. Miss Worthington and I are not to be disturbed for anything less than the death of the king." Though Old George had been going barmy for some time. "Make that the Second Coming."

"Very good, milord."

"And that goes for the nosy little tweenie who always seem to be making up my bed before I've left it, too."

Gareth skipped the society pages, knowing he would find more than one allusion to the broken-hearted Marquess of H_____, whose personal assets were so bewilderingly large he'd been dropped by a certain retiring Miss W_____, and so on ad nauseum.

Thankfully, by the time the Season began in earnest, a half-dozen new scandals would come toddling along to entertain the idle people whom Gareth called his peers. He took little comfort from that thought, though, and decided he'd spend some time on Andrew's estate in Sussex once he'd concluded his dealings with Felicity.

Because, a voice in his head taunted, watching a bunch of smelly old sheep be divested of their wool had to be more fascinating than drinking, dancing, and whoring his way through yet another spring-time in London.

He threw down his paper in disgust, and heard the clock chime ten times. The pile of correspondence still lay on the sideboard, and hours ago—it felt like days—he'd been intent on reading Callista's will. The very document, bound with a thick black ribbon peeked out at him from a stack near the wax jack. He withdrew it from its hiding place and began to read, only to be cursing fluently within minutes.

Lawyers, damn the lot of them, never wrote in plain English, and reserved their most arcane and ridiculous language for wills and trusts.

"I, Callista Marie Hemmings, being of sound mind and reasonable health, do hereby make, devise, create and declare this to be my last will and testament, hereby revoking any previous wills, codicils, or other testamentary documents and utterances of any kind whatsoever, whether created by me in my hand, or created for me with my seal affixed thereto..."

He put the thing in the center of his desk, and rose, wondering if, when the good fellows at the Inns of Court climbed into bed at night with their spouses, they "made, devised, created and declared" love to their spouses, or simply swived them like the rest of humankind.

He ploughed through two more pages before fatigue became a

crushing weight on his mind. As he stretched out for a late morning nap, it occurred to him that in the past week of sleepless nights, he should simply have forced himself to read legal documents until slumber claimed him.

ALWAYS BEFORE, Gareth had been on hand to escort Felicity up the stairs to the private areas in his house.

"His lordship has been keeping late hours," Hughes said, and for him, this was a significant confidence. "Not that he's socializing much, you understand. Mr. Brenner has been much in evidence of late. Much in evidence."

The butler gazed up the steps, as if his lordship had been carried off by wolves, and wasn't expected to survive the ordeal.

Hughes would not ascend those steps to disturb his employer. He'd see Felicity installed in the yellow drawing room, only the tea tray and her nerves to keep her company until Gareth came down.

"I'll just see myself up."

For the first time, a hint of sympathy clouded Hughes rheumy blue eyes. "If you think that best, Miss. You'll ring if the staff can be of service."

She started up the steps, realizing that Hughes did not judge her, but rather, regarded her the way he might a young lady on her way to make the hangman's acquaintance.

No footman stood at the top of the stairs, no maid hurried by bearing a silver tea service. This execution of every dream, hope and wish Felicity had harbored, was apparently to be conducted with utmost discretion.

Gareth was not in his sitting room, and not in his dressing room, which left only...

She closed the bedroom door softly, and regarded the Ninth Marquess of Heathgate, fast asleep, naked as a newborn, face down upon his barge of a bed. Without being told, she knew that Edith Hamilton and those of her ilk had never seen him thus—innocent and vulnerable in sleep—and soon, Felicity would also wish she'd been denied this privilege.

She undressed quietly, but not quietly enough.

Gareth rolled over amid his sheets and pillows. "That you, love?"

"Because you've probably called everybody who ends up naked in your bed 'love,' then I suppose that includes me," Felicity said, climbing into bed lest he lie there, inspecting her nudity.

His gaze lingered on her bare shoulders before traversing her bare everything. "Been busy, haven't you?"

She pushed a lock of dark hair off his forehead. "You needed to sleep."

"I was out like the proverbial candle. If you're here, it must be after two."

"It's probably two now," because yes, for the first time, she'd arrived a bit early. "Hughes was courting apoplexy because you'd left orders not to be disturbed."

Gareth wrapped an arm around Felicity's shoulders and pulled her against him. "I am such a burden to poor Hughes."

Felicity wouldn't argue that. She cuddled into Gareth's body and stifled a yawn.

"If you really need a nap, Felicity, I can leave you in peace for a while. I left endless mountains of paperwork downstairs."

So accommodating of him. Felicity had been enjoying the feel of his smooth abdomen beneath her hand, making lazy circles with her palm as she watched Gareth's chest rise and fall. Her hand stilled at his words, which sounded curiously like *stalling*.

"Let us proceed with our business, Heathgate."

"Please, God, Felicity do not *ever* refer to me by my title when we are in bed," he ground out, flinging the covers aside and getting out of the bed.

"And please, God, *Gareth*, don't you offer to tend to paperwork—that has been sitting on your desk all day—when you are finally supposed to be making proper love to me," Felicity spat back, rising to her knees on the mattress. "And we won't ever again *be* in bed so I hardly think it matters what I call you."

She saw Gareth pause in the act of pouring himself a drink—at this hour?—but it was the smallest hesitation, and he turned to regard her as she knelt, naked and uncomfortable on the bed.

"My apologies, Felicity, I meant only to show you consideration. Would you like a drink?" he asked in chilly tones.

How could a man be so intimidating—and so dear—stark naked with his hair rumpled from sleep? She subsided against the headboard and drew the covers up to her chin, because for once, Gareth needed her to show him how to go on.

"Can we please get this over with?" she asked in a small, unhappy voice.

He came back to the bed, and sat, drink in hand, with his back to her.

"I am sorry, Felicity, but with you, I do not want to be simply a stiff prick with a title and a good eye for a pretty bauble." He sounded beyond weary, he sounded forlorn.

"I am sorry too, Gareth," she said, her hand on his back.

He didn't acknowledge her touch, but instead lifted the covers and lay beside her.

"Come here," he said shortly, wrapping an arm around her. "Let's begin again, shall we? Hello, my name is Gareth, and I am just the randy bastard you've been looking for."

He would break her heart many times this day. The notion should not be surprising.

"Hello, Gareth," she responded gamely, "My name is Felicity, and I am the spinster-turned-madam whom you will never have to see again after tomorrow."

She'd failed to accept his challenge—failed miserably. Her voice had broken, her bright tone revealed for the lie that it was. "I am not very good at this," she said, burying her face against Gareth's neck.

"Oh, love." He wrapped Felicity in his arms and brought her

under his body, sheltering her with his limbs, his weight, his warmth. He braced himself above her, but let their bodies touch. Beneath him, Felicity gave in to her weeping, crying in silent shudders, tears leaking from the corners of her eyes and sliding into her hair.

He kissed those tears, kissed her damp eyes, her hair, her nose, her cheeks, her neck, but he let her cry until she was still and relaxed beneath him.

"It isn't what you think," she whispered against his chest. She needed for him to understand this.

"What is it?"

"I am not crying because I will no longer be a virgin."

"Why are you crying, Felicity Worthington?"

Now he was willing to talk—now, of all times. She took in a deep breath, and let it out slowly. She'd purchased some sandalwood soap from the shop he patronized on Oxford Street, and despite the extravagance, had made sure she could torment herself with his scent even after today.

"I am crying because I will no longer be *your* virgin, or your whore, or your spinster, or your anything. You have become dear to me, Gareth Alexander, and I do not know how I will cope without your friendship in my life. I am sorry to burden you with these untidy emotions, but you should know somebody cares for you."

He dropped his forehead to hers. "Your untidy emotions are part of what makes you dear to me as well, Felicity. But we must not let such feelings cloud our judgment, as much as it pains us. After tomorrow—"

She placed her fingers against his mouth, lest he make himself say impossible things for her sake.

"I cannot think of 'after tomorrow,' I cannot conceive of it, I cannot bear to imagine it. But I know it will come, and if you please, I should like a few more memories to sustain me through those days after tomorrow."

FELICITY TOOK HER FINGERS AWAY, but before Gareth could launch back into his rehearsed pontifications, she replaced her fingers with her lips, and drove every noble, selfless thought in his head to perdition.

He kissed her back, kissed her like his life depended on it, memorizing the feel of her mouth with his own. Behind the languor in her kisses, though, he felt a desperate grief, even as he felt Felicity's hands tracing the length of his back, his hips, his backside.

She was saying good-bye with her body, and the insight was devastating. For days, Gareth had been preoccupied with the conundrum of preserving her virtue without jeopardizing her future, but that riddle had blunted the reality that *she was leaving him. By this time tomorrow, she would be gone.*

He wrapped his arms around her, and rolled so Felicity was above him, barnacled to his chest in a position they both could take comfort from.

"I shall miss you," she said miserably.

"Don't say the words, Felicity. Don't say the damned words. Not here, not now." She would start crying all over again, so Gareth distracted her by brushing his fingers over her nipples.

"Yes, please, Gareth." She brought her hands up to hold his palms over her breasts. He obliged, watching her expression gradually ease from anxiety and grief into arousal and sadness. Her nipples ruched against his palms as he gently kneaded her breasts, and by slow degrees, even the sadness faded.

So he continued, with one hand, to pleasure her in that fashion, but his other hand drifted down across her abdomen, to pet and tease at her sex.

"On your elbows, sweetheart," he urged, letting her come down over his body to rest her weight on her knees and forearms. He used the small distance that created between their lower bodies to ply his thumb gently on the seat of her pleasure, then used his fingers to stroke and limn her sex.

She was gratifyingly slick, and when he allowed his finger to slip inside her, she sighed against his neck.

"Soon," he crooned, giving her shallow penetrations then increasing pressure with his thumb.

"That feels *heavenly*."

"It would feel more heavenly if you'd move too."

She complied, rocking her hips the least amount, so the pressure he applied with his thumb would surge and ebb, but never leave her completely.

"Will you come for me?" he whispered. "Come against my hand. Come soon, and come *hard*." He emphasized that instruction with a particularly firm pressure, and she moaned softly. Wanting her responses to build, Gareth gave the nipple between his fingers a slow, equally firm, rolling pinch, and was rewarded by an increase in the tempo of Felicity's hips.

"You're close," he breathed, watching desire suffuse her features. "So close."

He curled up against her, and took one nipple in his mouth, suckling strongly while he closed his fingers around the other. With his free hand, he applied a similarly unrelieved pressure with his thumb, while his fingers slid deeply inside her.

Within moments, she was convulsing around him, her body shuddering with pleasure as she hilted herself on his fingers. He drove her on with little flutters of pressure and release on her nipples, then drew the pleasure out by doing the same with her sex.

When she collapsed on top of him, sated and spent, he breathed in counterpoint to her while he felt her heartbeat gradually slow.

"Dear God in heaven," Felicity breathed. "I begin to see why people make great fools of themselves over this whole business. If I didn't hold you in high regard before, I'd become your most devoted supporter after this, Gareth. Such pleasure ought to be illegal."

"Always nice to be appreciated," he said, patting her bottom. "And some forms of it are illegal."

"Hush." She emphasized her request by kissing him with the

voluptuous languor of a well pleasured woman. "I need a crane to hoist me off of you—no, don't touch," she admonished as Gareth would have helped her swing a leg over him. She managed to get situated beside him, her head on his shoulder, one leg thrown across his thighs.

"If you don't mind, I will pause here for a few minutes," she said, yawning. "You have done me in, Gareth, and we are still not finished."

His caresses to her neck and arm paused, then resumed. "We are not done. Unless you're sore?"

He'd taken great pains to tell her about how delicate ladies' parts could be, and how to care for herself after an overzealous bout of lovemaking—another of the asinine lectures he'd inflicted on her.

"I feel fine," Felicity said, stretching like a cat, "Naughty, but fine." Her hand wandered over his chest, then down, rib by rib. Gareth braced himself for the inevitable, and soon enough, her hand drifted lower.

When Felicity encountered Gareth's flaccid cock, several heartbeats of silence ensued.

"What is this about?" She waggled his member gently as she spoke.

"What is what about?" Not that Gareth would be able to bluff his way through this.

"This." She waggled him more firmly.

"I like how that feels." And he did actually, though he couldn't recall a touch of hers he hadn't liked.

"Gareth, you mean to tell me I'm plastered to you, carrying on at great, strumpetous length—and don't tell me strumpetous is not a word—and the *marquess* here"—she gave him another wiggle—"is not aroused? Please explain this."

He heard the consternation in her voice, and knew where her practical, virginal mind would take her next: She wasn't desirable enough.

"Calm yourself, love," he said, urging her back into his embrace.

"This circumstance is one the professional ladies probably encounter fairly often. We men don't like to speak of impotence, as if doing so will conjure it."

"You are not having me on, are you?" She sounded not suspicious, but distraught.

"No, love, I am not having you on, not about something like this. I am puzzled though, because until this day, I had no personal acquaintance with this phenomenon."

With this *problem*—though in truth, he couldn't really regard it as a problem. More of a blessing, oddly enough. Perhaps St. Jude had taken a hand in matters after all.

"You are tired." Her fingers around his cock took on the oddest, protective feel. "And you've been drinking more. You said that doesn't help a man's performance."

His drinking had nothing to do with anything, and his fatigue was similarly irrelevant.

Gareth would have felt concerned, except he was too relieved. The decision of how to avoid debauching the spinster-madam had been taken from him, and time had run out. Somehow, he knew that between now and their meeting with the solicitors, the *marquess*, as Felicity had christened his cock, would not be a party to any mischief involving her.

Whoever would have thought a man's conscience could be located in his underlinen?

Though beside him, he could *hear* Felicity worrying.

"What am I to do about this?" she asked miserably, patting his genitals.

"There is nothing to do, Felicity. Sometimes, a fellow's spirit is willing, but his flesh is weak, so to speak. You are not to fret." He heaved her up to straddle him again, and gently forced her back down to his chest. "Your maidenhead, if you had one, has been destroyed. Of that I am certain." He kissed her brow, but it didn't make her scowl go away.

"I may not have a maidenhead, Gareth, but how do you know that's all a midwife would look for? Even Crabbie knows not all women bleed on their wedding nights."

Felicity Worthington was born to challenge every reassurance he could possibly give her—and she'd been interrogating the help rather than bring her questions to him.

"I am *almost* positive you cannot be found to be a virgin with any medical certainty, but we won't let it come to that, Felicity. Nobody will subject you to a medical examination. I won't have it."

"Pronouncements, no matter how confidently made, may not carry the day."

Gareth knew Felicity's mental gears were turning, but so were his. His were revolving around the thought that he'd never again hold Felicity naked against his skin this way, never see the desperate look in her eye when pleasure overtook her, never feel her indignantly waggle his limp cock while she interrogated him about his failure to ruin her entirely.

So many nevers...

"You're sighing mightily," Felicity observed, her chin resting on his sternum. "I can hear your mind parsing the problem. We shall contrive."

That platitude should have irritated him, but it didn't. Her faith in him, and in their ability to cope with what lay ahead, echoed his own certainty that his failure to perform today had been a final step in the resurrection of scruples that had lain dormant too long. Somehow, he and Felicity would contrive, and he would see her future secure.

As he pondered the angles on that challenge, Felicity grew more relaxed. Her breathing deepened, her limbs went slack.

Gareth wrapped his arms around her, and held her as tenderly as he dared, letting the shadows in the room shift into twilight as she slept on. When she finally stirred, full darkness had fallen, and still, he kept his arms wrapped around her.

"IT'S LIKE THIS, BRENNER," Gareth said, "Miss Worthington came to me claiming that as a condition of the will, I had to educate her regarding the duties of a madam—including the most intimate ones. In that last regard, I have failed." A failure of which Gareth was inordinately proud, and how long had it been since he'd felt any pride in himself at all? "What does the will *require* in terms of proof she in fact complied adequately to inherit?"

Before Gareth's eyes, Michael Brenner, competent if unassuming man of business, took on the raptor's visage of a lettered legal clerk.

"Perhaps your lordship would like to have some supper while I look over the relevant documents?"

"I couldn't eat, though I will leave you alone. Would you rather work here or in the library?"

"The library, with the legal references," Benner said. "Is there anything else I should know about this situation, your lordship?"

Gareth trusted Brenner, trusted him more than he'd realized.

"You should know there is gossip in the solicitor's offices," Gareth replied. "The details of this will are already circulating on the fringes of society, and we can't afford for them to go any further. It is imperative we conclude this business tomorrow, and without physical examination of Felicity's person."

"Solicitors will gossip," Brenner allowed, in a virtuosic understatement. "If you'll excuse me?"

Garth waved him on his way, and remained seated behind the desk, mentally pacing the bounds of the problem.

First, why would Callista do something like this to her cousin? Neither Gareth nor Andrew, both of whom had known the woman well enough, found such viciousness in character for her. Second, how had the rumors started, and why were they—now—so close to the truth? Third, how did David Holbrook figure into the equation?

Gareth turned over each question until he was ready to hit something—David Holbrook's handsome face, for example, or Callista's solicitors. When he heard the clock chime ten times, he made his way to the library.

"Almost done," Brenner said, for once too absorbed in a task to rise in the presence of his employer. "There's good news and bad news," he said, scratching some notes on a sheet of foolscap. Gareth stood by the hearth, waiting with as much patience as he could muster.

Which was to say, precious damned little. "Bad news first."

"I LIKE YOUR CHOICE OF ATTIRE," Gareth said as he settled into the coach.

Felicity had chosen a dress of deep green velvet, an ensemble that would have been suitable for church and a little severe for social calls. At Gareth's approval, the knots in her stomach eased fractionally.

"I see you're every inch the marquess today as well." And heavens, he made an impressive show in his elegant attire.

"One goes into battle as well armored as possible." He took her gloved hand in his, then scowled, stripped off their gloves, and laced his fingers with hers. "You shall not fret. Brenner and I were up half the night going over Callista's will, and he gave me plenty of ammunition."

Ammunition because this *was* a battle.

"We'll need it. The solicitors were very clear with me, Gareth. I was to be subjected to every possible indignity should I not be convincingly..."

She trailed off, frowning. What exactly had they said to her, and what she implied or been led to imply?

"Yes?"

"The will is legal," Felicity said. "They assured me of that at great length." *They had bludgeoned her with a falsehood, probably an entire lecture full of falsehoods.*

"Brenner gave me leave to doubt that." Gareth sounded viciously pleased to announce this. He was thinking clearly—thank God some-body was.

"This will grow complicated, won't it? Should we have brought Brenner?"

"He offered," Gareth said, drawing the shade down the last inch. "I may have to fight dirty, and Brenner is somewhat of a stickler." Gareth's thumb lazily rubbed circles on the back of her hand, while his mind was likely miles away.

"You relish the thought of playing dirty."

"I think somebody has played *you* dirty," he replied. "I relish the thought of being your champion."

Gracious. She had not recovered from that broadside before he brought her knuckles to his lips for a kiss.

"Are you sore today?"

"Gareth, how can you possibly think of such thing?"

"Your welfare is never far from my thoughts."

Gareth Alexander spoiling for a fight was a formidable compan-ion. "I took a soaking bath last night, and another this morning. I am in good health." Felicity regarded their joined hands. "We should not be having this discussion." She could not make herself use his title, not quite yet.

Beside her, Gareth shifted subtly, so his body was closer to hers and the light, spicy scent of his shaving soap stole through her senses.

"I told myself, Felicity, that for today, I would treat you with the distance and decorum you truly deserve. I told myself it would be kinder—and easier for us both—if I maintained some propriety between us, and kept my infernal paws to myself." He paused as if to gather his composure. "I simply *cannot* do it, not when I know that when I drop you off at home after this meeting, I will drop out of your life, and you out of mine, for all practical—and impractical—purposes."

Her champion was very fierce, also very brave. She would reward him with as much bravery of her own as she could muster.

"I am glad your noble resolve failed you. As it is, I wondered why you didn't kiss me, why you didn't put an arm around me. When you took my hand, my fears abated, but this decorum you refer to, it would have cut me to the heart."

Though she knew well, as he no doubt did too, that cut awaited them both.

~

ACCORDING TO BRENNER'S RESEARCH, the firm of Willard and Willard was the enterprise of two brothers, one a good deal older than the other, assisted by a younger nephew, as well as various clerks and secretaries. The offices gave every appearance of prospering, but the address was of middling prestige, the place smelled of books and coal smoke, and Gareth noted that the clerks were thin and poorly attired.

Gareth and Felicity were ushered into the office of the senior brother Willard, Thaddeus, by name, and joined by the other brother, and the nephew. They were then offered tea, and a polite ration of small talk while they stood around a long, gleaming table waiting for documents to be produced.

Gareth ambled around the room, handling whatever struck his fancy, then taking a seat at the head of the table, though it certainly hadn't been offered. Frowning, he stood right back up.

"Miss Worthington, I am remiss, and do beg your pardon." He held out the chair directly to his right, causing the other gentlemen to exchange uneasy looks. Of course they should have offered the lady a seat, but this was a *marquess*.

"Our pardon, Miss Worthington," The younger brother, Abernathy, offered her a bow along with the apology, and Gareth mentally labeled him the brains of the operation.

"And gentlemen?" Gareth made a gesture designed to invite them to sit as well.

As the solicitors were flipping their coattails and clearing their throats, an office boy came in, carrying a stack of beribboned files, which he laid on the table by the nephew.

Suggesting the nephew was the one who actually did the work.

"The Hemmings estate file, if you please." Thaddeus held out a peremptory hand toward his nephew. The nephew passed the file up while Gareth silently bided his time.

"Ah, yes, here it is." Thaddeus enjoyed himself for long minutes, perusing the documents, muttering to himself and occasionally frowning. "And is the mid-wife expected soon?" he asked his nephew.

"I believe so, uncle."

Gareth glanced at Felicity, and found her engaged in a battle of direct gazes with Abernathy. Utterly expressionless, she let the weight of her stare rest on the man, until he glanced away, a frown replacing his earlier jovial expression.

"Is somebody anticipating a happy event?" Gareth asked.

"Why, no, your lordship," Thaddeus looked up, his surprise to Gareth's eyes no more convincing than it was genuine. "We are preparing to comply with the terms of Miss Hemmings' will. The language is specific, you see, and as her solicitors, we have a solemn duty to ensure the terms are complied with in every respect. This has all been explained to Miss Worthington."

Thaddeus continued to smile benignly, even to the point of bestowing a small nod in the aforesaid Miss Worthington's direction.

Gareth endeavored to look perplexed when what he felt approximated the intent to do treble murder. "The language is specific, you say?"

"Quite." Thaddeus nodded so vigorously his prosperous chins jiggled. "Miss Hemmings was *very clear*, your lordship."

"I don't recall any such language in the document, gentlemen, and because Miss Hemmings is *very dead*—may she rest in peace—her oral instructions matter not one whit."

Glances ricocheted around the table, none of them happy.

"My lord." Thaddeus cleared his throat. "My lord, you must

understand the law is an arcane undertaking. The language in the document refers to an examination of the beneficiary, one undertaken to ensure qualification for all—"

"The only reference I saw was to written questions, Mr. Willard, which I'm sure Miss Worthington is prepared to answer."

The nephew's brows drew down in an expression Gareth had seen on Michael's Brenner's face when he was about to invoke Blessed Saint Ives, whoever that was.

"Miss Hemmings devised a series of inquiries," the nephew said, "and provided us the desired answers in her own hand."

Both Thaddeus and Abernathy glared daggers at their nephew, while Gareth gave the young man points for integrity, if not brains.

"Shall we have a look at the questions, then?" Gareth suggested. "After all, if we are to comply with the terms of the will, the questions must be answered, correct?"

"Yes, my lord," the nephew agreed, his gaze darting from one uncle to the other.

Abernathy spoke up. "Then let's get to it, boy. The young lady can answer the questions while we await the mid-wife. And as I recall, if the answers are in error, then we'll have no need of the midwife, isn't that so, nephew?" Something in Abernathy' too-pleasant smile communicated itself to the nephew.

"I defer to your superior understanding, Uncle," the nephew murmured, pulling the file onto his lap and rifling through it. "Here," he said, sliding a piece of paper across the table. Gareth's perused the paper, then slid it back across the table, his eyes boring into the nephew's.

"You must have inadvertently pulled out an earlier draft, young fellow, for that page includes some forty questions, and was not written in Callista's lovely hand. I had occasion to correspond with the lady. We were in fact, intimate correspondents."

If Gareth had had any doubt previously regarding the probity of the proceedings, it vanished with this lame ploy. Callista had had a proper upbringing, and her penmanship had been lovely, not that slashing, sloppy, *masculine* backhand.

The nephew seemed to grow smaller as he put the offending *draft* back in the file. After more nervous glances at Thaddeus and Abernathy, he rifled the file again.

"I suppose it's possible, your lordship, that the boy made a mistake. The file is quite extensive, as you can see," Abernathy commented, looking none too pleased.

"Perhaps this is the final draft?" The nephew slid another piece of paper across the table, one covered over about one quarter of its surface with a tidy, feminine hand.

"Much better. And where are our answers?" Gareth asked. Because under no circumstances would he allow this trio of jackals to leave the room without confirming that Felicity had answered every question correctly.

"Here, my lord."

Gareth glanced over the answers in comparison to the questions, and handed the questions back to the nephew.

"You may put these to Miss Worthington, and she will write down her answers." Felicity whipped off her gloves, slapped them onto the table, and picked up a black quill pen. While she scratched away, Gareth stood behind her chair and started making a list of his own. Upon reflection, he found he was on lunching terms with at least three sitting judges and four barristers, any one of whom could start exactly the sort of gossip that would see Willard and Willard's doors closed.

Saint Ives might approve.

A tap on the door was followed by an office boy sticking his head in the door. "Mrs. Burton be here, milords. Says she be a midwife."

"Send her away," Gareth snapped.

Abernathy shook his head, the office boy closed the door, and Thaddeus rose from his seat.

"Lord Heathgate, you cannot think to prove that a young lady who has never known the blessings of matrimony is fit to assume responsibility for a bawdy house if she's still, as it were, intact."

Five judges, and six barristers, one of whom, Gervaise Stoneleigh, was equal to any three of the others in influence. By Michaelmas at the latest, the firm should be rolled up.

CHAPTER FIFTEEN

Plotting the dissolution of a law firm was great good fun, but it would not see Felicity freed of these scoundrels—and whoever guided them —in the immediate term. Gareth offered his lady an encouraging and pleasantly proper smile.

Felicity passed him a paper, which Gareth studied for a moment and did not pass to the nephew, who nearly quivered on the edge of his seat.

"What I think, gentlemen, is that I am loath to offend Miss Worthington's sensibilities further than necessary, but I must point out that the duties of madam are quite different from the duties of the women she employs. I believe you would agree I am something of an expert on houses of pleasure, would you not?"

He waited before going on until each man had given him some sign of agreement.

"I can cheerfully assure you, then, that a madam does not entertain clients, though that might be an aspect of her past. A madam is usually past the first blush of youth, possessed of a cool head for business, and adept at managing more emotionally volatile females and their gentlemen customers. Are we agreed on that?"

This agreement was more conditional. "Well, yes, typically," or, "I suppose in the usual case," but a legal broadside was being fired, and the Willards knew it.

"I am glad we are agreed a madam's job differs from that of her employees." Gareth plucked the list of answers from under the nephew's nose. "For I do understand enough about business to comprehend that *ambiguity* in any kind of legal document is a sorry thing. Am I right?"

It was still slow in coming, but the uncles quietly agreed to that as well.

"And if that wasn't the case, then we can all agree that a document purporting to pass along ownership of a common nuisance is an illegal document at best, and thus void in its entirely."

Felicity turned a vapid smile on Gareth, suggesting she followed his reasoning perfectly, and wanted him to hurry the hell up.

"Let's see how you did, hmm?" He laid the two pieces of paper down side by side. "On what day does the Pleasure House do the least business?—Sunday. On what day does the Pleasure House do the most business?—Saturday. Where do the footmen sleep on grounds?—Above the carriage house. Where is the stillroom located? —Between the larder and the laundry. Where is the ladies' private sitting room located?—At the end of the hallway on the third floor. There, gentlemen, I believe you have a perfect score. If you would be good enough to make a countersigned copy for the lady, I would appreciate it."

Abernathy wrinkled his nose, the nephew made a show of rummaging in a drawer for an inkwell.

"I tell you, my lord," Thaddeus sputtered, "an examination of the woman is required."

"I tell you," Gareth said, quietly, almost pleasantly, "it is not. Nowhere in that document is any reference made to anything but a written examination, which has been successfully completed. If you argue that something more intrusive is required, I will counter that your document must fail in its entirely due to a fatal ambiguity in draftsmanship. A will must be clear, and the requirement you insist on is nowhere in evidence. *Nowhere.* Furthermore, if you posit that the will intends that the business itself be transferred to Miss Worthington's keeping, rather than its simple physical assets, then the intent of the will is illegal."

He spoke very softly, softly enough that Brenner would have been backing up a step at each word. "If the will is invalid, then *the Worthingtons simply inherit the entire estate outright as a function of consanguinity.*"

An uneasy silence descended. Gareth glanced over at Felicity, who was pale, unsmiling, and likely ready to throw anything within reach at the buffoons trying to create evidence that this bequest had made a strumpet out of her.

Before either uncle could respond, the nephew slid two pieces of paper across the table to Gareth.

"Your copies, my lord."

Gareth took a few moments to look them over, making sure one was a true copy before sliding it back to the nephew. "I believe you neglected your signature as clerk," he chided gently. The nephew complied, his ears turning an interesting shade of red.

While Felicity's knuckles as she gripped her reticule were white.

"As the trustee representing Callista Hemmings' estate," Gareth said, "I must consider one of two options. I can take this matter to court, because the document contains material ambiguities and illegalities which I believe make it impossible to enforce. I am reluctant to do this, because of the expense, the delay, and the undesirable publicity for all involved. I can, in the alternative, accept title to the deceased's assets—her assets only— executed in favor of Miss Worthington *immediately.*"

In either case, he would ruin this firm and enjoy doing so. His smile likely said as much.

"Might I have a moment to confer with my uncles?" the nephew inquired.

"You may. I will await your response here with Miss Worthington."

The Willards trooped off to some other location, but not far enough to completely obscure their exchange. Muffled shouts of "... he's a marquess, for pity's sake!" and "...damned idiot scheme..." reached their ears, along with "...he has the damned means!" and "... buy and sell you old scheming windbags...."

Young Mr. Willard returned alone some few minutes later, carrying more legal documents.

"These," he said, sitting down and addressing both Gareth and Felicity, "are written as quit claim deeds, which is the simplest way to transfer a title. If you will sign as trustee and beneficiary, respectively, Miss Worthington will own the property. The only condition of title is that you can't sell the property until the one year anniversary of Miss Hemmings's death."

Felicity looked at Gareth, who nodded that she was to sign the documents. When they were finished, young Willard saw them out, the uncles no doubt being occupied packing for an extended stay in the Antipodes.

Gareth handed Felicity up into his coach, and settled himself beside her. "Talk to me, Felicity."

He reached over to lower the shade and saw a petite blond alighting from a plain town coach. From the back, she looked suspiciously like Edith Hamilton. When the woman turned to see if her lady's maid was at her side, Gareth's suspicions were confirmed.

"What are you staring at?" Felicity asked.

"Merely the passing scene." Interestingly, the passing scene had made her way directly to the offices of Willard and Willard. "How are you, Felicity?"

"Shaken. Those two horrid old men were determined to humiliate me. What on earth were they up to?"

Shaken was better than screeching hysterically for half the City to hear, which she ought by rights to be doing.

"The point, Felicity, is that they failed. I suspect their goal was to blackmail you or more likely, to blackmail *me*, which would have been possible even if you'd been found to be chaste, had I in any way intimated that I accepted and supported the purpose of an illegal will."

The longer Gareth thought about it, the more he became convinced the entire exercise had been aimed at *him*—though not by Callista, and certainly not by a bumbling trio of solicitors. The question was, who had put them up to such venery?

Felicity looked at him aghast. "And if you hadn't been there, and hadn't beaten them at their own game, then I would have had no choice but to comply with their requirement for an examination, and with the resulting blackmail," she concluded bitterly. "I feel violated, Gareth."

"You've had a near miss," he corrected gently. "It doesn't help to dwell on such things." He had taken off their gloves again so they could link fingers.

"Then what am I supposed to dwell on?" Felicity asked with some asperity. "Perhaps you'd rather I fix my feeble female brain on that fact that in fifteen minutes, you leave my life forever?"

She was winding up, working herself into a tantrum, a female twitteration of grand dimensions. Given the penury she'd coped with since her father's death, the folly in her life over the last four months, and the outright insult of the past hour, she was entitled.

"Felicity…"

"Don't you 'Felicity' me, Gareth Joyce Alexander. You enjoyed that little imbroglio with those vermin. You consider I had a narrow escape because nobody actually thrust their dirty fingers into my body, but I… but I—"

"Hush, Felicity. Come here to me." He wrapped an arm around her, but he was too slow. She'd thrown herself against him, sobbing, before he could get his handkerchief free.

"Oh, Gareth, what they wanted to do to me…" she wailed. "Why would they be so mean?"

He let her cry and rant and ruin his linen and cry some more.

When she'd subsided, he held her, stroking her hair as they approached the turn to her street.

"You are *not* taking me home," she informed him shakily.

"I'm not?" He had enjoyed that exchange with the solicitors. He'd enjoyed championing her causes, and taking a stand on moral high ground for a change. He would not enjoy parting from her, not at all.

"No, you most assuredly shall not deposit me at my doorstep and toddle along your way."

Bless her, she sounded so very certain, not that he'd ever toddled anywhere. "And why aren't I?" he asked gently. "We have concluded our business Felicity, in every sphere. Further association with me would only do you harm, and I fear, increase the heartache awaiting when we part. I would spare you that."

"There is no sparing me, you wretched man. All you can is offer me is comfort against the separation to come. And I will have it," she said, a martial light in her eye.

"What comfort would you have of me, love? I cannot part from you and yet be with you, though I would if I could," he said, stroking his fingers down her cheek.

He wanted to close his eyes, the better to feel the pleasure of touching her one last time, and he wanted to stare at her, to memorize her every feature yet again.

"Take me home with you, Gareth, just for tonight. I want to make love with you."

He shook his head, but she kept on speaking, slowly, with a fierceness that reached out to his heart and sliced at it with relentless precision.

"Just once, I want to make love with you, face to face, so I can kiss you as I open my arms and my heart to you. I want you for a lover, not as some bedroom toy, or sexual pedagogue. Just once, Gareth. May I *please* have who and what I want?" She was weeping again, the tears coursing down her cheeks, tears not of fear or rage, but of grief and longing.

Yesterday, making love to her had loomed as part of some complicated moral choice between protecting her innocence or protecting her future. No matter what choice Gareth had made, Felicity would have lost something necessary to her. Today, the executed deed in her reticule and her own determination swept that question—with its moral implications and losses—right off the table.

He ought not. He ought to kiss her forehead, hand her down, and be on his way. And yet.... He could give her pleasure, he could be her lover—for one night. Felicity Worthington was stubborn enough and decent enough to go for the rest of her life without ever permitting herself the pleasure she begged him for now.

He shifted away, so they weren't touching. "Felicity, you have to be very, very sure. This thing you ask, it will bind us in ways that can only hurt. I cannot encourage it. There are steps we haven't taken yet, true, but if we take those steps, you can't ever take them again with anybody else, and you can't un-take them. You must be positive you want to take them with me."

He made the effort to dissuade her, even as he felt his own unruly heart soaring at what she offered.

Say no. My lady, don't do this to yourself.

"I have never been more certain of anything in my life."

She looked certain, too. Certain she wanted this time with him, regardless that it was all they could have of each other.

"Then, my dearest Felicity, I promise you, you shall have what you want."

He signaled the driver to take them back to his home, and drew Felicity against his side. By the time they reached their destination, he was already regretting their decision, because, upon reflection, he realized he too, would be taking steps he'd never taken with anybody else, steps that couldn't be untaken.

Steps that for one as lonely and weary as he, would be fraught with feeling and meaning. Steps that would bind him to her, as he was bound to no other. Fortunately for his regrets, he had given her his word, and a true gentleman would never break his word once given to a lady.

FELICITY HAD BEEN surprised when Gareth sent her upstairs without him, but as she'd had a brief soak in the scented bath he'd ordered for her, she'd enjoyed the chance to gather her scattered wits. When Gareth arrived, he came bearing fruit, cheese, and champagne.

"This is pleasant," Felicity said, sipping her wine in a cozy corner of the couch.

"You've never had champagne before?"

"Of economic necessity, ours became an abstaining house." And her various wine tastings under his roof hadn't included champagne.

"You can have all you please, now," he reminded her as he sat to wrestle off his boots.

Felicity used his change of position to trail a hand down his spine, feeling the bumps of his backbone under her fingers. He paused, and looked around his shoulder to shoot her a bemused smile, but didn't sit back until both boots had thumped to the floor.

"Andrew's running off," he told her, accepting a sip of her drink. "He's taken it into his head to go see the capitals on the Continent, complete his education as a gentleman, and 'that sort of thing.'"

"Do we blame Astrid for this sudden urge to see the world?"

"I think she's part of it," Gareth said, "maybe not all. Somewhere after the accident, I lost track of Andrew. I am beginning to think he's more upset than I knew, but I can't put my finger on why. He's always so hale-fellow-well-met, but I know he holds himself responsible for the fact that only he and Mother survived."

Felicity liked that Gareth would talk to her this way. She hated that after today, he'd have nobody to discuss family concerns with.

"From what you've said, Andrew and your mother were the only ones not inebriated."

Gareth paused, his hands at the knot of his cravat. "That never occurred to me. In years of tormenting myself with what-ifs and if-onlys, I never put together that everyone who died was drinking heavily, while those who survived were not. Interesting." He regarded their drink as if it contained hemlock.

"You won't die in a boating accident because you shared a bottle of wine with me, Gareth."

"I know," though his tone was unconvinced. Then he offered her a piratical grin. "Maybe I'll expire of an apoplexy in that bed in the next room." She hit him with an embroidered pillow for his impertinence. He lunged at her to divest her of her weapon, and they both ended up tangled lengthwise on the couch.

Felicity smacked him again with the pillow. "Get off me, you awful man."

"A blow to the head can have serious consequences," Gareth chided her, kissing her nose as he rose partway off her. "You must take more tender care of my person, Felicity, or I will conclude spirits make you violent."

He did get up, and held out a hand to assist her to her feet.

"Spirits don't make me violent, but dirty old solicitors surely do," Felicity said as she gained her feet.

"What about a dirty, not quite old marquess?" Gareth murmured as he slipped his arms around her.

"Him, I have a decided fondness for." If fondness could apply to the love of one's life. She leaned into him, felt his hand stroking down her unbound hair, and never wanted the moment to end.

"Seeing as you're so fond of me, how about if I take you into that bedroom and make passionate love to you for the next twelve hours, hmm?" He nuzzled her neck, addling her wits with the scents of sandalwood and spices. And with his kindness.

This flirtation, this banter, was Gareth trying to be kind—as if their assignation were merely another of his casual liaisons, undertaken for pleasure and easily forgotten.

Perhaps she could learn even that from him.

"Passionate love would be quite acceptable." Though twelve hours was far from enough.

He made sure it was lovely, made it everything she'd dreamed shared intimacy could be. They took their time stroking, petting, teasing and talking without any particular urgency or agenda. Felicity reveled in the pleasure of being able to see Gareth's face as he touched her, as his own arousal built and ebbed. She reached over again and again to touch his features as he lay beside her, to kiss him while his hands left trails of pleasure all over her body. The room had grown dark when Felicity felt Gareth's hand go still on the side of her face.

"Soon, Felicity, I will love make love with you. You will sleep in my arms this night, and we will rise and break our fast together. But then, my love, we will part. Do you promise me when the time comes, you will accept my farewell?"

My love. For one night, she was his love. He leaned down to kiss her before she could reply. When he paused, his mouth poised above her, she realized all his petting and stroking so far had been so much teasing before he turned his attention fully to her pleasure.

"I promise, Gareth." He was demanding a price from her for this night in his arms. The price was an absolute parting. He would start collecting on her promise tomorrow morning, but the price would never be paid in full.

Gareth made no further comment, but in the deep shadows of the firelight, Felicity saw him close his eyes briefly before she felt his lips on her forehead.

"So be it," he murmured, grazing his mouth over each of her features. His hands roamed her body, as if memorizing the landscape of her bones and muscles. He touched her softly, sweetly, and with such care Felicity's worries and fears melted under his caresses. When he shifted to rise over her, she wanted to lift herself up into him, to capture him with her limbs and her mouth and *her love* and hold him to her heart.

Gareth laced his fingers with hers where they lay beside her head on the pillow. In the same moment, he joined their mouths, and began the joining of their bodies. His tongue, his shaft, his hands, melded her body to his, slowly, gently.

Felicity felt an instant's panic—equal parts desire and anxiety—as the length of him filled her, but then he glided away, and the panic was replaced by loss. He eased forward again, watching her now, then forward a bit more. She raised her head off the pillow to recapture his mouth, and flexed her hips to follow his retreat. By slow degrees, her body accepted him, until she caught his rhythm and he was moving easily inside her.

For long moments, he pleasured her thus, with a lovely, languid thrusting that allowed Felicity to kiss him while her hips undulated with his. She freed one hand from his grasp and explored his face, watching her fingers trail over each feature. She slipped her hand to the nape of his neck, then down the long muscles of his back, using the purchase she found to hold herself to him more tightly.

Never tightly enough.

"Easy," Gareth murmured. "I want to love you all night. There's no rush,"

"But I crave..." Felicity went silent as pleasure spiked upward on his next thrust.

"And you shall have." He moved in her just as slowly, but with a hint more power and depth.

"Better," she whispered. "But Gareth, please..."

"Hush." He bent his head to give her a deep, open-mouthed kiss that met her need for more, and enflamed her further at the same time.

"Gareth." She would beg, she would plead, she would make wild promises, if only she could form the words.

"I know, love," Gareth said, kissing her again. "I know. Trust me." By slow increments, he changed the depth, speed, and angle of his thrusts, joining their bodies ever more closely. Felicity realized he'd measured his breathing in counterpoint to hers, so their torsos stayed seamed together, even as their hips moved. Still, she rocked up against her lover in a desperate need to be yet closer to him.

She crossed an eternity of pleasure with him, holding him desperately tight as longing, love, loss and desire twined through her soul.

When the first tear seeped from her closed eyes, Gareth began to give her the deep, powerful strokes that would bring satisfaction to her.

She let herself be swamped by the delight he gave her, buried her face against his chest and rocked up against him, rocked up *into* him with every muscle in her body, clinging and crying out with the force of her pleasure.

And her grief.

He eased her down with a return to that languid, lazy rocking together, stroking her face gently and smiling down at her when she opened her eyes. His gaze was so tender, so unguardedly pleased and sad, she had to close her eyes again.

I love you, I love you. I will always love you.

GARETH GAVE Felicity a while longer to drift as he rested his forehead against hers. Were she more experienced, he could have made love to her for hours, but the day before he'd pleasured her thoroughly—and a bit roughly—with his hand. He could have offered her a joyous romp tonight as well, or an encounter laced with ribald good cheer. He knew infinitely many ways to share pleasurable sex with a willing woman.

But he wanted—he needed—to *make love* with Felicity on their one and only night together. He needed to grant her wish for the experience of having not a bed partner, but a *lover*. For that, only tenderness and care would do, and so, he gathered himself to complete their loving.

She responded to the change in him as he began to move in her again. Whereas before, he'd been attentive and arousing, now he was focused and aroused, truly aroused. A mild pleasure would not do for Felicity, nor did Gareth seek one for himself. He sought to possess her, and to give her everything of himself at the same time. He flexed into her more deeply, letting her feel the relentless power driving his desire. She brought her legs up to lock them around his hips, holding him to her even as he withdrew to plunge again.

Without increasing his speed, he levered himself more tightly into her, and felt satisfaction bearing down. Felicity curled up, fused her mouth to his, drawing on his tongue in rhythm with his thrusts. She broke off as pleasure overcame her, leaving her shuddering even as he continued to stroke into her.

"Look at me," Gareth rasped. "Look at me when I love you."

Topaz heat locked on him, and without breaking her gaze, he spent himself deep inside her body, letting her see, even as he forced her through the fire yet again, the desperate pleasure, the passion, and the peace that being her lover had at last had brought him.

AS FELICITY gradually regained her breath, thoughts were at first too hard to hold. She held her lover instead, this dear, precious, generous, wonderful man, whom she must leave in a few hours. In one sense, she craved that parting, because the emotions and sensations Gareth had created for her were too much, too intense. Only the comfort of his weight pressing her to the bed reassured her she would not dissolve from a pure, overloaded intensity of feeling.

And in another sense, she dreaded their parting.

"You are generous and brave," Felicity said, pushing Gareth's hair off his forehead.

"You inspire me," he whispered, laying his cheek against her temple.

In comfortable silence, they lay together a good long while. Felicity eventually felt him slip from her body. Oh, what a loss that was. Still, she didn't want him to take his weight from her.

"You'll be all right if I get up?"

"I will be immobile for the next age, Gareth, so thoroughly have I been ravished. Please notify my sister accordingly, sparing her the unnecessary details."

"I'm not that brave," Gareth muttered, climbing out of the bed. He retrieved water left to warm by the hearth and a flannel. Felicity watched him wash the evidence of his passion from his body, then spread she her legs obligingly while he did the same for her.

"How shameless you've become." He gave her a proprietary pat on her privy parts when he'd finished tending her.

"Beyond redemption," Felicity replied, drawing the covers up over them both and flopping over to her side. "By your most inspiring example."

"I will provide one more example for you," Gareth told her, stifling a yawn as he spooned himself around the curve of her back. "I will now demonstrate that behavior most common to the sexually satisfied male by closing my eyes and, quite shamelessly, going right to sleep. I suggest you do likewise."

He was dodging—or being as wise and kind as the situation would allow. Felicity closed her eyes and wiggled her backside into the warmth of his body. They had had a long, difficult day, and she hadn't the strength—or the courage—to ask him to stay awake merely so she could store up yet still more moments of his company before the parting that must occur in the morning.

❧

IN THE SOFT, dark shadows after midnight, Gareth showed Felicity the pleasures to be had when sleeping with her back cradled against her lover's chest. When she woke just after dawn, sprawled on his chest, he gave her new pleasures, ones that allowed him to stroke and fondle her breasts while she controlled the speed and intensity of their coupling.

He hadn't intended to ask so much of her, but he was able to bring her to satisfaction with the subtlest of touches, with tenderness and care. She showed no signs of discomfort, though he was wise enough to doubt she'd admit discomfort even if she felt it. As she drowsed in his arms, he wanted her yet again, and again after that, but having granted her wish for a night together, he held himself responsible for managing their parting as well.

And each time they joined, he made that parting more difficult not only for himself, but for her, too.

He left the bed to build up the fire, knowing Felicity watched him when he moved around the room rather than return directly to the bed.

"I'm not leaving you yet," he told her, finding the water and flannel and making use of them again before rejoining her under the covers. "We have a few hours, at least." He kissed her nose, then wrapped her in his arms. "I said we'd part in the morning, and morning lasts until noon, I'm told."

But Felicity had doubtless sensed the change in him, the slight withdrawal. She kept her hands above his waist, and made no move to ask more lovemaking of him.

"I know you'd rather I hopped out of this bed, threw on my clothes, blew you a kiss and scampered out of your life," Felicity said, curled against his side.

She was being brave, and her example, as he'd said, did inspire him. "I wish you would, and I'd be devastated if you could."

"To think of not seeing you again, not holding you again, not even knowing if you are well or troubled, or even alive—it unnerves me. How shall I—"

He silenced her with a finger against her lips.

"Hush, love. You must think only of the next moments, and the next, and the next, and you will, sooner than you believe, find you are not missing me quite so much as you feared you would. Besides, I suspect Andrew would tell you—despite my wishes to the contrary— if I were seriously indisposed. We will need to contact one another indirectly for the next several months, at least until the brothel can be sold."

He'd taken inordinate comfort from that realization, which was selfish of him—also stupid.

"What if I don't want to sell it?"

She would hold onto the brothel, risking all the damage it could do her, just to maintain a connection with him—a connection he was not worthy of.

"Then my purpose in your life is truly at an end today, and we will have no further dealings, indirect or otherwise."

"I gather you'd prefer I sell."

"Of course I'd prefer you sell, goose. The longer you are associated with that place, the more likely it is people will learn of your interest in it. Somebody at Willard and Willard has already been egregiously indiscreet. Not selling all but guarantees whoever sought to tarnish your name will succeed—and my name as well, come to that."

At that last thought she looked mortally disgruntled, while the way she stroked his chest was doing rotten things to his self-restraint.

"You are fretting," Gareth said on a resigned sigh. "I'll ring for breakfast and we can discuss how you can profit from this business without being seen to know it exists."

Felicity was an astute woman, and she had to know when she left the bed that Gareth had just shepherded her another step along the path leading them away from each other. She tried to pay attention over breakfast while he explained his plans for their business dealings, but her mind was no doubt on their looming separation, even he sat beside her on the couch and tried to feed her warm, buttered toast.

"My dear, you are not attending," he chided, offering her the toast. "Brenner and I arranged for your accounts to be handled by his old firm. Even as we speak, your files are being retrieved from Willard and Willard and sent to the new solicitors. Brenner will alert my own firm to the situation, and should it be necessary, you can have your solicitors contact Brenner through them. You aren't being cast completely adrift, you know. Brenner is nothing, if not conscientious."

She peered into her tea cup, as if the dregs might hold a picture of her future. "And if I have need of contacting you?"

He could smile and flirt, he could make her hope. He could provide her an address and an invitation "just in case," but as he considered her question, Gareth realized that despite all odds to the contrary, Felicity Worthington had made some sort of gentleman of him in truth.

Equal measures of surprise and resentment collided, along with a dash of rueful humor, and a sense of resignation.

He stirred his tea—weak China black because it was her favorite. "You must not contact me, Felicity. The only exception I would ask you to make..." he paused, and to his consternation, his hand trembled as he reached for another slice of toast. "The only exception I would ask you to make is if there is a child. I would not have our child raised as an unacknowledged bastard."

He managed the tea pot, pouring her a fresh cup he doubted she wanted.

"I thought you said a child wasn't possible because of the way we timed it."

"Much better men than I have been made fathers by the vagaries of nature, Felicity. I was conceived during my mother's courses, if my father is to be believed. The only way to prevent conception of a certainty is to abstain, so I would ask this of you: You will let me know?"

"Of course." The swiftness of her answer was some comfort, some very little comfort.

As Gareth consumed food he did not taste, he detailed for her what she could expect from her new firm of solicitors, and what steps would prepare the business for sale. He'd set it up so that very little would be required of her. Brenner, or an agent of his choosing, would handle the sale, though Felicity's signature would be required. He cautioned her to make her signature as illegible as possible without actually scribbling.

"Have you any questions?" *My love.* For she was his love, regardless that their time was almost over.

He had a question: How were they to live through this day? The depth of his heartache confounded him, made him resentful, and made him worried—for her.

"I comprehend, Gareth, and thank you for arranging matters. I would not have known how to change solicitors, much less how to sell a brothel. I am in your debt."

She smiled at him—the warm, dear, soul melting smile—and the last, desperate mental fiction that he'd survive this day as a whole man gave way.

"Callista is in my debt, may she rest in peace," he said. "Shall I help you dress?"

Felicity's expression said she knew this was more progress toward their parting, that she knew damned good and well he'd not taken her hand over breakfast, or put an arm around her shoulders, on purpose.

He was trying to ease her through the morning and hurting her brutally with each increment of distance he imposed.

She slipped into her clothes, and only approached Gareth when the hooks on her gown needed to be done up. Those, he fastened with brisk efficiency until he reached the nape of her neck. His fingers slowed as he brushed aside her hair.

"You had best brush your own hair," he suggested quietly. She nodded without turning, and found his hairbrush on top of the bureau. He did allow himself to watch her, and had the sense she took her time, making this personal activity as lovely and graceful for him as she could. When she'd braided her hair and pinned it into a coronet, she turned to him, handing back his brush. He was dressed informally, wearing only breeches, boots, waistcoat and a loose linen shirt.

"No cravat?"

"I don't anticipate leaving the house for some hours yet."

He made himself watch as she absorbed that blow. Saw her pain in the curve of her neck as she dipped her chin, in the way her hands clenched and unclenched twice against her skirts.

"Felicity..." He caught her by the shoulders when she would have continued to look away. He drew her against his body, knowing it was selfish, cruel, and necessary if he were to continue to draw breath. "I would have us say any private good-byes here, lest we embarrass old Hughes, hmm?"

As he rested his chin on her crown, and stroked her back in the sweeping caresses that had soothed him on so many other occasions, she let herself weep.

And with those tears, Gareth learned what it sounded like when a woman's heart broke. He did not remonstrate her—the tears were his fault, after all—but neither did he offer her comfort beyond his embrace and the touch of his hand on her back. He offered her no promises, false or otherwise. He offered her no hope. He offered her nothing but whatever consolation she could wring from knowing her sorrow was shared in that moment by the man who'd caused it.

CHAPTER SIXTEEN

As far as Felicity's heart was concerned, Gareth had already left.

In his place, the quiet, self-contained marquess held her, his very silence magnifying her sense of loss, her sense that soon even he would not be within the ambit of her touch. She clung to him, crying like a bereft child, missing the part of him he had already withdrawn from her, even while he stood with his arms around her.

And soon, it hurt too much even to cry. His lordship fished out a handkerchief and stepped back to mop gently at Felicity's face. He smiled at her sheepishly, and folded her fingers around his handkerchief.

"In case you have need of it later."

A final kindness, a token, a last whiff of his scent. She nodded her thanks, words being beyond her.

He watched her folding the little cloth into her fist.

"If you are sufficiently composed, Felicity, I'd like to escort you downstairs. We have yet a few more needful things to say to one another," He spoke gently, and Felicity knew he would not tolerate her procrastinating here for another hour.

Not for another minute.

He offered her his arm, and she wrapped her fingers into the crook of his elbow. When they reached the door, he turned to her.

"Good-bye, my love." He kissed her mouth, her cheek, her forehead, and her knuckles—left and right in turn. With each gesture, he became less intimate, more formal. He became more and more, Heathgate.

Without further word, he escorted Felicity down to the sunny little parlor where she had first met him. Felicity recognized the room, of course, and had a sense of coming full circle, of standing in the same place, but being a different woman.

"I have more difficult things to say to you, Felicity," he told her in that same, gentle, cultured voice.

But he did not touch her.

"If I should call on you, you must not be at home to me, for I would not be at home to you."

Felicity closed her eyes, his words landing on her heart like dirt on the coffin of a beloved friend.

"If you receive correspondence from me, you must return it unopened, for I will return any such correspondence to you unopened. If we should meet in public, and I sense the meeting is by anything other than purest chance, you must offer me the cut direct, or I shall be forced to offer it to you. You have means now. Take your sister to Bath, go on a walking tour in the Lake District, distract yourself from this dalliance you've had with me, and forget what you think you feel for me. Our business is concluded, and I certainly intend to move along to other pleasurable pursuits."

Felicity could not even nod. She knew full well what he was about. He was intentionally offering her the means to hate him. He was telling her he intended to dally elsewhere, soon and often, to put this bothersome little episode with her behind him.

"Felicity, do you believe what I've just told you?" he asked, a good impersonation of longsuffering condescension in his voice.

She turned from him, unwilling to watch the effort he was making on her behalf, for he wasn't convincing her for a single minute that she'd meant nothing to him. And she wouldn't let him have the last word, but she nodded affirmation—in return for his sacrifices, for all his sacrifices, she owed him that.

"Hughes is in the hallway. He'll escort you to the carriage awaiting you in the mews. There's the door, sweetheart, you have only to walk through it."

He hands settled on her shoulders from behind and turned her to face the door. He gave her a gentle push and his hands dropped, but she stood her ground.

"I will never," she said, facing away from him and speaking in a low, composed voice, "forget you, or that you are the man who came to be both lover and friend to me. You will continue to dwell in my mind and my heart as a friend at least, as I would be to you. And I will miss you, Gareth. I will miss you until my dying day."

Felicity was proud of herself for making her speech without turning and flying back into his arms, but having made it, she still lacked the fortitude to follow up with a grand exit. She took a breath, hoping to find courage enough to move her feet, when she felt the barest hint of a weight from behind.

Gareth's hand appeared in her peripheral vision, resting on her shoulder.

"My dearest love, if you would be my friend, then I must ask you —beg you—take your leave of me now." He spoke barely above a whisper, not the haughty, bored marquess, but the lover, the companion, the friend.

And he sounded every bit as devastated as she felt. Felicity wrapped her fingers around his hand, brought his knuckles to her lips for a kiss, then walked away without looking back.

~

FROM THE DEPTHS of the parlor, Gareth saw the coach roll past the house. Felicity had drawn the shades, but he made himself watch until the horses trotted around a corner and the whole equipage disappeared from view.

He heaved a sigh, trying to be relieved—congratulating himself would have been too great a farce.

He had done it—said his good-byes as if he meant them, and sent Felicity on her way, back to the life of genteel respectability she deserved. Well done of him, if he did say so himself.

Of course, he hadn't quite convinced her she was being casually tossed aside—she'd outmaneuvered him at the end—but still, she'd left him, knowing better than to expect impassioned declarations from the likes of him.

A decent job, all around. Felicity had her financial security; and she need never set foot on the premises of her business again. Gossip should die for lack of any new developments, and all should be well.

Because he was a man of relentless determination, Gareth continued to repeat these sentiments to himself in some form as he stood, staring sightlessly out the parlor window over the next half hour. Finding no comfort whatsoever in his own twaddle, he applied his determination in a more productive direction, and by noon had achieved a state formerly unfamiliar to him, that of complete, stinking drunkenness.

~

ASTRID WAS MORE than a little worried.

Felicity had returned from what had obviously been an entire night spent in the company of the marquess and had hardly spoken a word since. For several days, she had barely left her room, and even now, three weeks later, she spent much of her time in solitude, a monogrammed handkerchief clutched in her hand, grief in her eyes.

At first, she had told Astrid it was simply her monthly, hitting her harder than usual.

But monthlies came and went, and enough was enough. Pining for the marquess was understandable, but he was only a man, after all, and not that impressive a specimen, if a sense of humor and joie de vivre counted for anything. Something had to be done, but what?

Astrid's musings were interrupted by their new butler's announcement that a gentleman caller had arrived.

The caller was not Lord Andrew, whom she'd been telling herself not to miss for days now.

"Mr. Holbrook!" Astrid beamed at her guest, and when he would have offered her a bow, she took both his hands in hers instead. "It is positively lovely to see you. You are a ray of sunshine to one confined in the dungeons of Caesar's Gallic letters. You must make this a long visit, sir, or I shall be gloomed to death."

"Good heavens, not the Gallic letters." Holbrook passed his hat and cane to the butler. "Isn't it illegal for females to read Latin?"

"Probably." Astrid rang for tea and took a seat on the sofa. "But if I want to read all that naughty Catullus, I need to learn some grammar and vocabulary first. Interesting bunch, those old Romans."

"You are serious," Holbrook said. "I don't know whether to be impressed or suggest your sister confine you with Fordyce's Sermons. Will Miss Worthington be joining us?"

Astrid's feelings abruptly hared off in all directions—resentment, frustration, longsuffering—and no little consternation, because by herself, she should not have invited Mr. Holbrook to stay.

Which point, he'd just delicately raised, drat him and his pretty eyes.

"My sister is mildly indisposed, thank you for asking." She was spared further explanation by the arrival of the footman with the tray. He shot a slightly censorious look toward Mr. Holbrook and took himself off no doubt to tattle to Mrs. Crabble.

Astrid started to pour, only to realize she was preparing to fix her own cup first. "And how do you take your tea, sir?"

"Plain today. I hope Miss Worthington's indisposition is nothing serious?"

"Oh, it's serious all right. Serious, grumpy, arrogant. I refer, of course, to the Marquess of Heathgate, who figured prominently in some embarrassing pronouncements made by a young lady of your acquaintance as you strolled recently by a certain duck pond."

She handed him her tea, that is, tea made with plenty of cream and three lumps of sugar. When he looked down at it in a puzzlement, Astrid realized her error.

"Oh, for goodness sake. I do apologize. Let me try again?"

Holbrook passed her the tea and lifted the pot himself. "Why don't I pour, while you enjoy that? Your nerves appear to be need of settling." He poured himself a cup of black tea and sat back. "So Heathgate was jilted more thoroughly than your sister intended?"

He apparently knew the gossip, though Astrid had the sense his interest was kindly.

"It's such a muddle," Astrid muttered. "Heathgate's a rascal, to use a ladylike term, so he thinks he ought not to offer for Felicity, lest she be disappointed. But he's also quite the marquess, so Felicity thinks she ought not to encourage him, lest he form a union beneath his station, or some such nonsense. I could just slap that man for sending her into this decline."

Holbrook considered his tea. "I have the sense plain speaking is in order."

"Discretion is in order." But how did one pretend to swill tea and discuss the weather when one's only relation hadn't left the house in weeks?

"I am very discreet, Miss Astrid. I give you my word, as a gentleman, as a friend, and as a fellow versed in the medical arts, that I do not gossip where a lady's welfare is concerned."

She should not be sitting here with him, even with the door open and Mrs. Crabble humming off-key Handel as she swatted the sideboard in the front hallway with a dust rag.

"Your trust would mean a great deal to me, Miss Astrid."

Heathgate had not trusted Mr. Holbrook, but where was Heathgate now? "I fear Felicity has entered a decline," Astrid said. If Heathgate were to fret over something, that struck Astrid as an excellent place for him to start.

Holbrook lifted the plate of tea cakes and held it out to Astrid. "She is not eating?"

Astrid did not want to eat either, but took a lemon cake to be polite. "Barely. She does not dress, she does not go out, she does not even speak much."

Holbrook stirred his tea, which had neither cream nor sugar in it. "It could be, Miss Astrid, your sister, having become attached to Heathgate, is simply pining for a former amour. If he is her first, then she's likely to take it quite too much to heart that they don't suit. She strikes me, however, as a practical and resilient young lady. You must trust her to come 'round in her own time."

Astrid took a raspberry tea cake this time. The conversation was very adult, and she should be pleased Mr. Holbrook would speak to her so, though she was at a loss to recall why adulthood had ever loomed with any appeal.

"Felicity has been practical and resilient for too many years. I fear this business with the marquess has exhausted her reserves." For it had certainly tried Astrid's patience, and she'd barely had to deal with the man.

Or his handsome brother. On that thought, she followed the raspberry tea cake with one covered in chocolate icing.

Mr. Holbrook held his tea cup a couple inches above the saucer, which brought out the fact that his left eye was the same color as the Jasperware. "If Miss Worthington doesn't rally soon, will you send word to me, so I can guide you in seeking consultation with a physician who might offer her some assistance?"

As if Lissy would permit a physician within twelve yards of her. "In truth, Mr. Holbrook, it is a relief to talk to someone about this, because I do worry, but you are not precisely... I feel awkward, that is to say... oh dear." Astrid gave up in frustration, and was about to blurt out something far too blunt, when Holbrook spared her.

"Miss Astrid, I have already assured your sister, and I would like to assure you, I have no amorous intentions toward either one of you.

I would simply like to be a friend to this household, in whatever capacity a friend is needed."

She had read some Catullus and knew that friendship—particularly from gentlemen not in contemplation of marriage—could be a flexible and not always proper concept. "Why?"

Holbrook sipped his tea, looking elegant and composed—suspiciously so? Astrid was safe, receiving him in her own home, because the place was crawling with footmen and maids, but he didn't necessarily know that.

"Your question is direct, Miss Astrid, and I will offer you directness in return. I grew up without a father, and my mother did not live to see me reach adulthood, which gives you and me something in common, by the way. In any case, I know firsthand what challenges can befall people who are facing the world, particularly as young adults, without familial support."

He set his cup and saucer on the low table. "As a gentleman, I am also aware that females who lack concerned male relations are at a disadvantage. I own myself protective of you and your sister, though I am, as you point out, little more than a stranger. The sentiment is there, nonetheless, and it cannot be any great inconvenience to have me stop by to chat from time to time, can it? How long has it been since you've taken a turn in the park?"

Astrid frowned at her tea, because it had been an age since she'd heard a duck quack, and that was Heathgate's fault too.

"I shan't go driving with you, but perhaps you wouldn't mind a short stroll about the park? I haven't fed my ducks for days, and even Felicity must understand I won't be denied their company indefinitely."

Holbrook smiled at her then, a smile as different from his proper-fellow smile, as a male peacock was different from his drab little mate. He approved of her request, and that was more reassuring than it should be.

~

ASTRID WORTHINGTON WAS GROWING UP, the shift in her perceptible even in the few encounters David had had with her. As they walked along arm and arm, her footmen pacing them several yards back, he offered her one safe topic after another.

He managed to draw her out in conversation, even as he had no doubt they were being followed. Not only by the two footmen who had appeared several respectful yards behind them when they'd left the house, but by at least two others. They weren't casual idlers out to watch a pretty girl feed the ducks, either. The two Holbrook had spotted were exchanging discreet nods and glances, and the Worthington footmen were oblivious to them.

Beside him, Astrid was chattering on about the amount of gore and impropriety found in the Bible, and how she had always thought it a wonderful punishment to have to copy verses out the Old Testament.

"Miss Astrid, I believe you could find entertainment in almost anything, so creative is that mind of yours, but I would like you to stroll along casually while you attend me closely." He offered his arm to her without glancing in her direction.

"I can do that." For her age and inexperience, she was quick and canny.

"I noticed you took not one but two sturdy footmen with you when we left the house, and those fellows are fairly close at hand, which is a good thing, for we have company in addition to your staff."

"What sort of company?"

"I don't know," David said, patting her hand when what he wanted was to retrieve the knife from his boot. "I've spotted at least two other men, working in concert, who are observing our every move. I think it prudent we cut this excursion short and you not return here on foot."

Astrid looked out over her duck pond longingly.

"It *was* such a lovely day. These fellows you see are probably just more of old Heathgate's foot patrol. He has them keep a close eye on Felicity and me, though she hasn't left the house in days."

"I thought you said your sister sent Heathgate packing?"

"She did, or he cut her free, or whatever. They do not associate any more, but Heathgate was advising us on some matters of business, and so..." Astrid fell silent a moment. Two months ago, she would not have paused to choose her words. "They do not associate, but he is concerned for our safety, so he has his minions keep an eye on us. I hardly notice them anymore, but I suspect they are still about."

Now this was interesting. Heathgate advised the ladies on business matters, provided them bodyguards, and was no longer willing to associate with them directly.

The whole business made absolutely no sense, none at all.

ANDREW REGARDED THE UNSHAVEN, gaunt, specter that was his older brother and suppressed a shudder. If the servants were to be believed, Heathgate paced the house at all hours of the night, decanter in hand, and spent the days dozing and drinking still more. He growled and barked without even a pretense of manners, and had raised his voice at Brenner when that man insisted on some direction from his employer.

Brenner had taken it upon himself to ask Andrew to call. When Andrew joined his brother in the library, he felt a moment's shame Gareth had come to this state and Andrew had been too "busy" to notice.

"So who was it that went whining for you? Either Hughes or Brenner, I'll wager. Well, you've seen me, I am upright—more or less —and you may now depart. You'll pardon me for not offering a drink, but you'd have to swill from the bottle, and I've appropriated this one for my exclusive use."

Time to have a word with Hughes. Andrew moved toward the door, Gareth's voice stopping him.

"Don't look so prim and prissy, little brother," Gareth said, bitter humor in his words. "I merely smashed the glasses in a little tantrum. It's easier this way anyhow," he said, taking a swig of brandy. "You get drunk faster than if you sip like some old woman."

Andrew glanced around the chaos on his brother's desk. "Getting drunk has become a consummation devoutly to be wished?"

"Why no, brother mine, utter oblivion would fulfill that objective, but that would leave you brotherless and titled, and even I wouldn't purposely do that to you," Gareth quipped, drinking again.

The decanter went flying as Andrew pitched Gareth against the wall, am arm across his throat.

"Don't you *ever, ever* jest about that again," Andrew hissed, applying a savage pressure to Gareth's windpipe. "You may make me brotherless in spirit with this dramatic display of self-pity, but render me brotherless in fact and I will follow you into hell to take my revenge."

Andrew's forearm prevented Gareth from breathing, and Andrew saw the moment when Gareth welcomed the impending oblivion.

Fear replaced disgust as Andrew released his arm abruptly and backed away, leaving Gareth to stagger as he regained his breath and his balance.

"You reek," Andrew observed neutrally. "Your clothes are clean because the servants are loyal, but your person is unwashed, and you are drinking yourself into illness. If Felicity is worth this great excess of feeling, *my lord*, she is also worth a hot bath and a decent meal. Why are you abusing yourself this way when you know it would pain her greatly to know of it?"

"Don't say that name to me," Gareth rasped, rubbing his throat.

Andrew regarded him with growing consternation, and an odd thread of hope. "Why shouldn't I use the lady's name, Heathgate? Do you hate her so much?"

Gareth made a noise that might have been a laugh from a more sober man.

"No, dear brother. It isn't that I hate her so much, though I would if I could, it's that I miss her so much. You understand the distinction, I trust? For sometimes," Gareth concluded in quiet bewilderment, "I confess I do not." He sat on the cold stones of the hearth and dropped his forehead into his palm.

Gareth Alexander had gone from being the butt of society's cruel gossip, to being the man so oblivious to gossip, society gossiped about his indifference. He'd turned around an ailing marquessate, taken on responsibility for what remained of their family, and was in every way, an exemplary brother.

Seeing that same man scruffy, bewildered, and inebriated with loss, Andrew had the sense his brother's upset was even greater than it had been a decade ago. He sat next to Gareth, not knowing how to offer comfort.

"You are the envy of all who know you. The women want your escort, the man want to be you. You are wealthy, handsome, titled, and a law unto yourself, Gareth. You are successful—"

"Get away from me," Gareth protested wearily. "I stink," he added with the simple honesty of the grape.

"You do, and that can be remedied with soap and water, but this other, Gareth...You scared me badly enough when you latched onto that Hamilton woman and her ilk, but if this is what association with a decent woman does to you, then I shall have to hire you a troupe of opera dancers. I cannot bear to see you like this."

Though the problem wasn't association with a decent woman, it was apparently the absent of that same lady.

"Spare me the opera dancers, please. I thought you were off to the Constantinople." Gareth's gaze went to where a calendar ought to have been hanging on the wall. The spot was bare now, the desk itself a sea of random papers, a white quill pen atop the mess. "Why don't you just take yourself off if I'm such a disappointment to you?"

Andrew rose, paced off and turned to glare at his brother. "I can't very well leave my properties in the hands of a sot, can I?"

"Oh, very well," Gareth replied, waving a hand. "Ouch, that hurt. There, now, are you happy? You've proven conclusively I am not yet numb. One must resign oneself to diligence when it comes to inebriation."

Diligence was also useful when planning a trip one didn't want to take. "You are a damned amusing drunk. Not fragrant, but amusing."

"Amusing now, am I? Amusing and successful?" Gareth scrubbed a hand over his face, then seemed surprised to notice he was well on the way to growing a beard. "What I am, dearest brother, is lonely. When I was with Felicity, I was not lonely."

Andrew sat beside his brother again, put an arm around him, and rubbed a hand between Gareth's shoulder blades.

The man was too skinny.

"Is there anything I can do?" Andrew asked, surprised Gareth didn't heave him across the room for his impertinence. "I'll drag the lady over here, serenade her from the street with you, and even order you a bath, but I hate to see you this way. I cannot lose you too, Gareth. I simply could not bear it, not even for Mother's sake."

"I was such an ass, Andrew," Gareth dropped his forehead to Andrew's shoulder. "Not only with Felicity, but ever since the accident, I've behaved like the most spoiled, arrogant, worthless, embarrassment—not to the title, but to the family. How did you stand to be associated with me?"

What on earth? "It was endless work," Andrew said. "All that dash and carefully cultivated masculine appeal, the casual wealth, the sophistication. What fellow wants to be associated with that? Shall I see about that bath?"

Gareth glanced around the office, which compared to the order Andrew usually saw here, was a shambles. The ruins of the decanter lay near the desk, cold ashes spilled out of the hearth, and the scent of expensive brandy perfumed the air.

"I suppose so. I can always resume drinking when I smell better."

Andrew gave his brother's knee a pat. "That's the spirit. A fellow has to pace himself if he's to pursue true ruin, but Gareth?"

"Hmm?"

"Why in God's name don't you just go to Felicity, tell her you're a changed man, and you need her by your side no matter what? I doubt she'd turn you down cold, though she might put you through some tribulation first."

Gareth gave Andrew a thoughtful, almost cagey, look.

"The difficulty, Andrew, lies in the nature of the change you perceive in me. What if the change is temporary, an aberration from a course set years ago? What if it simply isn't in my nature to be a faithful husband? She has a particular aversion to the notion that a man should enjoy variety in his pleasures."

He pushed a shard of glass away with the toe of his boot. "One doesn't like to disappoint, you know, and it's quite possible I am only having this dramatic display, as you describe it, because the lady would not entertain the usual sort of liaison."

And Andrew was nearly certain Gareth had not even offered that sort of liaison to her, either. The seed of hope in Andrew's heart germinated, even as he resolved to stop talking about a tour of the Continent, and start putting his plans into effect.

"I leave that imponderable for you to soak on," Andrew said. "It seems to me, though, the issue is not so much whether Felicity could rely on you, as whether you could rely on yourself. You've disappointed the decent women and proud papas of good society for years without a batting an eye. What you are loath to do is admit disappointment in yourself."

Upon which topic, Andrew himself was an expert.

Gareth made a disgusted face. "My little brother is now a philosopher. I am not the only rank thing in this room."

"I leave you, since you are back to flinging insults, and I am thus encouraged you will eventually make a full recovery to your obnoxious self." Andrew bowed, and kept his tone light. "Do you need my help, or can you make it up the stairs by yourself?"

"Out, whelp," Gareth said, rising off the hearthstones. The left side of his seat was streaked with ashes, his hair was rumpled, and he sported at least three days' growth of beard, but a hint of his typical imperiousness had asserted itself. "Tell Hughes I want the water scalding hot, for I must wash off both my own stench and that of your interfering, meddlesome, presumptuous, pontificating self."

"I'll tell them to make it boiling," Andrew called over his shoulder.

Feeling ninety-four years old, Gareth made his way upstairs to his chambers, rooms he'd been avoiding for almost a month. As he pulled a green ribbon from the remains of his queue, the footmen trooped in with the tub, buckets of hot water, and a tray with hot tea, crumpets, and butter. He went through the motions of bathing himself and washing his hair, drank three cups of strong, hot tea, and dressed himself in clean clothing. When he'd shaved and forced himself to eat some crumpets—with lots of butter—he gave orders for the office to be put to rights, and summoned Brenner.

This process, of going through motions when there was no point, of doing the next appropriate thing when he wanted to howl out his misery, was familiar.

Gareth knew what would follow—more of same, and more after that. Grieving for his family had been like this, an exercise in deception that eventually tried to become an exercise in self-deception. The servants would see him as regaining his dignity, and getting on with life. He would try to see himself that way as well, but inside, where he'd almost succeeded in closing off his heart, he knew a grief of this magnitude really never went away.

Never.

DAVID HOLBROOK HAD the gentle persistence of a parson's wife intent on recruiting bachelors for the spring assembly. He teased, he small-talked, he smiled, and he kept coming around until Felicity had agreed to drive out with him mostly to get him to desist with his offers.

And the outing hadn't been awful, even if she'd spent most of it glancing around in futile hopes of spotting a certain marquess looking splendid in his riding attire.

When Felicity returned from her drive in the park with David— Mr. Holbrook, that is—she found Astrid had decided to go off to feed ducks on her own again. Unusual, perhaps, but not alarming because she'd taken a footman and would have timed her walk during the park's most crowded hours.

Felicity poured herself a cup of tea, and considered the growing conundrum that was her younger sister. Perhaps she and Astrid should travel before cold weather, as Gareth had suggested weeks ago.

"Miss Felicity, Miss Felicity!" Crabbie's voice was raised in panic. The older woman came bustling forward from the back of the house. "You must come quick, please. Young Tolliver is come back without Miss Astrid, and he needs the surgeon!"

Felicity went into the hallway where Mrs. Crabble was wringing her hands in her apron.

"I'm here, Crabbie. Take me to Tolliver and fetch the medicinals, please." Years of dealing with Astrid's scraped knees and the stable boys' mashed toes had taught Felicity the necessity of calm in medical emergencies, and then Crabbie's words sank in: Young Tolliver is come back *without Miss Astrid*.

When they arrived to the kitchen, Tolliver ceased bellowing at Mr. Crabble and tried to stand. He was a strapping young fellow, one of the extra staff Gareth had insisted on, but the back of his livery was streaked with blood. Felicity put a hand on his shoulder and pushed him back into his seat.

"You are injured, Tolliver," she said. "You must sit so we may tend to you." Crabbie appeared with the medicinal stores, then busied herself with heating water to clean the wound, while Felicity gently parted the hair at the back of Tolliver's head. The man had nigh split his skull. The skin was broken and bleeding sluggishly, and a considerable goose egg was fast rising.

"Mr. Crabble, if we have ice, we'll be needing some crushed in a towel. If not, have one of the footmen fetch it from the tavern. Tolliver, you have quite a bump on your head, but I don't think you'll need more than a few tiny stitches. Now, how is it my sister did not accompany you home?"

Tolliver, apparently not knowing how to interrupt his betters, almost yelled so relieved was he to have the floor.

"That's what I was trying to tell Crabble, here! They done took Miss Astrid, Miss Worthington. Two fellows came up behind me and conked me noggin, whilst two other fellows came aside Miss Astrid, each took her by an arm, and they hustled her into a coach in no time a'tall. You must summon the watch, Miss Worthington, and pray God do it now or the marquess will plant me for sure."

Felicity backed away from the table, the bloody rag dangling from her hand.

"She's fixin' t' faint," Tolliver intoned ominously.

"I shall not faint," Felicity said, even as she felt light-headed and sick to think Astrid had been abducted.

Oh, God... This was exactly what Gareth had feared might happen.

"Miss, you must summon the authorities," Crabble insisted, laying a steadying hand on her arm. "The sooner we get help, the sooner we're likely to find Miss Astrid, safe and sound."

Crabble was right, of course. They needed help. They needed every bit of help she could raise on both sides of heaven.

"Hitch up the pony cart," she told Crabble. "Send another footman to raise the watch. Have him meet me at Heathgate's house. Tolliver, I hate to ask it of you, but you will have to follow as well when Crabbie has you sewn up. I'll need a groom to accompany me to that same destination. I'm off to fetch the marquess."

That brought a collective sigh of relief from the staff, but Felicity couldn't share their optimism. What if the marquess were not at home? What if he were not at home *to her*? What if he received her only to pat her on the head and tell her to summon the watch, for Astrid's mischief was no concern of his?

A thousand fears flitted through her mind, each worse than the last, before she found herself pacing Gareth's elegant yellow parlor. Hughes was not on duty, for the butler who showed her in had simply bowed and gone to see if the marquess was at home.

"Tell him..." She couldn't find the words, could hardly find a steady breath. "Tell him to come, please."

The man bowed again. He didn't have Hughes' intimidating formality, or Hughes' great age to commend him, but he looked at Felicity with polite sympathy before going to fetch his master—if his master deigned to be fetched.

~

THE DAY HAD BEEN SO PRETTY, as benevolent a summer day as London offered, and on the strength of that omen, Gareth had saddled up his horse and ridden off toward the Worthington residence.

He'd missed Felicity, missed her until his heart was crowded with it, his mind preoccupied with it, and his soul overflowing with it.

With the passage of time, he'd hoped to become more secure in his conclusion that letting Felicity go had been the honorable thing, the best thing to do for her. He'd made that decision with the conviction that he'd never have been a faithful husband, never have been able to offer her a whole heart. Most of all, he would never have wanted her to change, to become a tolerant wife, willing to look the other way and busy herself with their children.

As her own mother likely had.

As the weeks had gone by, he'd tried, more than once to take himself out prowling, and he'd had offers aplenty.

None of which had held the least appeal. It was as if, having refused to take Felicity as a lover for anything other than love itself, he was now incapable of trading in lesser coin.

He'd rather sit with a bottle of brandy of an evening, twiddling a white quill pen, holding a lavender satchet to his nose, and losing himself in memories as heartbreaking as they were comforting.

And such a state of affairs was pathetic, sufficiently pathetic that he'd saddled a horse and turned the beast in the direction of the Worthington townhouse. What he meant to say to Felicity, he had not known, and it hardly mattered.

He had to see her, to see she was faring well, to see that she wanted for nothing.

As he'd rounded the corner to turn his horse down the quiet street where the Worthingtons bided, Felicity had come out of the house on David Holbrook's arm, and climbed into the man's curricle. She'd been comfortable with her escort, relaxed, smiling, and when the damned man had leaned closer to offer some aside, she'd laughed.

She had a beautiful laugh.

Gareth had watched the curricle roll away in the direction of the park, and turned his horse for home. A man, even a man determined on martyrdom, could chose to hear a lady's rejections in private.

"A Young Person to see you, your lordship."

Gareth looked up from the column of figures he'd been staring at for twenty minutes. Felicity could have added them in a thrice, but Felicity was busy enticing Mr. Holbrook's interest.

"Parker, I realize you are only the underbutler, but did you not retrieve a card from this Young Person?" The last thing he wanted to do with this afternoon was be sociable.

"*She* was distraught, your lordship, and appeared to be greatly in need of your assistance," Parker rebuked him right back, though in chilly enough tones Hughes would have been proud.

Gareth got to his feet, puzzled. Cecelia, perhaps, come to seek consolation, if her new love had thrown her over as new loves were inclined to do.

He really did not have the patience for that now, though he supposed he owed her a polite hearing. But when he let himself into the parlor, he was astonished to see a lady with cinnamon hair standing with her back to him, her face bowed into her hands.

Without conscious thought, he walked up behind her, put his hands on her shoulders, and spun her to face him.

He opened his arms and she flew home to his embrace.

"Oh, Gareth..." Felicity murmured. "Gareth...."

He couldn't say anything, couldn't do anything, save hold her against him, and breathe in the lavender-scented reality of her.

She came to me. If Holbrook had offended her, hurt her, upset her, or merely bothered her, he'd see the man drawn and quartered.

Felicity was trying to tell him something, but she couldn't catch her breath, so he rubbed her back in slow circles. She was near hysterics, something he hadn't seen in weeks and weeks of difficult circumstances with her.

"Felicity, whatever it is, it will be all right," he said as he held her to him. "I promise it will be all right, but you have to tell me what distresses you so. Easy, love... take a breath, then slowly let it out. That's my lady."

"Gareth," Felicity whispered, "somebody has taken Astrid. She was feeding the ducks, and Tolliver said two men struck him from behind, and two others grabbed Astrid by the arms and forced her into a coach. She's gone, Gareth, my little sister is gone and I am so *upset*... What if she's murdered, raped, or worse? She's just a girl, and so sweet..."

Gareth stepped back, keeping his hands on her shoulders. "Have you summoned the authorities?"

"I have, and I asked Tolliver to meet us here when Crabbie had him stitched up. I should not impose on you, but I could not think who else would help us. What if we don't find her in time?"

He pulled her against his chest, even as he bellowed for Parker, Brenner, and his brother Andrew. The first two came at a run, the third was nowhere to be found.

Gareth stood in the center of the room, his arms wrapped around Felicity, her face tucked against his throat, while he barked orders and questions in all directions. Brenner mustered the household such that half a dozen footmen were dispatched to the park to question passersby regarding the abduction itself.

When Tolliver joined them, a half dozen grooms and stable boys were given a description of the coach that had driven off with Astrid, and told not to return until they had tracked down its direction. The watch received a report of a kidnapping, complete with a sketch of the victim and Tolliver's statement.

Gareth would have paced with frustration, except Felicity was still burrowed against his chest, upset and shaky.

"Brenner, where would somebody hide a girl of Astrid's description in this city?"

Brenner was about to open his mouth on some no doubt painfully honest, inadequate reply when he was saved by a voice from the doorway.

"I know where she is," Andrew panted. "He's got her at the docks. Holbrook—"

"Holbrook has her?" Gareth roared at the same time Felicity murmured,

"That's not possible."

Andrew shook his head. "Holbrook is the one who flagged me down. I was at the piers, seeing about passage to Italy next month, when I saw him skulking around one of the warehouses. He was on his way home from driving in the park when he saw Astrid bundled into a coach that took off posthaste for the docks. He followed as discreetly as he could, and he remains there, watching from what I hope is a safe distance while I'm summon help."

"Sweet fluttering angels," Gareth muttered. "Brenner, do we have any men left?"

"What's in this room, your lordship, and few of the older stable lads."

Stable boys by were occupation a slight bunch, but strong and tough as hell.

"It will have to do," Gareth said, knowing sunset approached. "Arm those who can use a weapon, bring the plain town coach, and make sure there's some brandy in the boot. We'll need whatever assistance the authorities can render as well. Brenner, please get a note to my mother, asking her to attend me at her earliest convenience for we'll be bringing Miss Astrid back here before sunset. I want us moving in fifteen minutes. Andrew can you draw us a map of the location and sketch the surroundings for us?"

As Andrew bent to comply and Brenner scurried off, Gareth held the woman in his arms the same way he had the night her house had almost gone up in flames. Around them, he commanded activity and created a controlled chaos of preparations, but some part of him, too, was focused on her.

Pandemonium whirled about them, and some corner of Gareth's soul was grateful for it, because Astrid's abduction had restored Felicity to his embrace.

"I'm coming," Felicity said during a pause in the mayhem. "She will need a woman about if she's been hurt." Then, more desperately, "Gareth, I can't wait here talking about the weather with your mother. You cannot ask it of me."

"I wouldn't, but you will wait with Parker in the coach. Can you shoot a gun if you have to?" She nodded, earning a kiss on her forehead.

And soon they were rolling out of the fashionable neighborhoods and toward the docks. Andrew, Felicity, Brenner, and Gareth inside, a half dozen armed men on the roof, Parker beside the coachy. They arrived to a seedy dockside neighborhood, scattered quietly to reconnoiter, then gathered again at the coach to confer.

"I seen 'em through a window on the alley," one wizened old fellow said. "Miss Astrid is tied to a chair near the street side, your lordship, and I count five men, one of 'em in fancy dress. The other four is muscle."

"Did Miss Astrid look distraught?" Gareth asked.

"Nah," he said, grinning. "She looked barkin', spittin', hoppin' mad. But sound enough."

"Thank God for that. Still no sign of Holbrook, though."

"He might be inside, me lord," another fellow offered. "There's a back door, all locked up rusty and dusty, but the lock has been popped."

Andrew was the last one to join them, scowling mightily.

"It's a damned fortress," he bit out. "The windows are all too high to climb in, and too small for me to fit through. I count three doors, but Astrid is seated and tied, for God's sake. The first moment those men suspect we're out here, Astrid could be hurt, or worse. I say we negotiate with them."

"Gentlemen?" Gareth canvassed the rest of the group, most of whom agreed with Andrew that too many advantages lay with the kidnappers.

He wanted to tell the lot of them they were fired, except they were sensible fellows, brave enough, and dear to their families. Astrid was bound, unable to protect herself, and negotiation was not a bad plan.

Also not one he could endorse.

"Felicity, do we negotiate?"

All heads turned and some caps were quickly doffed, suggesting the men hadn't realized she was listening. Gareth held out an arm to her, bringing her into the circle of men.

"You're asking me?"

"I will walk in there this instant if you'll allow it," he said. "Unarmed, and prepared to barter my kingdom for your sister." To barter his kingdom and his *life* for her sister.

Andrew broke the ensuing silence. "Heathgate, you're daft if you expect criminals—"

Felicity held up a hand. "What Andrew is about to point out is that if you walk in there unarmed, they'll have two hostages, and we'll be short a man we cannot afford to lose. People who would prey on an innocent girl will have no qualms about doing you an injury or worse."

"We could wait until dark," one man volunteered. "Maybe sneak in..."

Nobody took up the idea, and when Gareth wanted to tuck Felicity against him, she instead turned to address his men.

"So we wait, and what do you suppose will happen to Astrid while we wait, and her captors become more confident of their success? They're no doubt drinking, and she's pretty—also too outspoken for her own good, and she knows nothing of men."

This was the argument Gareth could not have made. *Time was of the essence,* but he could not ask of these fellows more than they were willing to give, lest they waver when he needed them steadfast. Felicity's gaze touched on each man, while Andrew took to swearing softly in French.

"Do you have plan, then Miss?" the old fellow who'd spoken earlier asked. "None of us want the young lady to come to any harm. Any more harm."

Felicity regarded Andrew, who was glaring murder at his boots. "They snatched her out of the park without anybody raising the hue and cry," she said. "They think they've won, and they won't be expecting problems—not now when they have her half way across London, and nearly two hours have passed. If there are three entrances, then we create a distraction from the direction they're least expecting one, and that leaves two other ways into the building."

Andrew looked up from his boots. "It's already nearly black as pitch in there, given how few windows the place has. Felicity's idea has merit. If there are six of them, we have the numbers, and the element of surprise." A few murmurs of assent followed, but not the unconditional support any desperate plan needed.

Gareth considered the woman he loved, and considered the likely harm to Astrid if she weren't freed before darkness fell.

"What if Felicity and I stumble in the back door?" Gareth proposed. "A doxy and her mark would be looking for privacy in an alley, and the door is to Astrid's back. She won't see us, and the other doors should soon be in deep shadow so you fellows can slip in."

The men liked that idea, though Andrew was back to scowling. "I foresee a problem. As soon as those men know they're under attack, one of them will simply hold a knife to Astrid's throat and threaten her murder if we don't surrender."

Felicity pinned him with a look. "Then your job, your *only* job Andrew, is to free Astrid. You slip in first, knife at the ready, and get her away while the rest of these fellows do the fighting."

Thus ensuring both brothers were not equally at risk of harm. Gareth could have kissed her, but instead looked at his brother. "Andrew?"

"Of course I'll take that assignment."

"Then the rest of us are tasked with providing you safe passage to do that, and bashing as many heads as possible in the process—preferably not our own, right, gentlemen?"

A chorus of agreements followed, which was the predictable result of Felicity's courage added to their own better intentions.

"Weapons?" Gareth queried, provoking a reassuring display of pistols, knives and—from the oldest groom—a set of brass knuckles. "Ye, Gods, what have I been harboring in my stables?"

"Best fetch that brandy bottle, your lordship," Parker reminded him. "No self-respecting sailor drags his dollymop into an alley without appropriate libation—particularly when said bottle can also knock a man senseless."

Gareth managed a smile at the suggestion, then held up a hand for silence. "David Holbrook was in this vicinity not long ago, but we've seen no sign of him. This could be a trap, or in the alternative, the kidnappers might have found him and done him harm. He's tall, well dressed, blond, and has mis-matched eyes. Don't do him injury unless you must to protect the women. Felicity?"

Gareth shed his coat and cravat, she took his proffered arm. In no time, they were in the alley, surrounded by gloom and the stench of rotting offal.

This was the last place he'd seek to bring her, the last role he'd ask her to play, and yet, a kind of ferocious satisfaction coursed through him too: Felicity had come to him, and by God, he would not let her down.

"C'mere, lovey," Gareth drawled, stumbling against the unlocked back door. "I just wanna little kish." He pinned Felicity up against the door, twisting the knob enough so when he leaned into her for his "kish," the door gave and they tumbled in, Felicity doing a creditable job of squealing like a doxy enticing a customer.

"Now there, no kissin' until I gets me blunt," she remonstrated, even as Gareth wrapped an arm around her waist and half-fell on her again. From the corner of his eye, he spotted Astrid across the cavernous interior, tied to her chair, all six men standing in a dimly lit circle around her.

"No blunt until I get's me kish," he argued. "I don't buy a skiff without makin' sure she's seaworthy, loovey." He puckered up and chased her chin around with his lips.

"Here now!" a voice boomed. "Out you two, this building is in use."

"Whaddya mean in use?" Gareth said, blinking owlishly at a burly fellow who'd brought a lantern over to the door. "There ain't been no cargo stowed in here, and all I wants is a little private-sy," he enunciated carefully. Then he smiled beatifically at Felicity. "A lady needs her private-sy when she entertains, right loovey?"

"I'm talking to you, man! You have to take the bitch and get out, now."

Felicity pasted a smile on her face and sauntered toward the fellow trying to chase them out, perusing him up and down.

"Now why should I give lover boy here a quick poke in that stinkin' alley, when we can be done with our business here in just five minutes, and then I'll be happy to compensate you for the use o' this splendid facility, me fine man. What say you?" She draped an arm around his neck, and leaned in to flash her cleavage at him. "I think he likes what he sees," she said wiggling the brandy bottle at Gareth.

"God damn it," a male voice bellowed from across the cavernous room. "Ames, get back here, we're under attack!"

Before he could respond, Ames got the business end of the bottle on the back of his head, the blow no doubt propelled by every ounce of strength and anger Felicity possessed.

"Go!" Gareth hissed, shoving her toward the door, and she was off like a shot for the safety of the coach. He blew out Ames' lantern, and sprinted toward the fight ensuing with the other five men. When the remaining abductors realized they were outnumbered, they held up their hands in surrender.

"Where's Astrid?" Gareth yelled.

"I'm over here," came a feminine reply, "but he's got Andrew!"

Gareth turned toward the voice, and saw Astrid was right. At the back door where he and Felicity had come in, Andrew stood next to another man, unmoving.

"Walk toward your brother, Lord Andrew," came the cultured, sardonic command, "so we might have this discussion in the light like the gentlemen we are." Andrew took slow, cautious steps toward Gareth's end of the room, his face devoid of all expression.

Gareth turned to the nearest groom. "Get the young lady out of here, please."

He melted away, taking Astrid by the arm and drawing her out of the light, while Andrew and his captor walked ever closer.

"Good-bye, sweet Astrid," called her abductor. "Dream of me," he taunted, coming to a halt a good dozen feet from Gareth.

"Riverton," Gareth spat. "To what do I owe the honor?"

"You have no honor," Riverton retorted pleasantly. "And thanks to you, I have no heir, so this was to be a small compensation to me. I think the intimate company of the young lady might have had a salubrious effect on my ailing health, don't you? Not to be, I suppose, so I am off to the Continent, courtesy of your worthless self."

Gareth folded his arms and widened his stance, trying to give every impression of a man settling in for a distasteful negotiation. All he could think to do was stall Riverton, and perhaps one of the grooms could angle around in the shadows and clobber the bastard from behind.

"How am I to get you to the Continent, and why would I do such a thing when your only bargaining chip is my wastrel younger brother?"

Whom Gareth loved to distraction, and who had a double-barreled pistol aimed point blank at his head.

"Oh, you'll do it," Riverton replied. "You wastrel brother is your only heir, and you would never be able to face your mother if his blood were on your hands *too*. I've studied you too long, Heathgate, to be wrong about this. In fact, I like this better than disporting with that little bitch. I could have had a lot of fun with her, but this will hurt you more."

"Riverton, this grows tedious. You apparently took a fancy to an unwilling female. You needn't kidnap a hostage to slink off to Italy, if that's your game. Just leave. I'm sure I can control my brother long enough to give you a reasonable head start."

Riverton guffawed—and kept the pistol snug against Andrew's temple.

"Oh, that was creative, Heathgate, as if I would pursue any female who had caught the eye of an Alexander simply for sport. Not bloody likely," he concluded, his voice turning ugly. "Now enough of your pontificating. You will hire me the fastest ship on the docks, to depart on the evening tide, and it will have on board enough gold to buy your brother's life." Riverton emphasized his demands by giving Andrew's temple a solid tap with the gun barrel.

Gareth forced himself not to look into his brother's eyes, but returned Riverton's sneer. "You are an ass, Riverton, or perhaps disease is affecting your mind. You expect me to charter you a boat and stock it with gold at a moment's notice? We are on the *London docks*. Without coin, nothing happens. With too much coin, one's life is forfeit. Now be reasonable and bugger off. You are beginning to aggravate me."

Gareth took an experimental two steps forward, halting when Riverton drew back the hammer on the pistol.

"You bugger off!" Riverton retorted. "You won't get what you want this time, Heathgate. You get the title, you get the stinking fortune, you get the women, but not this time! Nothing, *nothing*, would give me as much gratification as spattering your brother's brains all over this warehouse, unless I could also blow off your balls in the process."

Andrew was going to die. Andrew was going to die if Gareth couldn't parlay with this madman.

CHAPTER SEVENTEEN

Gareth spread his hands, leaving himself open to one of the two bullets Riverton might aim at any party he chose. "Riverton, if that's how you feel, why not take me instead?"

"Gareth, no!" Andrew interjected.

"Silence, damn you!" Riverton used the pistol barrel again, preparing to deliver a punishing blow, when he crumpled, clutching his side and gasping. Andrew wrenched the gun from his hand and spun away from his captor's grasp.

"Christ!" Riverton gasped on the floor. "You've killed me! Fetch the surgeon, for the love of God, somebody..."

David Holbrook emerged from the shadows.

"My man of business has often admonished me that a knife carried in the boot should be more than a fashionable pretension," he said, jerking his knife from Riverton's side. "Perhaps if you shut your mouth, Riverton, we might see about finding a surgeon but wounds that bleed freely are less likely to become infected."

A collective sigh of relief went up from the stable boys, while Gareth snatched his brother into a back-pounding hug. "Damn you, Andrew. Damn you and your bravery, and your nerve, and your..."

Andrew pulled away. "Damn me later, brother. I'm off to find a certain young lady."

Which left Gareth face to face with David Holbrook. "Took your sweet time saving my brother's life, Holbrook."

"Took your sweet time getting out of my line of sight," Holbrook replied, and then his face broke into a smile—an astonishingly winsome, warm smile. This smile eclipsed the man's natural reserve, his peculiar eyes, the surroundings, everything. Gareth dropped Holbrook's hand, as a suspicion welled up from that place in his mind where his best hunches, his keenest intuition, and his clearest insights sprang.

He held out his handkerchief to Holbrook. "Would you be good enough to join my brother and me at my townhouse? I'm sure the Worthingtons will want to thank you for your role in averting today's near-tragedy, and I have some questions regarding what Riverton thought he was about."

Holbrook took the white square of monogrammed silk and wiped off his blade. "I will be happy to accept your invitation, my lord, but I will repair to my own quarters first to make myself more presentable." He spared Riverton a glance before bowing and walking into the darkness.

And like a thief in the night, Holbrook would steal Felicity away. Not exactly in the manner Gareth had feared, but she'd again be lost to him nonetheless.

Tomorrow. Tonight, Felicity and Astrid would enjoy his hospitality, and that was as far as Gareth's tattered nerves could plan.

When Andrew and Gareth returned to the coach, they found both sisters had indulged in a bout of weeping, but had been cheered back to rights by Parker, Brenner, and the other men. Riverton's cohorts were bound and gagged, while Astrid looked pale but composed.

Gareth distracted her by offering her his flask. "A restorative, my lady?"

Astrid batted the flask away and flung her arms around his neck.

"You are an awful man, arrogant, stuffy, old, pigheaded and odious. Thank you, thank you, thank you," she said, her voice growing wobbly.

If this lively, irreverent, insightful, lovely, pigheaded, odious young lady had come to any harm—

"What?" Andrew asked beside them. "No hug for me?"

Astrid withdrew from Gareth's embrace and turned to face Andrew. Rather than gawk, Gareth handed Felicity up into the coach, and took a seat beside her, closing the door behind him.

"They will either kill each other or make peace," Gareth said, taking Felicity's hand.

"Tonight, they will be at peace," she predicted, lacing her fingers through his as if they'd not gone for weeks as strangers. Gareth looked at their joined hands in the gloom of the coach lanterns, and realized this might be the last time they'd be alone.

"Felicity, there are some things—"

But his thought was not be finished, because Astrid and Andrew piled into the coach. When Astrid reached for Andrew's hand, Gareth met his brother's gaze, and saw humor, resignation, and bewilderment in Andrew's eyes.

Also sorrow, though Andrew did not withdraw his hand.

When they reached Gareth's house, they found the household already apprised of Astrid's rescue. Her ladyship ordered a keg tapped belowstairs for the grooms and stable boys, while trays were sent to the library for the family. Gareth found a quiet moment to make a trip to his study, retrieving a document with a black ribbon around it.

By the time he returned to the library, Holbrook had arrived, looking dapper and severe, and not at all like man who could aim a knife accurately in the dark. When everybody but Holbrook had found a seat, Gareth gestured Brenner into the room.

"You need to hear this, Brenner," he said as the man found a perch on the hearth. "You are nothing if not a friend to this family, and you'll find it interesting." Brenner blushed, even his ears going pink, his smile bashful.

"Friends, Romans, countrymen?" Gareth said over the buzz of multiple conversations. He came around the front of his desk and hoisted himself up to sit, leaning on his hands, facing the room.

"Whom are we burying?" Astrid asked.

"None of our own," Andrew said from right beside her. "Thank God."

"Thank God," Gareth said, "and thank Mr. David Holbrook, late of Kent, and elsewhere." Silence fell as all eyes turned to Holbrook. "Holbrook, don't you think it time you let your sisters thank you properly?"

Holbrook's face suffused with pain as he set his plate aside.

"Our brother?" Felicity gasped. "Mr. Holbrook? *David*?" She crossed the room to stand in front of him. "Look at me," she said quietly. When Holbrook did not comply, she said it again, more fiercely. "Look. At. Me."

"You," she said wonderingly, "have Papa's nose. You are my brother. Astrid, we have a brother! Oh, a brother..." She went from elated disbelief to delighted squealing, throwing her arms around Holbrook and squeezing him until Astrid joined the embrace—and the squealing—while Gareth's sat across the room feeling a sense of naked, burning loss.

And joy—for Felicity deserved to have family to love her, at least.

"Why, this is wonderful," Lady Heathgate chimed in, cooing and fussing, calling for champagne and reaching for her handkerchief.

"It is," Gareth said. For Holbrook, possibly for Felicity and Astrid. "But it's also difficult, isn't it, Holbrook?" The squealing died down as all eyes turned to question Gareth, but he only repeated himself. "It's difficult, isn't it?"

Holbrook slipped away from his sisters. "It's very difficult."

"Why should it be so difficult?" Astrid interjected. "We have a brother now, and that can only be a wonderful thing. And I don't care one bit that Papa was indiscreet." She glared at Gareth to make her point.

"Tell them, Holbrook. The truth need never go further than this room if that's what the three of you decide," Gareth said gently. "We would all protect Felicity and Astrid with our lives. You've seen that."

His eyes said the rest: *You're safe here. Your sisters are safe here. You owe them the truth.*

Holbrook shifted to stand in front of the hearth, facing his sisters.

"Papa was indiscreet, indeed. He attached the affections of my mother, one of the Holbrook sisters, knowing his family would not approve the match. She was but the daughter of a baron, and Fairly, being early in his succession, was expected to look higher. He *was* looking, and in fact found himself engaged to your mother. But by then it was too late."

Felicity finished for him. "For he'd already married your mother, making you legitimate, and us"—she waved to encompass Astrid—"the bastard issue of a duplicitous, bigamous relationship."

"My heavens," Astrid said, sounding, if any, pleased. "This is a pickle, indeed." When Andrew slipped his arm around her, she stayed right next to him.

Felicity turned a worried expression on her brother. "Mr. Hol—*David*, you should have the title."

Holbrook speared her with a chilly regard. "I will not be the cause of distress to my sisters. I've handled this whole situation poorly, and I refuse to make bastards of my own sisters into the bargain. I was supposed to see you never wanted for anything, and I wasn't even aware you'd been orphaned until long after it happened." He dropped wearily to the hearth, rubbing a hand over his face. "I travel a lot, and dear cousin Callista was supposed to keep an eye on things while I was absent. I can see now she was in no position to do that."

What emerged as Holbrook spoke was a picture of a young man, torn by familial obligations. Holbrook's very existence posed a threat to his sisters' standing, so he traveled abroad extensively. Callista—his cousin as well—was to have ensured Felicity and Astrid were adequately provided for in his absence.

"She assured me you were managing, but I saw when I entered your house, she hadn't looked closely enough—and really, how could she have? I suspected her will had thrown you together with Heathgate, but feared you were associating with him for financial purposes, either to make an advantageous match, or worse. And then it seemed to me both trouble and gossip were following you too closely. I became even more concerned."

"So you became our friend," Astrid said, beaming at him. "How lovely. I have a brother who has never once teased me or bashed my doll about."

"But you knew Riverton," Felicity said to her brother, "and he was apparently the source of our trouble. What was going on there?"

"That," Holbrook said with a grimace, "was sheer, blasted bad luck. My father... our father, wanted to transfer the unentailed properties to me without attracting notice, so he recruited his social acquaintance, Riverton, to accomplish that. Papa 'lost' the land to Riverton in a rigged card game. Riverton then sold it to me, keeping a share of the proceeds for his silence and returning the rest to Fairly. You inherited what little remained on his death. Riverton did not know I was anybody's legitimate issue, or I suspect he'd have made even more trouble with that information."

Holbrook pinned Gareth with a look. "When I was hiding in the warehouse, Riverton did a lot of talking, a lot of muttering and ranting. I recall he said something about because you killed the Ponsenby girl and deprived him of his heir, it was only fitting he deprive you of your heir. What was that about?"

Lady Heathgate fingered a string of jet beads around her wrist. "So it was Riverton who got Julia with child," she murmured. "How extraordinary—and how unfortunate."

On the sofa, Andrew went into such a coughing fit Astrid had to pound him on the back.

"And," Gareth added, "Riverton was too far gone with disease thereafter to get any woman pregnant, hence his fixation on that child. I wonder why Julia didn't marry him—he was a viscount, and not poor, while I was not even an honorable."

Brenner cleared his throat. "Er, begging your pardon, my lord, but Riverton is poor. I got to visiting with young Mr. Willard about this and that, and he complained the quality were shoddy customers at best, and he'd rather work for the merchants any day. Riverton was his example of a titled client who had no money and less integrity. The man was flat done up and had been for years."

"Interesting. So perhaps Riverton was after the brothel as a source of income and then decided Callista's will made a fine way to discredit me instead."

Holbrook looked distinctly uncomfortable at the mention of the brothel. "I believe Riverton's knowledge of that whole situation is my fault," he said, staring at his hands. "Callista asked me to name a fellow I'd find utterly beyond the pale, and having had dealings with Riverton, I picked him. I had no idea she was drafting a will, or that Riverton might get wind of it. Thank God Callista chose you, Heathgate, and Riverton only as the compelling counterexample."

Lady Heathgate frowned thunderously from her chair by the window.

"Young man, do you mean to tell me you approve of your sister depending upon the good offices of a notorious rake?"

"Mother!"

"It's all right, Heathgate," Holbrook said mildly. "Lady Heathgate, it will not shock you to know that Callista Hemmings was quite familiar with the notorious rake in question, and in hindsight, I see that Callista never intended for Felicity to cross paths with Heathgate. Callista intended, rather, that the marquess and I should make each other's acquaintance. If I'm to assume my father's title as an obscure heir, then nobody is better suited than Heathgate to guide me in such an undertaking. Having studied Callista's will, I can only conclude Riverton's influence with her solicitors—or perhaps his unpaid accounts with them—inveigled them into supporting his prurient schemes, despite what Callista wanted for her family."

Silence greeted his pronouncement, broken by a question from Felicity. "You knew Callista?"

"I did, both of us being estranged from the family proper. Very likely she assumed I'd take an interest in her estate, as her only male relation, except I've been traveling for much of the past year. She was dying, and from her perspective family was worth any price, even bastardy and scorn. She knew I would welcome you both into my life on any terms, and being legitimate could only stand me in good stead. In truth, I care not whether I am a bastard or a viscount, but in another year, the decision will be moot. It has been six years since our father died, and as a missing heir, I have only more year to post a claim."

Felicity still looked confused. "So the will was intended to pass the business on to you rather than me?"

"I can answer that," Gareth said, holding up the black-ribboned document. "If you read this will, it never mentions the word madam, but instead refers to a manager, or proprietor. Those are both masculine terms. It also refers to an eldest cousin, firstborn issue of the Viscount Fairly. If you are the firstborn of two siblings, you are elder. If you are one of three siblings, then you are eldest. It was there, I just didn't see it," Gareth said, handing Felicity the will.

He needed to ensure she'd absorbed Holbrook's earlier point: "It is also, as we established with the senior Willards, absolutely not a requirement of this will that Callista's heir acquire anything other than business expertise from me. Callista was consigning Holbrook to be my protégé, which Riverton could not have known."

Lady Heathgate was still frowning, though she sounded less truculent. "This explains the gossip," she said. "Riverton would have wanted to discredit you, Heathgate, first as a competent trustee of the estate, so he could get his hands on the income, then as a gentleman. When that failed, he resorted to kidnapping and attempted blackmail."

"Is Riverton dead?" Felicity asked.

Andrew answered her. "He is. There will be an inquest, but you needn't worry. You weren't there, Felicity, and neither was Astrid. Riverton was set upon by ruffians, nothing more."

Holbrook exchanged a barely perceptible nod with Gareth and Andrew.

"Oh, no you don't." Felicity said. "You are my brother, David Holbrook, but you don't make decisions or attend inquests in my stead."

"Think of your sister," Andrew said, keeping Astrid's hand in his. "If Astrid is an acknowledged relation of a viscount, she can bear the stigma of unfortunate birth, particularly if she has some sort of dowry. If she might have witnessed a murder, and was kidnapped, trapped for two hours alone and bound in the company of criminals, what do you think her future holds?"

Felicity's shoulders sagged. "We weren't there."

Gareth wanted to tell her, "that's my lady," except she wasn't his anything. She was a woman with a titled brother, a fellow who could provide for her lavishly, and take on her problems as family was supposed to. What a damnable, depressing thought.

Brenner spoke from a perch on the raised hearth. "There is one bright side to all of this."

His ears turned pink as the company pinned him with incredulous looks. "Well, Miss Worthington is no longer the owner of a bordello," he stammered. When that met with silence, he blundered on. "The will left the brothel to the eldest, and that would be Holbrook, here...Why are you all looking at me?"

Felicity's expression shifted to that soft, dazzling, enthralling smile Gareth had fallen in love with months ago. "You are quite right, Mr. Brenner, that whole exercise was a waste of my time and the marquess's. I should never have bothered him in the first place, but I didn't find Callista's clues, and so I am the proud owner of a useless business education."

Her words cut Gareth, but she was smiling that special smile at him, and he was at a loss as to her meaning. Was loving him a useless education? *Had* she loved him?

His thoughts were interrupted by a loud sigh from Astrid. "I guess that leaves us with one problem. Who gets to be the bastard? Shall it be David, or me and Felicity?"

Lady Heathgate smiled for the first time that evening. "Neither," she said, looking at Gareth.

Gareth glanced at Andrew, then Holbrook, and saw no resistance.

"What do you have in mind, Mother?" Though he knew exactly what she had in mind and approved wholeheartedly. Better the idea come from her though, as a grand dame in polite society.

"I posit we simply embellish the tale David's family has already started. His mother married, became pregnant, didn't get on well with her husband—different strata of society, you know—went to Scotland to visit cousins and died in childbirth. Her estranged husband remarried. It's done all the time."

Brenner looked thoughtful rather than appalled. "All it would take is a change in date on a death record, your lordships." He included Holbrook in that courtesy. "And Holbrook—er, Lord Fairly —can claim his legitimacy, but if the late Viscount Fairly is revealed to be a bigamist, then all three of his offspring will suffer by association, title or not, legitimate or not. He could be found guilty of a felony posthumously, in the eyes of society if not the courts. This subterfuge would spare them that."

"I leave it to my sisters," Holbrook said. "I don't think my mother would have minded, if it makes a difference. She eventually accepted she would not have been comfortable in Fairly's world, and saw that the love of a lifetime for her was no more than a rebellious infatuation for him. What I want now is whatever would make my sisters happy."

Gareth watched Felicity, who was watching Astrid. He addressed the assemblage with a smile he didn't feel. "Why don't we

replenish our plates and leave Felicity and Astrid to consider their
situation? The day's events, while safely concluded, have to be overwhelming for them. Ladies, it is pleasant out in the garden, and I've
had torches lit if you'd like to stroll there."

He ushered his guests out of the library, but touched Felicity on
the arm when she would have passed him. "You'll be all right?"

"Gareth, I hardly know."

"Take it from me, Felicity, the acquisition of a brother can only be
a very great blessing. When you and I parted, were it not for
Andrew."

Felicity regarded him curiously. "Will you spare me a moment to
speak privately?"

His heart started hammering against his ribs. "Do you *want* me to
spare you such a moment?" A lifetime of such moments?

"I do, very much."

He leaned down to kiss her forehead and to breathe in lavender
and hope. "I've asked my mother to spend the night so you and Astrid
might remain as guests. I will join you later, and we can talk. For now,
I think your most pressing task is to talk Miss Astrid out of becoming
a bastard."

A BROTHER! Felicity still could not credit that it was so, much less
such a one as David Holbrook.

David *Worthington*. What a lovely name. If everyone was to be
legitimate, then they had the same last name. They had a *brother*. He
would be a splendid addition to the family, and Felicity had already
admired his ability to deal with Astrid.

Astrid, who had been through so much today, but who had
turned for comfort and support not so much to her sister, as she had
to Andrew Alexander. Andrew had been overtly protective and affectionate toward Astrid, and Astrid had tolerated his behavior.

No, not merely tolerated it. Astrid had returned Andrew's attentions. But then, it was a day for odd twists. And an exhausting day.

Felicity glanced at the bed, turned down to warm the sheets. She should blow out the candles and climb in bed, not wait up here in her room for that private moment Gareth had promised her. "Later" for a busy man whose day had been interrupted could mean next week, and her discussion with him was not, despite her desperate longing for his company, truly urgent.

"Something has you smiling," said a quiet male voice.

Gareth stood just inside her door, looking tired, handsome, and so very, very dear.

"I didn't hear you knock." He was undressed down to boots, a loose linen shirt, and breeches. His cuffs were undone and turned back to reveal his forearms, and he held a drink in one hand.

"I didn't knock, because I didn't want to wake you if you were asleep. Did you still want to have that private discussion?"

Her caller was Heathgate. The new and improved version, with better manners and a thread of humility, but still a reserved, cautious man who did not easily reveal himself.

"I want to have that private discussion. Won't you come sit with me?" Felicity bounced onto the bed, and patted the mattress beside her. Looking wary, his lordship crossed the room to put his drink on the nightstand before he took the proffered seat. He chose his spot carefully, so their thighs just touched. Just.

"How are you feeling about the day's developments, Felicity?"

She would rather he took her hand and called her *my dear*. "There have been so many. I am at sea, but very happy to have both brother and sister hale and hearty. And you and Andrew as well—I haven't yet thanked you, Gareth. There simply aren't words to do so properly."

"You still use my name."

His tone gave away nothing, not surprise, not amusement, certainly not pleasure. "Would you rather I didn't? We are sitting on my bed, and our attire is hardly decent. Still, I suppose I should have asked if you'd—"

He interrupted her by taking her hand. "Hush," he said, lacing his fingers with hers. "I want to be Gareth to you always. How is Astrid?"

He held her hand. Felicity took courage from that.

"Astrid is oddly quiet, though I think Andrew is a comfort to her. David seems to have a rapport with her that will help as well. She will be fine, in time, if Andrew can behave himself."

They both fell silent, but before Gareth could kiss her on the forehead again—God help her—Felicity seized her courage in both hands.

"I went completely to pieces, before. When we parted. I cried for days, stayed in my rooms for more days, left Astrid to fend for herself, and barely left the house. I am not proud of myself, but it just.... Everything hurt, though I sound melodramatic when I put it that way. I missed you, is all."

She got up and paced to the hearth because Gareth was still giving away nothing—not one thing.

"You missed me?" He might have been asking if the entertainment was a cellist or a pianist at some musicale.

"No, no I did not *miss* you. I *missed* you."

He regarded her warily, likely a man dreading to witness a female fit of the vapors.

Bother that. Felicity plopped down on the bed next to him, took his arm and affixed it around her shoulders. She possessed herself of his hand and tried again.

"I *grieved* for you. My heart became this aching, inert thing. I could not think, I could not speak, I could only watch myself suffer and pity the poor, helpless creature I'd become. I was ashamed of myself, and that, eventually, is what motivated me to drag myself from my bed. Do not be deceived though. I have learned how to miss you even as I comb my hair, don my clothes, and manage my household. I miss you still."

Which ought not to be possible, not when his sandalwood scent was teasing her nose, and the warmth and strength of him were right there beside her on that very same bed.

She gathered her resolve to abandon that bed, because clearly, Gareth—Heathgate, blast the man—did not reciprocate—

A large male hand gently pushed her head to his shoulder. "You missed me?"

"Shamefully, wildly, passionately, disgracefully. Need I go on?"

He held her snugly for a full minute, during which Felicity did not dare so much as breathe, before he began to speak.

GARETH WAS on a bed with Felicity, his arms wrapped around her, and he never, ever wanted to let go.

Which meant, he had to say something, the right something, to make her understand. "I... got drunk." She remained where she was, letting him hold onto her. "I know now where the term stinking drunk originates, because by about the third day, my own putrid stench no longer mattered to me. I yelled at the servants, stayed up wandering all night, drank some more, and missed you, and missed you, and missed you."

He paused because the next part required yet still more courage. "I probably would have drunk myself to death, Felicity, except Andrew paid me a visit, and told me, essentially, to stop feeling sorry for myself, because he hadn't survived all the same losses I had just to watch me commit a slow, odoriferous suicide. He was very understanding, but also very honest, and he managed to shame me into at least trying to be worthy of the regard you once showed me."

Which was all important to tell her, but not what really mattered.

"I am sorry, Gareth, that you suffered so. I should not have asked of you what I did."

Gareth felt a suspicious dampness trickle against his neck. Merciful God, he'd made her cry.

And yet, she did not leave him.

"I saw you today, with Holbrook on the way to the park. You looked so happy, and I told myself he had to be paying you proper addresses after all. I had been screwing up my courage to approach you, thinking perhaps we could negotiate *something*. Then I saw you with him, and I wanted to get drunk for another month."

"Oh, Gareth," Felicity wailed softly against his neck. "I did not mean to cause you distress, and you seemed so determined to be free of me."

He held her for long moments, thinking only that he had caused her spirit, his practical, vibrant, lovely Felicity's spirit, to flicker, and dim. Bad enough he'd stolen her virtue, stolen her innocence, put her at risk for social censure, and entangled her in his past with Riverton, but to have broken her heart like this... Desperation nearly choked him, but they both spoke at once.

"Will you marry me?" and

"I would be your mistress if you'd have me."

She'd spoken as humbly, as hopefully, has he had. Gareth rested his chin on the top of her head and swallowed twice before speaking again.

"I would rather marry you, if you don't mind. You've proven you can walk away from me once already, and I would not..." He took a slow, deep breath. "You have made me a better man than I ever thought I could be. You have restored to me the man I should have been, and I would not *survive* the loss of you again. I simply could not."

"Nor I the loss of you." Felicity agreed, wrapping her arms around him "Gareth?"

"Hmm?"

"I have one favor to ask of you."

"Anything, love." He would do anything for her in that moment except let her walk away from him again.

"Stay with me tonight?"

The Creator in his all wisdom had never fashioned a more

wonderful female. "My love, it shall be my very greatest pleasure to grant that request."

True gentleman that he was, he ensured it was *her* very greatest pleasure as well, and through all the years and decades of their long, happy and prodigiously fruitful union, Gareth continued to ensure Felicity great pleasure as often as she'd allow it.

Which was very often indeed!

AUTHOR'S NOTE

AUTHOR'S NOTE

As Gareth notes, a woman could not inherit a brothel in Regency England, not the way I might inherit my grandmother's candy store in modern times. Even in Georgian England, no court would enforce a will whose purpose was illegal, and bordellos were considered illegal. Felicity could, however, inherit property (all the assets of her cousin's enterprise) from a family member, and could still substantively inherit a going (if illegal) concern.

This story, of a rake charged with the ruin of a lady, only to find the lady instead redeems him, took shape as one of my first historical romance manuscripts, and I became enthralled with it the instant it popped into my head. And yet, I'm a lawyer, and so I wanted more information about the legalities involved in prostitution and brothels in Merry Olde England two hundred years ago.

My editor, too, wanted the context for the premise researched, and thus I had not only permission, but encouragement(!) to go down a particularly interesting Regency rabbit hole.

I found, to my surprise, that prostitution per se was not illegal, but that soliciting was, and living off the proceeds of "immoral commerce" was also illegal. A woman fallen on hard times, between legitimate employments, or otherwise cast adrift in Regency London, could thus entertain a few customers without much risk of arrest and with an expectation of immediate, direct compensation for her efforts.

And apparently, many, many women did just that.

In 1806, as part of a larger effort to quantify livelihoods in London, the Scottish statistician Patrick Colquhoun estimated that 50,000 women in the greater metropolitan area were engaged in some form of prostitution—or about one in ten women. That total of 50,000 was also cited for a study of eighteenth century London, at which point it would have amounted to *one in five* women.

Consider that Colquhoun was not asking women if they had EVER been paid coin for their favors, but only if they were engaged in such trade at the time of his study. The (perhaps Victorian?) notion that prostitution was a secretive undertaking for the immoral or unfortunate few flies directly out the window.

In fact, the ladybirds, soiled doves, streetwalkers, courtesans, demireps, and bits o' muslin—they had dozens of names—were very much in evidence in the better neighborhoods, around the best theatres, and in the elegant West End parks. I found two reasons for this. First, that's where the wealthy fellows were. (I found at least one reference to brothels for women who preferred their own gender. I could not find evidence of one for women willing to pay for male attentions, though I've seen mention of handsome shop clerks being available to wealthy women for this purpose.)

Some sources suggest that Haymarket was a popular place for prostitutes to gather, in part because the country girls would come into the city with the produce sold at the market, and any madam looking for new employees would have many to choose from. The myth of the abbess who took advantage of such girls was at least familiar to Jane Austen (she joked about it in her letters when discussing her own trips to London), and had more than a little grounding in reality.

The second reason brothels in particular tended to flourish in the West End, and even in Mayfair (St. James especially—don't tell the men's clubs) is that what police resources the authorities had tended to be deployed in the financial district, or "The City." In the wealthiest neighborhoods, the residents themselves—by virtue of hired muscle, stout locks, and social and political consequence—kept their environs safe.

Thus did the brothels locate themselves in the safest neighborhoods, proximate to the deepest male pockets, with the least threat of police interference—pretty savvy, considering how little access women had to anything like an education in commerce.

It's also the case that prostitution could result in significant social advancement—for the very, very few. Beau Brummell's mother was his father's mistress prior to becoming that wealthy man's wife. Harriette Wilson's younger sister took her first protector at thirteen, and by the age of seventeen had married the Baron Berwick (and though they attended her wedding, her three courtesan sisters never spoke with her again).

Elizabeth Armistead was working in a brothel when she met her future lover and husband, the Hon. Charles James Fox. She was by far wealthier than he at the time of their marriage, and yet, after his death, three successive English monarchs (including Queen Victoria) approved pensions for her, as the beloved widow of a revered statesman.

Most prostitutes were, of course, nowhere near that lucky. Ian Kelly, in his wonderful biography, "Beau Brummell: The Ultimate Man of Style," posits that when the great armies of Europe mobilized for the Napoleonic conflicts, a particularly virulent strain of syphilis mobilized with them (and Brummell was one of its victims).

While the symptoms of syphilis could be (somewhat) controlled by virtue of what amounts to mercury poisoning, the treatment was expensive and not a cure. Increasing life expectancy in the Regency meant more people lived to experience the horror of tertiary syphilis, and thus every woman engaged in prostitution would have known full well she risked her life for a few coins.

And a final word about nomenclature: My reference of choice for matters linguistic is the Oxford English Dictionary online (OED.com). If I ever turn up missing, you will find me nose down in this marvelous website. OED suggests that "madam," in the sense of a female brothel-keeper, did not come into common parlance until the 1870s. Nonetheless, as early as the 1650s, "madam" referred to a prostitute, courtesan or fallen woman. A female brothel keeper would have thus very likely have been referred to as a madam, though not with the precise connotation we give the word.

Because the historical meaning is close to the meaning I needed, and because I thought it would make for a smoother reading experience, I've appropriated the term "madam" for use in Gareth and Felicity's Regency love story.

CPSIA information can be obtained
at www.ICGtesting.com
Printed in the USA
LVHW091420020422
715151LV00015B/803